*By the same author*

DEATH ON WIDOW'S WALK

# THE
# FACE
## OF
# DEATH

# THE
# FACE
## OF
# DEATH

## LESLEY
## GRANT-ADAMSON

CHARLES SCRIBNER'S SONS
NEW YORK

This novel is a work of fiction. Names, characters, places and inci-
dents are either the product of the author's imagination or are used
fictitiously. Any resemblance to actual persons, living or dead,
events or locales is entirely coincidental.

First published in the United States by Charles Scribner's Sons 1986

**Library of Congress Cataloging-in-Publication Data**

Grant-Adamson, Lesley.
The face of death.

I. Title.
PR6057.R324F3 1986  823'.914  85-25076
ISBN 0-684-18588-1

1 3 5 7 9 11 13 15 17 19  F/C  20 18 16 14 12 10 8 6 4 2

Printed in the United States of America.

For my parents

# 1

The garden blurred beyond the window pane. Its bordering fence was a brown smear, its lawn patchily green. Rose bushes, burdened with the unfulfilled buds of summer, merged into February rain. Nearby grew the ghostly form of a rockery, too new for greening.

Peter Dutton shuddered and turned away from the scene with its sickening memories. He poured water on his breakfast teabag. The stillness in the house exaggerated his movements.

He carried his cup of tea and scant breakfast into the adjoining lounge and set them on a teak-veneered coffee table. He had moved the furniture round, bought a rug, tried to change the room into a different one without a past. Every morning now he sat here alone, spurning the cosiness of the kitchen, and waited for Shepherd Road to come to life.

The paper boy would be the first to appear, slouching through the wind or rain to thrust the *Daily Post* through the front door of number 7, then tramping the dividing flower bed to reach the Parkers' house, then on up the street and out of sight. As the weeks went by his satchel grew heavier because the occupants of Shepherd Road were multiplying.

In the beginning, when the first group of anaemic brick houses were completed but the roadway and pavements were not, there were only the Duttons. Then the Parkers came. Then the idea caught on and every week at least one removal van was disgorging its contents.

After that there was a lull. Phase One, as the developers put it, was completed. Phase Two was still being built and so builders' lorries rumbled by spewing mud and rubble, and serious-faced couples came, armed with tape measures and dreams and building society promises. When the houses which Peter Dutton could see from his lounge window were ready for occupation Phase Two would be complete.

He finished his breakfast and went to look out of the bay window, which the estate agents, with a paucity of choice, had made such a feature of the property. The agents, in the way of agents, had used nebulous words like 'attractive' and, when several of the houses had been sold, felt free to move on to 'popular'.

Quite probably none of the new owners gave a thought to their bay windows until they confronted the practical matter of curtains. Then the disadvantages became apparent: would it look funnier to hang short ones around the bay or floor length ones inside the room? The dilemma faced each pair of arrivals and they waited to see what the neighbours did. The couple who fitted blinds were thought to have ducked the issue and, more damaging, to be unable to afford curtains. For although the people of Shepherd Road may not have concurred with the agents' theories about the charms of their new homes, what *had* attracted them was the hope of a house at a reasonable price in Spinney Green, a north London suburb which, while never fashionable, had always been considered 'good'.

Peter Dutton craned to see to the far end of the street. The mere possibility of doing so was the only use the ugly-looking bay had. At one time he had run to it frequently, cold with sweat and expecting to see a police car. The panic died. He controlled it. He set a new pattern for his days and its momentum carried him through the worst. Now when he peered out the police were thrust to the back of his mind. He believed he was only looking for the paper boy.

He was rewarded. Head bent against lashing rain, the boy was turning the corner. Then Dutton found himself looking into the next bay, not the Parkers' home but the Siamese twin of his own semi-detached house. Number 5 was still empty although bought several weeks ago.

The Parkers, Jean Parker especially, had hinted concern about the absent neighbours. One liked to know, after all, whom one was to live next to. Peter Dutton did not care. He would keep himself to himself as he had always done, even in his miserable childhood in the battered terrace in south London. He intended to see little of his new neighbours and wished he saw less of the Parkers. She worked only part-time, in a baker's shop. He was a sales representative and often at home. They seemed always to be around, watching.

Dutton went to the kitchen and poured another cup of tea. A grim smile shaped his face. Let them watch. There were some things even those Nosey Parkers would never know about number 7 Shepherd Road.

The newspaper slapped on the doormat. The boy tramped past the lounge window and through the flower bed to the Parkers' front door. Dutton yawned. Time to shave and get dressed, begin the unthinking routine that took him to Spinney Green station and his menial job in a publisher's office.

He would have another day of receiving and sending memos, shuffling paper, telephoning people who were out and missing calls that came for him. He'd do his bit to keep the flow of ironic backchat going, so the manager's secretary could continue to boast it was a happy office. And at lunchtime he would slip away to stroll through bustling West End streets. In the evening he would feign surprise at his watch, murmur goodnight and hurry to the station. His working life had gone on like this for five years and he had no wish to change it. Jobs were no longer easy to come by, he would stay at Pegwoods.

He was thirty-three but beginning to look older – the greying of the temples had accelerated. Recently he had lost weight, although he was still solidly built for his medium height. It was the shadowed eyes, telling of anguished nights, that won him the protective sympathy of his female colleagues.

Before Carol went – the phrase he preferred – he had not roused an iota of interest in them. Now they all, from the manager's motherly secretary down to Mary Partridge, the youngest of the clerks, were worried for him. Mary Partridge threatened to become a nuisance. There was the embarrassing day when a fruit pie appeared on his desk and he had to

11

shove it in a drawer, quickly, before Johnson and Lewis, who shared the room with him, came back from the pub.

Of course, it was unfortunate that he had mentioned Carol at all, but with the office Christmas party looming and the department's theatre treat being planned, it was unavoidable. As he could not produce Carol he must explain.

He did not elaborate, his colleagues did that for themselves. The version which travelled back to him was that his wife had run off with another man and he was taking it badly. The gestures were not all fruit pies: there were little kindnesses he would never have suspected of them. It was the wispy Lewis, for instance, for whom he had never much cared, who saw to it that Mary Partridge's ploy to sit next to him at the theatre (with Johnson and his wife on her other side) failed. The athletic Johnson was generous enough to invite him home one day over Christmas, although he did not go.

The manager's secretary gave him the choice of holiday dates, tacitly suggesting he might welcome a break while his private life was in turmoil. None of them could imagine his turmoil. They could not know of the wide-awake nights that gave way to repetitive nightmare, nor of the nightmares that, waking, turned into truth.

In the first days after Carol went he felt constantly sick, unable to think about anything except her face as he had last seen it. He learned to calm himself, to adapt and look ahead. He took the early holiday offered, and spent the time perfecting the rockery begun in haste earlier. The planning, the choosing of the stone at the garden centre and the physical work of fetching and carrying, soothed him. The project was not finished. Developers would say Phase One was completed. Phase Two would not be until the pockets of earth were each filled with plants and the whitish stone spread with green.

There had been no more projects. The Parkers, frequently at work in their garden, hinted that he ought to persist but he brushed away their encouragement with remarks about waiting for better weather. In truth he was no gardener. The rose bushes had been Carol's idea, and now Carol was gone.

His comfort and his company was television. From his evening meal, in the kitchen with the portable set perched on the worktop, until he dozed off shortly before transmission shut-down, with the set balanced on the dressing table in the bedroom, he let it wink and chatter at him.

The sound of the Parkers' back door opening and closing, with the resistance of new wood on a wet day, told him Shepherd Road was fully awake. A car swished by, confirming. Dutton carried his cup of tea upstairs ignoring the newspaper in the hall. It was Carol's choice, not his, but he thought it best not to cancel it. He would leave it at home for the television programmes as he always did, and buy something else to read on the train.

In the bedroom, shaved and choosing a clean shirt, he flicked on the television. Socks and underpants, washed the previous evening, were crisply dry on the radiator and he gathered them up. And then he saw her. Carol. On the screen. She was lying in a hospital bed and the camera was moving in on her. There she was in close up: wide grey eyes, mousey hair wandering over a pillowcase.

Dutton stood open-mouthed, his mind a jumble of hope and conflicting knowledge. It *was* her – good God, he should know his own wife! And yet . . . how *could* it be? He heard nothing but the thrumming of his pulse and then he ran from the room to the spare bedroom and pressed his face against the window. Raindrops glided down the glass. The garden lay before him: the brown smear of the fence; the uneven green of the lawn; the winter-shaded rose bushes; the pale rise of the rockery.

His skin burned on the glass. Slowly he withdrew, went back to the main bedroom. The television had changed key. Time for the Problem Page of the Screen: would anyone like to phone in? The woman presenter was pleading. Peter Dutton roared hysterical laughter at her. How about *his* problem, then? How would her expert, on the left of the frame and casually picking lint from his newly pressed trousers, handle this one? But someone else phoned in, with a difficult wart, and Peter Dutton left them to it. Although his insides were churning he mustn't break step. Catch the usual train, buy the usual paper, get through another day.

Jean Parker, a scrawny woman in her forties with hennaed hair, was taking in her morning milk when he stepped on to the front path. They good-morninged and she followed up with an oblique suggestion that he remove his dustbin from the front of the house to its special shed near the back door. One had to keep up appearances, she believed. He'd told her it was none of her business when she tried the straight attack on the subject once before. This time he ignored the hint.

She was a well-meaning woman and soon after Carol went had offered to clean the house for him. For a spell it was a satisfactory arrangement. Then she made several of her 'little suggestions', and Dutton decided she was less committed to dusting than snooping. So he told her not to come any more.

He left her, a milk bottle in each hand, as he raced through the downpour to the station. The woman in the kiosk had his usual paper ready to hand to him, he flashed his season ticket at the barrier, and then the train was there and he was away.

Usually he detested travelling to work on a rainy day. The carriages were always crowded and the smell of damp clothing repellent. Naturally, no one would dream of opening a window and no one would dream of suggesting it. Instead weak smiles were exchanged between fellow sufferers, and they found solace in that.

Today he did not notice any of it. He manoeuvred himself into a position where he could read the paper while standing. She was on page two, the woman in the hospital bed. Newsprint had not improved on the image on the screen, but he would have known her anywhere. She was a Mystery Woman, according to the headline. She was no mystery to Peter Dutton. She was Carol.

Apparently she had been injured in a road accident in Leamington Spa. Her physical injuries were mended but she had no recollection of the accident or of whom she was or where she came from. The hospital was publicizing her plight in the hope someone would recognize her. Well, someone had; but he wondered how many other people had, too. Perhaps the lunchtime edition of the evening paper would say she had been claimed? He bought it, scanning the stop press box for the up-to-date news, and it didn't. The morning's appeal was repeated word for word.

He threw the paper away, went back to the office clutching a plant a stallholder promised would do well on a rockery. Perhaps the evening television news would say she was reunited with her family? It didn't, and all evening he channel-hopped from one news programme to another, watching over and over again Carol's sad face.

The doctor, a pleasant man called Michael Renfrew, repeated to reporters that accident victims quite frequently have no recollection of their accident or the period leading up to it and often never remember. Sometimes traumatic amnesia can go much further, wiping out far more memory. Rarely, his patient could recall nothing at all of her own life before the hospital bed. Yes, if the reporters insisted, she might never remember.

That night, in the worrying hours when the worst and the best seem possible, Peter Dutton imagined Carol coming home to him. When he slept he dreamed it was true. When he woke he was sure it could be.

# 2

There were two television crews. The companies could not agree about sharing film so she had to endure it twice. Dr Renfrew was displeased, she could tell from the way the warmth faded from his brown eyes.

The first crew were pleasanter because they worked more smoothly together. Each one did his job and the others knew it was being done and didn't fuss. With the second crew there was a man who kept ordering them about. Do this, have you done that, are you ready for so-and-so, what about such-and-such? He was a worried man, a little man – regardless of his stature. Possibly, she thought, he was the only one who was unsure what was happening and what he ought to be doing. Fussy people were generally like that.

The best thing about the swift, efficient visit of the first crew was the West Indian cameraman who coaxed her co-operation, made her relax, called her princess. Who knew, she might really be one? Everyone came up against the problem of what to call her. The staff at the hospital used 'dear' or 'love', except the ward orderly from Leicester who preferred 'my duck', and got around it that way. But it was absurd. She knew all their names yet not her own.

Memory began with a blur of faces above her and low-voiced conversation. The scene repeated itself, like a favourite dream, until the faces resolved into individual doctors and nurses. Soon she could put name and rank to those faces, they peopled her existence. Her acquaintance spread: the patients in her first ward, then the women in the next one she was moved to as she recovered. Some came, some went. She knew the names of each, a little of their lives, but nothing of her own.

The medical staff explained she would quite probably never remember the day of the accident which left her lying at the roadside, flung high in the air by the glancing attack of a black Citroen. The rest, they said, would filter back. And supposing, she asked, that it didn't? None of them had ever heard of an instance where it hadn't, when recovery in all other respects had been complete.

They were too careful to betray that she might be the exception. Only Dr Renfrew's persistent interest made her conscious that there was anything special about her. He looked in on her frequently, brought colleagues to talk to her without explaining who and why. Over the rim of the sheet her trusting grey eyes met theirs – Dr Renfrew, mildly disordered and looking more boyish than his years; his fellow doctors, older, wiser heads. All gave her their practised reassuring smiles and put the basic questions she could only fail. Then they went away.

There was a Malaysian student nurse on the ward, a diminutive creature. Her flat face and bright eyes never ceased smiling. The woman asked her once to fetch a mirror. It was three and a half inches long, two and a half inches wide, borrowed from the slot in someone's handbag. The woman held it up and adjusted its angle. By holding it at arm's length and vertical she could take in the whole of her face. By moving it downwards she could see how her hair drifted beyond her shoulders.

She now knew what she looked like. Her grey eyes were set wide apart, her eyebrows finely curved, her skin clear, her nose neat. Part of her scalp must have been shaved when they brought her into casualty because one area was tufty and the rest much longer. In later weeks she would stand in front of the hand-basin in the patients' lavatory and stare at her reflection in the wall mirror. The cropped patch of hair was lengthening, the rest needed trimming and tidying. She wondered who her hairdresser had been, in that other mysterious life which ended when she set out to cross The Parade, Leamington Spa.

As she grew stronger it became easy to pass time absorbed in such nugatory detail as which hairstyle would most

17

flatteringly disguise the evidence of her injury. She did not want a very short layered one, but when she next got near a hairdresser there would be no alternative.

At other times she could think of nothing but her mislaid identity and weary herself striving to remember it. There was the story of the accident and her arrival in Princes Hospital and there were a handful of clues.

She wrote a list of the clues, subconsciously scared she could be robbed of this information, too. The list began with a description of her physical appearance. Grey eyes, light brown medium-length hair, height 5 ft 4 in. The hospital estimated her age at between twenty-five and thirty years. Her weight told her nothing: she might still be regaining the loss suffered since the injury. Her voice was low, without obvious regional inflection. She was articulate, her hand-writing a confident sprawl across a page and she created sophisticated doodles.

She came to the hospital with only the clothes she wore and no bag. No one in Leamington reported seeing her until a few seconds before she stepped on to the zebra crossing near the town hall. The rest of the clues were negative. She had worn no rings, which could mean she was unmarried although that was no longer the foolproof test it would once have been, and there were no signs on her body that she had borne a child.

The hospital had shown her the clothes she came in, ruined garments she was excused from recognizing. She presumed they still had them, filed away somewhere, evidence of her identity. The hospital social worker had seen to it that a hospital charity bought her some underwear; other garments came from a mysterious supply to which they would return when she went away.

She wrote another list, a record of the tantalizing moments when she felt close to remembering. Turning a page in a magazine she would be held by a certain photograph, perhaps a country scene where cottages wandered down a lane or else a room which was a comfortable jumble of old furniture. Sometimes a phrase would leap out of an over-heard conversation and she would puzzle why it felt significant. Perhaps it was not the phrase but the tone of voice in which it was spoken which mattered to her? She tried to analyse: the only common feature was that the voices were alway female, but that was unremarkable in a hospital where so many of the staff and all the patients near her were women.

Her list was interrupted by the approach of Dr Renfrew and a senior nurse they called Dorcas because her surname was something complicated and Polish and by general consent avoided. She enjoyed the gentle undercurrents that ran between them. The doctor was at the beginning of his career as a consultant, the nurse nearing the end of her working life. It amused the woman to guess what the nurse was really thinking while she murmured 'Yes, doctor' or inclined her head in mute approval of his suggestions which, if carried out, would upset the comfortable running of her wards, alienate the kitchen staff and have the rest of her patients petitioning for similar favours. She imagined Dorcas, off duty and at home, telling with dry wit what that nice Dr Renfrew had done now.

The nurse waited as Dr Renfrew came up to the bed. After the preliminaries he would have delicately to broach the matter of publicity, and he would have to do it with the nurse watchful at his elbow and daring him to muff it. So first there was the jolly chat the doctor and his patient always enjoyed, and the nurse threw in the odd quip too. Then Dr Renfrew was saying: 'We will have to make you famous. The press have found out about you. I've had the *Leamington Morning News* on the telephone twice and the local freelance was caught wandering around the wards looking for you. If you agree to it we would like to make a public appeal now to find your family. As you know, the police records of missing people didn't help and although we might have got something from dental records that's a lengthy business and the press are already snapping at our heels.'

The woman noted his kindly inaccuracy that it was her family which needed finding. 'What will happen?' she asked. He explained that there must be photographs of her in newspapers and on television but that the stress would be limited as far as possible: one agency photographer would take pictures for all the papers and, he hoped, there need be no more than one camera crew for television coverage. She agreed to it, of course.

Later the tears came. 'Supposing', she asked Dorcas, 'no one recognizes me? Princes Hospital won't want to keep me here for ever – what will they do with me?'

Dorcas, who had been wondering the same thing herself for several weeks, gave her a comforting smile and said there was nothing to worry about, someone was certain to recognize her.

'And when they do, do you really think my memory will come back?'

'Once you are in familiar surroundings with people you know, your memory will have all the encouragement it could want.'

But first someone must take her home.

# 3

The opera singer had cried off. He was saving his voice. The atmosphere of an early morning television studio would do him no good at all, so during the night he changed his mind.

'A pity,' said Rain Morgan, the gossip columnist of the *Daily Post*. She had agreed to be on the chat show because she wanted to meet Lamberhurst and he was famously shy of journalists. She muffled a yawn.

'But we'll be all right,' the producer said, reassuring himself. 'Just one phone call and we've filled the gap.'

'And who have you got?' Beyond the bright smile Rain's spirits sagged. It was sure to be a politician. Who else would take kindly to being phoned in the night and asked to report to a television studio before the milk was delivered?

'David Rokeby.'

Ah, yes. That was who else. A psychologist with a chatty line in prose and a string of popular books alongside the learned material which had earned him a chair at a northern university. He seemed never to be at the university, he was mostly in London promoting Professor Rokeby.

'You know each other, I think?' the producer said, but he was losing interest. An argument was growing between a couple of his crew across the studio. He went to grub it out.

Rokeby arrived then, wearing his most dishevelled look. Rain remembered her student days when she had found it charming, the mark of the little boy lost. The discovery that Rokeby fluffed up his hair, deliberately set his tie askew and spent inordinate time deciding what to wear had astonished her. It was a secret very well kept from his admiring colleagues and his adoring public. No one would rumble it unless they lived with him. Rain had.

She took in with a glance the mismatched socks and was tempted to ask whether he had never considered odd shoes? Perhaps not, wasn't the whole point to look 'interestingly different' rather than plain eccentric? Wasn't it the art of knowing just how far to go, where to draw the line? She was no longer clear, and doubted whether Rokeby was either.

'You're standing in for Lamberhurst,' she said in greeting. 'Just the odd aria and a chat with me and Betty Blount about what's in the papers.' After a series of much publicized coups the rotund former actress Betty Blount had emerged as the show's presenter. With her had emerged a new set. Gone was the livid plastic and chrome look which had harked many a memory back to provincial airport lounges. In came 'something more feminine' as Betty herself said at the time. The set was now referred to as Betty's Boudoir, although not necessarily by those who wanted to be on the show.

'Those are the easy bits,' said Rokeby.

'Ah, yes. You're going to find a way of plugging your new book and the producer has set his face against such evil practices.'

'But you will help?'

'Will I?'

'It's called . . .'

'. . . *Naughty but Nice*. I know. I heard you plugging it on the radio: *Start the Week, Midweek, Woman's Hour, PM* . . .'

His tie was slipping dangerously towards the vertical. Rain tweaked it to the left.

'You've forgotten the repeats on *Pick of the Week*.'

'And the version printed in the *Listener*.'

'Quite.' He ran a cautious hand over what looked like three days growth of beard. It always did. How did a man contrive always to have three days stubble? Rain was not in on that secret, there had been a full beard in her day. He looked contemplatively at a scuffed toecap. 'Mind you, I was entirely ignored in your paper. Nothing on the books page, not even a mention in the scurrilous Rain Morgan column.'

'David, I promise if you attempt one of Lamberhurst's arias this morning I shall personally write the lead item about it for tomorrow.'

The producer interrupted with another attempt to reassure himself everything would be all right. They assured him they were reassured and he faded away. They looked through a heap of the day's newspapers, guessing what topics could be tossed at them for discussion.

'They'll want you to talk about this,' said Rain, tapping a front page story about the woman with amnesia.

'Like this, you mean?' He addressed her as though she was a lecture room full of medical students, pacing about in front of her, gesturing. It was an act she'd seen often before, begun as a send-up of a tutor from his own student days. She wondered how much of it he used during his real lectures, whether there wasn't a student somewhere who could ape Professor Rokeby rather well?

'Memory,' he said, and paused for effect, 'depends on the fornix, the hippocampus and the mamillary bodies. Therefore, if there is damage the result is amnesia. We see this where a patient suffers head injuries. But there can be other causes for amnesia.' Long pause for maximum effect. 'For example, stagnate hysteria and mental aphasia are both incurred by *emotional* stress.'

He paced and cleared his throat. 'Of course, life is seldom so straightforward and amnesia may not be due to any individual cause but to any combination of possible causes. Also, it can be a temporary condition or it can be a permanent one. Where a patient presents physical wounds there may well be damage to the hippocampus, mamillary bodies or fornix – and physical damage to the brain can mean the patient is no longer able to associate the information he has with his past. A shoemaker, for instance, may retain his skill at making shoes but have no recollection of where he worked. A linguist will not lose knowledge of the languages he has learned but will not remember that he made his living by teaching them. The gaps in these lives are *not* going to be filled by the patient remembering, either suddenly or gradually, because the physical conduits of memory have been physically destroyed.'

More pacing, another throat-clearing. Rain noticed the producer and Betty Blount watching. Rokeby didn't. He went on: 'There have been many instances where people have been put under what proved to be intolerable strain and have responded by forgetting. After the First World War there were men returned from the battlefields of France with no memory, because they were protecting themselves by wiping out the horror they had lived through, and with it they had wiped out everything else. In some of these cases the condition persisted for years, maybe to their deaths. Some of them were numbered among the tramps who roamed England, unable to call any place home. Sometimes they turned up in their home villages, drawn there in a mysterious way, and then they were recognized and taken home and often their memories returned. Once the distress which triggered their amnesia faded, the need for protection was diminished and so they were able to remember. Unless, of course, there were gaps caused by physical injury, and . . .'

The producer intervened. 'Betty's ready for you now.'

Rain and Rokeby took their places on the set and the show began. They got to the bit where they were asked to comment on items in the newspapers.

Betty Blount, in a flowing dress which might have been a peignoir, leaned forward in her deep armchair with its frilled cushions and invited Rain's comment on the Mystery Woman story. 'Amnesia is a rather interesting condition,' said Rain. And talked about the hippocampus and the mamillary bodies and the fornix, about the physical and emotional causes. Beside her she felt David Rokeby shuffling in irritation but knew he could not flaw her paraphrase. At last she drew him in, with as neat a link as any television presenter could have managed, to talk about *Naughty but Nice*. It was Betty Blount's turn to flinch, there was no hope of stopping the illicit plug.

They broke off while someone on another part of the set read the news. After that Rain, who had no books to promote, expected to be asked about the life of the Fleet Street gossip columnist because that was the reason the producer had given for wanting her on the programme. But Rokeby took his revenge. He seized on a tiny item about a police hunt for a murderer to tell all he knew about the criminal mind, with repeated emphasis on a television series called *The Face of Death*. He was both a backstage consultant and an on-screen expert for the series and had much to offer.

With minimal protest from Betty Blount he gave a rundown of the mental states familiar to criminologists: schizophrenia, revealed by callous detachment, where the right hand is prevented from knowing what the left hand is doing; paranoia, otherwise delusional insanity; sadistic psychopathy . . . Betty Blount exerted herself and lunged forward on the cushions with a series of gunfire-fast questions about notorious murderers of the twentieth century. In the control box, Rain saw the producer holding his head.

Later on Betty Blount remembered Rain and tried a jokey link to draw her into what passed for the discussion. 'I don't suppose you have much contact with murderers on the *Daily Post* gossip column?'

'Oh yes,' Rain said with her sweetest smile. 'One tried to kill me and very nearly did.'

Betty Blount gaped. This was going to be great television, the victim's eye view of murder. Well, *almost*. But it was too late. The floor manager was making winding-up signs with his hand and the credits were rolling.

Rain gave David Rokeby a lift home in her car. He said he would wait for a taxi instead, but she couldn't leave him there, hanging around after the programme in his odd socks and probably without the right sort of money. Islington was only a minor detour on her route so she drove him there.

'It's a mistake', he said with a yawn, 'to take television seriously.'

'I don't.'

'Nobody absorbs what you're saying, they only want to see what you look like.'

'As most of my appearances are confined to daft panel games or chat shows at unhealthy hours, I'm relieved to hear it.'

'Print is much more effective. Now suppose I had made *Naughty but Nice* as a television series . . .'

'Promise me you won't.'

'Why not? It would adapt rather well. Of course, most things *can* adapt if you know what you are doing . . .'

Rain only half heard the rest. She was wondering why she had let herself be talked off the programme, whether Rokeby realized or cared he had done it, how she would have felt if she'd walked out in protest, why she'd recited his speech about amnesia, why it annoyed her he had not thanked her for contriving that plug for his book, and whether some murderers weren't ordinary people who over-reacted in extraordinary circumstances. She thought that if she had known a good psychologist who would stop talking about himself for long enough she might have got at some of the answers.

# 4

Peter Dutton had loved Carol. He was sure of that. Their eight years together had been harmonious although, sharply defensive, she had a cruel tongue. Other people suffered from it, rarely Peter, and they kept few friends. Carol's astringent personality and his suspicion of the world made them a secure, self-sufficient unit. Or, put another way, lonely.

Without her he was lost. She was not a gap to be filled by a Mary Partridge. Soon he had forgotten the irritations which speckled their married life as they speckle everyone's: her habit of reading bits from the newspapers at him when he was watching television, or her muddy shoes kicked off anywhere around the house and left for him to fall over, or her greed. Soon he forgot them, but he never stopped thinking about her.

He carried the new plant out to the rockery early the day after he bought it, hoping to have the job done and be indoors before the Parkers could snare him into conversation. The February sky was clear but the grass squelched beneath his feet. Earth had washed out of the rockery and streaked the stone. Using a trowel, from a low shed near the back door, he refilled a crevice. He put the plant in position, splaying its roots and covering them with more soil.

The effect was pathetic but he trusted spring and summer to bring transformation. This was a plant to provide cover, his earlier efforts were bulbs. A few had been washed out by downpours but the rest were thrusting up blades of green and some were flowering. A pity, though, that the snow-drops were barely visible against the pale stone.

Dutton stood thoughtfully for a moment more, weighing the trowel in his palm. His plan, concocted in the night, did have snags. It might fail, and what then? Nothing then. He could back off at any point, and it would be much worse not to begin. Besides, even if the plan collapsed and he could not bring Carol home, at least he would have seen her again. Then his mind would erase the memory of the awful way she had last looked at him.

But if the plan succeeded he would be turning the clock back, and there need be no more nightmares about losing her. He would be protected, too, from ever having to explain what had happened to Carol. With her beside him again the question could never be put.

The Parkers' back door opened, but Dutton was already scuttling indoors. Today he was going to break step and he did not want to tell them why. He set out from the house earlier than usual, picked his way over builders' debris that littered the road and pavement near the Phase Two houses and went to the newsagent's. That was a mistake because the woman behind the counter expected him to pay the quarterly bill for the papers delivered to the house. He wrote a cheque he would rather have delayed, bought a selection of that day's papers and a plastic carrier bag to conceal them. Then he returned home.

It was curious, walking the opposite way from the station-bound commuters and seeing, instead of their fleeing backs, their vacant morning faces. Three from Shepherd Road, who would nod acknowledgement to him on the platform most days, sped by unheeding. Out of place they had not recognized him. Unfortunately, there was no escaping Jean Parker. As he came up his path she popped out of her front door, ostensibly to take in her milk. She wondered at him coming back to the house. He got his key in the lock while replying that he had taken the day off work.

'Not ill, are you, Peter?' She peered at him to see where the trouble might be. She was always saying to Ted that Peter Dutton didn't look well.

'No, just a day off.' Escape, the door was swinging before him.

She lobbed him her most detaining piece of gossip. 'They're going to have blacks over there.' She nodded across the road to the unfinished houses.

'Really?' Utter lack of interest.

Jean was indignant. 'Well, I mean, it's not what we were led to expect, is it? Not in executive homes . . . we're entitled to a decent class of neighbour. I'm sure we'd have thought twice about it if we'd known they were going to sell to . . .'

'I'm sure,' he echoed and closed the door.

She was still on her step, thwarted. Until he heard the thud of her door he would keep away from his lounge where she could see right in. He spread the newspapers on the kitchen table and went through each one looking for stories about the Mystery Woman. The only mention was that she was still in hospital and still a mystery. Today the story had shrivelled to two paragraphs. Newspapers lost interest so rapidly. Now the big story was the powercut which had condemned huge areas of the country to cold and darkness. Tomorrow they would have forgotten that and be on to something else.

His pulse was racing again. He rubbed his palms together nervously. His face felt hot. The real point of decision had been reached. The rest had been preliminary, *this* is where it would begin. A cup of tea, a delaying tactic. Then he must telephone. The phone was in the lounge, in the bay window. Carol had asked for it to be installed there, not finding any other means of making use of the space. He hesitated. Jean Parker was in her front garden, commiserating with the plants that had been battered by the paper boy. She could not fail to notice Dutton when he went to the phone. Let her. She had missed her chance of seeing anything interesting.

He sat in the bay, his back to Jean Parker, and rang Directory Enquiries. Then the Leamington hospital. He heard his voice cogent, belying his nervousness. The hospital switchboard operator asked him to hold, which was the most trying part. There was time to backtrack. He steeled himself not to ring off. Then he was speaking to another woman, explaining the Mystery Woman was his wife.

They arranged for him to visit the hospital that afternoon. He rang Pegwoods and left a message that he was unwell and would not be in the office that day. And after that he paced the lounge, concentrating, smoothing his plan. His fingers

29

flexed and his hands stressed points to the empty air. He was excited but confident. As long as he prepared thoroughly, thought it all through, he was sure to succeed.

He had been in hospital himself once so he knew how it would be. He remembered sitting, seven years old, on the edge of a high metal-framed bed and watching the hands on the ward clock slide around to 6 p.m. before his mother arrived to take him home. He was both frightened of her and afraid she would not come. The last of the other children being discharged were collected soon after lunch. Nurses tried to cajole him into occupying his time but he was stubborn about moving. His mother knew which bed he had been in, that was where she would seek him, and if she did not find him there she might go crossly away.

She was often cross. Cross with his father, cross with her son, cross with the neighbours in the terrace, cross with the supervisor at the school kitchens where she worked, cross with everyone and everything. He did not want to risk her leaving him in the no man's land of a hospital. And then she came, face puckered in a frown. Grabbing his hand, she dragged him home. She had preferred not to leave the kitchens early and lose an hour or two's pay on his account. Her own inconvenience at having to walk the half-mile to the hospital was more important to her than his childish worry that he had been overlooked.

Dutton never forgot that trudge home through shadowed winter streets, his mother smoking and coughing, smoking and grumbling. He felt his brief relief at her arrival snuffed out and a familiar resentment harden within him. Other children's parents didn't have rows as his did; or complain incessantly about him and about each other; their fathers didn't erupt into violence and their mothers did not bully and taunt. He wondered at the secretiveness that made him lie to the doctors, supporting his mother's explanation for the injuries which put him in the children's ward. He had never liked telling lies. Often he had wished himself older, old enough to be free of his parents; but when a word to the doctor might have freed him he withheld it. His mother had made sure he would. 'If you say anything they'll put you in a

Home,' she said and that was enough. Blackmail. Bullying. Any name he later liked to call it. She always knew how to manipulate him. Yet the sorest memory of that journey home was that not once had she bothered to ask him how he was. Everyone else, all week, had been asking him and caring about his answers. He was the model patient: polite, compliant, uncomplaining. And if their concern touched him, then he was too wary to show it.

Turning, a movement through the bay window caught his attention. Jean Parker. He had forgotten Jean Parker and there she was, stooped above her snowdrops, staring with eager-eyed fascination at his odd behaviour. He glared at her, knew that was the wrong response and managed a slight smile and a wave as he went out of the room. He left her more confused than ever.

Upstairs he opened the trap on the landing ceiling and pulled down the loft ladder. There was ample space up there. When they were new to the house he had boarded the floor so it was safe to move around. He switched on the electric light and saw deepening dust on tea chests, suitcases and a metal trunk. What he was looking for was in the trunk.

Carol had found the trunk outside a junk shop and bought it for fifty pence which at the time he thought too high a price. She made him carry it up the concrete stairs to their flat. 'What on earth do you want with this?' he'd said.

'It'll be handy. We can put things in it.'

'Quite. But do we want to?'

'I do, and when we move to the house you'll be glad of it.'

And he was. The life-scarred metal trunk, bereft of most of its paint and adorned with rust, proved its worth.

'You can always pretend it's a relic of your schooldays,' she'd said. And he remembered the sarcastic edge to her voice. She was always mocking his childhood, no one needed a trunk for a council school in south London. But they had ended up the same, even though she had started life with more. His parents had died and there had never been brothers and sisters. Her parents had emigrated to New Zealand and she had no siblings either. Aunts and uncles were sparse. The only reminder that Peter and Carol Dutton were not equally alone in the world was the regular payment into her bank account of some profits from her father's business, and occasional letters between Carol and her parents.

Dutton unfastened the trunk. He swallowed hard and threw back the lid. Dust was shed into the air, motes prancing in the vein of light. The trunk was full of clothes. Women's clothes neatly folded. Carol's clothes. After she went he could not tolerate seeing them. There was not the faintest chance of avoiding the pain as long as her things were all around the house. As Carol foretold, he was glad of the trunk.

He carried the clothes down and laid them on his bed. Then he checked the time. It would not do to be late at the hospital. If anything, he must be early. Peeping from the lounge doorway he made sure that Jean Parker was no longer in the front garden. Then he telephoned Paddington station, asked the times of trains to Leamington Spa and realized he must leave the house in a quarter of an hour.

He dashed upstairs, wrenched open the wardrobe which ran the length of one bedroom wall, plucked out some of his things which had strayed on to Carol's rails and thrust them in among his own. He set about the pile on the bed, rounding up spare hangers, and arranging all her clothes on the rail. Below them he stood her shoes, lined up in pairs. On a shelf above he put handbags. He emptied the drawer he had encroached on in the dressing table and laid her underclothes in it.

There was a stale smell about the clothes and they were creased. The effect was more like an Oxfam shop than what the estate agents and Jean Parker called an executive home. However, it was the best he could do. An idea came and he ran to the kitchen, returning with a fresh-air spray which he hissed around the clothes. The room filled with the unconvincing scent of sweet pine and his eyes prickled.

A squirt in the drawer for good measure and he was ready to begin his journey. And then, as he left the house, he gave himself a fright. Through the bay window he spotted the silver-framed wedding photograph on the mantelshelf. With trembling hands he unlocked the door and went back to hide it. He did not look at the happy confident faces but plucked it up and consigned it to the trunk. Then he ran to the station.

But what else was there? Surely he had forgotten something else, overlooked something crucial? His anxious mind insisted while he was on the train from Spinney Green to King's Cross and on the Underground to Paddington. But once he was settled on the train to Leamington he was no longer uneasy. Everything was ready for him to bring the Mystery Woman home and in an hour or two the hospital would let him take her away. He remembered how it had once been for him. The doctor said you were fit and then you just waited until someone collected you. He breathed steadily, relaxed. Whatever lay in the future, he had come through the worst. Whatever happened, he must always remember that.

# 5

When the first of the hopefuls telephoned Princes Hospital to say the Mystery Woman was his missing daughter, Dr Michael Renfrew was ready to watch the meeting between father and child. By the time the third claimant was on her way the doctor had learned better.

Peter Dutton was the fifth. Renfrew knew he was coming because Dorcas mentioned it. When the message reached her that Dutton had arrived, she sent her Malaysian student nurse to fetch him. It would not do to have him blundering into the patient's ward. She wanted a good look at him first.

The hopefuls were not cranks, far from it. They were people grasping at straws, impervious to the evidence. How could a man, who must understand his daughter would be almost forty years old now, have supposed she was the young woman whose age the hospital put between twenty-five and thirty? Or how could a woman, whose child's body was never recovered after a boating accident, nurture the belief that this was her June, miraculously safe all along and now grown up? They couldn't. By all rational tests they couldn't. And yet they did. It was hopeless trying to sift them out on the telephone, these implacable people had to find out for themselves.

Dorcas was capable of dealing with them once they were there, letting them see her patient while they were unobserved so that nobody became upset. And she prepared them for disappointment by dangling the flaws in their claims. 'But you do see, don't you, Mr Hall, that your daughter Alice would be nearly forty by now?'

'Yes, nurse, but she'd look young for her years. Her mother always looked young for her years, and that's the truth.'

'Any woman who looks fifteen years younger than her true

age is remarkably fortunate, Mr Hall, and extremely rare. But tell me, didn't Alice have your Yorkshire accent?'

'I thought she might have lost it.' Wavering, afraid of being turned away as a lost cause.

'Then come along. You shall see the patient.' Through a chink in the curtains along a wall of glass Mr Hall looked at the Mystery Woman chatting to a patient who shared the two-bed room. Mr Hall met disappointment and headed for Huddersfield. No need to trouble Dr Renfrew this time.

Peter Dutton came into Dorcas's office. At least, she thought, as her welcoming smile encompassed him, this one's got the age right. A twenty-seven-year-old wife fits. It got better. She wanted to hear when he had last seen his wife. He said November and, with embarrassed agitation, explained that there had been no word from her since. Dorcas herself filled in the detail of a row and, perhaps, another man. It was touching that he was so uncomfortable telling her his wife had run off, people thought so little of it these days. She asked a few questions about his Carol – where she had grown up, what sort of family background she had, where she had worked.

He replied: in the Home Counties; she did well at grammar school and then worked as a secretary; her parents had always run their own business and were abroad now; Carol had spent some years in New Zealand with them after they emigrated; she had a small private income from them. He hoped he was not saying too much, but sticking to the facts was the easy part.

Dorcas was satisfied and offered to let him see her patient, although he was not as fortunate as Mr Hall. 'She's asleep, I'm afraid, and we don't want her disturbed now.' It was the first stumbling block. Dutton realized he was not going to be allowed to take her home as easily as he had expected. There was a hollow feeling in his stomach. The nurse saw his frown and misinterpreted. She reassured him. 'She has recovered from her injuries and built up her strength but the publicity has been upsetting. When she's on television and in all the papers it is rather unsettling. Here we are, you can go in.'

Dutton stood where Dorcas indicated, a short way into the

room, and gazed at the placid features of the young woman in her drugged sleep. The bedclothes had been straightened so her chin jutted over a pristine sheet. That was all he saw of her, just her sleeping face. He caught his breath. He knew what he would do. Dorcas, at his elbow, studied him closely. They both ignored the room's other patient and her female visitor and the pair tactfully pretended to be unaware of what was going on.

Dorcas touched Dutton's arm and gestured to him to approach the bed. He moved forward. Now he could hear the sleeping woman breathing, see the tentative rise and fall of her flesh. The nurse who had tidied the Mystery Woman's bed had smoothed the mousey hair, too, but perhaps he only invented that and sleep had come so fast that there had been no preparatory head-tossing and settling. Just one strand sketched its way across the pillowcase. He wanted so very much to put out his hand and touch her hair, feel its warmth. Despite the heat of the ward a chill moved along his spine. A dreamlike quality came over the scene. He felt like observer as well as participant. Time slowed. The inner voice that phrased his thoughts was wordless. There was only emotion. Apprehension. Excitement. Guilt. Love.

Dorcas was taking in the intent look on Dutton's face, the way he struggled to restrain himself from gathering the sleeping figure to him. She saw him swallow hard, close his eyes. Dutton fought to speak. His voice came in a croak, the first part of the sentence lost. Only one word was clear. 'Carol.'

From her office Dorcas telephoned Dr Renfrew. He was busy, she left a message. Then she showed Dutton her patient's belongings. The student nurse brought them and they were unwrapped on a trolley in a corridor. The coat was navy blue but torn and marked with what might have been blood. On the dress there was no question but that it was. The garment had been cut right along the length.

Dorcas said they had cut the clothes from her body when she was carried unconscious into casualty. 'There wasn't a handbag, or its contents might have explained who she was.' She asked whether his wife had clothes like these. He said

36

she could have done but Dorcas was not troubled by the doubt. Men were notoriously vague about what their wives wore, and any man might fail to recognize garments in this state. The blood must be quite disturbing. And she remembered how shaken the woman herself had been when the clothes had been shown to her in an attempt to stir her memory.

Dorcas indicated to the nurse to roll the bundle up again. 'What would you like us to do with them? I really don't think they would ever be of use and we can get rid of them here quite simply.' Dutton thanked her, with a nod. She said: 'In the meantime we will put them back where they came from,' and sent the nurse away with them.

Then Renfrew was free and Dutton let himself be led to the doctor's room. He listened to his steps sounding steadily along the corridor, taking him towards the next hazard. His scalp tightened, sending quivers of fear down his back. He had not been prepared for any of this, although the nurse had been eager to believe him and the doctor would have no choice. Whatever Dutton said there was no one to contradict him and by sticking to the truth about his wife the one enormous lie would be ignored.

They reached Renfrew's room and Dorcas, with time only for a brief introduction, was called away. Renfrew stood to shake hands. He was smaller and jollier than he seemed on television. 'Well, Mr Dutton, you have solved our mystery for us!'

'Yes.'

'But she was not able to recognize you?'

'No.' The men looked at each other across the desk. Dutton felt he ought to say more but the words would not come.

Renfrew gestured him to a chair. 'If you wouldn't mind, I'd like to go over what you've already said about your wife.' He paused. Dutton nodded. 'You say you last saw her in November. Was she quite well then?'

Renfrew ran through the questions, elaborating on those Dorcas had already put. Dutton had the answers pat. He felt easier. He knew he could not be faulted. But if only they would just wake the woman up and let him take her away!

Suddenly Renfrew was moving on to new and unexpected ground. 'I don't suppose you thought of bringing your wife's medical card, did you?'

'No.'

'Well, give me the name of your family doctor and I'll get the number from him along with the medical history.'

Dutton was allowed no time to think. He stuck to the truth. 'We are still registered with a doctor near where we used to live. He's called Andersen.'

Renfrew wrote down Dr Andersen's address. 'We'll telephone him today. Then I'd like you to come again and bring some things – photographs and anything else that seems appropriate – which you think might trigger her memory.'

'Yes.' Dutton was alarmed at the way things were snatched out of his control. He had imagined he would have the initiative, the hospital would be so pleased to hand their Mystery Woman over he would be on his way home with her by now. Instead Dr Renfrew was virtually asking him to provide proof of her identity. If the things he was asked to bring were purely to jog her memory then why wasn't the doctor waking her up and asking her whether she recognized Peter Dutton? And then he guessed: Renfrew was unaware that she was still asleep.

He felt Renfrew waiting for him to enlarge on the monosyllable. A telephone on the desk rang and saved him. When Renfrew had dealt with the caller Dutton had his own question ready, a question to which television and the papers had already given him the answer. 'Would you tell me about amnesia, how it is affecting her?' He barely listened to the reply, he was thinking ahead to the next danger. He would have to go through the greater ordeal of presenting his proof on another visit and he could not avoid doing so. He had been honest about all the information he had given: his own identity, his home address, the details about his wife, the name of his family doctor. There was no possibility of backing away now. The trap he had laid for others had already sprung and he was its first victim.

There was one danger he thought he could ward off. 'Can

you keep it secret when she leaves hospital? I don't want reporters on the doorstep when I get home.'

'No, and neither do I want them giving her a send-off from here. It is better for her to be kept calm and quiet. We will conspire to silence.'

'And the hospital won't even say where she has gone?'

Renfrew smiled. 'There will be no clues.' Carol Dutton, he thought with unprofessional selfishness, would once more vanish without trace. He added: 'She should be ready to be discharged at the weekend, if you can fetch her by car. Would it suit you to come again on, say, Saturday?'

'Yes. I'll telephone to confirm she is ready and then drive up.'

Dorcas, joining them, put in: 'But don't forget to bring clothes for Carol to travel home in.' The details were fixed and Dutton was free to leave. The nurse and doctor smiled at him, showing they shared his relief at finding his missing wife. Dutton walked away down the warm corridor.

Dorcas stayed with the doctor. She wanted to give a report on one of his other patients. That was her pressing matter but she must also underline that Carol Dutton had been asleep when her husband called, although she assumed that Dutton would have already explained that. Renfrew was still looking after Dutton. He sighed. 'Well, Dorcas . . . he's not exactly what I expected . . .' The telephone rang again. He was needed on a ward. With a show of weariness he got to his feet. Princes Hospital was short-staffed and he had been on duty a long while. Dorcas knew it and without waste of words told him about her sick patient. By the time he got to the ward he had twice been intercepted by urgent calls and Dorcas had gone off duty.

Renfrew wasn't concerned about the meeting between Carol Dutton and her husband, just sorry he had not been there to see her reaction. But as there had not been one it hardly mattered. He'd asked Peter Dutton whether she had recognized him. And Dutton had said: 'No.'

# 6

Dutton bought the *Standard* next day and studied the cheap car advertisements. He wanted a quick deal, a kerbside sale where an offer of cash would bring the price down. At a garage they would want him to sign a hire purchase agreement because the salesman would be after commission from the finance company. Dutton had found that out when he bought a car in the past.

His eye stopped at a promising advertisement. He lifted the telephone on his desk. Johnson and Lewis were at lunch, Dutton had returned early with the paper so his enquiries would be private. A man answered him. The car was not yet sold. They discussed it. Dutton said he would call round on his way home from work. It wasn't on his way from Oxford Circus to Spinney Green, but he would let the ambiguity stand. It was just as well to be wary of everything and everyone, but he did not want to tell lies. He had always hated them, since early childhood when his mother who was none too fussy whether she told them or not accused him of lying whenever she chose to disbelieve him. Dutton had learned to avoid the direct lie and the avoidance gave him a moral superiority.

He was a bit early. The man was getting out of the car, and Dutton guessed it had just been driven round the block to make sure it started easily when the owner showed it off to him. A young woman and two small faces peeped from a ground-floor window in a council house and watched as Dutton pored over the vehicle. He was pleased. He pieced together the situation. The man was out of work, the family car had to go.

Dutton scanned the documents. 'You haven't had it long?'

The man fingered a wing mirror. 'No.' A break. Then: 'It was my mother's. She always looked after it, and then when she . . .'

Dutton nodded. 'So you got the car.' The papers seemed in order so far as he could tell. There was nothing to suggest the man wasn't the real owner with a legal right to sell. 'The tax runs out at the end of the month.' Obviously the man could not afford to renew it. The circumstances were just what Dutton had hoped for: an owner desperate for money and unwilling to spend a penny he didn't have to.

They drove down the road, looped around the housing estate and parked outside the house. Dutton made his offer, his mean offer that took into account the cost of renewing the road fund licence and the reduction he would demand for paying in cash. He saw the man wanted to reject it, but Dutton ignored his disappointed face and looked about the street as if to point out there was no sign of anyone else arriving with a better price. The man sighed. 'It's a lot less than I was hoping for. In the advertisement I said offers around . . .'

'I can give you cash. Tomorrow.'

The man put out a hand to the car's polished sleekness, then drew it back without touching. It was a gesture that relinquished possession. Dutton knew he had won.

'All right,' the man said. 'If you bring the cash tomorrow.'

Dutton glowed as he walked back to the Underground. He had got a bargain, he had got it quickly and whether or not the story about the careful lady owner were true the car would suit him very nicely. He was smiling to himself, a thin smug smile. Everything had gone exactly as he intended.

The train arrived as soon as he reached the platform and it was empty enough for him to find a seat. There were a number of people opposite him but he took hardly any notice of them: a black youth listening to music on earphones, a middle-aged woman with her nose in a pulp novel, a man doing the crossword in the evening paper, a few others. Dutton's mind was running ahead, imagining himself at home and gathering together the things he would take to Leamington. He was deciding which photograph would be best, what other items he ought to choose.

41

He was jolted back to the present by the sound of his name. 'Peter? It is, isn't it? I couldn't be sure. I've been trying to decide whether to speak to you ever since you got on. You feel so foolish if it turns out to be a complete stranger, don't you?'

She might have *been* a complete stranger. He could not place her at all. A short, plump, dark-haired woman in her twenties dressed fashionably but cheaply. 'Marcia,' she said. 'Marcia Cohen. I used to work with Carol. Met you once or twice when we . . . So how *is* Carol? It's ages since I've seen her. What is she doing now?'

'Oh . . . Er . . .' Fortunately the train was rattling and bouncing and he was able to get away without a proper answer. It screamed into a station. He struggled to his feet, the woman backing off to let him stand.

'Is this your stop? Before we've had time to talk? Well never mind, tell Carol you've seen me. Ask her to phone me. I rang your flat but the people there said you'd moved and they didn't know where you'd gone . . .'

The doors hissed to a close behind him, cutting her off. He made a show of walking up the platform towards the exit. The train passed him, Marcia Cohen waving from the seat he had vacated. Then he wandered about the platform and waited for the next train to continue his journey. Marcia Cohen. Marcia Cohen. Yes, there was a glimmer of recognition. Not the name, he would never have drummed that up but the whining voice and the way she pressed her face towards his to shout above the noise of the train . . . He knew that was familiar. He thought she had worked with Carol, she was also a secretary. How long had Carol known her? A couple of years? Three? Possibly even further back because Marcia Cohen was the sort who never let go. The thought struck him like a blow. Marcia Cohen could be extremely dangerous, because Marcia Cohen would pursue Carol.

For the rest of the journey he tried to prove he was exaggerating the significance of the chance meeting. He had been many miles from Spinney Green but Marcia would assume he was on home territory. He was quite likely to be safe in assuming that *she* was. In fact, they might never meet again. And if they did, how much would it matter? It would be a nuisance to be pestered with messages for Carol, but when there were no messages back even Marcia would be forced to give up. Yet he had a gnawing apprehension that would not go away.

He fetched the car next day as arranged, handing over an envelope containing cash drawn out of the bank that lunchtime. The drive to Spinney Green was marked by nothing more worrying than uncertainty about the route. By now he had decided what he would take to Leamington with him: a poor photograph of Carol and some letters. The business of choosing those things and the activity of buying the car had helped him through the waiting time.

On Friday evening he was taut. The tasks were all done, the decisions taken. He had nothing to occupy him. He jumped from one television channel to the next, impatient for distraction. Nothing was any use. He sat through an American-made series where the cops predictably closed in on the robbers at the end of half an hour. A doyen of television naturalists droned through a wildlife film about plankton. A blonde woman, Rain Morgan, led her team to victory in a panel game. The news programmes came and inattention left him confused as countries and crises flashed over the screen. Finally there was *Chapter and Verse*, a books programme, which was hogged by an untidy Professor Something talking about a book called *Naughty but Nice*.

Dutton took the television set up to the bedroom and fell asleep in front of it long before transmission ended. It was his usual, precarious sleep. He was downstairs again very early in the morning to check through the stuff to take to Leamington and to torture himself with fears of what the day might bring. When it was time to set off he felt distinct relief.

Doubt and fear revived as he walked into the hospital, putting his future in the hands of others. He believed he could carry his plan through. Intellectually, he believed that. But the way he braced himself for the ordeal, the knowledge that all his muscles had tensed and that he was poised for flight undermined that belief. He delayed before reaching the reception desk, blew his nose, creating a little activity to mask his real preoccupations and to earn a short space in which to compose himself. When he was as steady as he knew how to be he went up to the desk and said who he was and why he was there.

Dr Renfrew was not alone. In his room was a social worker called Irene Yarrow, a dark woman with a professional smile and keen eyes. Dutton felt her eyes searing into him, exposing every dishonesty, showing up the liar who was so particular about avoiding lies. Beneath his clothes he was unbearably hot, on his forehead a cool sweat formed.

He was carrying a very large plastic carrier bag holding everything he had brought. Suddenly this seemed silly, he wondered why he hadn't put the clothes into a small suitcase. Surely he was creating the wrong effect? Renfrew and Miss Yarrow were staring at the bag. He set it down beside a chair, but it wouldn't stand up. He grabbed at it. Renfrew invited him to sit down. He lowered himself on to the chair, still with one hand on the unruly bag. It seemed important not to let it fall over and spill the clothes, like secrets, on the floor.

Renfrew said: 'We telephoned Dr Andersen to tell him your wife was here and he has given us your wife's medical records, Mr Dutton. The only thing of possible significance is that she has suffered from stress-related conditions in the past. Insomnia and tension headaches seem to have been a problem for her over some years.' He was reading through the papers on his desk as he spoke, but Miss Yarrow was giving Dutton all her attention.

'Yes,' said Dutton, not knowing how far it was wise to enlarge.

He adjusted his position in the chair. The bag slipped from his grasp and he lunged at it. He knew he was making a fool of himself, his nervousness was going to give him away.

Irene Yarrow was speaking: 'Are those the things you have brought to show your wife, Mr Dutton?' She had a soft Birmingham accent. Kindly. Not accusing, despite the vigilant eyes.

In reply Dutton took the package of photographs and oddments and held them out to her. 'I don't know if they will be any use, it was hard to know what to bring.'

44

There were murmurs of sympathy. Miss Yarrow spread the things on the desk in front of Dr Renfrew: a photograph of Carol, windswept, by a beach; a photograph of her parents posing outside their New Zealand home; a letter from her mother; and so on, pieces of paper that might mean anything or nothing. Dutton knew they were going to mean nothing.

They talked some more. Their questions, Dutton's guarded answers. He wished he could loosen up inside, expand on his replies, behave in a more natural way. He could not do it. The tension was stultifying. It was a tight band around his chest, crushing his freedom to act and speak as he wanted. He willed them to get on with it, bring the woman in, get it over, let him leave.

Renfrew was saying: 'I think the best thing we could do now, Mr Dutton, would be to ask your wife to join us.' Dutton nodded, mute. Irene Yarrow's eyes noted his failure. With the briefest delay the Mystery Woman came into the room.

Dutton registered the warmth of the smiles Renfrew and Irene Yarrow turned on her, the gentle touch on her arm by the nurse who had fetched her. 'Hello, Carol,' Renfrew said and Irene Yarrow moved up a chair for her to sit. Dutton knew then he had got away with it. Unless something terrible happened, some catastrophic blunder, then he had got away with it. *Because they were calling her Carol!* They would never have told her that was her name unless they had swallowed his story on his first visit. Today's was almost a formality.

'This is Peter Dutton, Carol,' Renfrew said. Everyone looked at the woman, and she looked at Dutton. She was wearing a hospital dressing-gown, her fingers twisting the cord. She appeared pale, anxious. The little hope that was in her grey eyes faded and Dutton turned his head not able to bear her gaze.

He heard her voice, 'I'm sorry, I can't . . .' It was a pretty voice.

Renfrew said: 'Don't be upset about it, it would have been very surprising if you had suddenly remembered. Now, have a look at these.'

Dutton felt the pressure lifting. No one was interested in

him now, he was just an exhibit as the photographs and pathetic bits of paper which were meant to represent a life, were exhibits. He sat silent, watching as Irene Yarrow invited the woman to study each item in turn, encouraging her to say if there was anything the least familiar.

Eventually they gave up, asked her a series of questions based on information Dutton had given them. Repeatedly, the woman shook her head. She managed to laugh off the disappointments. 'Nothing seems to connect,' she said. 'My only glimmers of memory seem more to do with the countryside than London.' She turned to Dutton. 'Did I ever live in the countryside?'

'Not that I know of . . .'

'You see, I sometimes get a very strong feeling – I can't explain it, it's a sort of recognition but it isn't actually memory. When I'm looking at photographs in a magazine, for instance, I'll suddenly find my attention being held by one in quite an intense way . . . It's the same with television but, of course, that's more ephemeral . . .' She let it trail away.

'Go on,' said Renfrew when Dutton did not respond.

She said: 'I'm afraid I'm not making much sense. But what it comes down to is that these pictures are usually rural subjects and so I thought the countryside was important to me.'

Irene Yarrow picked up the letter Carol Dutton's mother had written to her. 'You say your wife was in New Zealand with her parents for a few years after they emigrated, Mr Dutton? They live in a small town, so isn't it possible that Carol could have developed an attachment for the country-side during that period?'

Dutton said: 'Yes, perhaps she did.' He looked at the woman whose hands were still worrying the dressing-gown cord.

She gave a weary smile. 'I have no idea.'

The session went on until day faded. Despite diminishing hope of success Renfrew and Irene Yarrow pursued every possible strand of information that might lead back to their patient's memory. From time to time they were joined by doctors, some, Dutton suspected, psychiatrists. Dutton's tension turned to resentment. He had won the game, it was obvious so why didn't they give up and give in?

When they came to the end of it he was taken by surprise. Irene Yarrow was handing back to him the package of documents, a nurse was accompanying the woman to a room where she could change into the clothes he had brought.

Renfrew said: 'Before you leave I'll give you a letter to take to Dr Andersen. If you are lucky she will begin to recover her memory in the familiar surroundings of home, but if not, Dr Andersen may want to refer her to a consultant in London.'

Dutton was in control again now. The band of tension had weakened as triumph became surer. He promised not to leave without the letter for Dr Andersen. He stood up, putting the package into his overcoat pocket. As soon as the woman was dressed and Renfrew had scribbled his letter he would be free. Then Irene Yarrow was speaking and Dutton's hand tightened on the package.

'We'll follow up, of course, Mr Dutton. I'll set things in motion so that someone goes to see Carol and how she's coping.'

She was smiling at him, a comforting silly smile. He said: 'Yes. Yes, of course.' His hand released the package. His palms were sweating.

## 7

Her break with Princes Hospital was painful. A nameless anxiety made her want to cling to the place, which was all she knew. She blamed it on tiredness. The day had been exhausting.

She went to change. The student nurse was there to help. There was a grey wool and polyester skirt, a green blouse and an acrylic waistcoat with a Fair Isle type of pattern encompassing most colours. To wear with them Dutton had brought tights, green boots and a grey winter coat. A faint sweet smell hung about them.

Her hair had been cut so the tufty part was no longer obvious and she hoped that, wearing her own clothes at last, she would look and feel good. Instead, she was demoralized. Dorcas put her head into the room as Carol buttoned the waistcoat. 'Oh dear, Carol,' she said with a chuckle. 'You *have* lost weight!'

The nurse handed her the boots. They were a little too big, she guessed she usually wore socks in them but Dutton had not brought any. Dorcas said, taking up the coat: 'Oh, this is a nice loose style so it should be all right.'

Carol put the coat on. She gave a brave smile. 'I'm ready for home.'

She went to say goodbye to Dr Renfrew, conscious how impatient Dutton was to be gone. She knew she was stretching everything to its limit because she was afraid to leave. When she went she would leave behind everything she knew and her only company would be a man who might as well be a stranger.

There was a call for the doctor and she had no excuse to delay him. He gave her a final reassuring smile and went one way down the over-heated corridor while she and Peter Dutton went the other.

At the front entrance to the building there were a few shallow steps. She faltered. It was a long time since she had worn anything except slippers on her feet. The ill-fitting boots made her falter. Dutton took her upper arm and led her down. 'That's it,' he said. 'Take your time. We're in no hurry.' But she sensed that despite his words he wanted to get away quickly and so she tried, striding out across the car park where his car waited. Some nurses coming on duty stared at them. Carol waved but Dutton had her arm and steered her to zigzag between parked cars. She resented that. She had an urge to break free of him, run to the nurses and beg to be taken back to the world she knew. Tiredness was making her irrational. The hospital did not want her, she belonged with Peter Dutton. Behind her she heard the women's voices start up once more as they passed without having met.

The car Dutton brought was a fawn family saloon, several years old but spruce. As the hospital was on the north of the town he had to find the road which would take him east and towards the motorway. Carol noticed how he fumbled with the controls, muddling the windscreen wiper switch with the indicators. When they joined a line of traffic at lights she said: 'Haven't you had this car long?'

He shot her a surprised look. She said: 'I only thought . . . because you keep mixing up the controls . . .' He was silent and they moved forward. At the next junction he took the wrong lane and was swept into the town centre. The street was garlanded with lights, as far as the eye could see. Pedestrians overflowed the pavements, took their chances crossing the road. 'We're on The Parade!' she said.

'How do you know?' His voice was casual but she saw his fingers tighten on the wheel.

She laughed a rippling laugh. 'I've seen the Parade Dry Cleaners and now I've seen a street sign.'

Soon they were in country darkness. The miles sped away. Carol could not think what to say to him but hated the silence.

Real conversation was ruled out while they were travelling. Inconsequential chat, with the serious waiting to be said, was awkward. They had nothing but the rumble of the engine, the hiss of the telegraph poles passing, and the intermittent scream of other vehicles.

Carol wanted to look at him. She wanted to swivel round in her seat so that she could study him, get to know him as one does a new acquaintance. She moved a fraction, began to watch unobtrusively. It was a strong face that passing cars illuminated for her. Dutton looked like a man who knew his own mind and how to get his own way. Yet there was tension, too, in his rigidity and the set of the jaw. Ever since he had met her at the hospital he had been discernibly nervous. The voice was steady and matter of fact but anxiety revealed itself in a way he could not disguise. On his left temple a tiny pulse throbbed.

He felt her eyes, turned with a smile. 'We'll stop for tea on the way, if you like.'

'Yes, thank you. I'm quite thirsty. Heaven knows why they keep hospitals so hot, one just wants to drink the whole time.' Caught spying, she shifted to watch the swathe of road ahead. She was tired. It was alarming how she so often felt tired.

He heard her yawn. 'Why don't you put the seat back and rest?'

'How do I do it?'

'Isn't there a catch at the side of the seat?'

She was right, he wasn't used to this car. She groped along the side of the seat and discovered how to adjust the backrest. Then she slid down, willing sleep until it was time for tea. Sleep would shut out her unnamed doubts and the discomfort of Dutton's company.

Carol curled her hands into the pockets of the voluminous grey coat for warmth and dozed. The fingers of her left hand closed over a card. She wondered what it could be and whether it held the vital clue to her past? But she already had the vital clue. That was Peter Dutton, beside her and driving her home where she was almost certain to rediscover herself. She left the card where it was and slept.

50

Waking, as Dutton pulled off the motorway into Todding-ton service station, she felt the card again. Her inclination was to pull it out and read it, but some instinct refused while Dutton was there. He held her arm again as they went into the cafeteria. Near the entrance she tripped but his firm grasp saved her from falling.

'I'm sorry, it's the boots,' she said.

'The boots? What's wrong with the boots?'

'Well . . .' a pause as he held open the door . . . 'they're loose, I imagine I usually wear socks in them.' He was leading her to a table. 'In fact, all the clothes you brought are a bit too big.' She laughed her low rippling laugh. People at the next table looked up. Dutton leaned across to her, obscuring their view. The pulse in his temple ticked.

She said: 'Oh, don't look so worried about it. I lost weight after the accident. People do, it's partly shock and partly lying there with tubes and that sort of paraphernalia instead of three good meals a day. I've regained most of it – at least I *thought* I had but this just shows how much further I've got to go!'

He went to fetch tea and teacakes. Carol watched him walk away, this stranger she had to learn to know and love all over again. She wondered why he was so tense, so taciturn. Surely he ought to be happy and excited to have found her? And then she understood. She had left home three months ago; besides giving her details of their ordinary lives he was going to have to tell her why. And she could not tell him where she had been or whether she had been with anyone else.

Fears and doubts that had made her cling to the hospital were crystallizing: she had given herself into the hands of a stranger and she would have to take on trust everything he told her about herself.

The cafeteria was busy and most tables occupied. Couples were comfortably paired, families grouped congenially. They were confident and secure in their self-knowledge. Only she, Carol Dutton, was adrift. Even her own name meant nothing to her.

She imagined, to lighten her mood, how she would have

felt if one of these families had come to Princes Hospital to claim her. That one, with the gingery-haired daughter squeaking a straw at the end of a cherry-red drink? No. She wouldn't have picked that one, given a choice. Or that family, where the teenage daughter in jeans and anorak had the country-red cheeks of a girl who'd spent the day riding a horse into the wind? Carol halted the diversion abruptly. So, she thought: I've remembered about riding horses into the wind.

But as soon as she snatched at the recollection it faded. This was how it so often happened to her. She formed an opinion and realized that it could, logically, only be formed of experience. It was close to remembering, but not quite. She sighed. Well, never mind. Don't mope, play another round. Now supposing that other family had said she was one of them? Would she be pleased? Yes, she rather thought she would. They had an aura of self-confidence, their clothes were good. She pictured that outside in the car park they would have the sort of small Continental car people opted for because it was fun. Probably the car would be a few years old but it would say all the things which, for the same money, Peter Dutton's second-hand car didn't.

Carol bit her lip. She stopped the game again. She could sense where it was leading and it was far too early to pass judgement on Peter Dutton or his choice of cars. If she had been with him when he went to buy it then perhaps she could have persuaded him into something jauntier, the type she was so vividly assuming for the young family nearby. Yes, of course, she would have done.

Dutton was leaving the checkout, giving her a cautious look across the tables and carrying the tray towards her. She rearranged her face into a smile of welcome. The family she had chosen to be hers finished their tea and rose. The mother swung a fine cashmere sweater over her shoulders. It toned perfectly with the rest of her outfit. The action jarred Carol. Here was she admiring the quality and style of the woman's clothes while she herself was dressing in garments which, quite apart from the poor fit, she disliked. Instinctively she knew that however poor the Dutton household, she would

52

starve for a cashmere sweater and leave its sad acrylic cousin in the shop. Yet she was dressed in the proof that this wasn't true. She was utterly confused. Instead of things becoming clearer to her now that she was going home, they were growing more mysterious.

Dutton arrived with the tray and they talked generally, about the relative busyness of motorway service stations at different times of the day and week, about tea and about teacakes. Before they continued south Carol headed for the door marked Ladies. While she was rubbing her hands under a hot-air drier she remembered the card in her pocket. With damp fingers she drew it out and stared at it until another woman, impatient to use the drier, asked her to move.

Carol roused herself, apologized, went to the mirror to comb her hair. But she had no handbag, no comb, no anything. She studied her reflection, as she used to in the hospital. She looked drawn. Then she tried out a smile and the face lit up. She would buy lipstick on Monday, when the shops opened, and perhaps a good night's sleep in her own home would do wonders for her pallor.

Briskly she went to join Dutton. He led her back to the car she so unkindly despised. Settling back to rest, her hands found her pockets and in the left one the card. An appointment card. As the car joined the motorway once more she frowned into the darkness.

# 8

Spinney Green meant nothing to her, nor Shepherd Road. The headlights of Dutton's car focused on raw new houses, unfinished buildings, trails of rubble shed by lorries. Carol saw light-coloured brick houses with dark woodwork and peculiar bay windows. Then Dutton was swinging the car up to one, letting her out and hurrying her through the front door. He sounded cheerful enough now. 'Here we are. How does it feel to be home?'

It was an ironic joke, they both knew that. She laughed. 'I'll have to let you know when it *feels* like home.' They were in the hall. She paused like any first-time visitor to a house. 'This way?'

'Wherever you like.' He pushed open the door she'd indicated and flicked on the light. She stepped into the room with the bay and waited, feeling hope recede.

Then she looked shyly up at him, shaking her head. 'Sorry, Peter, it doesn't mean a thing to me. I really want it to, but . . .' There was a moment when they both thought she was going to cry. He put his arms around her and pulled her to him. She pressed her eyelids tight. She must not become upset now. It had been a testing day for both of them. He must be as miserable as she was that their home had not captured that elusive memory. He was concealing his disappointment from her, and she was grateful.

They stood like that until car lights approached along Shepherd Road and Dutton released her and closed the curtains. Jerky conversation revived and he took her around the house, accepting that she must be introduced to everything afresh as though she were a stranger. Upstairs he showed her first the main bedroom where her clothes hung in a wardrobe beside his. They were creased and she imagined him bundling them out of sight after she left. A faint scent of pine wafted as he opened the door but he did not comment on it, and she did not like to. For all his talk of other details it was the double bed which dominated the room and her mind. She was relieved when Dutton said: 'I made up the bed in the back room for you. I supposed you would prefer to be on your own.'

Obediently she followed. He put on the light and drew the curtains. The back room was cell-like: a single bed, a chest in pale blue laminate and a matching bedside table.

They spoke at once. She said: 'Well . . .' and he said: 'I thought we'd . . .' Embarrassed they laughed and he began again, suggesting they have a meal of steak and kidney pies and oven chips. They ate in the kitchen, Dutton getting the meal and insisting she watched television. There was a quiz show on, a puerile one where contestants were asked elementary questions by a compere exhibiting all the composure of a chicken with its head cut off.

Over their meal she and Dutton agreed to defer serious discussion until next day. She was thankful, being far too tired to cope and not managing even token argument when he urged her off to bed to leave him to the washing up.

From the kitchen he heard her movements in the bathroom and bedroom overhead. The tension which had gripped him all day was suddenly released. He sagged against the kitchen doorpost, exhausted. His legs felt weak, his body leaden. Breath was a painful rasp. The dreadful moments of the day returned to torment him. He winced at the pitiful naivety which had ever let him believe the woman would be handed over to him and no questions asked. How on earth had he kept control when Renfrew had asked those questions about the photograph? Or when the social worker said she would make arrangements for her to be followed up? And when he was pressed about the idea she had lived in the country? But he had, he *had*! He'd taken a huge risk but he'd won. He was euphoric.

For all their smart questions and bright ideas he had outwitted them. Right under their noses he had carried out the most audacious deception and they would never find out. His whispered words were an ironic understatement of his feelings: 'So far, so good.'

Then he pulled himself up. No, it hadn't been all good. She was quick-witted and had noticed his unfamiliarity with the car. He could not help that: he'd had to dash out and buy a car to collect her, the train journey would have been too tiring and perhaps the hospital would not have let her undertake it. Well, so what? He would tell her that. Always stick to the truth, the facts are easier to handle than any amount of clever fabrication. The only dismaying thing about the incident was that it revealed how observant she was. He would have to be constantly on guard.

But he *had* made a mistake, a fundamental and avoidable error. He believed he had thought the whole thing through, and yet he had blundered. The clothes were the wrong size. And the *boots*. Oh, worst of all the boots! When people lost weight their shoe size did not change so radically. Holding her, in the lounge when she was on the verge of tears, he had felt how slender she was beneath the bulk of the grey coat. He had felt, too, how very vulnerable and trusting she was. He would look after her. He had never had anyone dependent on him before. Looking after her would not include passing on to Dr Andersen the letter Dr Renfrew had handed him, and he would have to dream up a way of stopping Irene Yarrow's local colleagues following up the case. He didn't think that would be beyond him.

Dutton planned a treat. He would take her out to lunch tomorrow. They'd go to the Halberd, a steak house, a pleasant drive away. It was an extravagance but he wanted to make her happy and that would get them off to a good start. In a way, he thought, it would be like remaking his marriage, starting again at the beginning when he and his wife were happiest and their relationship could have grown in any direction. It would be easy to love her. He had felt it so strongly when he looked at her in the hospital on his first visit. When he was no longer a stranger to her she would be ready to give up the bed in the spare room and join him. But he would not rush her. He would move as stealthily in that direction as in every other.

He washed up and went to the front bedroom for a dreamless sleep. His mistake about the clothes was there to confront him next morning. She came to the kitchen door, dressed only in the nightdress she had rummaged from the dressing table in the front bedroom last night. She had been too sleepy to wonder at the sweet smell which clung to it but had dragged it on and toppled into bed.

'I couldn't find a dressing-gown,' she said by greeting and Dutton started at the sound of her voice.

'Tea?'

'Yes please.'

'Milk? Sugar?'

'Just a little milk, please.' While he poured she went on. 'Do I have a dressing-gown somewhere?'

There was a tremor in his hand as he passed her a mug. Oh yes, Carol Dutton had owned a dressing-gown, he was sure of it. Creamy nylon lace, it was, and when she went she took it with her. He said casually: 'Perhaps you took it with you.'

She shied away. The accusatory words made his point. She had left him and now here she was with no excuses, no explanations. She desperately needed to know where she had been, why she went. Dutton must have the answer to the second question but she was too embarrassed to press him just then. The story would inevitably be one of her desertion, possibly her unfaithfulness. She felt ashamed. She hid her face in her mug. Then the garden took her eye. She went to the sink and scanned the long strip surrounded by its wooden fence. A few young rose bushes no one had pruned. An ugly, mis-shapen rockery. A cat was doing unspeakable things to a mouse. She could not bear to watch the torment, so she turned away.

'I'm going to look through all the clothes in the wardrobe and see what fits,' she said. And away she went to discover the best was a heavy cotton smock, one of those amorphous garments designed to bury all shapes and sizes. There was a ribbed woollen sweater that worked fairly well under it and, with a pair of socks in them she was able to wear the green boots comfortably. At least she looked as though the clothes belonged to her now. She ran downstairs to show him. His face lit. She held out the smock and twirled round. 'Everything else feels a size too large.'

'I always liked that dress.' He turned back to the frying pan.

'But I must have some new things. Everything else is hopeless.'

He made a vague sound which she took for agreement. During breakfast he told her he was taking her out to lunch, if she felt well enough.

'Oh, yes, I'm quite well. I just tire easily, but I've had a good night's sleep and I can cope now.' There was a pause. They both knew what had to be coped with.

Dutton said: 'Would you like to talk this morning? If you feel up to it there's no point in putting things off. Then afterwards we'll go to the Halberd.'

'The Halberd?'

'Sorry, I forgot. It's the restaurant we used to eat at sometimes.'

She gave her rippling laugh. 'No, you mean *I* forgot. I'm afraid we're in for a lot of that.'

Dutton was worried about what questions she might have that he could not or would not wish to answer. They sat on either side of the teak coffee table in the room with the bay window, like people in a posed television-studio interview. Carol asked, Dutton answered. She noticed how the situation made him tense, how the pulse in his temple raced. She felt sorry for him and deferred the questions she knew would be most troubling. She started with the easy ones.

'I feel a fool,' she said with her shy smile, 'having to ask such basic things.' Things like how long they had been married, where she had lived before then, what his job was, what hers had been, where their relations were. And on and on until he looked at the brass and pine clock (a wedding present) on the mantelpiece and said he really thought they should set off for the Halberd.

'You're just saying that to spare my shame,' she laughed. She had got to the question of her weight problem. 'Why on earth didn't you force me to go on a diet? I must have been hideously fat.'

But he didn't respond to her self-criticism, it was as though a shutter had dropped down and cut off contact. She had far more questions, especially those about why she had left home, but his manner forced her to accept that the question and answer session was over. He fetched the baggy grey coat, she swaddled herself in that and they went out to the car. She was disappointed with herself for not having asked, right at the beginning, why she had left home. She had intended to lead him gently towards it, but she did not understand his nature. Of course, he had realized where the questions would lead and he had effectively refused to be led there. Now she would have to wait for another chance, maybe another day.

Shepherd Road was lazily coming to Sunday morning life. Cars, ancient and modern, were being washed on the concrete run-ins outside several of the houses. Small children played in immature gardens. Couples squinted through the windows of the nearly finished Phase Two houses opposite the Duttons' home, and other house hunters distinguished themselves by driving at crawling pace up the street, the drivers gazing sideways and leaving the road ahead to trust. Carol was loath to be confined in the car again but after lunch at the Halberd she might have the chance of a walk.

Lunch was a shade easier than breakfast, and breakfast had been less onerous than supper. Everything must, she reasoned, be gradual. Unless something gave her memory the shove it required she would have to settle for slow relearning. And patience. One thing she had discovered about herself was that she was short of patience. And how lucky for them both that Peter Dutton had an abundance. He was not pressing her, not becoming exasperated (as she did with herself) but willing to lead her gently along until she knew all she should know about Carol Dutton. Her only criticism of him was that when she tried to tell him about those moments when she felt near to memory of horse riding or views along steep valleys, or honey-coloured houses on a hill, he brushed them away, and recommended her to do the same. That was frustrating, but she could see that he believed it was for her own good.

The Halberd was a 1930s roadhouse which flourished in the steak and chips age by installing a few plastic beams and a fake log fire whose 'smoke' was meant to drift up a copper canopy tacked on to a wall which had no chimney. The red paper napkins had been bought, the red carpet laid and the Halberd was ready for success. Like all its kind it was dependable, inexpensive, aiming for and achieving the mediocre. It was extremely popular.

Dutton had booked but although he told her they had been there a number of times before, none of the staff recognized them. The Halberd had arranged matters so that access to the restaurant was through the bar. Everyone was shunted into it and kept there until they had spent the requisite amount of time and money.

The ploy, so flagrant, amused Carol but she said nothing, unsure whether Peter Dutton would share her humour. They were talking easily now, the new setting giving them fresh subjects. Dutton was attentive, caring. She forgot yesterday's impulse to flee from him.

It was after the meal when the waitress came to invite the Duttons to the coffee lounge that Carol knew something was wrong. Perhaps the sherries followed by wine had come as a surprise to her system after the hospital months. She felt queasy, and mumbling an excuse, made for the ladies cloakroom. She was almost there when an elderly man's badly parked walking stick tripped her and she fell. There was a gasp from the tables nearest and then hands were clutching at her, helping her up, propelling her into the cloakroom.

The waitress and a customer held her, pushing her down into a soft chair and talking to her simultaneously. 'You're not going to be sick, are you?' she heard one say.

'No, I'll be all right in a minute.' She took steadying breaths.

'I expect it's the heat, dear,' said the waitress, fingering an ear-ring. 'It gets very hot in there. Honestly, the first day I worked here I thought I'd die.'

When they had gone there was a deep stillness, broken at last by the sound of Carol sighing, going to the washbasin and splashing cold water on her face. She looked pale, the good work of the restful night was spoiled. All she wanted was a corner to curl up in and sleep. She did not think of the back bedroom at 7 Shepherd Road. With clarity she knew that would never feel like home.

And the thought was followed by the wild idea that this was an opportunity to slip away, disappear from Shepherd Road and Peter Dutton as she had done before. If she could get unobserved from the cloakroom to the exit from the restaurant then she would be free. She could cadge a lift from a car, going anywhere, and then . . . and then she would be stuck, because she had no money, just the ill-fitting clothes she stood up in. At least she had taken her dressing-gown when she had run off in November!

Her eyes met their reflection in the mirror and there was accusation in them. She was being mean, ungrateful and very selfish. How could she even think of running off now? It would be unforgivable, Dutton had done nothing to deserve that. She could not understand her panicky urge to flight, although later she would wonder whether it was not premonition.

She went back into the restaurant. Dutton was hovering near the cloakroom door with her coat over his arm. He had paid the bill and was keen to get away. A few heads looked up as they went out and Carol smiled back at them. 'Come on,' Dutton said brusquely, holding the door for her.

'They probably thought I was drunk,' she said laughing.

'Probably.'

'Do see the funny side of it, everybody else did. There's nothing as funny as someone falling flat on her face.' He was offering her the coat. She demurred. 'What about coffee?'

'We can have coffee at home.' He wasn't open to argument. He gripped her arm and steered her towards the car. So that was that. Back to Shepherd Road. No coffee, no walk, end of outing. Dutton did not speak on the way home. She slid a sideways look at him but the strong features were revealing nothing. She hoped he was not sulking; it would be intolerable to live with a man who sulked.

Then she grew warm with indignation. So he was angry

because she had fallen over in a restaurant and 'shown him up'. Well, it could have happened to anyone. If that old man hadn't been so careless where he left his walking stick . . . She hoped the next time it would be Peter Dutton who went sprawling. But it was a futile hope. Dutton was too methodical to be hurrying about, not looking where he was going.

She wondered how often in the past he had been ashamed of her behaviour, whether the homing instinct always prevailed when things went awry. But they weren't questions she felt able to ask him. However, there were some things she could learn without asking. If she were to live amicably with this near-stranger then she must discover how to do so. All it took was observation. Instead of obsessive self-concern, searching for her own identity, she would study Peter Dutton.

The car turned into Shepherd Road, deserted now as late Sunday lunchtimes claimed the car washers. But as Dutton drove on to the run-in a man and a woman popped out of the front door of number 9. Carol's face glowed with interest. Dutton cut the engine, dashed round to open her door. She was on the side next to the man and woman who stood there like a reception committee waiting to greet her.

Carol managed 'hello' but the balding man and henna-haired woman only opened mouths to reply before Dutton had his front door open and Carol inside. She wrenched herself free of him. His grasp had been quite rough. Beyond the front door she could hear the woman saying 'Well!' in disgust and the man's mumbled answer.

Carol hung her coat in the hall and went upstairs to the bathroom. Emotion had brought colour to her cheeks again. Perhaps the waitress had been correct: the heat might have made her feel unwell. Since leaving the restaurant she had been all right. Downstairs she heard water running, pictured Dutton making coffee, pictured them in silence in the kitchen or at the low teak table in what he called the lounge. She did not want to go down. Her head was beginning to ache. She opened the bathroom window and stayed there, looking at the view and breathing the cold air.

After a while she closed the window and went to the kitchen. Coffee was made and Dutton had left a mug for her on the worktop along with the sugar bowl and milk bottle. She spooned in sugar.

Fancy Peter Dutton, the well-ordered Peter Dutton, forgetting whether his wife took milk or sugar in her tea and coffee. She smiled a private smile at this failing and then carried her mug into the next room. As she sat opposite him she caught the woman with the reddish-brown hair peeping in, under the pretext of doing something to the flower bed which separated their properties. 'Who are the neighbours?' Carol asked.

Dutton didn't look up from the television guide. 'Jean and Ted Parker. I call them the Nosey Parkers.'

'They sound just like neighbours.' She drank.

He flipped over a page. 'They don't bother me.' He read a paragraph then added: 'But *you've* never got on with them.' That, he told himself, was pure inspiration. It was the kind of verbal trickery he enjoyed. She was bound to think he meant she was on bad terms with the Parkers and so she would avoid their company, which was what he intended. But there was another way of interpreting his words. They could suggest she had never met the Parkers.

## 9

The next morning, Monday, Peter Dutton pushed into his pocket a letter which came from New Zealand for his wife, took a cup of tea up to the back bedroom and then walked to the station. She drank slowly, deferring getting up. She had not slept well. There had been turbulent dreams about restaurants and hospitals and one where she was being chased by a man whose face she could not see. She had woken agitated and lain there for a long time while the sky lightened and birds started to sing.

Something of the nightmare was with her now, casting its shadow over her day, cramping her spirit. She finished the tea, made herself bound out of bed and break free. Yesterday with its tribulations was over. Today she had the house to herself. She ran a bath and persuaded herself that the green blouse did not look hideous beneath the cotton smock.

Over breakfast she browsed through the *Daily Post*. She had read it each day in hospital and turned to Rain Morgan's gossip column. An opera singer called Lamberhurst had backed out of a Covent Garden production pleading ill health – but been photographed the same evening in a West End night club with a new mistress. Professor David Rokeby was to be offered a plum job in television, an appointment he would take up once he had finished work on a series called *The Face of Death*. A murderer whose story was told in *The Face of Death* was complaining of his ill-treatment by the producer. The editor of *Jet*, a black newspaper, was celebrating startling new circulation figures. Then an item about a doctor sent her thoughts flying back to Leamington and she felt what she could only call homesickness for Princes Hospital and the people she knew there: Dr Renfrew, Dorcas, Irene Yarrow, the petite Malaysian nurse, the friendly patients. It was as though, instead of being found, she had been lost.

She made a mental list of all the information Dutton had given her about herself. They had covered the ground but she wanted more detail about some points. She needed to know precisely where she had worked so she could find out whether any of her former colleagues were familiar. He said she worked as a secretary but gave it up when they moved to Shepherd Road because it was too far to travel. The idea was for her to find another job near home but that hadn't happened. She also wanted the addresses where they lived before the move to Spinney Green because she intended to visit them and any friends or neighbours she might recognize.

Dutton had been doubtful. He said she had lost contact with friends as she changed addresses, moved jobs. He could not name any of her friends. She decided to urge him to try – and then remembered how the conversation ended. It ended with Dutton getting her to agree to keep her condition secret. If anyone asked tricky questions she was to say she had been in hospital but was all right now. At first she wasn't sure but he had been persuasive. If word got around, she would have newspapers and television after her, much worse than it had been in hospital. She knew he was right. She could not bear that.

She had asked him whether she ought not to write to her parents who might be worried about her, but he said there was no point. They would not know she had been injured and to write and tell them she had lost her memory would only upset them.

Her tour of the house on Saturday had been cursory, her true degree of inquisitiveness unacceptable. Today she could tug at drawers and count up the towels and do anything that took her fancy. She began in the lounge. Besides the teak coffee table and another with the television on it, there was a three-piece suite, a new fitted carpet and, in front of the fireplace with its brick kerb, a new rug. There was a gas log fire. The only other furniture in the room was a modern pine desk with three deep drawers down one side. They were locked. Abutting the drawers, at a right angle, were four shelves. On three of them books flopped loosely. The bottom shelf held television guides. Most of the books were popular pulp novels, two were cookery books which depended more on lavish photography than tempting recipes, one was an English dictionary, and one a gardening book. All the collection betrayed was that Peter and Carol Dutton were not readers.

There were two bedrooms. The front one contained a double bed, a painted wooden chair, two bedside tables and a fitted wardrobe finished in white laminate which matched the dressing table and its stool. The carpet was new. She skipped the back bedroom and went to the bathroom, the only item of interest being the bathroom cabinet which housed, along with shampoos and plasters, a collection of ointments and pill bottles. She plucked out a bottle at random. It was half full of white tablets and its label was indecipherable except for the name Carol Dutton.

'Carol Dutton,' she said aloud, daring the sounds to release something within her. 'Carol Dutton.' Louder. Nothing. She grabbed, in a flurry of anger, at the chemists' bottles and ranged them along the window sill. 'Peter Dutton, Carol Dutton, Carol Dutton, Peter Dutton, Carol Dutton . . .' there were more bottles for her than for him, she had acquired a stock which ran back years. Several of the bottles appeared to contain identical prescriptions, a few tablets left in each bottle.

On the landing she investigated a linen cupboard with an immersion heater below a selection of sheets and towels. Then, in the kitchen, she delved in cupboards and drawers to discover what equipment she could call on. It was quite limited, although there was a simple liquidizer, but when she came to the food cupboard and freezer she saw that it hardly mattered. There were packets of mixes or ready-prepared frozen foods. Much of the freezer was taken up with a big bag of oven chips and some packs of hamburgers and peas.

Her heart sank. She was willing to put together a meal for the evening but there was no scope, and she had no money to go shopping. While she thought about it she made a cup of instant coffee and sat with it watching lorries and occasional pedestrians negotiating the mud of Shepherd Road. It was very strange to be on her own when all she could remember was the crowded hospital, where there was always the sight and sound of other people, where she never had to decide what to do.

She looked at the car on the run-in outside the front door. Again she had the urge to flee. She could drive away from this meagre little house. But Dutton had told her she could *not* drive, contradicting her conviction that she loved it. She was suspicious: his denial had been so swift, and men like Dutton were often unwilling for their wives to drive and for no very good reason apart from masculine vanity. She warned herself against being unfair to him – wasn't it possible she had learned during the time she was away from him? She did a calculation. If that were true then she would have had to learn extremely fast because she left Spinney Green in November and had been in hospital for longer than two months when he came for her in February.

She took her empty mug to the kitchen, then once more wandered around the house. This time she took a duster and cleaned as she went. Superficially the house had been clean before, but her duster found its way into corners and crevices that had escaped attention for months. Lightbulbs and lampshades, the high rims of cupboards, the backs of pictures . . . she had time and more to spare so she could afford to be scrupulous. Then she got some cleaner and polished the mirrors and the glass in the pictures, buffed doorknobs and wiped over light fittings.

After that she was back in the kitchen, wondering whether to vacuum the floors which showed no need of it. 'So this is how it used to be,' she said. 'Women used to have to sit at home without jobs or money, and try to occupy themselves until it was time to feed their men. How on earth did I do it, even for the few weeks before I ran off? It's not yet eleven and I'm bored already.'

She wondered whether it had not been the sheer boredom of her existence at Spinney Green which had driven her away, and what excitement she might have found in the life she had escaped to. She went into the garden. The day was mild and grey and the garden uncheering.

From over the fence came the noise of a back door being pushed open and Jean Parker was calling. Dutton's remark came back to her: she had never got on with the Parkers. Cautiously she returned the greeting. 'It's too cold to talk out here, come in and have a coffee,' Jean offered.

Carol let herself be persuaded. 'Ted's out, he's gone to see a customer,' Jean said leading her into her lounge. 'Milk and sugar?'

She returned with cups on a tray and set it down on a table between a pair of matching sofas. Jean gave a small laugh. 'I'm afraid I don't actually know your name,' she admitted.

'Carol.' So Peter Dutton was wrong when he suggested she was not on good terms with the neighbours. There had been so little contact that Jean Parker had not found out her name. She became aware that Jean was struggling with her curiosity.

Jean Parker thought better of it and didn't ask Carol where she had been since November. She pitched into the subject of Shepherd Road and the sort of people who were moving in. Nodding her head towards the Phase Two houses opposite, she said: 'They've sold four of those now, they'll be in by Easter I shouldn't wonder. Then we'll see if I'm not right. I told your Peter last week they've had blacks and all sorts going round them. It's not right, not with these being executive homes.'

Carol said something non-committal while wondering how Jean would have fared in hospital where the staff at all levels came from the full gamut of colours. She moved the conversation to gardening.

'Oh yes, I'd call myself a keen gardener, Ted too, for that matter. Wherever we live we always have a nice garden, except when we were in the high rise, obviously. But you should have seen those window boxes!' She grew dreamy at remembered window boxes.

'I was wondering what to do with our garden.'

'You could do a lot out there. There's a start been made, true enough, but you could still do a lot. I'm sure I could make one or two of my little suggestions, if you wouldn't mind, that is.'

Carol listened to a few of Jean's little suggestions and then Jean offered to fetch anything Carol wanted from the shops when she went to work in the baker's that afternoon. Carol asked for chops and vegetables and Jean said: 'You can pay me tomorrow.' When Carol got up to leave Jean rummaged in a bookcase and lent her a couple of gardening books in the hope she might 'get some inspiration from them'.

Carol went home sure Dutton had lied to her about not being friendly with Jean Parker. She took the borrowed books into the lounge and planned to browse through them that afternoon until Jean and the chops came home. She would fantasize about turning the drab patch behind 7 Shepherd Road into a compact splendour.

But first, and more practically, she would draw up a list of things she needed to buy. Clothes, food, a few items for the kitchen. On the desk was a pad of writing paper and a biro. Carol made her list, her vigorous writing winding across the pages. She became ashamed at the length of the list, because she doubted that the Dutton household had much money. She crumpled it and began a fresh, briefer one. Then she compromised on that, too, going down it with her pen and underlining the essentials. She left it on the desk where it stayed while she had lunch and then she curled up on the settee and read about gardening. Jean's books were extravagantly illustrated. One picture in particular caught her eye. A mellow stone house among old-fashioned cottage-garden borders. She did not know whether it was the house, or the borders, or the combination which tugged at her memory. But for a breathtaking second it reminded her of somewhere.

She let the frustration pass. She would show the picture to Dutton and hope he would explain. Until then, there was no point in fretting over it. She resumed reading. Before many weeks had passed she would look back on this innocuous afternoon as the time she first put her life in danger.

# 10

Dutton read the letter from his wife's parents. It was written in his mother-in-law's spiky handwriting, contained a little family news and the usual grievance about Carol not writing home as often as her parents wished. Her mother referred to a letter and a Christmas card from Carol along with a parcel. Dutton knew they had been posted in November.

He meant to let the correspondence die altogether but could not settle whether to break off immediately or write back this time. Yet Carol herself had regarded the occasional letter as a tiresome duty which had to be fulfilled in case her parents took umbrage and stopped sending her money. The balance, Dutton thought, was in favour of writing a typed letter or two a year bearing Carol's signature. He could manage that.

But the New Zealand letters were a serious hazard. Whether or not he replied this time, Carol's parents were certain to write again and eventually the day would come when he failed to be the one who opened their letter. He could not see what to do about this, but he had plenty of time to think. He pushed the letter beneath papers in a drawer of his office desk to keep it safe and private. Lewis and Johnson were chatting, as they did most mornings, about what was in the papers. They had the *Daily Post* spread on Lewis's desk. Lewis read from Rain Morgan's column the item about Professor Rokeby moving into a top television job.

'What does he know about television? It's always the same, isn't it? It's not what you know but who you know that gets you the plum jobs,' said Johnson.

'Oh yes? So who did you know who got you a job at Pegwoods?'

'Only Dutton!' They collapsed in laughter. It was true. Johnson had met Dutton and Dutton had mentioned the vacancy.

'Actually, it amazes me how much people do know. Has anyone computed it, do you think? Totted up all the bits of information we carry around in our heads?'

'I doubt it.'

'And it's not only the extent, it's the quality of some of that knowledge which impresses me.' He prodded a finger at Rain Morgan's byline picture. 'She's a gossip writer, right? But on breakfast television she was explaining all the physical and psychological causes and effects of amnesia. She was incredible! See what I mean? You never know what people carry around in their heads.'

Dutton went out of the room. Lewis pulled a face at his retreating back. 'Another quiet day at the office! He's getting worse. At least he used to join in the conversation a *bit*.'

Johnson agreed. 'I've always said he isn't normal.'

At lunchtime Dutton went for his walk. That was when the horror began.

He was waiting to cross at traffic lights and a young woman came up to the other side of the road and joined waiting pedestrians. She stood opposite Dutton, her mousey hair tugged by the wind. She reminded him alarmingly of Carol and he could not shift his gaze from her. When the lights changed and they passed in the centre of the road she gave him a puzzled, irritated look. Dutton's stomach contracted sickeningly. He did not dare look back. He moved on, oblivious to everyone and everything around him. He could see nothing but her face.

Reaching a garden square he hovered by a bench until the gossiping occupants moved up and let him sit. He was limp and frightened and hardly cared if anyone saw it. That look, that woman's look, was a faint echo of the expression of astonishment and horror he had last seen on his wife's face. Dutton put his head in his hands and moaned. For two nights he had been able to sleep without seeing that shocking face in his dreams and now this. Was he always to be haunted by that look?

A cold fear ran over him. He faced up to the craziness of what he had done. It had all seemed so manageable. There was Carol in her hospital bed, all he had to do was fetch her home and then everything would be all right again. The night terrors would be over, history would be unmade, his future would be protected. All would be well.

There was a moment when he felt a heartbreaking surge of self-pity. He cut off the emotion, turned it to anger, turned anger to defiance. That had always been the better way. Self-pity left you prey to other people, anger bred violence and destruction, but defiance helped you rise above your circumstances. He had given up self-pity as a child when his only defence was to ignore his mother's barbs and the well-meaning sympathy of neighbours and school teachers. His father's blind anger had led to a prison sentence for assaulting a man. As a schoolboy Dutton had cultivated a quiet defiance that made him invulnerable, unapproachable.

His mother died of cancer and his father killed himself months later, unable to face life without what, to the rest of the world, had always appeared a completely unsatisfactory relationship. Dutton, watching the second of the cheap coffins glide away at the crematorium, had wondered at the sad faces of the handful of mourners. He felt no agony of loss, only an emptiness which had always been there.

The gossipers on the bench moved away and it was time for him to go too. Dutton dragged himself back to the office, to Lewis and Johnson with their similar grey suits and their similar grey minds, to Mary Partridge and her pathetic role of office vamp. But all afternoon he was bedevilled by the face of the young woman on the crossing.

He could not fathom why she had looked at him like that. Surely it was not possible that she knew anything about Carol Dutton? He began to tremble and tried to concentrate on the papers on his desk. He never succeeded. Each time he was becoming engrossed a different aspect occurred to him and he was reliving the night when he and Carol had the terrible row. He could picture her, sarcastic and mocking, for once turning that bitter tongue against him. And

72

then her face was anger fading to amazement as his fury exploded. He had loved her and it had ended like that.

Mechanically he began the homeward journey. Shop windows and street lights gave the illusion that the February evening was light, but for each patch of pretend daylight there were dark unbeckoning corners. He had not far to go from Pegwoods office to Oxford Circus Underground station, normally the detail of the walk went unnoticed. This evening he was edgy, afraid of meeting the woman with his wife's face. Then it happened. A cry behind him. He did not look back, he might have misheard. He knew he had not. He increased his pace.

Amidst all the other noise he picked out quickening footsteps. Dutton was sure he was being followed. Abruptly he turned down the dark slit of an alley. A few yards on he plunged into a shadowed doorway. The sound of high heels pursued him.

He swore under his breath, sprang from cover and darted away from her. He broke into street light. Market stalls were being unloaded at the end of the day. There were people, and vans and noise and confusion. The cry was repeated. His name. Involuntarily he glanced back, to see her lit by a shop window. A young dark-haired woman in boots and a winter coat. Not the woman from the crossing. Marcia Cohen.

Dutton raced, dodging among the stalls and discarded cabbages, bumping into people. Angry words chased him and he ran. At a crossroads he hesitated, doubtful which way to go. He must reach the Underground. For the second time he looked back. He had shaken her off.

Someone gave directions: go to the end of the road, make a turn, he couldn't miss it. But he missed seeing her. In the passageway leading to the platform he discovered with shock that he was now following her. He held back, someone banged into him and loudly cursed his awkwardness. Others looked round. So did she. She waited for him. 'Peter!'

She had won. He was face to face with her. Marcia Cohen, his wife's friend. The friend who so much wanted to see her again. He mumbled a grudging hello. People were pressing past them, they had to go with the tide. She said: 'How is

Carol? She didn't ring me. Did you remember to ask her? Give me your phone number and I'll call her.'

They were on the platform, a tube train rumbling towards them. The noise excused him from more than vague mutterings in reply. In the carriage he wriggled away from her, letting it appear that the crush of bodies was carrying them apart. The last he saw of her was a resigned smile. When he got off at King's Cross it was impossible to say whether she was still in the carriage or not.

His hand trembled as he showed his season ticket before boarding the Spinney Green train. The detour while trying to throw off Marcia Cohen had made him late, he could not get a seat. He wedged himself against a door just at the end of the carriage and let it take his weight. He would have given much for a seat, to be able to open his newspaper wide and shield his reddened face until his pulse slowed and his composure was regained. He knew it was nonsense that anyone could hear another's heart pounding, but the sensation that everyone was aware of his was very real. He bent his head to the folded newspaper, the print a mere blur in front of his eyes. The train moved off with a lurch. The rhythm of its movement and sound comforted him. Soon he was breathing normally. He began to organize his thoughts.

Bad things had happened all day but Marcia Cohen could be the worst of it. Meeting her among the homegoing commuters, it was reasonable to guess that she was now working close to Pegwoods. As she did temporary secretarial work for an agency she might leave the area at any time, although probably not before the end of the week. As long as she was there he risked running into her again.

He remembered now about Marcia Cohen. She had persuaded Carol to give up her last permanent job and take to temping. Marcia had recommended Carol to the agency, and had kept in contact with her, comparing notes about the offices where they worked. When there was a vacancy at a congenial place where she was berthed she tried to get Carol in there too. He didn't recall her ever visiting his home but he remembered that Carol and Marcia had often lunched together. Temps stuck together, Carol had explained. They were the outsiders in every office where they worked, they didn't build up friendships there because it wasn't worth anyone's while. They would be moving on and forgotten. It was an unlikely friendship because Carol made it plain she felt a cut above Marcia. She joked about her to him, deriding Marcia's East End Jewishness and her failure with men. Dutton never understood why Carol chose a friend she believed inferior. But Marcia was missing Carol and showed no signs of forgetting her. Dutton was sickened by the knowledge. Somehow he would have to deter Marcia.

The train was slowing. He peered through the window and saw the Spinney Green sign sliding by. He offered the paper to a fellow passenger, as he often did, and got off. It was a relief to be in the cold fresh air. He shuffled with the other commuters along the platform, more slowly down steps, through a mere formality of a barrier, and out into the quiet streets. A couple of hundred yards from the station most of the group veered off down a side road leaving only Dutton and a handful of others to take the rising road to the less affluent part of the suburb. In the end, he knew, there would be four of them going along Shepherd Road. Unless one was ill and missed a day it was an invariable pattern. Today, outwardly, everything was as usual although inwardly it was chaos.

Dutton pulled up his coat collar and moved on, dreading getting home. He wished himself anywhere else. He had so much wanted his wife back, he had become so overwrought that he had fooled himself it was possible. And now he had at home a vain silly woman who grumbled about clothes and tripped over in restaurants and drew attention to him. He meant to love her and care for her, but she was making it impossible. It had been beyond recklessness to bring her home and it had not saved him from being reminded of his wife's final look.

He let himself into the house and found her in the kitchen. There were pans on the stove. Carol – he was going to have to go on calling her that – said: 'I didn't know what time you would be back.' She lit gas beneath pans.

'It's always this time.' He went to hang up his coat.

'I've got some lamb chops. I hope that's all right? Isn't it ridiculous that I don't know what you like to eat? I'll have to learn that all over again, too.'

He looked at the chops curling in the pan. 'Where did you get those?' He had a shrewd suspicion.

'Jean Parker offered to fetch some shopping for me . . .'

He was right. He snapped at her: 'I want you to keep away from Jean Parker.'

She was bewildered. 'But she came and . . .'

'I don't want to hear what she did. I just don't want you having anything to do with those Parkers.'

'Why ever not? She seems . . .'

'Because I don't. She's an interfering busybody and I won't have her in here again.'

'She didn't come here, I went to her house.'

'Then I don't want you to. You will keep away from her, do you hear?'

She turned her back on him, busied herself with pans. She no longer felt hungry. Dutton went into the lounge, switched on the television and brooded. 'Jean Bloody Parker!' he muttered. 'I might have known she'd be trouble.'

Then he noticed the list on the desk. He was jolted by what he saw and quite forgot what he would like to inflict on Jean Parker. The length of the list was extremely disagreeable, but the shock was the handwriting. Bold, distinctive, it was unlike any woman's handwriting he had ever seen. Certainly it was nothing like his wife's. In trepidation he put the list back.

She came in. 'You've found my list? It's not all crucial, I've underlined the most important stuff. We can buy the rest later.'

He nodded. She said: 'We must talk about money, and the sooner the better. I'll have to have some – I already owe Jean Parker for the food and I said I would pay her tomorrow.'

'All right.' He felt in a trouser pocket and brought out a handful of notes. 'Take that for now. I'll go to the bank tomorrow and get some more.' He knew she hadn't meant only that. She wanted to agree regular housekeeping payments and find out the details of his finances. The longer he could prevent her doing so the better.

She took the notes, warm from his pocket, and slid them into her own. She opened her mouth to try again, but something boiled over and she darted to the stove. Preferring to be alone she stayed there. Dutton was in a peculiar mood and that vein in his temple was throbbing.

While she cooked he considered his next step. He would open a new joint account at Spinney Green. The original accounts would stay near Oxford Circus and Carol's father's money from New Zealand would continue to be paid into hers.

Dutton sighed. Eventually he would have to mention the money and pray she did not take to frittering it. He could not keep the knowledge from her because from time to time the bank would send statements or other correspondence and he could not guarantee being able to intercept the post. Once she saw a statement she would want to know how the money had dwindled while she was in hospital and unable to draw on it. Then he would have to confess to forging her signature.

The truth was that without Carol's New Zealand money to top up his income from Pegwoods they could not afford to live in Shepherd Road. Worse, he had just been cornered into buying a car. He told her: 'I'm going to move our bank account to Spinney Green, that will be more convenient for you.'

It was the first time he had spoken since giving her the cash. His temple had ceased throbbing. She said: 'Perhaps I can start buying some of the clothes I need this week? I need some shoes rather urgently because those in the wardrobe are all so high. I got used to slippers in hospital and seem to have lost the knack of walking in them. I'd like to go to the West End if I can, I don't think there is much of a shopping centre near here.'

'You shouldn't go rushing about. Remember Dr Renfrew said you have got to take things quietly, get plenty of rest.'

'I feel as though most of my life has been taking things quietly and resting. There isn't much opportunity for any-thing else in hospital.'

He finished his chop. She asked him about the picture in the book, why it looked familiar. He brushed it aside. She persisted but things were moving dangerously close to argument. 'We've been into that business about the countryside. I don't know what this could mean to you.' Not long after Dutton said: 'You look tired. You'd better go to bed early tonight.'

'Do I? I don't feel it.' Then she thought of the sleepless night and assumed he must be right. Quite early she accepted his repeated advice and went to bed. He brought her a hot drink and a sleeping pill. 'You used to find these helpful,' he said, holding out the white tablets she recognized from the bathroom cabinet. He stood over her as she swallowed a pill.

Dutton sat in front of the television for an hour, then crept up to her room to make sure she was asleep. Gently shutting her door he ran downstairs, reached into his coat pocket for his key ring and unlocked the drawers of the desk. He worked his way from the top drawer to the bottom, throwing out on to the carpet any piece of paper, no matter what the document was, which bore Carol Dutton's tiny childlike handwriting. On top of the desk he laid the cheque books and file of bank statements relating to the existing accounts in the names of Peter and Carol Dutton. Beside them he put one sheet of paper with his wife's signature on it.

When he was confident he had sifted out everything which must be kept secret, Dutton relocked the desk, put the key ring back in his pocket and gathered up the papers from the floor. Suddenly he stopped. He could not burn them, which would have been ideal, because the only fireplace was fitted with a gas log fire, and it was unwise to entrust them to the dustbin. Her curiosity might be aroused when she emptied something on top of them or else the dustbin men might let a few flutter off down the street. They would have to be tucked away somewhere until he could get them out of the house and destroy them. It might even be that waiting for a garden fire in the summer would be safest, but meanwhile . . . he knew of one good place.

Dutton carried the papers and cheque books up to the loft and hid them in the metal trunk. His framed wedding photograph smiled up at him as he swung back the lid and he looked once more into his wife's face. Then he let the papers flop down to bury her. Offcuts from the lounge carpet were to hand and he tossed them in, too, so that anyone opening the trunk would see nothing but carpet.

The day had been too full of fears and frights and he slept badly. The recurring dream woke him around three and he only dozed after that. Reverting to the pattern of recent months he was up early and watching for the paper boy. But he felt more confident after the evening's work. He had taken care of another detail and now he could put the whole story out of his head and go to work. He would fob off Marcia if he saw her and he would refuse to be frightened by the woman with the look of his wife.

When he left the house Jean Parker was taking in her milk. 'Look at that,' she said with a snarl. 'What did I tell you?'

A smile of amusement at her disgust brightened his face as he walked away. It was taken as a greeting by one of the black men unloading furniture into the house adjoining the Duttons.

# 11

Daniel Marcus and Joel James were grappling with a chest freezer which teetered between them on the lip of their hired furniture van, Dan wary of pushing too hard and Joel doubtful of the wisdom of pulling it on top of himself.

'You know what's wrong with this?' Joel called to the partner he couldn't see beyond the white sheen of the freezer. 'You got the wrong kind of freezer.'

'You mean you got the wrong kind of van,' Dan countered, rubbing damp palms down his trouser legs and trying again for a grip. 'Should have got one with a board that lets down.'

'With a what?'

'Nothing. Doesn't matter. Are you ready? I'm going to shove now!'

Joel staggered backwards as the freezer lurched towards him. 'Hey, not so hard, you're throwing it at me.'

Dan stopped thrusting and flopped against the other contents of the van. 'Are you OK, Joel?'

'Sure.' Joel sprang into view around the side of the freezer to demonstrate that he was sound in wind and limb. 'What are we going to do, then?'

Dan took a long slow breath. Then he said: 'We'll try changing places.' Joel, his younger, wiry cousin, had insisted on doing it his way and it hadn't worked.

'Sure,' said Joel again, gesturing Dan to come out so he could squeeze through the gap and take up position inside the van. There had been many helpers last night when they loaded up but everyone else was at work now. Only Dan, whose shift started later in the morning, and Joel who had no work to go to, were available to unload.

As Dan poised to grab the freezer a small car came

swerving and hooting up Shepherd Road. 'Here's Holly,' Dan called, hoping to delay Joel. He was too late. Just as Holly Chase ripped on the handbrake and leaped from the car so the freezer came hurtling out of the van.

Holly shrieked: 'Don't drop it!' and ran to plonk an ineffective hand on the enamelled surface which was dangerously near the tarmac. Dan grunted a reply probably best not understood. Holly stuck her head into the van. 'Joel? Joel! Stop pushing and come out here and catch. And bring that doormat. There, behind you.'

Together the three of them manoeuvred the freezer down on to the doormat which Holly had dropped on the roadway to protect it. The men stood getting their breath, but Holly was up in the van and announcing what should happen next.

'I'll tell you, Holly,' Dan said at last, 'what we want next. We want the front door unlocked. You have the key, remember?'

She switched her gaze to the semi-detached house with furniture littering the front garden. From her pocket she took the key, squealed an apology for being late with it, and ran into the house. They could hear her feet pounding over bare boards, her occasional whoop of delight. Joel shook his head. 'She's a real case, your Holly.'

She appeared at the front bedroom window, her hair tight to the scalp in tiny braids, her big ear-rings dancing madly. Dan waved to her, Joel stuck out his tongue. Then they were moving the furniture from the garden and into the house, leaving the next adventure with the freezer until strength was restored.

Holly Chase and Daniel Marcus did not have much furniture. There were the pieces from the flat Dan had shared and the things Holly had cadged from her parents' home. There was an equally small number of things they had bought in anticipation of setting up home at 5 Shepherd Road: carpets for the lounge and front bedroom, a fridge, a cooker and that huge freezer. Neighbours, craning into bay windows, took note.

It was all too exciting for Jean Parker. She urged Ted to share her woe at black people being permitted to buy executive homes. Ted put on his glasses for a surer view. 'She's a pretty girl, though,' Ted admitted.

'Ted! How can she be? She's black!'

Ted said no more. He still thought Holly Chase was a pretty girl and took delight in watching the pert little figure scampering in and out of the house. In a while Dan and Joel had the freezer hoisted and were tottering up the front path with it. Unfortunately they went out of sight of the Parkers, who then decided that this was the perfect time to weed the border between their front garden and the Duttons'. Out they went.

Their true motive was not lost on Joel, who had been whispering to Dan a commentary on their antics for some while. Seeing them actually outside, to stare and not say hello, was too much for Joel. He slapped a hand on the freezer, which was at a standstill before the awkwardness of the doorstep, and called over in a stage Jamaican accent: 'Day gonna keep all dem bananas right in der, man!'

'Cool it, Joel!' Dan said sharply.

'Isn't that what they want to hear? Isn't that what they've come for?'

'That's their problem. I don't want any trouble with our neighbours and I especially don't want it from you. Right?'

Joel shrugged. Dan turned to where the Parkers seethed, and he called a good morning to which there was no reply. In a few minutes the freezer and the Parkers were all indoors. Joel looked around the dumped furniture, boxes and parcels. 'When's the housewarming,' he asked ironically.

'Right now,' said Holly, passing him a cup of tea. 'The great British ritual – a nice cup of tea as soon as you move in.'

'I thought the neighbours did it for you, as a welcoming gesture.' Joel's edge of irony was still there.

'Some neighbours, some places, sometimes,' said Dan.

'Whoever heard of a pioneer being welcomed with a cup of tea?' asked Holly. 'That's what we are in this street – a couple of pioneers.' She climbed into the bay window, coiled there with her cup of tea. 'We'll be fine,' she said with determination.

Dan, squatting on the bare floor of the lounge, looked up at her in admiration. Once he'd persuaded her of the economic and practical advantages of buying a house in Spinney Green, Holly had become wholehearted about it. He said: 'What time are you going to the *Post*?'

Joel cut across her answer, with a roar of laughter. 'Sounds like she wants to send a letter.'

At last, when the familiar jokes were finished, Holly said she had to be at the newspaper office around noon. She was assistant editor on the *Daily Post* Diary and Rain Morgan, whose byline the column carried, was busy away from the office that day.

'Tough you couldn't get the day off for the house move,' said Joel.

'It doesn't matter, there's not such a lot to move and I've told Rain she's got to make it up to me.'

By late morning she had driven to work, Dan had set off in the hired van to return it before going to the television company, and Joel was whistling in accompaniment to a transistor radio as he fitted the front bedroom carpet. Next door Carol Dutton was washing clothes by hand. There was no washing machine in the house and so she presumed there was a nearby launderette. Although she had the money to use it now, she was reluctant to ask Jean Parker for directions. Dutton's anger the previous evening had shaken her and her reaction was to withdraw into herself.

She began the tedious job of rinsing the garments. Then she sighed, and stood, her arms deep in cold water, and stared out at the February garden. 'I don't like this boring little house and I don't see how I could ever have loved Petter Dutton.' Tears pricked her eyes and her wet hands could not help them. Then she bent her head and went on rinsing and wringing until her hands were numb and her ingratitude punished.

In the Parkers' house Ted had gone up to the back bedroom which was his office and begun a series of phone calls to existing and potential clients to arrange interviews. He was quite effective as a salesman and his appointments diary began to fill up. Ted was in gromets. He'd been in Wellington boots, and he'd been in safety-grip handles and now he was in gromets.

Downstairs Jean was contemplating the knitting pattern in a women's magazine, reading it as though it were a story and wondering whether it was too complicated for her to tackle. She liked to knit but only if she could watch television at the same time.

Tuesday was not a day when she worked at the baker's and if it was fine she gardened. There was always something to do in the garden, she always said, whatever the time of year. The sight today of Carol Dutton attaching a washing line to two likely posts attracted Jean out of doors. She went straight to the fence for a chat.

After a few remarks about the weather, Carol began to hang out the washing. Jean stayed at the fence. 'You've seen your new neighbours?' she began, lowering her voice.

'Yes, I suppose the woman and the older of the two men will live here.'

'I don't know so much, it's the more the merrier with their sort, isn't it?'

'Is it? I shouldn't worry, the house is so small three would be a crowd and any more impossible.'

'Oh. Do you think so?' Jean was deflated. She hadn't expected to draw criticism of the houses.

Carol, unaware that they could be regarded as anything other than small, went on oblivious. 'I'm going to do some sketches this afternoon for the new garden.'

The gibe at the house upset Jean but she wasn't sure Carol had meant it. She took her revenge on the Duttons' garden. 'You ought to shift that rockery for a start.'

Carol, not knowing this was meant to wound, agreed. 'But I don't think I can, not now Peter has done so much work on it.'

All afternoon she drew and redrew her plans. She enjoyed drawing them, pausing once to ask herself whether she hadn't just felt the most slender memory of sitting at a drawing board, creating a design for something else, somewhere else. The pages fluttered on to the settee beside her and from there to the floor. She tried every possible revamp, but the only schemes that satisfied her were those which ignored the present position of the rockery. Tactfully she rounded those up to destroy them. If Dutton himself suggested it she would jump at the chance, but it would otherwise be out of the question to shift the rockery. Leaving it where it was, there was only one scheme which worked and so she chose that. The other sheets of paper were ripped up and dropped in the dustbin.

She folded the acceptable garden plan and slipped it in her smock pocket. The action reminded her of that moment in the car when her hand closed over an appointment card. In the next instant she was in the front bedroom, needing to remind herself of the name on it. She pulled the grey coat towards her and reached into a pocket. She must have the wrong one. Carol lifted the coat out and plunged into the other pocket. Empty.

It had been a small yellow card with the name of an employment agency on it. Now it had gone, taking with it another little bit of information about her life, possibly the piece which might have helped. She could have gone to the agency, just to look at it. She could have gone in and met the interviewer and perhaps that would have been enough.

She slammed the wardrobe door and sank down on the edge of the double bed. For the second time that day tears damped her face. She was sure she had kept the card and that could only mean Dutton had removed it. But why? It would be as if he did not want her to remember her past.

Through the wall a transistor radio throbbed out the beat of a reggae band, a song about a lost tribe wandering far from their home. She sobbed aloud. Perhaps there had never been a card. Perhaps her disordered mind had made it up. She was after all certain of nothing. Nothing.

# 12

Peter Dutton found her red-eyed. 'I feel as though I shall never remember anything,' she wailed, her body aching with unhappiness. He put a soothing hand on her shoulder and felt pity, but there was nothing he could do. His decision had been made and he was regretting it for both of them.

He talked her into another early night and again watched as she gulped down a sleeping pill. He promised it would soothe her and deal with the headache she had developed.

Downstairs he switched on the television. There was a soap opera with a scene in a hospital and it took his mind back to Leamington and Dr Renfrew as he wrote the letter to Dr Andersen, the letter Dutton had since destroyed. Renfrew had been explaining he must be patient and gentle with her and it had been easy to agree when he could not visualize the difficulties. Renfrew would be picturing his Mystery Woman in the care of her own doctor and possibly a specialist by now, but Dutton had to cope alone.

He was certain his entire plan had been a dreadful mistake, that he had been carried away by fantasy nurtured on fear. The misgivings on the train to Leamington had been well founded. He doubted whether he would have gone through with it if the woman had been awake when he first saw her. If they had spoken and he had heard that low voice, seen those mannerisms, listened to that laugh, he could only have backed out. Yet, even though it was tougher than he had imagined, he was still sure he could cope. Coolly critical of his mistakes, he did not believe any were serious. What did they amount to? The clothes were the wrong size. He had taken her to the Halberd where she might have been recognized by any newspaper reader or television viewer. He had not checked through the pockets of the garments he took from the trunk. By the time he did, the grey coat had been twice worn with an employment-agency appointment card in a pocket. He had thrown it away, thanking his luck that she had not noticed it and demanded to go to the agency and meet the people she was supposed to know there. It was unthinkable that she could have discovered it and not told him.

He gauged he had allowed enough time for the sleeping pill to have its effect and tiptoed to the landing. In the tin trunk in the loft he routed out Carol Dutton's personal cheque book, made a note on the stub and tore out a cheque. Then he found the piece of paper bearing the good example of her signature.

In the kitchen he filled out the cheque in his normal handwriting and made it payable to himself. Then he went out of the back door. The light was on in the kitchen and by holding the paper bearing the signature against the glass and the cheque on top of the paper he was able to trace his wife's signature. He slipped the cheque into his wallet and hid the paper in the bottom drawer of the locked desk.

Next day he paid the cheque into his own account. He ought to do nothing more until it was cleared because his account was low, but there was some shopping that could not be delayed. He decided to compromise and do it on Friday. When he got back to Pegwoods from the bank there was a telephone message from Marcia Cohen asking him to ring her. He could guess what she wanted. He thanked Johnson for the message, and tore it up.

In Shepherd Road the Parkers were still scandalized by their new neighbours, Carol pottered about the house trying to keep herself busy and her spirits up, and the new arrivals got their house into shape and showed it off to visitors. Both Daniel Marcus and Holly Chase had jobs that sent them from home at varying times of morning and returned them at curious times of evening. Consequently, they saw less of their neighbours than might have been expected.

On Friday lunchtime Peter Dutton left Pegwoods office early and walked up Oxford Street from Oxford Circus to the Marble Arch store of Marks and Spencer. The shop was reliably crowded and as usual there were plenty of men, mainly Middle Eastern types, buying clothes for stay-at-home wives. One more man at the pay desk with an armful of women's clothes would not be noticed.

Dutton studied the window displays, to get an idea of which garments would go well together. The models on the showcards were wearing lightweight casual garments and thin suits. The sun shone all around them. It seemed rather early to be buying spring clothes but packed rails and the press of customers snatching at them confirmed that this was indeed what one bought in February.

He was relieved. He could hardly go wrong with a suit. He chose a blue tweed one with a blazer-style jacket. Then he considered blouses but was doubtful about picking a good design, so he paid for the suit and went downstairs to the ground floor counters of woollens where he settled for a blue lambswool sweater with long sleeves and a neat round neck.

He had no worries about getting the right size. He had looked at the things in the wardrobe, knowing he needed a size smaller. But he was troubled about the shoes until the showcards proved the blue tweed favoured low-heeled grey shoes with bar straps. He sought them out, spotted they were displayed with smoky grey tights and bought a pair of those, too.

The expedition was marred only by the sour remarks of Johnson who had been left to manage while Dutton was out. Dutton put the green plastic bags on the floor behind his desk and hoped to avoid comment. Johnson was too busy and grumpy to show any interest in something as dull as a shopping spree in a chain store. The bags went unremarked until late afternoon when Mary Partridge came in with a query on a stock order.

She perched on the edge of Dutton's desk, an irritating way she had which he supposed she thought coquettish. 'You see it says here, Peter . . . Oooooh, who's been shopping, then?' Leaning across to show him the order she had given herself a good view of the bags.

'Would you believe *I* have?' No point in being touchy about her impertinence. The manager's secretary liked to boast it was a happy office and this afternoon the reputation was being heavily dented by Johnson. Johnson looked hard at Mary: 'You know what curiosity did to the cat?'

She laughed at him. 'Peter doesn't mind, do you, Peter?'

Johnson bent his head to his work.

Mary opened her eyes wide to Dutton and gave an exaggerated shrug as though Johnson's objection was inexplicable. Then she strained further over towards the green bags and whispered, cajoling him: 'Go on. Let's see what you've bought.'

She was wearing a perfume he did not care for, and her dark hair swung in front of his face. When he stooped to open a bag the move was as much to duck out of contact with her as to satisfy her curiosity. He picked one at random and it flopped open to reveal blue tweed. 'Oh,' said Mary Partridge, surprised, although she could have had no notion of what to expect.

Dutton could see the way her mind was working. His wife had left him and now he had got over it and there was another woman. Which might mean there was also a chance for Mary Partridge, after all. He said: 'It's for my wife.'

Mary said 'Oh' again, and then: 'Why couldn't she go and buy it herself?'

Johnson gave her another look. She saw him and shrugged again but Dutton was not watching her. He was doing up the bag. Mary slithered off the edge of the desk, exposing a lot of thigh, put the stock order form down in front of him saying: 'I'll leave that with you,' and went.

Once or twice Johnson looked up under his brows but Dutton appeared absorbed in his work and so nothing was said about Carol's return. That was the trouble having Lewis off sick, there was no time for conversation. Unless you were Mary Partridge, of course.

At the end of the day Dutton gave his regular performance of showing astonishment at his watch, taking up his things and rushing out of Pegwoods. It had crossed Johnson's mind to suggest a quick drink at one of the nearby pubs. That would have served as an apology for his bad temper and have been the thank-God-it's-Friday celebration that he and Lewis normally shared. It would have been the perfect opportunity to find out about Carol Dutton's return. And Johnson might also have mentioned that someone called Marcia Cohen had phoned again and he had given her Dutton's home address.

## 13

Dutton clutched the bags on his lap on the train home. On the whole it had been a lucky sort of day. The only blot was Mary Partridge drawing out of him the news that Carol was back. He quite saw that Johnson was avid to hear more and if Lewis had been there too, then the topic would have surfaced again. He could picture them inviting him to join their Friday evening session so they could squeeze the details out of him. Anyway, the deed was done, the words had been spoken. The world now knew his wife was back. But how long before someone would say the woman at 7 Shepherd Road was *not* Carol Dutton?

Carol had met his colleagues a few well-spaced times. She had been sarcastic to Johnson's wife, which was to say Johnson's wife was a fool and asked for it. But Johnson's wife would remember Carol Dutton 'clearly. Looking ahead, Dutton saw the real danger as Christmas. The office party and theatre outing would put Carol under scrutiny. A wife who had left and come back was always interesting. He would have to find an excuse not to go, book the tickets and just fail to turn up, then plead an emergency like one of Carol's nervous headaches. His wife had been no stranger to them: he believed they were provoked whenever she failed to get her own way, but their series of family doctors had been more sympathetic and doled out the tranquillizers and sleeping pills she insisted on. She rarely finished a bottle. The bathroom cabinet was witness to that.

Then Dutton realized with a pang that he was wrong about Christmas. The challenge would come much sooner. There was the summer cricket match and that would be more difficult to get out of. The department would be relying on him to bat; if he didn't they would have no one in the team. He had an empty feeling in the pit of his stomach. Sooner or later he was going to be found out. His chances of getting away with it were negligible. He shuddered and the green bags slipped forward. He grabbed at them. A woman tried to help, clawing at them with savage red nails. Dutton wrested the bags from her. It would never do to have women's clothing tumbling on to the floor of the 5.45. That was the kind of incident everyone noticed. He shut out of his mind the idea of failure. He would ward it off, he was sure to think of a way.

The clothes were a success. He shook the bags out on to the settee. She said: 'Oh, they're lovely! Such pretty colours. I must try them on right away.' And she gathered them into her arms, the fabrics vibrant against the drab cotton smock.

Upstairs her fingers quavered with excitement as she unzipped the pure wool skirt and stepped into it. She was transformed from a waif in cast-off clothing to a smart young woman. For the first time she felt both comfortable and attractive. In the top drawer of the dressing table was a box containing odds and ends of make-up. She spared another moment to put on a dash of lipstick and a touch of colouring to her cheeks, then flashed a comb through her hair and went downstairs.

'Look at me,' she said, whirling round. 'It's smashing, and it all fits. So clever of you, and such a lovely surprise.'

She darted towards him, flung out her arms and kissed him. With a split second's anticipation he tried to draw away. His heel scuffed the brick kerb and he stumbled. Her embrace prevented him falling. 'Be careful,' he snapped, and thrust her roughly away. He hurried out of the room.

Carol was shaken by his hostility and strangeness. For a few seconds she was unable to move. Then, her pleasure spoiled, her gratitude rebuffed, she went upstairs. She did not understand his reaction, any more than she understood his bad temper at the Halberd, or why he had lied to her about not getting on with Jean Parker. He had become unapproachable but only he could give her the information she needed about herself. She supposed everything that was causing difficulties between them now was linked to her reasons for walking out on him. There was nothing else to be done, she would have to insist he gave her those reasons. But she would have to pick a time when he was in a calmer mood.

A mischievous smile shone in her eyes. It was bad enough that he recoiled from physical contact with her, but wouldn't it be unbearable if he wanted her to share his bed? Having found the brighter side of the situation she went downstairs. Dutton was in the kitchen but went out of the back door as she came in.

Later, when he was choosing their evening's viewing, she tentatively mentioned her idea for improving the garden. 'Everything could be made ready now so plants can go in during spring and summer. Then some shrubs in autumn, and maybe a tree.'

There was a lengthy pause in which she doubted he had heard what she said. Then: 'That's a good idea.' He saw no reason to discourage her. A little pruning and titivating would keep her busy and at home. He couldn't think of a better occupation as it happened, especially as he hadn't the heart to work out there himself.

During a commercial break between two bits of a soap opera, Carol raised another matter. She expected it to be safer. 'Where shall we go to buy the rest of my clothes?'

He looked blankly at her. 'What do you mean? I've just bought you all those . . .' His hand made a gesture from her head to her toe.

'Yes, but . . .' She cringed under his forbidding gaze and her face grew pink. 'I will need more than this one outfit, lovely though it is.' He must be able to see that. He had read her list.

'Can't you wear the other stuff at home?'

'No . . .'

'What's wrong with it all of a sudden?' His tone was unpleasant.

She floundered, her hands making a helpless movement. 'You know what's wrong with it, it doesn't fit.'

'You'll have to wear it at home.'

'I'll tell you what I need, it's not really much but I need some more underwear . . .'

'Nobody sees that.'

She ignored him. '. . . and another skirt and a sweater and a blouse. That's the minimum. I really do have to have a complete change of clothes.'

'You've got a whole wardrobe of them upstairs.' He switched his attention to the television.

'Yes, but . . .'

'Shhh.' The soap opera was moving off again.

'Don't hush me, this is serious.'

He didn't take his eyes from the screen. 'Oh, yes, it was always serious when you wanted to spend money, wasn't it? Especially when it was on something for you.'

She had no idea what he meant. She could not argue about it so she ignored it. She said: 'I thought you bought me this outfit so I would be decently dressed when we went to buy the rest of my clothes.'

'There aren't going to be any more. Not until there's some more money.'

He was making her feel mean and greedy. Her face grew redder and hotter. Could it really be that the price of a chain-store suit was enough to break the Dutton bank? And had she been the spendthrift who had brought them to that? She swallowed hard to calm herself. 'Look,' she said, knowing his eyes would not leave the screen. 'Perhaps you ought to tell me about the money. How am I to know what the financial position is if . . .'

'. . . "I don't remember"!' He ended her sentence with sarcasm. 'You don't remember any of the times I've spelled it out to you that the financial position is that there isn't any money?'

'No, I *don't* remember!'

His temple pulsated. His anger boiled. 'You've never bothered to remember, have you? All that's concerned you is that you should have exactly what you want. Well, you've got what you wanted. You've got your precious house in Spinney Green. I told you we couldn't afford it and now you can forget about buying any more clothes because there is nothing to buy them with.'

He slammed out of the room. The television burbled to itself. Carol sat, feeling crushed, a headache establishing its rhythm in her brain. His accusations were unanswerable. She remembered nothing and had to take his word for everything. Deep down she felt again that nagging suspicion that she was unwise to do so.

After the fiasco at the Halberd his attitude to her had changed. The gift of clothes was welcome but she was no longer happy about his motive. Why had he not taken her shopping at the weekend? Did he imagine she would run off on a wild spree? Could it be true that she ever had done? The clothes upstairs did not suggest it, there were enough of them but they were inexpensive. And then there was the house. She did not like it and yet he said it was bought at her demand. She flopped back on the settee, her confusion complete.

Something else was bothering her, too. Why was he choosing her clothes as though she were a child or housebound? The word echoed in her mind. Housebound. Tied to the house. Was that what he was achieving? Was he deliberately making it unnecessary for her to go outside? Supposing he had lied about her ability to drive a car, as he had lied about her being on bad terms with the Parkers? Were all these things attempts to isolate her? If so, why?

She had expected life to open up for her once she left Princes Hospital. Instead it was closing in. Her misgivings about putting herself into his hands had not been unfounded: she had found so little to like. And yet it seemed he disliked her, too. Again, why?

Carol was aware she was prowling round and round the subject, failing to understand what was at the heart of it. The process was wearying, taking her nowhere and her headache was mounting. She did what she always tried to do when something was oppressive. She looked for the more heartening aspect. She seized on it. Whatever Peter Dutton's motive in bringing her the clothes, here they were and they gave her the confidence and freedom to venture out. She would, too.

# 14

Peter Dutton stood in the darkness of the kitchen, gripping the edge of the sink. He wrestled with his temper. His face flushed and his left eyelid flickered. Releasing a hand he tried to calm the eye but the lid agitated beneath his finger tips.

Dutton moaned in incoherent agony. In the next room the television talked at a woman he knew was not watching it. Everything was her fault, if she hadn't flown at him like that he could have stayed in control, but her action had tipped him over the edge. Suddenly, coming like that, she *had* been his wife and he was terrified. He had re-created her, brought her ghost into his house and it was taunting him to re-enact that evening in November.

Since November he had mourned the good things about his relationship with Carol but there had been other things he would rather forget. This woman was reminding him of them. He cursed her for that.

What he had said just now was fair. Carol Dutton was always spending money, and that was what they had rowed about. She insisted on the move to Spinney Green, which they could ill afford. He recalled her saying: 'We can manage it with my New Zealand money, until you get a better job.'

And he had replied: 'But I like it at Pegwoods.'

'It's hardly well paid, is it?' The gibe was not new.

Once the move to Shepherd Road was over, she had no job herself. Her visits to the employment agency did not yield anything and her New Zealand money was essential to supplement the Pegwoods salary. Whether Carol Dutton was there or not her New Zealand money was indispensable.

Dutton groaned. Still in darkness he went into the garden and stood on the concrete strip the estate agents called a patio. The weather was cold but he did not feel it. His face burned, his eyelid danced. His breath was painful in his throat and he was sweating heavily.

He walked back and fore, fists clenched in jacket pockets. 'I've come through the worst, I must remember that,' he repeated. But the thought was no longer the encouragement it had once been. There were things happening now which he had not bargained for and it was feasible that the worst was, after all, still to come.

From over the garden fence he heard a kitchen window pushed open and laughter. He stepped on to the grass, a rose bush snagging his sleeve. There was light in the downstairs rear window of 5 Shepherd Road and he had an unobstructed view of the black woman and her man. The man was recounting a funny story, acting two speakers and using his hands to describe things in the air. The woman was leaning back against the sink, head bobbing with laughter. The happy sounds of Holly Chase and Dan Marcus brought an extra dimension to Dutton's misery.

They were like figures in a television play, framed by their uncurtained window. There was some business at a stove and a steaming pan was carried to the sink. The man had plates in his hand, and then the couple disappeared from view as they sat to eat.

Their voices continued but Dutton lost interest. The February dampness was seeping into him but he preferred not to go indoors. He would have to speak and he did not know what to say.

Close up, the rockery lost its silvery sheen and was an undistinguished heap of stones. Dutton put out a brown toecap and touched it. Then he wrapped his arms around his body to still the spasms which racked him. The nerve in his eyelid jumped. He had rekindled fear.

'I must put it out of my mind,' he said in a savage tone. He swung away from the rockery, action imitating thought, and strode to the end of the garden until he met the barrier of the fence. A tangle of dead weeds brushed his trouser leg. Well, if she wanted to garden she could start by tearing these out, clearing the miniature wilderness!

Beyond the fence there would, before much longer, be another garden and another house. Until then the land was rough and waiting. It had been part of a farm until a few years ago, and then the open land had been built over and the woodland left. After a skirmish or two with the conservation lobby the trees had come down and Shepherd Road had gone up. Soon there would be a Woodman Road backing on to it. Perhaps the rural names were the developer's sop to those who would have preferred the area to keep its rural nature?

Dutton stabbed at the weeds with his foot. He forced himself to take his mind off other things by concentrating on remembering what the plants were. There was rose bay willow herb, he was definite about that. Around it were low fleshy plants and a tangle of others. When he had first seen them, when he and his wife were house-hunting, there had been a pungent smell. Cats, he'd thought. But she had said no, it came from one of the plants. She had ripped a leaf from it. 'Try it,' she'd dared him, and pushed it at him until he took it and sniffed.

'It's disgusting!' He couldn't get the stench off his fingers.

Undaunted, she tore off another leaf and put it in her mouth. Then her face contorted and she spat fiercely, complaining at the bitterness. He remembered her saying: 'You wouldn't think anything that looked so ordinary could be so vicious.' And it *had* looked ordinary, although why she thought she could eat it he never knew. Later, after they had bought the house and moved in, she identified it from a book. The plant was slender and many-branched with skimpy daisy-like flowers. She told him it was feverfew.

Over the Duttons' fence the weed patch continued a short way and then petered out. Jean Parker, who had several times hinted that Dutton ought to clear his weeds to improve the appearance of his garden, had a theory about the patch. It proved, she said, the presence of an earlier house, maybe a farm building, on the site, because weeds like that would not grow in a wood. She developed her theory into imagining a shepherd's hut in a clearing.

'What would sheep be doing in a wood?' Dutton discounted the idea, but she was not to be put off. The idea had a sentimental charm so she stuck to it.

A light came on in the bathroom and brought his mind back to the present. Through the frosted glass he saw a figure, then the light went out to reappear in the adjoining room. The woman came up to the window and drew curtains. Dutton let the minutes pass, guessing whether she had gone to bed or was keeping out of his way as he was keeping out of hers. It was the cold that finally sent him indoors. The house was disturbingly silent so he switched on the television for company while he went into the kitchen and made a warming mug of tea.

Clasping his hands around it he stayed there, back to the window. In the mornings he hated this room with its sharp view of the garden, but for weeks after Carol went he dreaded the lounge even more. Irrationally, he had been afraid of finding his wife lying by the hearth where she had fallen and looking at him in the way which haunted him.

In those days he forced himself to keep calm, to keep up appearances, to carry on as though everything was normal. He almost managed it. If it had not been for the torturing nightmares he would never have conceived the dangerous game that meant he was no longer in sole charge of his precarious situation. It was no longer enough that he should keep up appearances and carry on. Now he had to get the co-operation of the woman upstairs and the task was too much for him.

He set the empty mug on the draining board and went into the lounge. The television was offering a solemn discussion on the world's latest hot spot but Dutton slumped in his chair brooding. There was only one acceptable solution. The woman would have to go. Leave. This wouldn't sound too odd to the ears of his colleagues nor to the neighbours. Carol Dutton had gone once before, and she would go again.

He wore a sly smile. Her departure shouldn't be difficult to organize. They did not get on well, tonight's scenes emphasized that. He would create more difficulties and that would eventually persuade her she would be happier to leave. He hoped 'eventually' would not be long.

Pacing the room, he planned. He saw only one major obstacle to prevent her getting up and going at any time. Money. She had none and in her present state could earn none. The New Zealand money was needed for the mortgage and, anyway, the account was bare until the next instalment arrived. The only possibility was to sell the car. He was not eager to do that having owned it so brief a time and been to the expense of taxing it. But, if that was the only way, then he would sell it.

He modified the plan. Initially, he had assumed he would come home from Pegwoods one day and find the house empty and a note by the pine clock. But to flit like that she would need money. The revised version saw them reaching an amicable agreement to part and civilly passing a few days until the car was sold and he was able to give her the cash from it. All of it? Perhaps not, but a decent share.

The programme ended and Dutton unplugged the set. His mood was lifting now that he had arranged the future. He moved more lightly and his features softened. Quietly he went upstairs. At the door of his room he stopped and listened. From the back bedroom came the slurred sound of a woman speaking in her sleep.

Dutton tried the handle of her door. It twisted noiselessly and he looked in. The landing light threw a shaft near the bed. The face was very much like his wife's. He closed her door, lowered the loft ladder. In the roof space he hunted in the trunk and came up with the wedding photograph.

Taking it into the bedroom he stood near her, holding out the framed photograph so the landing light let him compare the faces of the sleeper and his smiling bride. He saw very little likeness. Horrified, he shrank from the bedside but as he drew the door to close it something else struck him. The blue suit hanging on the back of the door, the suit he had been so confident about choosing could almost be the one Carol Dutton had worn on her wedding day. Behind him the woman stirred and Dutton's heart thudded. She muttered indistinctly and then spoke a name he did not know. He staggered on to the landing. Although he waited there, straining to hear, there was no more.

Dutton leaned against the wall, his head ringing as if he was about to faint. His stupidity shamed him. It was cruelly plain his modified plan was no use either and he ought to have known it. He had been wilfully oblivious to the core of the problem! Not just this evening but all along he had shut his eyes and ears to it. He had been so intent on getting her out of hospital that he had ruthlessly edited what Dr Renfrew had been telling him. He had been desperate for his scheme to work and he had refused to consider the fundamental reason why it was doomed. And tonight he had been so anxious to dream up a way for her to leave Shepherd Road that he had not noticed that ultimately it made no difference whether she did or not.

Throughout he had failed to ask himself what happened when part or all of her memory returned. It had been easier to believe her mind was a blank page where he could write any story he chose. With arrogant disdain for the facts he had fooled himself her memory was dead, whereas it was only sleeping. Fantasy had taken over and he reproached himself bitterly. The shock of realization was more than he could bear. Dutton wondered whether he might not be mad.

# 15

Holly and Dan did not disappoint Joel. They announced a housewarming party for Saturday evening and allowed him to invite some of his flatmates and friends from the black newspaper, *Jet*, he sometimes worked for. 'But I'm busy today, mind,' Joel cautioned when he went to Shepherd Road on Saturday morning to install a borrowed music centre for the occasion.

'For *Jet*?' asked Dan taking down a frighteningly long list Holly was dictating.

'And rice,' said Holly.

'For *Jet*,' Joel confirmed. 'The sports page. Winston Broad's playing today and I want a nice big picture right across three columns of him doing something spectacular.'

'And if he doesn't?' asked Dan who was dubious of the *Jet*'s coverage of sport and of life as an extension of sport.

'And tomatoes,' said Holly.

'In that case it'll be a nice big picture of him doing something else.' Joel was equable.

'Like being sent off?' Dan said.

'That only happened once,' Joel said.

'And you got your picture and *Jet* wouldn't use it.' Dan wrote down rice and tomatoes.

'Editor's decision is final,' Joel said. He didn't sound unhappy about it but he'd been grieved at the time.

'So what if someone else, say someone white, does something spectacular?'

But Joel had heard Dan criticize the *Jet* this way before. 'Like I said, the editor's decision is final. He sends me out to take pictures of Winston Broad, I take pictures of Winston Broad.'

'And Coke,' said Holly.

'*Who?*' said Dan and Joel together.

'Hey, wake up!' shrieked Holly. 'We're planning a party not a sports edition.' She made Dan write down Coke.

'Anyway,' said Joel, tipping music cassettes from numerous pockets and piling them high in the bay window. 'You can argue that out tonight with the editor.'

'Dewinton's coming?'

'Sure.' Joel glanced at Holly. 'Don't ever tell me I don't bring interesting people to your parties.'

She laughed. 'I just hope you don't all turn it into an interesting political fight.' And then, on second thoughts: 'No, I know what will happen. Dan will deliver a lecture on murder.'

'That's a good subject,' Dan said. 'Everybody's fascinated by that, it cuts across class, creed, colour. And you must admit this series I'm working on is the best thing that's been done on the subject for . . .'

But they were both laughing at him. His enthusiasm for the programmes he worked on was endearing, but he was always puzzled that those around him did not share it.

The series, under the working title *The Face of Death*, was scheduled as a solemn six-part prime-time study of the who, how and why of murder. It was trundling out retired forensic scientists and newly appointed police chiefs to discuss detection; re-creating the scenes of horrific crimes; and had persuaded several murderers to appear before Dan's camera. The material for the series had also been cobbled together into a book with a massive print run and there was even talk of marketing a recording of the introductory and intermittent music.

Joel slid one of the cassettes into the music centre and turned it on at low volume. He began to dance around the lounge. Then he held out a beckoning hand and Holly joined him. Dan tossed aside his pencil. 'Is this a private disco or can anyone dance?'

They danced across his outstretched legs. Then they ignored all his other comments until the number finished and they sank down on to the carpet beside him. Holly took up the list. 'OK, that's it. All we've got to do now is go and buy it.'

'All!' Dan remembered the slog of previous party preparations.

'Sorry folks,' said Joel without sorrow. 'I'm a working man this afternoon.' They left the house together in Dan's car. Joel was dropped off near the bus stop so he could get back to his dismal flat. It was on the third floor of a dilapidated walk-up block which the council were intending to demolish. Families and other council tenants had been moved out as better accommodation was made available. The block was now occupied mainly by young single people who, like Joel, would have been homeless otherwise. Joel shared the damp flat with three other men, but there were frequently more people than that living there as friends came and went.

As Joel bobbed along on the bus home, Holly and Dan shoved a trolley around a supermarket and lobbed into it the items on their list. There was no supermarket at Spinney Green so they had driven to the adjoining suburb with its much bigger shopping centre. They opted for what they thought was the shortest checkout queue and waited their turn. Dan revived the matter of Joel and *Jet*. 'He takes good pictures, I'd love to see him get a proper job.'

'There ought to be something one of us could do, with me in Fleet Street and you with a television company . . .'

'The most we could do is say we know someone who is keen and has got talent and needs experience. Nobody these days has a job for anyone like that.' He and Holly had both made it, from humble beginnings and hard work. But he didn't underestimate the amount of luck that had come their way.

'If only he could get better freelance work.'

'Don't forget Joel has no space to work in. He can't even develop a film at the flat. Dewinton understands that situation, so the freelances use the room at *Jet*.'

An idea was forming in Dan's mind. He decided it was too fresh to try it out on Holly. Joel was his cousin and perhaps he was being too protective. Besides, he did not want to pressure Holly. Holly read his thoughts. 'How would it be if Joel moved in with us? Would he be able to work there?'

By the time they reached the till they had agreed to ask Joel whether that would suit him, and whether a makeshift darkroom might not solve some of his more urgent problems. Then, as they walked out of the shop, Holly nudged Dan. 'Look, isn't that the man who lives next door to us?'

'I don't know,' said Dan who had seen only the Parkers so far.

'Yes, I'm sure it is. He looks a bit gruff, doesn't he?' They watched while Peter Dutton tussled with the stacking trolleys which refused to come apart. It was a matter of sixteen or nothing.

'Those things would make anybody gruff,' said Dan and they walked away. If they had left the supermarket a minute earlier they would have seen the odder spectacle of Peter Dutton pressed up against the dirty window of the empty shop next door. It was a modest lock-up, dwarfed by the supermarket, and had been vacant for some months. Through its glass door, set back in a porch, free newspapers and junk mail accumulated like flotsam deposited by the tide.

Back at Shepherd Road, Holly made her duty call next door. She wanted to explain in advance of the noise that there would be a party at number 5 and invite the neighbours to drop in. Holly promised Carol Dutton: 'We won't be going on very late. I've got to go to work tomorrow and Dan might have to as well.'

Carol raised an eyebrow. Work? On a Sunday? Holly said: 'I work for the *Daily Post* so some of us have to go in on Sundays, or you don't get a morning paper on Monday. And Dan is a television cameraman so that means all kinds of hours. If the weather is kind his producer will want to shoot tomorrow. If it rains, he gets the day off.'

Carol wondered whether there was a scarf or some jewellery which would add a touch of frivolity to her new outfit and make it more suitable for a party. But the scarves in the dressing table would not do and the costume jewellery was tawdry.

She was disappointed and puzzled. Even if she had taken away with her all the jewellery and clothes she liked, why had she ever acquired all this stuff she hated? She sat on the dressing table stool and examined her face in the mirror. The large wide-set grey eyes, the short hair . . . the soft lambswool sweater flattering her fair skin . . . All she knew about herself was what she could see and what Peter Dutton chose to tell her. It was nothing like enough.

Her reflected face clouded and she looked away. Somewhere she must have friends. She wanted them now, *needed* them. Yet Dutton told her she was a woman with little family, no friends, very few possessions, no job, no skills except shorthand and typing, no money, no ambition except the house in Shepherd Road. Carol Dutton, as he described her, was nothing. She had lived for nothing and might as well be dead.

# 16

Peter Dutton stayed out until mid-afternoon on his super-market trip. He was going to stock up on food and although she wanted to go with him, he persuaded her to stay at home. 'Dr Renfrew said you must rest,' he repeated.

On his return she was watching sport on television as she had nothing else to do. She had coaxed herself back into a positive frame of mind which she trusted to see her through the difficult moments ahead. She would tell him she was going to Holly and Dan's party, and she intended to get from him some answers about her past.

'Guess what?' she said, going through to the kitchen and helping him unpack the carrier bags of food. Her cultivated cheerfulness prevented even an inward wince at the packets of processed food. 'We've been invited to a party tonight.'

He laid a bag of oven chips on a freezer shelf. 'Whose?'

'Our new neighbours. They're called Holly Chase and Daniel Marcus, I've met her but not him. She's very friendly.'

He did not reply and she went on. 'Holly came round to invite us and I said I'd love to go.' She handed him a bag of frozen mixed vegetables.

He was relieved. He had never known the Parkers have a party and did not think he could bear an evening at their house. They were much too probing and could cause all sorts of difficulties. But the new neighbours . . . That was different. There shouldn't be any problem there.

'What time?' He took the frozen cheesecake she handed him.

'Any time after nine.' His facile acceptance surprised her. She thought he was in a suitably calm state for her to tackle more serious matters. Afterwards, when they were seated in front of the television with mugs of tea, she said: 'I know you don't find it easy to talk about all this, and neither do I, but I must know why I went away in November and if you've got any clue to where I went.'

Curtly he said he saw no purpose in raking over all that again.

'But we haven't raked it over at all! You haven't told me what my reason was for going – whether we had a row and what it was about.'

'You went and I fetched you back, that's all you need to know.'

'But it isn't. How am I ever going to remember anything if you don't help me?' The fragile cheerfulness was crumbling into exasperation. 'Honestly, it's as though you are *afraid* I might remember.'

She saw the pulse in his temple jerk to life, his hand clench on the arm of his chair. For an instant she feared he was going to spring at her, forcibly silence the questions that would not go away. Instead, he snorted derision.

She stood her ground: 'Whatever happened between us I have a right to know.'

'Nothing happened between us.' On the screen a sports presenter read a sing-song list of soccer results. Carol tried again.

'I want us to go right through everything you told me last Sunday and this time I want to ask questions. There was too much to take in then. Now I've had time to think and there are so many questions.'

He said nothing but the twitching temple was eloquent. His jaw set and he gazed at the television. On impulse Carol jumped up and touched the control which changed the channel. The sports presenter was replaced by two groups of people playing a recorded panel game. The camera zoomed into close-up on one of the panellists, a pretty blonde curly-haired woman of about thirty. She looked familiar. She and the chairman swapped banter and then she made a witty guess which won her team a point. The camera pulled back to reveal her colleagues' thrilled reactions. The card in front of the woman identified her as Rain Morgan.

No sooner had Carol read the card than there was a knock on the front door. Peter Dutton pushed past her without a word and opened it. He returned in seconds and hissed. 'Go into the kitchen and stay there. Someone's coming in to use the telephone.'

Dutton joined her until he heard the ping of the receiver being replaced on the cradle. Then he showed the visitor out.

Carol had only heard it was a woman speaking to someone called Oliver. Once Dutton shut the front door he went through to the garden and Carol peeped from the bay window. On the path outside Holly's house was a shortish blonde with bouncing curls. She was talking to Holly and there was much laughter. Carol shrank back before she was caught spying, but she saw the woman's face as she turned. There was no doubt, she was Rain Morgan and Carol had missed meeting her.

Carol picked up the coins Rain Morgan had left by the telephone. Then she thought better of it and put them down. She suspected it would antagonize Peter Dutton if she helped herself to them. Yesterday's accusations about her greed were an unhealed wound. She encouraged herself, with platitudes about looking on the bright side and finding silver linings. After all, she had Holly's party to look forward to and it appeared likely Rain Morgan and some other lively people from the *Daily Post* would be there. Holly's front door banged shut but no one walked away down her front path.

In Holly's house a number of friends had arrived to help her with food, Dan was cursing the slowness of the people installing the telephone, and Rain Morgan was deciding whether to go and come back or to stay. She hated to be in a party-planning house at this stage when there were too many helpers and she could usefully do nothing. But she had managed the important thing, she had tracked down Oliver West at the first attempt and he had said he would drive over. Perhaps she had better stay. She caught Dan Marcus watching the thought flicker through her mind. He laughed and shook his head. 'You and Oliver . . . but you seem to survive.'

Dan wasn't the only one. Everybody marvelled at the

ridiculous way they went on. And yet they did go on. **And on and on.** She described her relationship with Oliver as undulating, because it had as many downs as ups. For most of the last four years they had lived together but she several times left him when his behaviour seemed singularly charmless and she thought of better things to do with her life.

Each time she had gone back, with not much persuasion, and partly because it was absurd that she should be the one to leave her own flat. On other occasions it was Oliver who had upped and gone. He had done it last on Wednesday, going off in a huff, shouting that was definitely *it*, this time it was *final!*

Even so, it wouldn't have been fair to let him miss Holly's party and Holly and Dan especially wanted him there. Rain guessed where he would be on a Saturday afternoon even if she had only a hazy idea where he had slept the previous two nights. And Saturday afternoon found him imbibing behind the locked after-hours doors of a Chelsea wine bar.

He sounded pleased to hear her and pleased to be invited to Holly's party. There was no reference to the hiccup in their relationship. Perhaps there hadn't been one. Perhaps this simply *was* their relationship.

Oliver was tall and elegant and ducked his head past a low-slung lampshade when he stepped into Holly's hall. He kissed Rain in greeting, but not in any special way. She anticipated no more than a casual picking up of the threads that had been snapped on Wednesday. Their earliest reunions had been marked by a tension and a passion which had become out of place when parting and reunion became so regular.

'Show Oliver the house, Rain,' offered Dan who did not understand they had no need of time alone.

Rain showed Oliver the house. It took very few minutes but they lingered talking in the back bedroom, looking down on the darkening gardens. A man was in the one next door.

'Say something nice to Holly about the house,' Rain advised.

'Like what?' Oliver glanced helplessly around. They were

standing in a bare uncarpeted box. His pretence was that it was all like that.

'Well, how do I know? You're an imaginative fellow, you'll think of something.'

'What did you say?'

'That's cheating. You think up your own politenesses.' Rain had a troubled thought. 'And for heaven's sake don't say anything patronizing.'

'I'll try the script out on you first, shall I?'

'It might be safer.'

When they rejoined the others and Oliver told Holly how comfortable the house would be and how the garden was big enough for some really good barbecues when summer came, they discovered the Duttons were the topic downstairs.

'I was saying', Holly repeated, 'that the woman next door reminds me of someone and I can't think who.'

'Gosh,' said Oliver teasing, 'I thought they all looked the same to you.'

Holly tried to kick him. She went on: 'Rain, who do you think she looks like?'

'I didn't see her, I only saw him.'

Holly, who prided herself on her memory for faces, was frustrated by the lapse. 'Never mind, we can all take a good look when she comes in later.'

But Carol Dutton didn't go to Holly's party. Peter Dutton picked a quarrel and then told her she was too nervy and upset to go out. He said Dr Renfrew had said she was to get plenty of rest. He fetched a sleeping pill and waited while she washed it down with a hot drink. Then he sent her up to bed and watched television while the house rocked to a reggae beat from next door.

The happy bounce of the reggae was accompanied in Holly's lounge by Dan Marcus telling his guests about *The Face of Death*. The episode which he had just finished shooting was the one where some convicted murderers who had served prison sentences discussed their experiences and their current attitudes to their crimes and murder in general. The presenter did not forget to ask them about their opinion of the death penalty. They were all against it.

Dan said: 'Three of the four think they had a subconscious wish to be caught and punished, and that's why they made what look like pretty stupid mistakes.'

'That's amazing!' said a girl in a white spangled cat suit. She had been finding things amazing all evening.

'Three of the four', said Dewinton in his droll way, 'have spent too long in the prison library reading pop psychology from the pen of Professor David Rokeby. If you've done something wrong the last thing you want is to be found out and hauled into court. By definition, your programme is only dealing with the failures, the ones who get caught.'

'How come you can speak for the rest?' piped up a youth at his elbow.

There was laughter through which Dewinton appealed: 'Do I look like a murderer?' No one answered him.

Dan said the series wasn't light on serious psychology, pathology and sociology and all the other ologies but in his view the most riveting sequences would be those where the murderers appraised the matter of murder. 'Unfortunately,' Dewinton's voice came again, 'even the might of your television company cannot balance that with the victims' opinions of it. A comparison would be most illuminating.'

'Amazing!' said Spangles.

'So what's the conclusion?' asked a man in a red shirt.

Dan was lost. 'The what?'

'The conclusion – what's the message the series punches to us? There generally is one.'

'Oh, I don't know. They haven't quite finished shooting yet and the commentary script will be written last.'

'Amazing!' Spangles moved closer to him. But Dan didn't feel like justifying the curious ways of television programme makers who worked often in a vacuum and relied on good luck and a following wind to bring a project safely home. His guests wouldn't want to understand that a great idea with no filmic possibilities was no idea at all, or that the art as practised was not perfect planning but flying by the seat of the pants. He excused himself and went to replenish his beer.

'That', he said to Joel in passing, 'should be turned down.

112

The neighbours might want to go to bed.' Joel's hand reached out and the music was imperceptibly softer.

Later on Peter Dutton unlocked the pine desk and took out a sheet of writing paper and the slip with Carol Dutton's signature. He went out of the house and, with the help of the light shining through the glass of the back door, traced her name on to the writing paper, low down where one would sign a letter.

# 17

Around two in the morning at Holly's party Oliver West asked Rain Morgan: 'Your place or mine?'

There wasn't a choice. For the previous two nights he had slept on a friend's floor in Earl's Court. They said their goodbyes and went out into the peaceful dark of Shepherd Road. 'We don't need both cars,' said Oliver. 'We'll go in yours and collect mine tomorrow.'

'Fine.' Rain unlocked her small Italian car and they drove away. The only house in Shepherd Road with lights blazing was Holly's and the street lights had gone out long ago. Rain's headlamps picked up a few bricks and some stray bits of rubble on the road. The houses across the street from Holly's had a For Sale board and some words beginning with Phase Two. 'Fancy one?' asked Oliver.

'Not my style. Nor yours, I think.'

'Nor Holly's and Dan's. Did you make out why they did it?'

'The best of reasons. A low deposit because it's a new house. A good suburb not too far out, so the investment should be sound. Oh, and they needed somewhere to live.'

'The best of reasons.' He rested a hand on her thigh. The car swerved a fraction.

'And your reasons for coming back to Kington Square? Are they any good?'

His fingers crept along the inside of her thigh. 'It comes cheap, it's a good address, it's central. Oh, and I need somewhere to live.'

She removed his hand and changed gear. 'Holly was a shade hurt none of the neighbours came in.'

'Holly looked all right to me. I shouldn't think she cared.'

'She cared. But you know Holly, she puts on a big smile

and keeps on batting.' Rain drew away from deserted traffic lights, feeling disappointment for Holly that her friendly overtures had been rejected.

Oliver yawned. 'Did they say they were coming? It was rather late notice, wasn't it?'

'One set said they'd try but might be going out. The others – where I went to borrow the phone to call you – said yes, please. Holly thought the woman looked genuinely pleased to be asked.'

'That's the woman she wanted you to see?'

'Yes.'

'Perhaps her husband didn't want to go. He must be the odd fish we saw from the window.'

'Yes.'

Oliver yawned again. 'Looked just like a man who'd turn down a party.'

Back at Kington Square Oliver grumbled that he couldn't find his toothbrush and demanded to know what Rain had done with it. She replied that it was one of the three things he had taken with him on Wednesday, but if he stopped complaining he could borrow hers. Oliver said he already had borrowed hers and could they please stop arguing about toothbrushes. Everything was back to normal.

They made love tenderly, and then Oliver promised he would never leave her again. Rain thought that was an extremely rash thing to say and she would be even rasher to believe it. To avoid replying she kissed him. Oliver interpreted the length and energy of the kiss as a rapturous endorsement of the notion that they would part no more. Any decent fellow, he thought, would feel ashamed. It wasn't as though he had intended to say that. He'd been lying there congratulating himself on not having to sleep a night further on that dreary floor in Earls Court and suddenly he'd heard a voice and it was coming out of his mouth and making crazy promises.

Oliver's way of describing his four years with Rain was to compare it to a lumpy mattress: one knew things ought to be smoother but the discomfort was a challenge. Rain was soon asleep, an arm wrapped around him. Oliver redistributed the duvet rather more in his favour than hers and followed. His thoughts on drifting off to sleep were that it was a bore that they would have to go back to Spinney Green to collect his car, especially as they would have to drive in the other direction, too, to fetch his things from Earls Court. Still, if Rain had any money perhaps they could do something more enlivening in the evening?

They woke late next morning, a very mild day with the sun streaking the bedroom and an insistence of spring in the air. There was also the insistence of a telephone. Rain tugged on a dressing-gown as she ran to the sitting room to answer it. The flat was at the top of a white-stuccoed Georgian terrace and spacious. The handsome sitting room ran the length of the original house. At the front were floor-length sash windows and at the rear french windows leading on to a roof garden above an extension built to accommodate bathrooms and plumbed kitchens when the property was modernized by the Victorians.

The current arrangement meant that Rain had only one bedroom, the flats on the lower floors more. Yet she would not have traded her garden for the amenities of her neighbours, and when guests suggested remodelling her flat to create a more roomy bathroom, another bedroom, a bigger kitchen, she listened with amused interest. She liked it the way it was, particularly that long, light sitting room with its tranquil white walls. They were the perfect display space for the things that took her fancy: colourful weaving and embroidery from South America, vigorous pictures from North Africa, silks from China, mirrored quilts from India, and more.

Her bedroom, an ample room, housed her bookshelves and desk but if she worked at home she was more likely to be curled up on a long low couch with a telephone beside her and a typewriter a step away on the dining table. Of Oliver's four years – since she had rescued him from a west London house shared with fellow Australians and helped him to a job as one of the cartoonists on the paper – there was little to be seen.

He followed Rain into the sitting room and hovered,

116

waiting to know who was on the phone. He wrote a question mark in the air. She began to write 'Dick' but only got to 'Di' when Oliver rolled his eyes skywards and sloped off to the kitchen to make coffee. 'What was it this time?' he called through as the filter machine began to splutter and he heard her ring off. Dick Tavett was the features editor.

'He's seen an item in the Pendennis column of the *Observer* and wonders whether I've got it.'

'And you haven't.'

'No, and as it concerns Lord Bromfield and some of his famous string of horses . . .'

'. . . you'd rather not.'

'Quite.' Together they assembled mugs, milk and sugar. 'It's Holly's turn to go in this Sunday and not mine. I'll have to brief her.'

'Can't have your deputy getting out of step, can we?' He tweaked a blonde curl which fell over her forehead.

'You know what happened last time he made her run a story about Lord Bromfield. We had to publish a grovelling apology.'

'Which isn't to say it was wrong.'

'I've no doubt it was true, but we couldn't prove it. Unfortunately, he never learned the journalists' maxim: when in doubt, leave it out.' The coffee machine gave what sounded like a sympathetic sigh and was silent. Rain poured.

Holly greeted them with noisy pleasure at Shepherd Road. Dan had the bleary look of one who had been at a good party but also had to clear it up.

They took discussion of Dick Tavett's failure to balance enthusiasm with caution out into the garden. Oliver repeated his assurance that Holly and Dan would have some great barbecues out there. Having thought of a good line he was prepared to make the most of it.

Over the fence Holly spotted Carol Dutton. Holly nudged Rain who nudged Oliver and they all watched for a few seconds, Oliver in comfort, Rain and Holly on tiptoe. But Carol did not see them. Holly was frustrated, she wanted Carol to turn so that either Rain or Oliver would be able to tell her who the neighbour reminded her of. Dan, who might also have helped, had gone back into the house.

Carol heard the voices but was too self-conscious to go and speak to Holly. She was afraid she might have caused offence by not going to the party and had decided to apologize, saying she had been unwell on Saturday evening. But she could not face mentioning it unless Holly was on her own.

She had left Dutton lolling in front of the television, a scatter of Sunday papers on the carpet beside his chair. From her smock pocket she took the plan for remodelling the garden. The gardening books Jean Parker had loaned her spelled out what she had previously known by instinct: a rockery ought to appear to grow out of the setting, like a natural outcrop of rocks; it ought to be constructed not of rubble topped with chunks of hard material like granite or marble, but of easily-weathered stone such as limestone. Dutton's rockery did not comply with any of the guidelines. The crocuses he had planted were beautiful in the sunshine, but their success in disguising the ugliness of the crude heap of stones was minimal. The pitiful new plant that he fretted over showed no signs of taking root: each shower dislodged it and earth had washed from its crevice and pooled on thin grass below. Carol went in search of a spade.

The Duttons had no garden shed, but there was a low wooden shed near the back door and a few tools were kept there although, as Jean Parker had been known to point out, that was where the dustbin should be hidden. Carol thought she would like to have a proper garden shed at the other end of the garden, as the Parkers did, and keep the dustbin in the one designed for it instead of by the front door. She returned to the rockery with a spade. Men's and women's voices came over to her, talking and laughing and intercepted with whoops of delight which she knew to emanate from Holly. Carol smiled. It was good to hear people enjoying themselves, to have someone as irrepressible as Holly close at hand.

The ground was spongy beneath her feet, but poor drainage would not matter because she wanted a pool in front of the rockery and a tree behind it. Although it would be on a small scale, the effect could be pleasing. She would refine her plan, cost it, get Dutton to agree and then she would be free to work outside doing something positive and creative instead of moping indoors. Her face was still relaxed in a smile as she bent and lifted the first spadeful of earth back on to the rockery.

She tamped it down in one of the emptied pockets. Then another spadeful was lifted and replaced. But as she thrust the spade beneath the last of the dribbled mud, there was an explosion of angry noise and Dutton had burst out of the back door and was running up the garden shouting. 'What do you think you are doing?' His face was twisted with rage, the rest of his words unintelligible. He snatched the spade out of her hands and held it between them, threatening.

Carol was petrified. A terrible silence came, broken only by Dutton's jagged breathing. In that silence Carol was acutely conscious that beyond the fence Holly and Dan and their visitors were listening. The knowledge sustained her. Whatever madness was in Peter Dutton she would not be harmed when there were people so close. Her mouth was dry, there were no words to deal with her situation. Dutton, glaring, lowered the spade until it hung innocuously in his right hand. He asked in a broken voice: 'What were you doing?'

Carol did not answer him at once. She marvelled at his rage and his violence, but there was something else in his eyes. He put the question again. She told him, in a steady voice: 'Replacing the earth which had washed off the rockery. It rained in the night.'

He did not look at the rockery, he kept his eyes on her. She faced him squarely, seeing how the temple pulsed and his left eyelid flickered. She read the message in his eyes. It gave her confidence. She asked: 'And what did you think I was doing?'

She didn't get an answer and didn't expect one. Dutton went lamely away, shoved the spade in the shed on his way indoors. Exhausted, Carol followed. There was nothing to sit on in the garden or she would have stayed. Instead she went straight upstairs and lay on her bed. She had made a discovery but it was a tantalizing one. The discovery was that Peter Dutton was frightened of her. She was certain he was more frightened of her than she had yet been of him.

## 18

Monday brought the respite of Peter Dutton going to work. It
also brought a letter signed 'Marcia'.

'Hello, Carol,' it began. 'How are you after all this time?
You won't believe what I've been through to find you.
Chasing your husband up the street, phoning him at work
and making a real nuisance of myself!! Anyway, in the end a
man where he works told me where to write to you but he
couldn't give me your phone number and you aren't in the
directory. So as *soon* as you get this, phone me here and we'll
catch up on the news and fix a lunch date. I'm here for
another week, then moving on. Ever the gypsy! Love,
Marcia.'

Marcia had not given her home address or phone number,
she had typed on a sheet of headed stationery belonging to
the office where she was working. It was in the West End.
Carol lifted the telephone receiver. Considered. Set it down.
If she got through to Marcia, whoever Marcia was, what was
she meant to say? 'This is Carol who doesn't know a thing
about you?' She needed to think before she launched into a
difficult telephone call. She reread the letter.

How long was 'all this time'? Did Marcia mean they had
lost touch in November when she left home or later when she
had the accident and forgot everyone and everything? Or was
it even earlier than November? Did it happen when the
Duttons last moved house? And was it by accident or design?
Why did Marcia say she had been chasing Peter Dutton? Did
she mean he had been trying to avoid her? Had they both
tried to shake her off – by dodging her in the street and by
not telling her where they had moved to? There might be
very sound reasons for the Duttons to be cutting Marcia out

of their lives. And yet *any* contact with Carol's past must be welcomed. She made up her mind to ring Marcia and arrange to meet her for lunch.

She lifted the receiver again. Put it down again. Marcia *what*? How could she ring a busy West End office with a request for 'Marcia' and no surname? She shrugged. The first name was all she had to offer so she would offer that. She got through with speed and tried her luck. 'Marcia Cohen? One of the temps?' asked the switchboard operator. Carol said yes, and took a chance that it was the right Marcia. The operator put her through.

A strong London accent said: 'Carol! Wonderful! How *are* you? I was beginning to think you'd run off. Where have you been? Peter is so difficult to get any information out of. Did he even tell you I was asking after you? But tell me, what have you been up to? We must have lunch and catch up on all the news. It's been ages.'

Carol slotted in a murmur now and again but wasn't allowed scope for much more. Just when she'd got used to Marcia's prattling it halted. 'What's your phone number?' Marcia said, and waited.

Carol told her. Then: 'Marcia, I'd like to meet for lunch, as you suggested. Can you manage it fairly soon? This week?'

Something had caught Marcia off balance. Carol heard her voice slow to a cautious drawl. 'Ye-es. Any day's fine.'

'Oh, good. Tomorrow, then. If you are sure that's all right?'

'Meet me here at 12.30.' Still that doubt in her voice. She said: 'You're all right are you, Carol?'

'Yes, why do you ask?'

'Well . . . it's just that you sound a bit . . . well, a bit strange.'

'Do I? I feel fine. It must be the line.'

'Yes. See you tomorrow then.'

They said goodbye and rang off. Carol took up the letter again. She'd been a fool, she'd found out nothing important from the phone call except Marcia's surname. She still didn't know who Marcia was – a relative or a friend? The only thing she had not known before was that Marcia Cohen was a chatty temp. She hid the letter in her pocket. Peter Dutton had not mentioned Marcia was asking after her so she would not tell him Marcia had written or that they were to meet. It was not a tit-for-tat reaction but she believed there was a danger that if Dutton knew about the meeting he would prevent it.

The prospect of meeting Marcia thrilled her. Whoever Marcia was she could not have the same reticence as Dutton about discussing the past. Carol would break her agreement with him about keeping her loss of memory secret. She would have to, Marcia would find out something was wrong as soon as they began to talk.

Her heart leapt. Marcia already *had*. As soon as Marcia heard her say a few words she had asked whether she was all right. Carol's instinct was to phone and ask Marcia exactly what was strange. On second thoughts, it seemed better to be patient until they met. Everything would be easier face to face and she had not long to wait.

She would take with her a mental list of points she wanted Marcia to clear up for her. Who her friends were, where she had worked, why she had left home, so on. But meanwhile there were other things she needed to do.

First she took a sheet of paper and jotted a list of the times Dutton had upset or startled her by his ill-temper. It began with her accident at the Halberd on the first Sunday and ended with the incident at the rockery eight days later. Parallel with that list she wrote another, setting down what seemed to be the cause of his switches of mood. The first occasion was passed off as embarrassment at her making a fool of herself falling over, but that did not apply to scooping up fallen earth or any of the other occasions. At the end of an hour she was no nearer understanding the common thread and, setting the list aside, she carried out her next task. She called on Jean Parker and invited her for coffee.

Jean, who was doing her weekly wash before walking to her job at the baker's shop, downed soap powder and dirty socks, roared upstairs to Ted to keep an eye on the washing machine, and out she went. Carol and Jean talked of this and that and the tiresomeness of household chores, and then Jean let it out that she used to clean the house for Peter Dutton.

Immediately, she grew uncomfortable. 'Well, of course, it was while you . . . I mean before you . . .'

'Before I went away?' Carol helped her out, thinking Jean meant Carol had known about it.

'No, before you came.' Jean looked even more awkward. She hadn't meant to blunder into the business of where Carol Dutton had been or not been. She took a gulp of coffee and blundered on. 'We moved in just before Christmas – now take my word for it, don't ever move house just before Christmas, it was *murder*. So, seeing Peter was all on his own I said to him look, why don't you let me come in and put a duster and a vacuum cleaner round?'

'Are you sure you only moved in at Christmas? Late December?' This did not tally with something Dutton had said.

'I'm sure all right. Ask Ted if you don't believe me.'

'It's just that . . .' Carol faltered, made a decision. 'Tell me, Jean, when did we meet?'

Jean's eyes narrowed. 'That's a funny question. It was only last week. On the Monday. You drove up with Peter on the Sunday afternoon and ran straight in the house so we didn't meet until a week ago today.' She couldn't make out what Carol was getting at, asking such an extraordinary question.

'I see.' A lengthy pause. Neither woman knew how to go on. Then Carol said: 'When you first met Peter . . .'

'The day we moved in.'

'. . . where did he say I was?'

'Peter didn't say anything about you. To tell the truth Ted thought he might not be married, but it was always my idea that he was and his wife . . . you . . . had, well, you know . . . I mean, why would he want a house like this all on his own?'

'What about the other people in the street? Didn't they tell you anything about me?'

Jean gave a nervous laugh. Wherever was this conversation leading? She said: 'But you and Peter were the first people to move into the street, weeks before we did. We were next but by then you had . . . er . . .'

'I see.' What she saw was that Dutton had lied to her. She

could not possibly have been on bad terms with neighbours she had never met. It crossed her mind to confide in Jean that she was suffering from loss of memory but she was not convinced Jean would be a good confidante. Carol did not care about breaking her promise to Dutton to keep the matter to themselves – she was going to break it when she met Marcia Cohen – but she doubted whether she would be helped by Jean's ensuing pity. She gave Jean enough to satisfy her. 'I was in hospital for a time, after a road accident.'

It was Jean's turn to say 'I see' although she didn't. Carol escaped to refill coffee cups and Jean meandered about the lounge. Something, she knew, was missing. What could it be? Ah yes, the wedding photograph in its plated silver frame. She had polished it when it was kept on the mantelshelf, that's how she was sure it wasn't solid silver. There'd been no hallmark although she'd taken it to the window to check. Funny she should forget the photograph when it was the reason she gave up working for Peter Dutton. Well, she'd been given the sack if the truth was wanted. He'd been really put out and all she'd done was make a little suggestion about putting the photograph somewhere else. He hadn't understood she was only trying to be helpful. She'd never been totally sure it was Peter Dutton in the photograph, the man looked a lot younger – not so nervy, not so grey, a better head of hair. But, of course, it might not have been a good likeness at the time and it probably *was* him because people seldom showed off anyone else's wedding photograph on their mantelshelves.

Jean cast around for it. Her eager eye fell on Carol's list on the desk and she drifted over to read it. Jean read across the page from Carol's note about the Halberd episode to her one-word suggestion for its cause: embarrassment? Jean got a third of the way down the page like that. She could make no sense of it. She wondered whether it wasn't a poem. Carol Dutton behaved rather oddly, so it was quite possible she was the sort to write a poem.

A creak of the door as it swung back to admit Carol with the tray sent Jean wandering in casual style back to her chair. To deflect attention, in case she'd been spotted reading, she said: 'You've moved the photograph, then?' She indicated the mantelshelf with a jerk of the head.

'What photograph?'

Jean gave a mirthless laugh. 'Your wedding photo! It used to stand on there.' Another nod at the mantelshelf. Inside her head she could hear her own voice relaying to Ted how oddly Carol was behaving.

Carol managed a weak smile. 'Oh, that.'

Once Jean had returned home and was indeed recounting to Ted the strange conversation, and wishing she could remember a line or two of the poem to recite for him, Carol's hunt for the missing wedding photograph began. The desk drawers were locked so it might be hidden in there. Dutton would not have wanted it on view as a constant reminder that she had run away from him, but now she was back what could be the objection to reinstating it? Especially as it might help her lazy memory.

Carol went through the dressing table drawers and the cupboards but there was no sign of it. She gave up and was going downstairs when she realized there was one stone left unturned. The loft. She hesitated. Lofts were dusty and she dared not get her only good clothes and shoes dirty or damaged. Before going up to the loft she would have to change into the smock or some other garment she didn't care about. And she didn't have time to do that because today she was going out.

She walked as far as the shops in Spinney Green, having gleaned from Jean's earlier conversation how to reach them. The weather was kind enough for her to wear the suit jacket and spare her the grey coat. She stepped around the dried mud and rubble, like the stools of a giant animal, outside the Phase Two houses.

Carol was happy, despite so much to be unhappy about. The sun was out, she felt fitter than she had done for days, she gained confidence from dressing presentably, she was not on bad terms with her neighbours and tomorrow she would renew a friendship. Whatever Peter Dutton did or had done in the past he would not be allowed to break her spirit.

There were six shops with flats above them in a block called

Station Parade. A smattering of dark wood about the gables was a nod in the direction of Tudor and a clear indication of low-grade 1930s. The walk itself was the real purpose of the outing but it was convenient that at the end of it would be a newsagent's where she could browse among magazines. The sight of them brought her mind back to Princes Hospital where friendly faces had offered her a constant supply of reading matter to occupy her mind. At least the magazines were familiar things when everything else in Spinney Green felt foreign.

She chose a gardening magazine and *House and Garden*, strolled passed the rest of the shops and headed home. Until she reached Shepherd Road her buoyant mood persisted, but she was undeniably reluctant to enter the house. She put a brave face on it: Peter Dutton would not be home for a long time. A lorry, racing from the site at the far end of the road, came by in a haze of dust which stung her eyes.

As she rubbed them she noticed a woman on the doorstep of 7 Shepherd Road, a young bird-like woman with a bulging document case. Carol thought she might be selling door to door, but decided that was wrong. Sales representatives were neater, more conventionally dressed. They went in for suits or tailored coats. This woman wore flat black canvas shoes with patterned dark green tights, a flowing black cotton skirt and a pink quilted jacket.

'Carol Dutton?' she asked as Carol started up the front path. 'I'm Ellie Gray, from the social services department. We got a request from a hospital in the Midlands for someone to call on you.'

Carol took her in and made tea. Ellie Gray sat at the kitchen table in the warmth listening to Carol's strange experience of forgetting. 'But why haven't you been to see your doctor yet?' she wondered.

'I didn't know I was supposed to. There isn't anything he can do, is there?'

'They should have told you at the hospital to go and see him. Maybe they mentioned it to your husband instead.' Ellie Gray looked at her notes. 'The social worker at the hospital, Irene Yarrow, said they'd written to your doctor. He's quite a

126

long way off, isn't he? Why don't you switch from Dr Andersen to a local doctor?'

'Yes, I must do that.'

'It's quite simple. You just go and ask the doctor if he'll take you and he gets all your records from Dr Andersen. You won't even have to queue up to see the doctor when you go to register, his receptionist will deal with it.' She wrote down the names of some local general practitioners. 'Dr Hubbard is your nearest, close to Spinney Green station.'

She checked her watch against the Duttons' kitchen clock, bundled papers back into her document case and stood up. 'I'll try and find time to drop in again sometime and see how things are progressing. But it's up to you to get yourself to a doctor.'

She hurried off, a full caseload of other people's disasters keeping her in perpetual motion. Most of them she had been trained to help, but not someone like Carol Dutton. What had that Irene Yarrow expected her to do? The social services department wasn't a repository of lost memories. Carol's treatment was up to the Duttons and their doctor, if they could be bothered to see one. If it had been a child who'd left hospital with a problem, then it would have been her duty to keep watch. Adults were supposed to be able to exercise some initiative themselves. Yet it was funny how slack quite intelligent people could be, especially when they needed help.

Carol decided to ask Dutton about Dr Andersen and then tomorrow, on her way to lunch with Marcia Cohen, she would call in at Dr Hubbard's surgery and register.

The rest of her day passed quietly, reading. She considered hiding the magazines from Dutton, in case they inflamed him to accusations about carelessness with money. She was right. He grumbled about *House and Garden* in particular. Even while he was watching television it rankled that she was feasting on pictures of fantastically grand homes. He switched off the lights in the room and then complained she would strain her eyes trying to read by the flicker of the set. She refused to be drawn. After a while he lost heart and left her alone.

She told him about Ellie Gray and he wanted to know in detail what they had spoken about. She had a suspicion this was more than normal interest, that he was checking up on something. Her answers apparently satisfied him. When she relayed Ellie Gray's suggestion about switching from Dr Andersen to a family doctor in Spinney Green he said he would see about it, she was not to trouble. She wanted to ask whether anyone at Princes Hospital had told him to take her to a doctor, but it was too easy to imagine him regarding the question as an accusation. Her courage failed her.

A play came on the television, about a couple on holiday in Italy. Afterwards she asked where they had been for their own holidays. 'Suffolk,' he said.

'I do wish I remembered.'

But he ignored her plaintive remark and picked up the programme guide. The patience he had shown at first had vanished days ago. He had started off being protective in not urging her to remember things, now she felt he could not care less whether she did or not. She said: 'Where did we stay?'

'At Southwold. In a hotel. You liked it there, we went three times.'

'I must have liked it a lot to want to go three times.' And then, taking a chance: 'As I liked it so much perhaps we could go again. It might help me to remember.'

'I don't see that it would.' He found the page he wanted and was intent on the rest of the evening's viewing.

'Perhaps a weekend.'

No answer.

'Or a day trip?'

'You wouldn't see much in a day, would you?' He got up and changed channel.

'Could we compromise and stay just one night? Soon?'

'The hotel probably isn't open this time of year.'

'But we could find out.'

'All right, I'll find out.'

They were twenty minutes into the next programme when she asked: 'Didn't we take any photographs in Suffolk? They might help me, too.'

'There are a few somewhere. I'll dig them out.'

Her eyes rested on the desk, assuming a camera and some packs of holiday snaps in a drawer. She feared she would put the whole delicate enterprise in jeopardy by pressing him, so she said nothing.

## 19

After she had gone to bed Peter Dutton took the key to the desk from his overcoat pocket. Out of the bottom drawer he drew a pack of photographs, his face impassive but his mind busy. There had seemed no harm in saying Suffolk, just like that. The mistake had been in letting her know the Duttons had been there three times because Carol had liked it so much. Now he might have to go to the trouble and expense of taking her there, and it was true, he had been there three times with his wife so what if one of the hotel staff . . . ?

However, he had his escape clause and he would use it. He would tell her he had telephoned the hotel only to find that it was closed until Easter. Many seaside hotels shut down until then so that would be plausible. Then he would persuade her to delay the visit until after Easter and that was late this year. By then there would be other reasons not to go, or she might have left him. Anything could happen.

He flicked through the photographs, tossing aside all those that showed his wife smiling into the camera or posing near a tourist attraction. Then he replaced the others in their envelope and, carrying those of Carol Dutton, he went in stockinged feet up to the loft, where he hid them beneath carpet pieces in the tin trunk. He left the pack on top of the desk where she would find it next day after he had gone to work. With the sketch of a smile he thought about the following evening when he would attempt to coax her memory with those photographs of Suffolk scenes and sights.

She would be despondent, of course, believing the hotel closed and the photographs no use to her. Well, she would have to put up with that as he had to put up with other things. That day had been a trying day at Pegwoods. He had wasted his lunch hour to use, unseen, Mary Partridge's typewriter so that he could type on the sheet of paper where he had traced Carol Dutton's signature. He was writing a brief letter to the bank manager advising him that she was no longer living at Shepherd Road. There had, after all, been a way to prevent the bank sending quarterly statements to the house, a way to keep the secret of the New Zealand money to himself. Quite simply, it was a flash of inspiration.

It irked that his two-finger typing was so messy and that Mary Partridge came back early from lunch and was cross that he had dribbled white typewriter corrector fluid on what she called her platten. He expected her to use the occasion to flirt with him but she stayed cross. In the end it had been all right: the letter had been completed and posted without Mary or anyone else reading it.

Next day Carol's mind was full of her plan to meet Marcia Cohen until she discovered the photographs as Dutton intended. She spread them over the carpet and crouched there studying them. Nothing. No trace of recognition at all. Dread filled her. She would never recall her past life. All she ever had were those slight brushes with memory which very nearly let her conjure up a country place, a voice, the scent and feel of a day.

The photographs were of average quality and type. Seascapes. Country views. Town scenes. A few close-ups of the detail of flowers and old breakwaters. Her hand went out to one of the town scenes. In the foreground was a man she now realized was Dutton. He was out of focus, his identity not apparent before. But what interested her was that he was coming down the steps of a small white-painted hotel. On a post beside him swung the hotel sign with its name and the promise of three stars. She had no doubt this was the hotel where they had stayed, and stayed three times because she was so happy there. In that case, she wouldn't wait for Dutton to find out whether the hotel was open through the winter, she would do that for herself.

Perching on the deep sill of the bay window she rang Directory Enquiries who came up with the telephone number of the Boatman Hotel at Southwold. Immediately afterwards she got through to the hotel and discovered that not only was it open throughout winter but the owners were offering inexpensive weekend breaks of one or two nights. They had a vacancy for the next weekend so she made a booking for a double room with twin beds.

Humming in cheerful anticipation of a weekend by the sea, she went about her chores. It jarred that there were no photographs of herself in Suffolk but maybe she had been the photographer? She rounded up the dirty washing and set to work at the kitchen sink grateful for another crisp day which would dry the clothes quickly. She had plenty of time before she need set off to meet Marcia Cohen.

While she was hanging out the washing, Holly Chase popped out of her back door and Carol took the chance to apologize for missing the party, using the excuse that she had been unwell. They had little conversation because Holly was late for work. Shortly after, Carol combed her hair, put on her suit jacket and was ready to walk to the station. Then the phone rang. Marcia Cohen. Today wasn't convenient after all. There was a young accountant she'd had her eye on since she was sent to the office and he'd asked her to lunch with him. She knew Carol wouldn't mind. They rang off without fixing an alternative date. 'I'll ring you,' Marcia said, and was gone.

As Carol coped with her disappointment Holly Chase was driving to work tussling with the certainty that she had seen Carol Dutton somewhere before. She had reached the stage of deciding she had not spoken to her, as Carol had shown no recognition of her. Holly fingered one of the fine braids of her hair as she waited for traffic to creep forward. She did not like this sort of nagging puzzle. She tried to recall the places she had been to during the past couple of weeks and asked herself whether she had seen Carol Dutton at any of them. She was convinced she had seen her no longer ago than that. Some of the places were straight away ruled out – Carol would not have been at press conferences or the other diary jobs she had covered, nor at the social gatherings of journalists. Others she was prepared to chew over. By the time she swung into the office car park to make her daily bargain with the attendant for unauthorized use of a space, she was sure the context was work and not social. There was the haziest picture in her mind of Carol's face seen above an expanse of white. Obviously, Holly thought, Carol must have sat near her in a restaurant, and the whiteness represented a tablecloth.

Rain Morgan was on the telephone when Holly arrived at the facing desk in the corner of the modern open-plan office allotted to the staff of the *Daily Post* Diary. They mouthed greetings and Rain continued to talk into the telephone. Holly asked who was speaking by sketching a question mark in the air. Rain replied with the slash and dot of an exclamation. She was saying: 'I'll ask someone to call you back. No. I can't promise it will be this morning . . . But the staff won't be in until later on . . .'

Holly made a dumb show of being the aggrieved caller on the other end of the line. Rain extricated herself and rang off. 'Hi!' said Holly.

'How's commuting?' Rain wrote a note on a scrap of paper which already carried a scribbled phone number, and slapped it on top of a typewriter on the desk abutting hers and Holly's.

'Commuting's fine. Was that true? That the staff's not in?'

'She's probably in the loo.'

The telephone shrilled again. Rain pulled a face and answered it. Then she put her hand over the mouthpiece and said: 'Send out a search party would you, Holly. This could go on all day.' And she picked up her pen and jotted notes, giving the caller the polite minimum of encouragement to go on with his tale.

A short, balding man in blue cords and a handknitted sweater of coloured stripes came and sat on Rain's desk and swung an impatient leg, urging her to end the call. 'Good morning, Dick,' said Holly with misplaced optimism. It was never a good morning for Dick Tavett, the features editor. The dearth of good mornings was making him prematurely middle aged. He smoothed a hand over the front of his head as though checking that the hair had indeed vanished.

Returning Holly's greeting he tacked on to the end of it the purpose of his visit: the non-appearance of an item he had passed on to Rain and expected to see in print that morning.

Holly decided to escape while there was time. When would Dick ever learn not to promise at the editorial conferences stories his staff saw no excuse to run? She opted to leave the argument to Rain who was tougher. 'Can't talk now, Dick.' She gave him her widest smile. 'I'm a bloodhound on the trail of the missing member of the team.' She mimed sniffing the air.

'Try the library,' offered Tavett. 'I asked Rosie to check up on something in the files for me.'

Rain, hearing, fixed him with a stern look. He winced and stroked the baldness. By the time she came off the phone Rain had marshalled all the ammunition required to see him off. How was she to get the column out if she was going to be on the phone all day because he had filched her secretary? Why couldn't he get himself a reliable secretary who got in on time, instead of poaching? Tavett was sheepish, very nearly apologetic. He made light of his own grumble and shrugged his way back to his desk further down the room. The bald head was polished by his palm several times before he got there.

Holly, meanwhile, had gone to the library to remind Rosie where her true loyalties lay. Several other people were using the room at the time, a knot of them, including Dick Tavett's secretary who still had her coat on, were chatting and drinking plastic beakers of coffee from a machine. Rosie, the Diary's efficient and fashion-conscious young secretary, was not with them. She was looking in a file of recent back numbers, turning the pages methodically, scanning each with care. Just before Holly arrived at her elbow Rosie turned over the page with the photograph of Carol Dutton in her hospital bed.

With Rosie back at her desk and manning the telephones, Rain scribbled the list of potential stories which she would discuss at the editorial conference that morning. Holly chipped in a couple more. Down the room Dick Tavett was trying to attract their attention to hurry them. He hated to set off for the conference without all of his staff who were needed (or *might* be needed) in tow. Demonstrably, he believed there was safety in numbers. It was unfortunate, for himself and for his staff, that he was scared of the editor and he was made no less faint-hearted by the way the man was commonly referred to as God.

'Come on,' said Oliver West. 'Dick's twitching. Put him out of his misery.'

Rain said: 'Dick's earned this bit of misery. He helped himself to Rosie and I've been on the phone ever since I got in.'

Oliver draped an arm around her shoulder and studied her list. 'What's that about?' He pointed at one of the cryptic items.

Rain explained as they walked towards the editor's office. 'A simple tale of a royal personage's blossoming liaison with a cabinet minister's secretary who was caught shoplifting but dodged prosecution when the boss had a word with the Indian shopkeeper.'

'As simple as that?'

'No.' She told him the rest. Oliver remarked that the story was sexist, racist and a treasure of innuendo. 'I know,' Rain said. 'What more could I ask?'

'I'll bet the lawyers won't let you run it.'

'Not as I've told it to you, but you know the rules of this game: blur the slur.'

'Has Dick seen it?'

'Dick loves it.'

'I still say the lawyers will stamp all over it.'

'How much are you betting?'

'I'll be kind – a fiver.'

'You're on.'

'I hate to take your money,' said Oliver, who hated no such thing.

Dick Tavett was holding the door of the editor's room open, chivvying them through. Rain dropped into the chair which Tavett believed he had reserved for himself and Oliver lounged against a filing cabinet on top of which he laid a note pad and doodled cruel caricatures of his colleagues: Tavett

135

patting his baldness; the insignificant editor behind the bombastic ties; the ragbag of out-at-elbow men who passed for the paper's intellectuals; the business editor who regularly gambled his salary on the horses; the partially deaf theatre critic no one had heard speak in the editorial conference for twenty years but whom no one had the heart to tell need not be there. And then Oliver toyed with cartoons of the cabinet minister's secretary stuffing her brassière with the Crown Jewels and sneaking out of a royal bedroom.

The door opened once more, to admit a thin careworn man – Wilmot, the lawyer who steered the paper around the libel laws. Oliver's pencil exaggerated the man's wariness into terror but then he checked himself, scribbled through the figure. Today he was on Wilmot's side, today there was a fiver in it.

# 20

Lewis had recovered from his cold by Tuesday and returned to Pegwoods. He and Johnson broke off conversation when Dutton walked into the room but Dutton had no doubt they had been talking about him, discussing Friday's revelation that Carol Dutton had returned home. He also had no doubt that sometime during the day Lewis would refer to it.

The memory of his colleagues' unexpected kindness when Carol went had faded. All Dutton could see now was that they were a gossiping and nosey crowd. He offered a brief good morning, a word or two about the delay on the 8.23 from Spinney Green and then made a show of being so busy that interruption would be heinous. Out of the corner of his eye he saw Johnson grimace at Lewis. Then they both yawned, reached simultaneously to their filing trays and plunged into their work.

Dutton thought he understood the plan. It would be: 'How about a quick one?' (which would mean at least three because they would each be obliged to buy a round of drinks) and a plot to delay him in the evening. Then he saw he might be wrong: Johnson and Lewis went to the pub only on Friday evenings, so far as he knew. And, yes, the athletic Johnson played squash on Tuesday evenings – Dutton could recall many a bruised Wednesday – so the ploy could not be an after work drink. Lunchtime, then. Johnson and Lewis sometimes ate a pie and drank a couple of pints at the Brewer's Arms at lunchtimes and sometimes asked him along, although the occasions were rare because his acceptances were rarer.

As the end of the morning came he was ready for them, mumbling that he would see them later and heading out of the room before they had a chance to speak. He thought he heard Johnson swear, and grinned at having cheated them. Outside Pegwoods he dithered. The day was cold although sunny and might be too chilly to sit in a garden square with a sandwich. There were only three tables in the sandwich bar he normally used, and they were certain to be taken. But in the opposite direction there was another, a slightly dearer one, which relied less on the takeaway trade. He could be lucky and get a seat in the warm there.

Dutton went left and wound through narrow streets, the wind razor sharp on his face. He pulled up his coat collar and dug his hands into his pockets. The wind flattened his trousers against his legs and tore at the old winter coat. Pieces of paper and flurries of dust spiralled, pedestrians leaned forward for balance. The sandwich bar came in sight, its broad window pane vague with steamy warmth. Dutton joined the queue at the counter. An espresso machine was noisily active and he had to repeat his order for a round of salt beef with coleslaw and a cup of coffee.

Down the room was a table with an empty space, provided the woman next to it would shift her shopping bag. He had to ask whether she would mind doing so and she put it on the floor, grudgingly, barely looking at him and without breaking off conversation with her two companions. They were grumbling about the morning's happenings in the office where they worked. Dutton wished he had brought a newspaper to read. He had no one to talk to and nothing to look at except his sandwich. Whenever he glanced up from his plate the woman opposite turned her face from her friends to him, making him feel an eavesdropper. Several times he lowered his eyes when this happened, but then refused to be intimidated in this foolish way and the next time held her gaze. It was she who looked away.

He was pleased at this tiny victory but in the next second he saw something which made him freeze. A young woman coming away from the counter with her tray was casting about for a seat. Her face was Carol Dutton's. She had shoulder-length hair of the right shade, large grey eyes and she was moving down the room towards him. He wasn't

138

aware he dropped the sandwich he had been about to bite into, nor that he was staring, nor that a pulse in his temple was working. But he felt breathless and panicky, dreading what might happen.

He could only believe that it *was* his wife and she was going to walk right up to him. Even when the woman rested her tray on the edge of another table, removed her plate and cup and saucer from it and then stood the tray out of the way by the table leg, he could not grasp that she was not going to confront him. His gaze was unswerving, like a rabbit watching headlights approach.

The woman took a knife and cut her sandwich into quarters. She spooned sugar into her cup and toyed with the espresso froth for a moment. Then she began to eat. As she chewed the first mouthful she saw him. She looked about the room and carried on eating, but the next time she caught him watching her the grey eyes grew hard and challenging. Dutton gulped and looked down. The sandwich had come apart when it fell to the plate. He fumbled to put it back together, scooping the scattered coleslaw on to the bread with his knife. The knife fell to the floor, he ignored it, crammed the top slice of bread on to the disarranged filling and tried another bite.

His mouth was parched. He felt he would choke. He set the sandwich down, it slid messily apart. Raising his coffee cup, his hand shook. The women with him broke off their chatter to watch him put the cup rattling into the saucer. He could not help himself, he looked once more at the woman with Carol Dutton's face. She was wriggling out of her coat now, finding the crowded café too hot. As the navy wool vanished she emerged wearing a cream sweater in a lacy knit. And then it happened. She raised her head and, seeing Dutton's unyielding eyes, gave him a look that was so like his wife's the last time he had seen her. He whimpered. The women with him turned censorious faces. Then he was on his feet and running out of the café, abandoning his lunch. He knew the whole world was watching.

Several streets away, walking furiously, battling against the wind he tried to rearrange his wild thoughts. Of course, it

139

could not have been his wife. And, of course, the cream lace was only a coincidence. And, of course, it was mere chance the woman had gone into the café while he was there. He argued it through, forcing himself to accept only what was rational and in the end failing because he was not in control of his reason. Whatever common sense told him, he was equally sure that Carol Dutton was haunting him.

Ice-cold rain stung his cheeks and he raced for the shelter of a corner pub. The noise of the jostling customers, each with scant room to raise a glass to his lips, was deafening but he welcomed the blanket of sound to smother what his mind was screaming at him. Despite the crush he was served quickly. Slopping the beer as he struggled back from the bar, he sought out a spot to stand where he could rest his glass on a window ledge.

The rain came like tapping fingers on the pane but the engraved glass prevented Dutton seeing out or anyone outside seeing in. He held his beer mug in two hands to keep it steady, but he had only drunk an inch or two when he had to put it down and try to soothe his jerking eyelid. Perhaps he should not have ordered beer, he thought. A brandy or a whisky would have done more for his nerves. So he downed the beer and thrust into the throng at the bar. When he returned with his whisky someone had taken his place by the window ledge and he had to find somewhere else to stand. He made his way towards a promising gap at the far end of the bar and next to the door marked Toilets.

Whisky warmed and calmed him and if the eyelid did not respond at least he gave up worrying about it. He reflected on what had taken place, deciding that the rational explanation did not necessarily cancel out the other. It was quite easy to understand there was a woman who looked remarkably like his wife and who worked near Pegwoods. He had seen her twice: eight days ago when they had come face to face crossing Oxford Street and today in the sandwich bar. She was not somebody he had ever seen before so the major coincidence was her appearance once Carol had gone. Whichever branch of fate was in control of the distribution of coincidences was piling them on. He would never be able to

140

walk the streets near Pegwoods without risking meeting the memory of his wife.

He ordered another whisky and wondered whether he could do anything to bring the situation to an end. What if he took evasive action? He could leave Pegwoods, get a job in another part of London and never see this woman again. Would that mean he had won, or would it mean another likeness would spring up to taunt him in the next area he went to? And how long would this persist if he stayed at Pegwoods? Would the woman give up working around there soon? She did not look happy, so perhaps she was already thinking of changing her job.

By the third whisky he felt it might be best to get into conversation the next time he saw her and find out what her plans were. If it wasn't essential it would be a pity to leave Pegwoods because he didn't fancy settling into a new office with new people, and, besides, jobs were not plentiful. By now the pub was emptying and Dutton tagged along behind a group who were leaving. The shower had finished, only the occasional puddle gleamed as wind dried the streets. Dutton tried to work out the route back to Pegwoods.

He was rather late on his return and it was noticed. The manager's secretary frowned as he passed her in a corridor. Mary Partridge and a typist giggled after him, and Johnson and Lewis were deeply interested in his awkward efforts at getting his coat on to its hanger. When he tripped over his wastepaper bin neither of them was surprised, and when he fell asleep at 3.15 it was no more than they expected.

Shortly afterwards Dutton began to talk. 'That's the most he's said to us for months,' Lewis said and they laughed. Dutton continued and Lewis pretended they were in conversation. 'Absolutely, old chap, couldn't say fairer myself.'

Then Johnson told Lewis to hush, he was trying to make out what Dutton was saying. Lewis, who thought he was being amusing, was a bit put out but hushed anyway. Yet neither of them could understand the words, and so Lewis said: 'Come on, speak up, Dutton.'

A bit louder Dutton repeated the mumble. Johnson said: 'I think he's saying something about Carol. Isn't that it?'

'Don't ask me, ask him,' said Lewis.

Johnson tried conversationally with: 'What's that about Carol?' Dutton continued the confused sounds. Johnson said to Lewis: 'You try, he responded when you asked him to speak up.'

'All right.' He waited until Dutton paused and then, slowly and clearly asked: 'Where's Carol?'

Equally clearly Dutton said: 'Carol's dead.'

Lewis always swore that if Mary Partridge hadn't bounced into the office at that point he would have got the rest of it out of Dutton. But in she came and away went the chance because her hoot of laughter at finding Peter Dutton asleep over the stock orders and Johnson and Lewis staring at him with the compelling eyes of a couple of hypnotists disturbed him. His face contorted and a moment later he woke, apparently from a nightmare.

Peter Dutton had no inkling he had been speaking in his sleep. Lewis and Johnson gave no clue and Mary Partridge had not heard. He only knew he woke from the dream of his wife's face as he had last seen it, but this time the scene his dreams repeated was not at Spinney Green but in a sandwich bar in the West End.

His mouth was dry and bitter and he went in search of a glass of water. There was a heaviness in his skull and he felt immensely tired but afraid of falling asleep again. He wished very much that he could walk out of the building and get some cold air to perk himself up, but he could not leave so early. He drank water and went back to his desk where he did some desultory work until it was time to slip into his nightly routine of dashing for the Underground.

He bought no paper on the way home as there was no change left in his pocket. He had spent far more at lunchtime than he meant, but he did not blame himself. It had, after all, been an emergency. Sitting on the 5.45 as it trundled up the line to Spinney Green he felt weary and depressed, a consequence of daytime drinking which usually deterred him from doing it. He knew the episode had been a mistake but had no idea of the magnitude of it.

There was nothing attractive now about the silly notion of

getting to know the woman he had seen at lunchtime. He would never have the courage to go up to her, his control would snap and he would flee as he had fled that day. All his plans were useless. The woman at home was a catastrophic error because one day she was going to remember who she really was. No man in his right mind would have dreamed up the crazy scheme he had brought to fruition. Except, though, that it had not come to fruition because it was not possible to have his wife back.

Dutton shut his eyes and leaned his head on the backrest. He could not think of a way out. He could drive the new Carol away by unkindness but one day she might rediscover her true self and be back on his doorstep to accuse. And she would not keep it to herself. He could fob her off all right, he was cleverer than she was, he was sure of that. But how could he fob off everyone else who would be asking why he did it? By 'everyone else' he meant the police.

He pulled himself up. Supposing he drove her away, sold the house and disappeared? Then she could turn up on the doorstep as often as she liked and he wouldn't be there. He would change his name, his job, go abroad. He'd never been abroad because his wife had hated travel after her journeys to and from New Zealand, but going abroad with a new name would save him.

The train reached Spinney Green. He joined the straggle of commuters passing through the token barrier and dispersing into the suburb. When he came to the corner of Shepherd Road he was still considering the practicalities of going abroad. There would be difficulties, but his spirits lifted as he reminded himself that nothing in the future could be as bad as what lay in his past

His brow puckered. Wasn't there something he had to remember to do this evening? As he was walking up to the front door it came to him. He was going to say the visit to Suffolk was off until the summer season.

## 21

'About the hotel . . .' Carol began once Dutton had hung up his coat in the hall. She wanted to get matters settled before he had a chance to pick a quarrel.

'I'd rather leave it until the summer.'

'I got through to the Boatman Hotel and they are doing cut-price weekends so I made a provisional booking for next weekend. That will be all right, won't it?'

His mind was working far too sluggishly to interpret what had happened. He could not recall mentioning the name of the hotel and she was saying she had telephoned it. She was looking pleased with herself. His heart sank as he wondered what she had been up to. She gave her rippling laugh. He did look odd standing there, almost dazed. She said: 'You're thinking I must have remembered the name of it?'

He pulled his wits together. 'Yes, how else would you know it?' Meaning he knew very well she couldn't possibly have remembered it, but was fearful of her explanation.

She held up one of the photographs. 'Because of this.'

He saw himself coming down the steps of the Boatman. Then he dropped into his usual chair facing the television set, the photographs in his hand. So everything was all right, he needn't panic. She had done no more than make an intelligent guess. He handed the snapshot back, yawned. The lunchtime drinks were still evident. He felt comfortable and lazy and rather fancied a couple of days at the Boatman. 'This weekend will be fine,' he said.

That night, when he woke up from his nightmares and went downstairs to sit wakefully in the kitchen drinking tea, he doubted the wisdom of taking her to Southwold. The owners of the family hotel and their staff would recognize him but not her and what would she make of that? And to think he had embarked on all this because he thought she was identical to his wife! He was sure he must have been mad to believe two human beings could be so alike, even in mere appearance, and even madder to think he could get away with such a deception.

He reverted to his escape plan. How would it be, he wondered, if he just disappeared while they were at Southwold? Could he go for an evening walk on his own, say, and just not reappear, leaving her to assume he had been caught by the tide? Of course, February was far too cold on the east coast for him to pretend to a swimming accident.

Then he saw objections to walking off. He would have to have a means of getting away from Southwold in the evening. There was no train service and he wasn't sure of the buses. Obviously, he would have to leave the car behind.

He pictured himself setting off along the windswept cliff top at dusk and then dashing across fields to reach a lonely bus stop just at the right time to catch a ride to the nearest town with a railway station. What should he take with him? Not much or he'd look exactly like a runaway.

His tea had gone tepid so he topped it up with thick dark liquid from the pot and set his mind to disappearing from Southwold. The concept excited him. He knew the impracticalities of it, because country eyes were everywhere. It was in the big cities with people all round that one passed unnoticed. And yet, and yet . . . He had a seductive idea that he knew how it might be done. The dangerous thing would be to construct an elaborate method which could tumble at various stages. The essence of success was simplicity.

For a while he sat there in the kitchen with only the drone of the fridge for company and he refined the plan for his disappearance. What came next was less clear, but going abroad wouldn't do because he did not have a passport. Once he had acquired one the whole world beckoned, but there were only three days to decide how he would vanish from Southwold and where he would go.

Dutton deserted his cold tea and paced the lounge trying to think of all the things he would need to prepare. If he went from Southwold then he must not come back to Shepherd Road, ever. So in his luggage for the weekend he must take whatever he wanted for the future. His departure was to look like an accidental death, he must leave behind the documents a dead Peter Dutton would leave. His cheque book and credit card could be left in the Boatman because a cheque cashed after his 'death' could trace him as readily as a bloodhound. And he must not take every penny from the account before going to Southwold because that would also look suspicious. But Southwold would not have a bank open at the weekend so it would be quite reasonable if he were carrying a more than usual amount of cash at the time he vanished.

Money wasn't an important problem because he held the ace which was Carol Dutton's personal account. Before going to Southwold he would drain it and hide the cash. Later, when the next instalment was transferred from New Zealand, he would draw on that, too, simply signing his wife's name on cheques made out to himself but in the new name he was about to choose.

By the time light was breaking beyond the Phase Two houses Peter Dutton had convinced himself that he must 'die' at Southwold and be reborn at an unspecified elsewhere. In one thrilling evening he could be free of all the horror which had dogged him since November.

The rooms were chilly and he went back to bed for warmth, although he was positive there was no chance of sleep. His mind had been far too active for him to drop off easily and he knew it would follow the pattern of other sleepless nights in recent months and race on, from topic to topic, until it was time to get ready for the working day. Today he didn't care, he had a new and absorbing plan to perfect and he was brimming with optimism. There was only a fleeting moment when he glimpsed the rest of his life as one escape plan after another.

There were no sounds to invade Dutton's thoughts until footsteps sounded on the stairs of the adjoining house and a distant radio blared and was quelled. Shortly afterwards a car drew up and Dutton squinted round his curtain.

It was an estate car with the back full of the protective metal cases that house valuable equipment like cameras. Daniel Marcus was a television cameraman, therefore the two casually dressed young men going up his front path were probably colleagues fetching him to go off on a job somewhere. Dutton heard the sound of next door's bell and then a babble of voices as the visitors were welcomed and taken inside.

Holly Chase, wearing light grey jeans and an enormous baby pink mohair sweater, was cooking breakfast and pouring coffee. 'Hi,' she called as Terry, the sound man, and Geoff, the producer, were ushered into the kitchen. 'You made good time.'

'On time, on budget, just as we should be,' said Geoff who, like most producers, appeared to think of little else. He gave Holly a kiss in exchange for a mug of coffee.

Dan joined them and they all discussed the route they were to take and the shooting schedule for the day. Unless the best-laid plans went awry this would be the last day Dan worked on the murder series. 'And then it's up to the rest of you,' he said. 'I'm into wildlife from tomorrow.'

'Soon he'll forget murder and there won't be anything I don't know about otters,' said Holly.

'From death to life in one easy move,' said Terry, who hadn't enjoyed the murder series much. The subject depressed him. He'd hoped to be moved to the crew for the wildlife series but Dan had been lucky and he hadn't.

'But *The Face of Death* will be fascinating,' said Holly. 'It's a subject that can't fail, isn't it? Think of the audience and forget the horrors.'

'They aren't forgettable,' said Terry. 'If the viewers respond to the series as I do there will be a nationwide movement to switch off television sets. Nil ratings. The Big O. All that electricity saved for the National Grid.'

She said: 'But they won't, they'll love it!'

'I'm afraid you're right. From the safety of their armchairs it will be just another half-hour thrill before the news comes on. But I've been through the reconstruction of two mass-murder cases – which our pundits say is the newest thing in murder so look out for it in your local high street soon, folks! – and

I've listened to some small-timers in the world of crime excuse themselves for hacking up a child and shooting a . . .'

'OK, OK,' said Geoff who'd heard Terry warm to this theme before. The series had been Geoff's idea and he meant to make his mark with it. Terry's scruples had become tiresome over the months of filming. It had been a mistake to have him on the crew, although Terry had been his first choice because of the reliability of his work.

'No, it isn't OK. I'm saying what all of us felt in some degree, including you. We felt revulsion at making entertainment out of savagery.'

Holly queried that. 'And is that all a television documentary is – entertainment?'

'No,' said Geoff.

'Yes,' said Terry. '*Ultimately* it's what you consider, which brings us back to your point about the ratings. People who switch on to *The Face of Death* aren't going to care what statistics Professor Thingummy has. And he hasn't got anything new, anyway: there've been around 50 murders a year in the London area since the beginning of the century and around 155 for the whole of England and Wales. The guesswork about what makes a murderer or about the numbers who get away undetected is pretty futile if you ask me. And at the end of the series all we will have told people about *The Face of Death* is that it doesn't change. We could have said that in one programme, but this is television so we have stretched it to six with our mock-ups and shoving Dan's camera into some rather ravaged faces.'

Holly countered: 'My feeling is that the public interest often runs along the lines of "There but for the grace of God go I." Victim or murderer, take your pick. The lost of temper that kills someone, unpremeditated, could be yours or mine . . .'

'Not murder, probably manslaughter,' said Dan.

'Technical,' said Holly. 'I don't suppose I'd stand over the corpse calculating which it was. *Inside* it would be the same. Killing another human being is the final horror, isn't it?'

'Oh no,' said Terry. 'Tune into *The Face of Death* and you'll see what some of our interviewees have to say about that –

the ones with personal experience I mean. They didn't waste much time being horrified: self-preservation was paramount. Getting caught was their final horror. And these are among the ones who didn't get away with it.'

Geoff drew their attention to the time and the need to be on their way before there was much traffic on the roads. As he turned the estate car round, Holly waved them off from the doorstep. She had worked Sunday and was taking Wednesday off instead. She was expecting delivery of a bed for the back bedroom and curtains for the main bedroom and lounge. She was also expecting Joel who had leapt at the chance of moving into Shepherd Road and organizing himself a darkroom.

He came mid-morning with a large old-fashioned suitcase containing all his clothes, and a large cardboard box containing everything else he owned. A friend with a battered car brought him, but if he hadn't had help he could have made the move with only two trips on public transport.

'You'll have to think of it as sleeping in your darkroom,' said Holly. They were in the doorway of the back bedroom which now looked pathetically small. 'Dan says we can run a pipe straight through from the bathroom next door for your water supply.'

'It'll be great, Holly.' In his mind's eye the equipment and furnishings were already there, the shutters made and fitted, the work coming in.

'Dan will probably be back tonight, but he's left a sketch and some measurements for the shutters so you can go and order them if you want to. He thought you might be impatient to get on with it.'

'Where do I go?'

'Not far. The other side of Spinney Green station there's a timber yard and they make up simple things.'

While he walked down to the timber yard, scarcely believing in his great good fortune, Holly made a hearty soup for lunch. She sang as she went about it. Quite suddenly she stopped singing and thought unflattering thoughts about the people who should have installed her telephone when she moved in and were still keeping her waiting.

It was very inconvenient. Dan wouldn't be able to tell her whether he was on the way home that night or not, she wasn't able to ring the furniture shop and find out whether Joel's bed was merely late or had been forgotten. Worst of all, she couldn't ring Rain Morgan and satisfy her curiosity about what had become of the story of the prince and the cabinet minister's secretary. It wasn't in that morning's paper and when Holly left the office on Tuesday evening Rain was in a huddle with Dick Tavett and Wilmot, the lawyer, and Oliver West was rubbing his hands like any pantomime villain and saying he was owed a fiver. All in all, a telephone was indispensable.

Holly could resist it no longer. She switched off the gas beneath the soup and went next door. While she was still on the pavement she could see her neighbour had company, but she had been noticed and could not retreat. Carol Dutton opened the door to her and introduced her to Jean Parker.

Jean was torn between curiosity and indignation. Holly Chase was not what one required of a neighbour and she had intended to be ostentatious in having nothing to do with her. And yet, thrust into acquaintance in this way, she was able to satisfy her other, deeper, instinct. She could already, in her mind, hear herself telling Ted about the encounter.

'Holly works on the *Daily Post* gossip column,' Carol Dutton was saying, to leave them something to discuss while she went to pour coffee.

'That's interesting,' said Jean, who found it more surprising than anything else. 'Secretarial work can be very interesting, especially I should say on a newspaper.'

'I'm not a secretary, I'm a journalist.' A correction Holly would have to make throughout her career.

The look in Jean's eye betrayed scepticism. 'I should have learned to type, I'm sure I should have liked being a secretary.'

Carol returned with coffee for Holly. Jean said: 'Can you type, Carol?'

Carol hesitated. She was not sure what her answer ought to be. Dutton told her she was a shorthand typist but she had no recollection of typing. She compromised. 'I used to.'

'It's like riding a bike, though, isn't it? Once you've learned you never lose the knack.' Jean appealed to Holly.

Holly said: 'You can get awfully rusty without practice.'

Jean said: 'If you want the practice, Carol, you can type some letters for Ted. We are both two-finger people.'

Carol gave her a discouraging look. Holly said: 'What does your husband do, Jean?'

'He's in rubber goods.'

Holly decided not to pursue this, fearing where it might lead. At that moment Ted appeared on the path outside the Parkers' house, gesticulating through the window at Jean. She made her apologies to Carol, ignored Holly, and left. Then Holly made her call to the furniture shop. The bed, the man promised her, was indeed on its way.

She had less luck with the telephone people. There was no ready excuse why the installation was delayed and she was asked to phone again during the afternoon. Carol said of course she was to try again.

Back home Holly finished cooking the soup and waited for Joel's return. She pottered about hanging a few pictures and doing some chores but there was very little she could get on with. It would be dreadful, she thought, to be home like this every day as Carol Dutton was. Holly hated to be under-occupied. If she had a telephone she would be catching up on friends or following up the suspicion of a story for the column. If she was not waiting for Joel and the delivery of the bed she would be dashing off in her car to buy some new clothes or something for the house.

Joel came at last with the news that the shutters were ordered and to be delivered early next week. Then the van with the bed arrived. The man who brought it said it was no part of his job to carry it further than the front door. He leaned it against the door jamb and pushed at Holly a chit for her to sign to say it was in good condition.

Hearing the man's belligerent tone, Joel came to see what was wrong and would have become embroiled in an argument about whether the bed was to be carried indoors or not. But a look from Holly dissuaded him and she signed. Then she and Joel moved the bed.

They got it into the back bedroom without difficulty or chipped paintwork. Joel sat down on it and bounced. 'Great,' he said.

'And it wasn't worth a fuss. You were here so even if he left it in the gutter he wasn't causing me any problem.'

Chided, Joel went to the window and looked down. Carol Dutton was in the garden, a cold wind blowing the baggy smock. 'Holly, have you remembered whom she reminds you of?'

'No, and I saw her again this morning and it's driving me crazy.'

'She looks just ordinary.' He picked up his camera and focused on Carol. As she walked towards her house he took a series of photographs of her.

By mid-afternoon he was wandering around Shepherd Road idly taking pictures of anything that caught his interest, compiling in a haphazard way a picture story that ended with the occupied houses with flower beds planted and curtains at windows, and began with men at work on the last group of houses at the far end of the street. The Phase Two houses opposite Holly's would come towards the end of the sequence, their sale boards making a very clear statement. It was a shame there were no hopeful buyers staring through the windows, but he expected the weekend would bring him those.

While Joel was out Holly took up Carol's offer of a second phone call to the telephone people. She was startled that Carol opened the door red-eyed and distressed. 'Whatever's the matter?'

'It's . . . it's nothing.'

Holly followed her into the lounge where Carol seemed about to explain then shook her head and hurried to the kitchen leaving Holly to phone. After the call Holly found her weeping. On the table was a pile of writing paper with the printed heading Grimbleys Grommets, and several sheets of the same paper on which bad attempts at typing letters had been made.

'I see,' said Holly. 'Jean Parker's given you Ted's letters.'

Carol nodded, unable to speak.

'And you can't do it.'

More tears. Holly said: 'Well I can, so there's nothing to cry about. You put the kettle on to make us a cup of tea and I'll rattle these off.'

Carol's gratitude was apparent but indistinct. Holly sat down at the typewriter. 'A copy of this letter to each name on the list?'

'Yes.' Carol blew her nose. She lifted mugs off hooks and fetched a teapot.

'Off we go then.' There were only half a dozen letters and in the time it took for the tea to be made and poured she had done three of them. She broke off to drink and looked questioningly at Carol who appeared once more on the verge of explanation. Holly tried to help her out: 'You're wishing you hadn't said you could type. You couldn't have guessed she meant to give you Ted's work.'

Carol held up one of her attempts. 'You said typists can get rusty but this doesn't look as though I ever learned, does it?'

'Frankly, no.' It revealed not only inability to hit the right keys and evenly, but also unfamiliarity with the mechanics of the typewriter. Holly remembered her reluctance that morning before she said she used to type. And Holly suggested that once these letters were completed and the machine returned to the Parkers it should be made to stay there and Carol should resist any further bullying to get her to work for Ted. 'But at least we now know what Jean means when she says he's in rubber goods.'

'I still don't,' Carol admitted. 'What *are* grommets?'

'Very dull – they're rubber rings. Ted Parker isn't nearly as interesting as I thought he was going to be.'

Carol made up her mind. Holly was kind and practical and she felt she could trust her. She *might* have been able to trust Marcia Cohen but Marcia had never phoned back. It would be incalculable relief to share her desperation with a woman like Holly. 'I really thought I must be able to type, or I wouldn't have claimed to, but the reason was . . .'

Holly rolled another sheet of paper into the machine and clattered through the next letter. 'The Parkers will never know,' she said above the din. She liked Carol and thought it sad she should get caught out in such a silly boast. She

153

guessed that Carol had claimed to be a former typist rather than admit to never having had any skills. People did not like to admit to that.

Holly believed it highly unlikely that Carol Dutton would ever do anything like it again. Carol made another attempt to explain but Holly skilfully deflected it. She was always to regret that.

# 22

Jean Parker and Peter Dutton met as he was leaving for work on Thursday morning and she was stepping across the dividing flower bed. She was on her way to collect the Parker typewriter and letters.

Dutton didn't know about the letters because Carol had hidden them and the machine beneath her bed. She did not want to jeopardize the Southwold weekend by a row about her developing contact with the Parkers. There was another reason, too: she did not want him to discover his statement that she was a typist had been challenged.

Jean Parker squeezed past the Duttons' car, forcing him back on to his doorstep. He did not care for this, feeling trapped. 'Good morning,' she was saying, 'is Carol about?'

'Er . . . yes.' What could she possibly want with Carol, and so early?

'I'm just popping in for my letters. I would have come yesterday as I'd told her but I got one of my bad heads on the way back from the baker's so all I was fit for the rest of the day was lying down.' By now she had closed the gap. He looked down at her from the doorstep, his back pressed against the glass-panelled door, her scrawny figure almost touching. His face was expressionless, hers enquiring. He couldn't think what she was talking about. Letters? Why should she be collecting letters?

She thought he was behaving oddly, standing there right in her way and not opening the door for her or letting her reach the bell. She said: 'I mustn't hold you up . . .' and waited some more.

Holly Chase bounded out of the next house into her car, but Dutton and Jean Parker ignored her good morning. Their impasse ended when the postman came up the Duttons' path with a handful of letters. Dutton reached forward to take them from him and Jean's hand made it to the doorbell.

Rather than squeeze by the car the postman cut across the Duttons' lawn to Holly's house. He and the paper boy and the milkman were wearing their own tradesmen's paths across all the lawns in Shepherd Road, an eventuality the developers had failed to consider.

At the ring of the bell Dutton stuffed the letters into his pocket, pushed past Jean and by the time Carol opened up he was well down Shepherd Road. Carol decided honesty was the best policy. When Jean looked over the letters and said they were 'beautiful' Carol said: 'Holly Chase did them – I'm afraid I couldn't cope.'

Jean's glee faded. It was one thing coercing Carol Dutton to help out, quite another to accept favours from someone like Holly. The letters now appeared less beautiful than she had at first thought.

Both Carol and Jean were confident Holly Chase would never again type any of Ted Parker's letters. Clutching the typewriter to her bosom and the letters in her hand Jean Parker stepped back over the border and home. Grimbley's Grommets had vanished from Carol's life as abruptly as they had entered it.

Carol resumed her interrupted breakfast and then stayed at the table reading the newspaper. She took a special interest in the gossip column now that she knew Holly and looked forward to finding out what went on behind the scenes. How, for instance, did Rain Morgan or Holly come upon stories like the one about the royal romance with the shoplifting secretary?

There would be no answers that day, she knew, because Holly had driven off early and was never home until mid-evening. Nor would there be any visitors because Jean Parker seemed offended that Carol had not typed the letters herself. She phoned Marcia. She had chosen one of her busy moments. 'Hello, Carol! How are you? I'm fine too. Look you'll never believe this but I'm actually rather busy for the next hour or two. Let me ring you back.'

'I wondered whether we could make another lunch date.'

'The thing is, there's this accountant. Takes me for lunch every day now. Until the end of the week, anyway. I won't be here after that, so who knows what will happen then?'

'Do you know where you will be working next week?'

'Shan't know that until Monday morning. You know what the agency's like, keeping everybody on the hop. But actually it's a bit quiet for them at the moment. Could be a week off. We could have lunch every day then! I'll ring you.'

Carol got the photographs again and pored over them, until she was no longer sure whether she remembered Southwold or just what the photographs said about it. She was setting much store by this weekend. Even if Southwold was no help in restoring her memory it would be a precious change from the boredom of Shepherd Road. She craved fresh scenes, new faces, and the mental stimulation they would bring.

Her twelve days at Shepherd Road had convinced her that she must have left Peter Dutton because he was selfish, had an unpredictable temper and she had been utterly bored. It seemed only natural when her day dreams about Southwold turned into plots to get away from him once and for all.

In one version she left him in a restaurant, believing she had gone to the cloakroom. In another she sneaked out of the hotel at night. In all of them she came up against the snag that she had no money and he was not likely to give her any. This made everything she thought up impractical, but could not deter her from dreaming. She no longer accused herself of ingratitude, her instinct to escape from him had been right.

She wrenched at the locked drawers of the desk frustrated at not knowing their secrets. The loft was the only other hiding place and today she was wearing the smock and old sweater and did not care if they became grubby. She pulled down the ladder.

When she had climbed up she noticed the light switch and the scene was transformed. The shapes became tea chests, suitcases and a metal trunk. Carol did not move to begin with. She looked at the illuminated scene, taking in the detail. Several of the tea chests were stacked on their sides, showing they were empty. Dust draped everything but there were scuffled patches on the tin trunk, near the fastenings. And on the floor was a track from the loft entrance to the trunk.

Carol followed the path, put her hands on the dust-free patches on the trunk and then stopped. Suddenly she was afraid of what she might reveal. But whatever it was Dutton was hiding from her she was entitled to know. Curiosity would make her lift this lid sooner or later. Dust swirled and then she was looking down on to offcuts of the lounge carpet. Tentatively, she lifted the top pieces but all she saw below was more of the same. Disappointed, she dropped the lid, snapped the fastening, and took stock.

Dust on the suitcases appeared undisturbed but she did not walk over to them because that would mark the floor and give away the fact she had been up there. Instead she switched off the light and went back to the landing. Apparently her conviction that she had been close to Dutton's secrets was false, the answers must lie in the pine desk after all.

Without hope she tried the back door key in the locks, but it was too big. She had no other keys. She knew where the desk key would be: on Dutton's key ring and that was with him all day. Was it feasible, she wondered, that she could tiptoe downstairs at night without waking him and take the keys from his coat while it hung in the hall? And if she succeeded, would she also be able to go through the desk, find whatever it was she was looking for, and then get back to bed undetected? The answers were not encouraging, and neither was the certainty that Dutton would be uncontrollably angry when he found out what she had done. From sheer self-preservation she dared not take his key.

The desk was an inexpensive affair but sturdy. After the Southwold weekend she might dredge up the courage to break into it, until then she would have to be patient. But perhaps the desk would be opened before the weekend as it would be possible Dutton would need to take something from it before they went away.

'The *camera*!' she cried aloud. 'This must be where he keeps the camera and all I've got to do is make sure he remembers to take it to Southwold with us.'

Everything was now straightforward. She would mention the camera, he would unlock the desk and get it out and she would show natural curiosity in the contents of all three drawers. She would do it this very evening.

The camera might solve another problem, if it were an expensive enough type. She saw herself taking it into a second-hand shop in Southwold and selling it so that she had the cash to carry her away from this dreary life with Peter Dutton. The suggestion foundered: why should she hope the camera was an expensive one likely to raise more than a few pounds? Nothing else in the Dutton house was worth much.

Yet the notion of selling the camera would not go away. Even if it raised only ten pounds it could pay for a train fare out of Dutton's reach. What else could she sell? She prowled round the house, appraising. Her first choice was the clothes that no longer fitted her. From the wardrobe she took some of the garments and then in the Yellow Pages commercial telephone directory she found Second Hand Rose, a nearly new shop with an address in Spinney Green.

The woman who answered the phone was politely discouraging. 'Our main demand is for children's clothes and maternity. If we take women's they have to be of very good quality or else we are stuck with them. It puts you off slimming, doesn't it? Finding you are lumbered with a cupboard full of unwearable clothes nobody wants to buy? I've been through it myself, I know how you must feel.'

'Can you suggest anyone who might want them?'

'You could put a card advertising them in a shop window, although I don't think that's very productive in this type of district. I gave all mine to the Oxfam shop, but if you were hoping to sell . . .'

'Yes, I must try and make a little money, quickly.'

'. . . Then Dobsons would give you something. They go by weight so style and quality don't matter.'

'Weight?'

'Yes, they're scrap dealers. They've got a yard off Orchard Road. They're in the phone book. I should ask them.'

Dispirited, Carol hung the clothes back in the wardrobe. She was convinced she would never be fat enough to wear

159

any of them again, but the amount of cash she could make from a scrap dealer wasn't worth the effort of taking them to him. Dobsons might offer to collect them but she couldn't allow that because Dutton might find out they had been to the house. There was no time to try a card in the newsagent's window and, again, she could not have people phoning or arriving on the doorstep without Dutton asking what she was raising money for. The very mention of money was sufficient to send him into a rage and this was no time for that to happen. It was too easy to imagine him cancelling the Southwold weekend and preferring to sulk at home.

Carol's eye rested on the hearth rug. Like the fitted carpet it must have been new with the house and was in mint condition. She bent down and felt its soft, strong wool pile. The ease with which she had another deceitful plan to hand was alarming.

There could be no difficulty in persuading a shop dealing in second-hand goods to take a rug like this and she ought to get a good price. All she had to do was telephone shops from the list in Yellow Pages until she found one which was definitely interested. Then she could take the rug to them. The journey would have to be made tomorrow because Thursday afternoon was almost over. On Friday evening Dutton would come home from work to find the rug missing and a story about Carol having spilled coffee on it and taken it to a dry cleaner's.

She grabbed the directory and flipped it open at the second-hand dealers section. There were several entries for businesses buying furniture and furnishings so she telephoned those, starting with the nearest. One had a Spinney Green number and she was soon explaining she had an unwanted rug for sale. The dealer asked a few questions about it: the colour, the type and the size. Until he saw the rug he couldn't give her an idea of how much it might be worth to him, but if she would take it in he would quote her a price there and then.

She believed she understood what that meant. Get the customer into the shop with a heavy burden and rather than stagger back home with it and have a completely wasted journey she would accept a pitifully low price. She pressed him. In the end he said he might go up to thirty pounds but it would have to be in exceptionally good condition for that.

Carol knew the rug must have cost several times that but she was ready to be tempted and to push him to his thirty-pound top limit if she could. Thirty pounds would get her a long way and pay for a cheap night or two until she worked out what to do next. If she was able to sell the camera, too, she would have a little more. All she had at present was four pounds, left from the money she had been given the previous week.

She looked for a piece of string to tie up the rug and make it easier to carry. There was some thin string in a drawer in the kitchen. And if it rained tomorrow? Then a couple of black plastic bin liners would protect the rug, one popped over each end. The only detail she could not take care of was the dry cleaner's ticket. If she truly had taken a rug to be cleaned she would be given a ticket to present on collection. She would have to hope that Dutton didn't ask to see it, which he might because cleaning a rug was not an inexpensive thing.

With a start she saw the flaw in all this. The sort of wool-pile rug she was going to sell was not the type that would go to a dry cleaner's. This was a job for a specialist. Feeling stupid that she had not spotted this before she once more turned to the Yellow Pages. There were no carpet-cleaning businesses in Spinney Green, but several further afield. She would have to discover which was the nearest one and claim the rug had gone to them.

Dutton would know she had next to no money, so she could not pretend to have made a journey of any great distance to deliver it. Perhaps she had better claim that once she spilled the coffee she telephoned one of the companies and they happened to have a van in the area and arranged to collect it. Yes, that was reasonable because although her rug was portable many people's would be far too big for anything but collection in a van. She chose a name from the directory and memorized it. When Peter Dutton asked she would say the rug had gone to Carpetcare.

Carol put the directory away and experimented with the

rug, rolling it up to make a neat and manageable roll when she carried it to the dealer the next day. She held it firmly, keeping the edges straight and rolling it tightly. And that was how she discovered the blood stain on Peter Dutton's lounge carpet, the hideous mark the rug had been bought to conceal.

## 23

Memories were running through her brain like speeded film. Peter Dutton had threatened to attack her with the spade; he had flung her from him in the lounge; she had been intimidated by numerous flares of aggression. There was no trace of doubt in her mind that the brown stain on the carpet was her blood, as the stain on the clothes they had shown her at the hospital had been.

The jigsaw was coming together. She and Dutton had alway been incompatible and eventually there was a row during which he physically attacked her. After that she left him. He did not know where she had gone but when she turned up in hospital less than three months later suffering from loss of memory he fetched her home. And all the time he had been afraid she would remember how he had assaulted her. That was why he was evasive and uncooperative whenever she asked pertinent questions. He would not tell her why she left home and to protect this secret he would not remind her who her friends were because he believed they knew what he had done and would give him away.

For the same reasons he must have tried to put her off being friendly with Jean Parker, forgetting that the Parkers did not move in until after she left. Or else reasoning that the more socially isolated she was the less likely that she would meet someone whom she used to know. All his disconcerting behaviour since she returned home pointed to his fear that she would remember how he had hurt her.

Carol unrolled the rug and hid the stain. She wondered what Dutton would tell her about it – he must have realized that one day she would move the rug instead of vacuuming over it. But she did not intend mentioning it, nor selling the rug. She would have to do without the dealer's thirty pounds because the exposed stain could not be ignored and a discussion of it would be critical. Not only might the Southwold weekend be abandoned but Dutton might be triggered into a further assault on her.

Unless the camera was valuable she saw no chance of raising enough money to be free of Dutton over the weekend. She fell back on the plan to get him to show her the camera that evening, then she would know whether it was worth concocting a plan around it.

'We must take the camera with us,' she said after supper, moving the talk from travel plans for Saturday morning.

'We haven't got a camera.'

Nothing had prepared her for his denial. She struggled to make her face express no more than mild surprise. 'But . . . the photographs . . .'

'I didn't say we *never* had one.'

'Why haven't we got it now?'

'It was stolen.' He got up and went into the garden. She believed he was smiling.

Dutton stood on the concrete strip which passed for a patio and laughed into the gathering darkness. She should have seen her face when he said there was no camera! It really was funny, women were so vain: she'd probably been meaning to spend her weekend posing for him to take photographs of her. She would never see why it was so comical that he'd said the camera was stolen. Well, soon she would be free to go and buy a camera if she wanted one.

A ragged rose bush clutched his sleeve as he walked out on to the grass towards the whiteness of the rockery. There was barely enough light for him to see whether the new plant was making an effort at survival but he was confident it had a chance. All you had to do was hang on, don't panic and never give up.

Throughout the day he had felt his spirits rising, sometimes reaching moments of near joy. The escape hatch was near, he was primed for action. Not long now and he would be free. He knew Johnson and Lewis were watching him closely in the office as his mood had become apparent. He even had a welcoming smile for Mary Partridge when she tripped in and flaunted herself on the edge of his desk with a flash of thigh.

In the kitchen of Holly Chase's house a light snapped on to show Holly and the younger man. Holly was wearing a warm jacket and a fluffy hat over the tight plaits which chequered her scalp. She removed the jacket and hat as the man spoke to her, then Dutton heard her giving a squeal of pleasure as she took a card held out to her. She was chattering and enthusing, then moved her excitement to the next card. Dutton knew then that they were photographs. 'Tonight everybody's mad about photography,' he said. And laughed, softly.

The Parkers' kitchen light was already on and Jean came to the sink beneath the window and turned on a tap. Dutton heard water gurgle away down an outside drain. She reached up and pulled down a blind. He saw nothing but her shadow as she washed up. Trust the Nosey Parkers, he thought, to have a blind so no one spied on them.

He swung back to number 5 where Holly had no such inhibitions. But the thrills of the photographs had died and the conversation was too low for him to catch more than an occasional laugh. He criss-crossed the garden and then went indoors. There was a programme on television he wanted to watch and there were the new television guides to be read. All in all he had a lot to be happy about.

That day he had been to the bank near Oxford Circus where he and his wife had always kept their accounts. He paid into his a forged cheque which drew most of the money out of hers. Then he cashed one of his own cheques for the same amount. The money was in his pocket, a slim wad of greyish-brown fifty-pound notes. That should speed him a long way into his new life. His fingers caressed the edge of the paper, he savoured having it close to him.

It would have to last him a long time because the New Zealand account was emptied and the next instalment not due until the end of April. It was paid every two months. Carol's father had wanted to pay it quarterly but she made a fuss, saying she needed it sooner. At the time Dutton thought this unnecessary and she should have accepted what was offered. Now he was glad she'd won.

Apart from the two months wait for the account to be topped up, there was another reason why the cash must last. He would not want to draw on the account again until he had his new identity and a bank account to go with it. Then Carol Dutton would appear to be making out cheques to someone other than Peter Dutton, and no suspicions would be aroused that he had run off instead of dying in an accident.

Back indoors he found Carol watching television. He told her she was on the wrong channel, the programme he wanted to see was on another. She didn't protest when he switched over. At the end of the programme he left the room, saying he was going to the loft to fetch a suitcase ready for the weekend. 'It'll be dusty, you can clean it up tomorrow.'

Carol waited nervously while he was in the loft. For all her carefulness she might have left a clue that she had been there and now it would be too late to pretend it was to look for a suitcase, an acceptable explanation. The minutes tripped by on the brass and pine clock and still Dutton did not appear. She wished she had the courage to follow and see what he was up to.

If she had done so she would have found him deep in the tin trunk, lifting out all the documents and the wedding photograph which she must never see and putting them into a plastic carrier bag. Then he dropped the carpet pieces higgledy-piggledy back into the trunk, put the plastic bag inside a suitcase and carried it down to his bedroom. He took the bag out and hid it under his bed. When he showed her the case it was dusty but empty.

Next morning he made the bundle as compact as he could and forced it into the inside pocket of his overcoat. The photograph frame was awkward but he had no time to remove the picture so the frame must go to Pegwoods with him, too. At lunchtime, in a bouncy mood, he went to one of the garden squares and got out the plastic bag to go through the contents. He left in it items to be destroyed. Things he meant to keep were pushed into a pocket.

Scruffy pigeons, equating rustling bags with offers of

scraps to eat, waddled around the wooden bench while he did this and were disdainful when, after a few minutes, he folded up the bag and its contents on the bench beside him. He did not notice their disdain. In his hands he held the wedding photograph, its silver-plate frame flashy in mild sunlight. He looked closely at the young couple with their self-conscious smiles. She had been slimmer then, he had yet to see his hair greying or his face lined.

Then he turned the frame over, unclipped the back and removed the smiling couple. He was going to put them in the bag of things to be destroyed, but the frame was harmless so he would leave that in his desk drawer. It was about the only decent thing that came from his dead parents' house in the shabby street south of the river. He shoved it into his pocket and opened the bag to receive the photograph.

He didn't do it. He wavered, his hand shaking and his mood clouded. To destroy this image of his wife was a symbolic repetition of what happened in November, as was covering the photograph with papers while it lay staring up at him in the tin trunk. He let go of the bag, the photograph still in his hand. Without the frame it fitted into the breast pocket of his jacket.

He tore up the items in the bag and as he walked towards Pegwoods he dropped handfuls of them into each litter bin he came upon. He was obliterating the evidence as thoroughly as he knew how, and even while he did it he was aware that the most damning piece was in his pocket. Reason and caution could not persuade him. This was Carol Dutton's smiling face and he needed to be reminded of it instead of the ghastly look he had last seen. Equally powerful was the need of proof that he had once been both loved and loving. If the photograph might one day be used as proof of something else, then that was a chance he was compelled to take.

While he was sprinkling the last scraps of paper into a bin and a chill wind was frisking them towards Oxford Street, Carol Dutton was rummaging in the loft in what was to be her last attempt to find something to sell. The dusty floor was more extensively marked than when she went up there before, showing how Dutton had moved around while fetching the case. She walked only where he had walked and lifted a suitcase which a dust-free patch on the floor told her he had moved. The case was light, empty and she set it down again. Standing near it she could confirm that the tea chests, souvenirs of the move to the house, were all empty. The only other container was the trunk. There were now hand prints on it and the floor around was imprinted where Dutton had stood things.

For the second time she undid the clasps and threw back the lid. The carpet pieces were still there but not exactly as she remembered. Some had their foam backing uppermost whereas yesterday she looked on pile. Reaching into the trunk she emulated what Dutton must have done, lifting out carpet to put the pieces on the floor until she came to the bottom. The trunk was completely empty but she was convinced that yesterday it had not been. Her instinct had not been at fault, because Dutton could have had no reason to remove the carpet unless something was hidden beneath it. No one else could venture into the loft, so whatever it was had been hidden from her.

The only hiding place he had left must be the desk and in moments she was wrestling with the locked drawers. She was all impatience, only the threat to the Southwold weekend restrained her but she vowed that if, as seemed inevitable, she came back from Suffolk to Shepherd Road she would break open the drawers and the secrets they held. There was no question that they were her secrets, too.

# 24

Rosie, Rain Morgan's secretary, tugged open a padded envelope at great risk to her fingernails and slid on to her desk a paperback book with the most repellent cover she had ever seen. She gave an exclamation and pressed back in her chair to escape.

Holly and Rain looked up. Rosie flushed. She was not the demonstrative type and a year working at the *Daily Post* had hardened her to many things. Colour photographs of dead bodies were not among them. Her typewriter hid from her companions what was on her desk.

'Dracula's calling card?' enquired Holly.

'A memo from God?' asked Rain. Rosie was always nervous of notes from the editor.

Rosie inched forward a finger and slid the offending book into view. 'Oh, that!' said Rain and Holly together. Rain reached out a hand for it, Holly was quicker and took it up.

'*The Face of Death.* At last I can find out where the authorized version differs from Dan's account.' Then she got the book the right way round and saw the picture properly. 'Good heavens!' She held it up for Rain.

'Anyone we know?'

'It can't be real, though,' Holly hoped. 'They couldn't do this with an actual photograph of a murder victim, surely?'

The telephone rang and Rosie became engrossed with a pop group's manager who was trying to persuade her there was no truth in the rumour the band was splitting up. Rain picked up a letter which had dropped from the book. It was written to her by Laurie Pegwood, the head of the publishing house, and after the familiar greetings which pass between journalists and the publishers who wine and dine them, there was the familiar assurance that the accompanying book was a supreme example of its kind and going to be so news-worthy she ought to start writing about it right away. There was a line about the many thousands of copies printed and the expected sensation when they hit the bookshops.

'Which will be nothing compared to the sensation as shop assistants and customers faint with shock,' Rain remarked to the signature at the end of the letter.

Holly handed over the book, swapping it for the letter. 'If we do nothing else, we'll ask him how they've got the nerve to use this cover.'

'As soon as we can get him on the line.' Rain scrutinized the offending picture for clues to its genesis. 'If it's a fake it's brilliant but disgusting. If it's real Pegwoods have gone mad.' She felt an untimely hand on her shoulder and tensed.

'What's that?' said Oliver, equally astonished by the cover.

Holly said: 'The book of Dan's television series.'

'Tell me honestly, Oliver,' said Rain, 'if you saw this on a bookstall, would you buy it?'

'No,' said Oliver. 'Definitely not. I'd borrow your copy.' He tweaked it from her hand and began to browse, then screwed up his face in distaste and gave it back. Holly said Rain was going to ring up Laurie Pegwood and ask him if someone had suffered a brainstorm.

'I expect', said Oliver, 'there's some perfectly logical explanation for this reaction against all that's good and worthy at Pegwoods. The new marketing director has proved Pegwoods customers are mostly necrophiles, or the art director has been told to cut his budget for live models, or . . .'

'Or somebody has told Laurie there's money in this approach,' said Rain. 'You have to admit it's a change from the staid image we're used to: all those misty impressionistic scenes or those jokey cartoons.'

'I've never thought much of their cartoons,' said Oliver who had failed to get a commission for one.

Dick Tavett loomed at Rain's other shoulder and made the

sort of exclamation Rosie had made. Rain held the book out to him. He took it but momentarily, then it was back on her desk. 'Is it real?'

'I'm about to ring Pegwoods and ask.'

Tavett said: 'There are some things that just shouldn't be published.' It was a remark which had never crossed his lips before and was never to be heard again. Other people on the staff would argue in the years ahead that Rain, Holly and Oliver had collectively misheard. Tavett was thrown by it, too. After polishing his forehead with his palm a few times he confessed he had forgotten what he had come for and went away.

Laurie Pegwood was unrepentant, arguing that the subject was conducive to nothing but a good strong cover.

'Strong? Laurie, this is foul.'

He laughed. 'Then say so, Rain, by all means say so.'

'Because any publicity is good publicity? But you still haven't answered my question: is this a mock-up or a photograph of a corpse?'

The laugh again. She pictured him at the desk where his grandfather, the founder of the firm, had sat, leaning back in the great leather chair, a portrait of his grandfather on the wall behind him. 'A real body? Rain, you have a lurid imagination. Would a company like this lend itself to a trick like that?'

'Would you actually know if it did?'

He gave bland assurances during which words like integrity were used but conveyed all the same that questions would be put to the agency who designed Pegwoods' covers.

'I think', she told Holly as she came off the phone, 'he hasn't seen this cover himself, and the minion who passed it must have left his pebble glasses at home that day.'

Oliver said: 'I'll bet they change it. For a cartoon.' He grew interested in the thought of getting Rain to ask Laurie Pegwood to let him do the cartoon, but then dismissed all hope. The timing was wrong, he would try another time. 'I'll bet they change it,' he repeated, and tried to get Rain or Holly to bet him a fiver this would not happen. They wouldn't play.

'You can read it over the weekend, Holly, and I'll have it

back on Monday,' Rain offered and gave Holly the book. The contents, if anyone got beyond the cover and read them, were a longer version of the material used in the television series. The pundits, including David Rokeby, had written chapters on their own special topics and the script writers had linked the whole with a pithy introduction and conclusion which Holly knew to be based more on the intention when the series was planned than on the contents of the programmes as they had evolved. The timing meant the discrepancy couldn't be helped: the book was to be published to coincide with the screening of the series, and the series was still being filmed.

Laurie Pegwood rang back to give Rain some more reassurance about the cover. He'd seen a copy and was sure it would have terrific impact on the bookstalls. And the design house had told him they had been to tremendous trouble over the mock-up.

Rain put the phone down with a grumble that she had been made to feel a prudish spoilsport. 'He's totally happy with that picture. He says it's not as extreme as some of the things to be shown on the screen and so how can it be wrong for a book cover?'

'Because the images on the screen won't be there as long as two seconds but a book cover won't go away,' said Holly. 'People are used to hearing that television images are the strongest medium – you should hear Dan argue in favour of that theory – but it isn't always true. In a fleeting appearance amidst a lot of other material, pictures don't amount to much. Taken alone, as this will be, it's far too strong.'

'I wonder whether the shops inundating Pegwoods with orders for the book have any idea what's coming their way? You know, we should have taken Oliver's bet: there isn't time for the cover to be changed. You and I could be richer by a fiver.'

Rain asked Holly to show the book to a variety of people, avant-garde publishers and guardians of good taste, who were reliably acerbic in their comments and eager to have them quoted in the press. At the end of the day Holly took the book home to read about the circumstances and psychological defects that caused otherwise ordinary people, the boy or girl next door, to become murderers.

'It's all a matter of identity, isn't it? A matter of how one sees oneself?' said Oliver West as he stretched his length on Rain's sofa. 'Laurie Pegwood's grandfather saw himself as a benefactor bringing the world the best of Victorian poetry . . .'

'. . . and some moral tales from the pens of narrow-minded matrons,' Rain said, interrupting her yoga-style deep breathing as she lay on the carpet.

'Well, yes. I don't suppose even he thought he could manage without making money. But the image was all to do with good writing and a fine name handed down to posterity. Laurie Pegwood sees himself as an *enfant terrible* and he's too old for it.'

'Objection. He doesn't see himself as that, he merely thinks he's perking up the family image. And he isn't old and he's very nice.'

'You mean he flirts with you over lunch twice a year.'

'At least twice.' She rolled over on to her stomach and began to play with the carpet pile. Any minute now, she thought, Oliver would be working round to the question of why she didn't get Laurie Pegwood to commission a cartoon cover from him.

'Then you might find time on one of these cosy occasions to ask him to let me do a cover.'

'I might, but he'd be unlikely to say yes.'

'Why?'

'You know why.'

Oliver groaned. 'That was years ago.'

'Not many. It was just after you moved in here, after I'd . . .'

'I know, I know. Just after you rescued me from obscurity and Earls Court and cleaned me up and got me a job on the *Post*.'

'I wasn't going to say that. I meant after Dick Tavett . . .'.

'Do we have to talk about *him*?' This was getting rather far away from the point, which was when she was going to coax a cover out of Pegwoods.

'No.'

Silence. Then Oliver said: 'That was actually a rather good

173

cartoon of Laurie Pegwood. Some people offer to buy cartoons of themselves which have appeared in newspapers. Doesn't he know that? Wasn't he flattered?'

'Hardly, it was scurrilous and it didn't have the cache of getting into print. People put up with a lot if it gets them into print. Laurie called in for a drink and found your vicious version of him pinned on the bathroom wall. You think he's going to forget *that* in a mere four years and ask you to do a Pegwoods' book cover?'

Oliver gave her his most disarming smile. 'If you ask him nicely, then yes.'

She weakened. 'I'll do it but at the right time, so don't push me.' The last words were without hope. Oliver would keep up the pressure until she did it, he was ruthless in the way he used her but she had given up caring whether that mattered. When he wasn't there, there was a gap in her life which was deeper than the loneliness of the flat.

Oliver had been told his talent was for drawing people's weaknesses and he had been delighted with the compliment. A thinner-skinned artist might have been abashed, wondering at the implications of always wanting to present one's fellow human beings in the cruellest way. Not Oliver.

In his craft he did not have to trouble with the journalist's slower way: listening to the story, seeing how the body language belied the words, probing, checking, deciding. Oliver's assessment of people was instant. He saw their weakness, and the why and the how and the whether-it-was-important did not concern him.

So Laurie Pegwood was posing as an *enfant terrible*, and Holly Chase was so ambitious she would steal Rain's job, and Dick Tavett was a neurotic, and Wilmot the lawyer had a pathological dislike of newspapermen, and the editor was a faceless despot who hid behind a flamboyant tie and sent out his henchmen to do the dirty work, and Daniel Marcus had a butterfly mind and would never be allowed to become a director . . . And Rain Morgan? Sometimes she dared herself to ask him how he saw Rain Morgan.

But she never asked. It was easier to overhear other people's opinions that Rain Morgan was indispensable to him than to listen to her own suspicion that she was a fool to put up with the worst of him, or to hear from him what might be more salutary. She couldn't believe he would make an exception for her, although his cartoons of her were gentle and humorous and unlike his others. He rounded her out, making her plumper and giving her features a provocative cast. She scampered over the sheets of paper, a fluffily blonde Marilyn Monroe figure – which couldn't possibly be how he saw her.

She left Oliver on the sofa and went to shower and change. He had collected several months backlog of expenses and was taking her out to dinner to celebrate. So long as he had the cash with him and wasn't secretly relying on her credit card, the evening should be a success. She thought, as she glanced at the Pegwood cartoon on the bathroom wall, that if she could draw she would capture Oliver at the moment of sliding a restaurant bill across a table to her, or creeping into the distance while she placated colleagues or friends he had upset by his tactlessness or scathing caricatures. If anyone saw himself as an *enfant terrible*, it was Oliver West.

## 25

The Boatman Hotel at Southwold teetered on the tip of South Green, with views of both a featureless sea and people walking inland to Queen Street and the town centre. In the first days of March the winds of Siberia licked the water white and the faces of Southwold's shoppers blue.

The Duttons arrived at the Boatman mid-afternoon, after a meandering route and a lazy lunch of game pie beside one of the alluring log fires at the White Hart at Blythburgh. While Dutton signed the hotel register and spoke to Mrs Moore, the proprietor, Carol accepted his suggestion and followed the suitcase and the porter upstairs. The Duttons were lucky: their room peeped obliquely out to sea and from the window Carol could study gulls tossed on the wind above waves or else take in the comings and goings on South Green.

The porter put the suitcase on a stand and Carol gave him a tip. Then she was alone, to consider not only the view but the twin-bedded room she was to share with the difficult stranger who was her husband. This would be the first time since she had come from hospital that she had slept in the same room with him and she worried that he would see it as a natural occasion to resume sexual relations. There was nothing she wanted less. He had made no advances to her over the past two weeks but his mood had changed as the weekend arrived. Now he was being kind and considerate, as he had last been before the calamity at the Halberd spoiled things.

He joined her then, looking relaxed and happy. Flipping open the suitcase and arranging his clothes on hangers and shelves he was boyishly excited. As he tossed the contents of his jacket pockets on to one of the beds he was whistling a tune. She stayed at the window, wondering. Suddenly he spoke: 'You'd better have this.'

To her astonishment he was holding out a couple of bank notes. They were greyish-brown. She thought she must be dreaming. 'They're *fifties*. That's a hundred pounds.'

He teased her. 'If you don't want them you can give them back.'

Bewildered she thanked him and held back the questions why and how. Sitting on the edge of a bed she saw him return cheque book, keys and other bits and pieces to his pockets. 'Tea?' he asked, once this was done, and she rose compliantly, her fingers tight on the precious money. 'I'd put that out of sight,' he suggested.

'Yes.' She folded the notes and tucked them into a pocket of her suit jacket where they lay with the rest of her cash: three pound notes and a few coins. The new shoes called for a grey bag but she had nothing suitable and rather than spoil the outfit had not brought a bag at all. But driving into Southwold she had registered an expensive shop which was selling its winter stock of bags, shoes and silk scarves at reduced prices. She had wished then for the cash to go bargain hunting and here it was. But the hundred pounds did not set her drooling over handbags. It unlocked the prison she was living in. As if by magic she had the money to buy her freedom and Dutton had given it to her himself.

She could not fathom why he had done so or where he had obtained the cash, although the only questions which troubled her were when she should go and how. The 'when' was easily answered: as soon as possible, rather than face a night worrying whether he would come to her bed. Also, Saturday gave her greater opportunity because public transport was more frequent than on a Sunday.

Her hands were sticky with ill-controlled nervousness throughout tea and she had to fight to concentrate on Dutton's conversation. She was afraid her agitated state would become obvious. Her hands trembled, her features tensed. There were about a dozen other people in the dining room and the Duttons' table was in the centre of the room. Whenever she glanced up she saw someone looking her way. A waitress, who recognized

Dutton from earlier visits, had several brief discussions with him and gave Carol sympathetic smiles.

The tea was excellent, the Boatman proud of its food. At any other time she would have loved being cossetted there, but now all she could think about was getting away. As she poured their second cups of tea she had the outline of a scheme. She said: 'I'd like to look at the shops this afternoon. I can't remember the last time I went window shopping.' She laughed. 'Of course, I can't.'

'Don't spend all your money at once.'

'No, but I might be lucky and find a grey handbag to go with the shoes.' She raised her cup, timing her question. 'What will *you* do this afternoon?'

'There's not much of it left and I want to take the car to a garage.'

'Is something wrong with it?'

'Don't worry, it won't break down.'

They agreed to meet back at the hotel at 5.30 and went their separate ways. As she ran down the front steps of the Boatman and on to South Green the icy wind snatched her hair and she regretted the thinness of the blue woollen suit. The grey coat was still in the car, folded on the rear seat, but she was reluctant to fetch it and meet Dutton again. So far things were working in her favour and she dared not upset that.

Her left hand closed around the bank notes and she hurried, the wind urging her along the gaping space of South Green and into the relative protection of Queen Street. It funnelled into Market Place, a triangle cluttered not with market stalls but parked cars. She saw a bank, a town hall, a hotel, shops – her eyes searching for a clue to the direction she ought to go. A thrill ran through her. She felt strong, determined. She would have her freedom.

Ahead of her was High Street, stretching into the distance and lined with undistinguished shops broken by the bulk of banks and another hotel. She started down High Street, then paused by a shop window giving herself time to think without the pressure of Dutton's conversation and the presence of the Boatman's other guests. Behind her, two men greeted each other and began a discussion which hinged on the relative merits of different types of fertilizer. The window pane reproduced them in green quilted jackets and thick tweeds.

Then a bus lurched into the kerb, drowning their words. Its throbbing reflection beckoned Carol and her legs were ready to rush her on board and away to wherever it went. But where was that? The destination board was displayed on the front. To read it she would have to walk the length of the vehicle and perhaps Dutton would be driving by and notice her. To leap on a bus without a clear route to freedom was reckless, she might be stranded out in the country with no return service all weekend.

The reflection juddered away across the window pane. Carol walked on to a newsagent's where she scanned racks of postcard views of the lighthouse and Market Place. She was looking for a map, a plan of Southwold, but they were not on display. Instead she picked up a new edition of *Country Life* and, paying for it, asked whether the shop sold maps. When she succeeded in buying one she would hide it inside the magazine. 'Sorry, we've sold out. We won't get the new stock in until the summer season,' the woman at the till told her.

She continued along the row of shops, looking up with hope whenever she thought she might have heard the sound of a bus. None came. She walked on. When she was at the distant end of High Street she was startled to see that on the corner was a garage. If Dutton came while she was there he would doubtless stay with her for the rest of the afternoon. Skirting the garage she ran across the road. She meant to keep her face averted but gave way to the impulse to check he was not following her with his eyes. She could not see him, but he had been there because at the back of the forecourt was the car.

Her footsteps faltered. If only she could drive she could collect the car and be away. Dutton would have left the keys at the garage and she could invent a reason why she had to have the vehicle urgently. She would pay whatever they wanted for the small repair and if they hadn't done it yet she could race away hoping that it was, after all, nothing serious. But Dutton had scorned the idea that she had learned to drive and a garage forecourt was no place to test whether he was lying.

Carol went on, back up High Street, eyes skimming the

Saturday afternoon shoppers for a sight of the man she was avoiding. She came to the shop with the sale. The goods were very good indeed, but one of the covetable handbags in grey leather would eat a sizeable bite of her hundred pounds. The silk scarves came cheaper and the wind at Southwold was cruel. Carol came out of the shop a few minutes later sporting a fluttering grey silk square at her throat. The purchase had allowed her to change one of the fifty-pound notes into more manageable denominations. Seeing Carol push the tens and fives into her pocket the shop assistant mentioned the handbags but Carol proved an intractable customer and the bags stayed where they were.

She tried once more to buy a map, but without success, and decided to chance a bus. The afternoon was slipping away. It was nearly five and she was still in Southwold. Any move now would be better than no move at all. Ideally she wanted a train to spirit her away but nothing she had seen of Southwold suggested it was important enough to be on a railway line. The next best thing was a bus to the nearest railway station, although she was prepared to settle for less. If she got only half a dozen miles and stayed somewhere overnight she would be free to continue her journey early next day. The drawback was that bus services would be negligible on a Sunday and she would waste valuable time while Dutton was hunting for her.

Back at Market Place she found herself outside the town hall and there, in a glass case, was what she had been seeking: a street map. Station Road was prominent but did not appear to lead to a station. She checked with a passer-by who confirmed that Southwold no longer had a line, and then darted off before she could ask anything else. Scanning Market Place, making sure Dutton was not coming up Queen Street, Carol went back to the bus stop in High Street and read the timetable. Her timing was poor, which she already suspected from the absence of a queue. An old man told her the time, and there was a long wait for the next bus.

Unrelenting wind wrenched at her blue skirt, she was hunched with cold. After a minute she ran away from the bus stop and down High Street to the garage. Her coat was in the car and the garage would have to let her have that. No one could deny her in such weather. And once she had the keys to fetch it she would see whether she could drive the car.

The fawn car was just where she had seen it, at the rear of the forecourt. She hurried over to be sure the coat was still there and Dutton hadn't carried it to the Boatman for her. But the back seat was empty. She swivelled her eyes to the front seat, thinking he could have moved it. But it was not in the car at all. Immediately she understood why not: the litter of papers and road maps explained this was not the Duttons' car, merely an identical one. Feeling foolish she turned away.

An overalled mechanic was coming up to her. 'Did you want something?' He looked suspicious.

She blurted out that she had thought it was her husband's car and meant to fetch her coat from it. She said: 'He was taking the car to a garage here and I guessed it was this one. Where is there another garage?'

He scratched his head with a spanner. 'On a Saturday afternoon? This is the only one open on a Saturday afternoon.'

Confused, she walked away saying she must have mis-understood. As she left the mechanic checked all the locked doors on the car. Carol burned with frustration. There were only two possibilities now: a bus to whichever was the nearest railway station or to an overnight hotel, or a taxi to the nearest station. If it was a long journey the taxi fare might be more than she wanted to part with. There was no way of telling how long she would have to make her money last. Returning to the bus stop she consulted the timetable again, careless now whether Dutton caught her at it or not. It was getting close to the time for her to meet him in the Boatman. An elderly woman joined her and remarked on the keenness of the wind. Carol set aside her need for secrecy: 'I've got to get to a railway station. Do you know which is the nearest one?'

'Halesworth would be your nearest. It's a way, mind. Sure to be ten miles.'

That settled it. A taxi must be her last resort, she would wait for the bus. But the bus was not due for another twenty minutes and she could not stand there all that time, partly because of the cold but also because if Dutton looked for her she would be easily found. She went back along High Street but after a short way crossed the road and followed her curiosity down the narrow slit that was Bank Alley. First it took her on to a cobbled area with a few cars, then she was in Victoria Street. Rather than turn left along Victoria Street which would lead her towards the garage, she turned right and came to East Green.

A white and blue painted Methodist chapel looked defiantly across at Adnam's brewery. Cottages in a jumble of styles – from red brick to cream and pink stucco – ringed the prettier part of the green, and she intended to make a circuit of it before returning to the bus stop. She went past the chapel and started towards the cottages – and then she saw it. Parked at the side of the green, in front of the cottages, was the fawn car. This time she made no mistake, her coat was as she had left it.

Carol looked about but the church and brewery were Saturday silent and the row of cottages told her nothing. She pictured Dutton emerging from a cottage, but then knew that was not going to happen as certainly as she knew there had been nothing wrong with the car and it had not been to a garage. She felt very uneasy.

Teeth chattering she ran across East Green and down Church Street to arrive in High Street near the bus stop. There she hid in a shop doorway. It sheltered her and if by any misfortune Dutton saw her he would not know she was waiting for a bus. Now it was impossible to tell whether she was quaking from the penetrating cold or trembling with emotion. Dutton was up to something, that was clear. He had been excited about the weekend, he had given her all that money, and he had hidden the car.

She attempted to work out the effect of hiding the car. Supposing she had turned up at the Boatman at 5.30 as arranged, would he have said it had been stolen? Or that it was still at the garage? Whatever he told her, it would mean they could not venture out of Southwold until it was back. There would be no trips to the nearby places which might jolt her memory as the Boatman and Southwold themselves had failed to do. Was that the idea? To make her a prisoner of this compact little place as he had tried to make her a prisoner at Shepherd Road?

Round and round the mystery went until the bus came thrumming to a halt. Boarding, she secured a seat on the offside where a passer-by would barely be able to see her. An age passed before the bus jerked away and left Southwold. Stuffy warmth thawed her and she settled into the rhythm as streets dwindled and countryside closed around the vehicle and its handful of passengers. Near the front the elderly woman was talking to the driver. Three school children were sprawling on seats and taking the attention of other people. No one gave Carol Dutton a second look.

Her magazine lay on the seat beside her. With her left hand she felt the bank notes in her pocket. And she leaned back and closed her eyes to dun-coloured fields and lapwings in young pasture and the signs of striving spring. Her body relaxed, the drone of the engine soothed her mind. It had begun. Her journey to freedom had begun.

## 26

Peter Dutton laughed aloud at his own good humour. A weight of anxiety had lifted from him and he was euphoric. He had just said goodbye to Carol who was going to look at the shops and he would never see her again. Soon he would stop being Peter Dutton. He had gone upstairs to their room and dashed to the window to watch the slim woman in the blue suit go up South Green and out of his life. It was then that he laughed aloud.

A hundred pounds was a lot of money and it would not be true to say he did not grudge it. But she had to have some means of getting back to Shepherd Road and coping with bills in the weeks ahead. The first demand would be the Boatman bill. In his prevailing good mood he felt that a hundred pounds was probably fair. 'Too bad if you spend it all on clothes,' he said after the diminishing figure. Then he left the window and got to work.

Sitting on the bed in which Carol expected him to sleep that night, he lifted the telephone and asked for an outside line. A garage offering cars for hire was one of the advertisers included among local services in the list the Boatman provided for each room. The woman who answered said she had a Ford Fiesta available late that afternoon and quoted him a price for the hire of it until Monday morning. He arranged to collect it.

Then he emptied his pockets on to the bed for the second time that day and set aside his cheque book, credit and cheque cards from the Duttons' new joint account at Spinney Green. He put them on the table with the telephone, and everything else back in his pockets. Then, as an afterthought, he put the cheque book and cards more discreetly on a shelf in the wardrobe with his clothes. On a sheet of the Boatman's writing paper he scribbled a note to Carol. 'Gone for a walk along the coast. Peter.' He left it on her bed where she could not fail to find it.

He pictured her, back from shopping and running upstairs to show him every extravagance. She would be eager and happy until she found the door locked and subsequently the explanatory note. Then he imagined her alone and cross as afternoon passed into evening and still he did not come. No, that image would not do. He had never seen her cross, this Carol did not get cross, not even when he had been in a fury. She withdrew into herself but she didn't get cross. It was the other Carol who had done that.

His next step was to move the car. With a final glance round the room to check there was nothing left that ought to be taken, he pulled on his overcoat and handed in the room key at reception. Mrs Moore had a few words with him: she hoped the room was satisfactory, that the Duttons were comfortable and enjoying their visit and wasn't it a shame it was so blustery this weekend? He did not waste the opening she had given him. 'I don't mind the weather. Carol's gone shopping so I'm going to take a walk.'

Dutton went into the cold, warmed by his success in deflecting suspicion about Carol. When he had sent her upstairs with the porter on arrival there was time for him to have a private conversation with Mrs Moore. He had said Carol had been seriously ill since they last saw her and had not long come out of hospital. The point had been taken and Carol left alone, except for concerned smiles during tea.

Dutton couldn't help laughing about it as he drove the fawn car from the Boatman car park to the garage. The tank was nearly empty, he needed a gallon of petrol. Then he went down the back streets. He would have chosen to park it more obscurely, in a narrow side street, but there were yellow lines along them and the best place he found was East Green. After leaving it there he walked to the sea front. There was an hour before he could collect the Ford and he must keep away from the shops in case Carol bumped into him and he was obliged to stay with her.

Near the lighthouse he passed a couple of scurrying figures, coat collars up and hands in pockets, then he was on the front and alone. The battering wind invigorated him. Soon he would be as free as the black-headed gulls screeching as they stalked about the roadway. He looked at his watch. When would it be? Which would be the exact moment he would stop being Peter Dutton and move into a new life unhindered by the dreadful past?

He wanted to run madly, to sing into the wind, to mock the fate he was outwitting. The habit of caution saved him as it had saved him so often. Soberly he went along the sea front with its beach hut reminders of summer days, until he came to the stump of the pier. Like the town, the pier had evolved from its Victorian heyday and the pavilion now called itself the Southwold Leisure Centre. Above its Neptune Burger Bar a camp Neptune reclined in a shell, a limp wrist letting his fork droop. Victorian vigour had grown languid.

Beyond the shut-up building the beach huts straggled again, like coloured matchboxes which ought, by the laws of nature, to have been carried inland by the wind. And beyond the matchboxes the low cliff ran the mile to where the next brave buildings waited on the brink of erosion. The coastline was constantly changing its identity.

Dutton passed the pavilion and sat for shelter in the lee of a beach hut, while his watch marked off the final minutes of Peter Dutton's existence. He was at the beginning of the enterprise but the early stages had gone smoothly. He was confident this would set a pattern for the rest. The car was hidden so he would not have to go back to the Boatman car park where he might be seen by Carol or someone from the hotel. Everyone was to be convinced he was taking a walk. His car would be found on a lonely reach of the shore, indicating he had walked along the crumbling cliffs or scrambled to the beach. But once he had driven the car there he would scuttle across country to where the hired car would lie waiting.

Before the evening was spent he would be on a train out of Ipswich, the hired car dumped near the city centre. Thinking of it, he clenched his hands with excitement and broke into a broad irresistible grin. He felt kindly disposed to everything and everyone just then. At last things were going his way, he had extricated himself from his folly and was going to be allowed to start again.

His plan was a model of ingenuity, he knew that. It relied on no one but himself and he was sure of the fundamental wisdom of that. Yet a flicker of doubt entered his mind. There was one stage where he would need luck. He shrugged, there was nothing he could do about it so he had to believe luck would be on his side at the tricky point. This point would come when he had collected the hired car, driven it a few miles out of Southwold and hidden it.

Luck would have to let him hitch a lift back to Southwold so he could take his own car from East Green to a spot further up the coast. When he spoke to the driver who picked him up he would try and sit on the back seat on the nearside. That would prevent the driver seeing much of him: the man would not be able to watch him in the rear-view mirror as they drove along. His excuse for getting into the rear of the car could be that he detested wearing seat belts. If he achieved all this, the driver would only get a good look at him as he got into the car.

Gulls wailing overhead took his attention. His wife had once said they were the souls of doomed men. She had liked them. She had liked less the sort of people who used the colourful beach huts. Her cruel wit had played with them, reducing to pathos their daily routine of shifting from hotel or boarding house to beach hut and back again. No matter that they were happy watching their sun tans darken and their children frolic in the paddling pool, and scenting their lunchtime hamburgers cooking at the Neptune.

Her own love was the unpeopled shore where the centuries had eaten towns bigger than Southwold had ever been. Together they had stumbled along the precarious cliffs, comparing this year's new path with last year's route which lay tumbled on the beach, sucked by the sea. Unbroken waters, the endless skies above a smooth land where massive churches rode like anchored ships, thrilled her. For all its openness this was a private country where each individual made his compact with the elements.

187

Together the Duttons had slithered down miniature cliffs to leave their trail over the sand, ending where tides creamed to an indecisive stop. Companionably, avoiding anyone else, they paid out the short rope of holidays. It seemed never to rain, always to be sunny, whether they came when golden whin scented the air or heather glowed. On these walks Carol Dutton had been truly at peace, released from the pressures which drove her. Her days on the Suffolk coast were a return to the simplicity of childhood when she had come there with doting parents.

Her parents had owned a Southwold cottage that faced the sea, and Carol's habit each time she came to the Boatman was to go down to look at the outside of it, noting how its current owner gave it annual facelifts which changed the paintwork from yellow to blue and back to yellow. In Carol's childhood it was always yellow. The last time she and Dutton came she brought a camera and photographed it. 'Where did you get the camera?' Dutton had asked, fearing the answer.

'Never you mind,' she replied, teasing. 'It's time we had a camera, everyone else has one, even those drones down at the beach huts.'

She had photographed him, stealing shots as he ran down the steps of the Boatman or walked on the cliffs. And he had relented, putting away his distaste, and photographed her against the unlikely red of a sunset reflected on a broad, as she strolled carefree and barefoot over the sand, posed against the white rail that edged the Southwold sea front, strode through the elegance of South Green and was captured by the fun of the regatta. He took scenes of town and countryside, with and without Carol. She was far more willing to be photographed than he was, encouraging it.

He looked at his watch. Time to collect the hired car. Back streets kept him hidden from shoppers most of the way, then he had to join High Street. His eyes swept the busy pavements but there was no sign of a blue suit. He entered the cramped and smoky office to ask after the Ford. The woman had the paperwork ready. He was going to pay in cash rather than let the bank trace what he had done on the day he disappeared. He counted out the notes, pleased that his hands were so steady despite the tension building within him. Then the woman spoke, bringing him up sharply: 'You've got your driving licence, have you?'

He had never hired a car before and was not prepared for that. He thought it was like other transactions where money spoke for itself. He had been naive. The garage would want his driving licence as proof that he was a qualified driver as well as proof of identity so that he could not vanish with their car. The woman was patient while he fumbled through pockets. He was deciding what to do, whether to hire the car in his own name and change the rest of the plan or to relinquish the entire plan and start again. He played for time. 'I'm sorry, I didn't think about it.'

'We must see it, we're not allowed to hire without the licence. It's to do with insurance, you see.'

'I understand. It's not far away.' He moved to the door.

'Don't be long, we close on the hour.'

Cursing, he went into the bitter air, down back streets the way he had come. Lights were being switched on in houses as day was fading. He had little time to rework his plans, none to spare for blaming his stupidity. As he walked, his hands emphasized the crucial matters he must take into account. But he was growing afraid the next plan might also contain its own fatal flaw. 'Keep it *simple*,' he heard himself say to the empty street. 'Stick to what you know.'

His licence was in his pocket but there was no point in getting a car in his own name because the police would find out. He had meant to give the garage a false name and address, to sign the form as Ted Parker which he thought a rather hilarious touch. He had even had it in mind to say Ted Parker lived in Grommets Lane in a London suburb, probably Pinner.

Dutton came to the end of a street and slowed to a stop. He was undecided what to do for the best, except that he had ruled out going to the garage or the Boatman. Cars lined the street where he stood and with black humour he told himself that if he were a criminal he would break into one and drive off. A woman studied him through net curtains and he moved on, winding his way towards the green where his own car waited. He got into it and sat there, for the first time knowing the coldness of the day. He started up the engine and put the heater full on.

'I might as well get out of Southwold,' he said, and took the car a mile or two inland, keeping a moderate speed some way behind a bus lumbering on the first leg of its journey to Halesworth. When it pulled into a stop he passed it and not long after veered right and down a wriggling lane which ran parallel to the coast.

Thatchers' reed was stacked at the roadside to dry, black trees fringed bare fields beneath a white sky and he made the tight turn to Covehythe. There was a farm, opposite it a flinty tower below which a tiny thatched church took shelter in the pebbled ruins of the vast original structure. Carol had loved that sight, the new church rising phoenix-like from the ruin of the old, and sharing the same triumphant tower. Ruined buildings, like the tattered coastline, had held her in thrall. 'Sometimes I think you only like destruction,' Dutton had said. It was half a joke.

'Can't you feel it, Peter? The atmosphere?' But he could feel the heat of the sun, the caress of the sea breeze. He had shaken his head, he could not feel what she felt. She was beyond him, she had always been beyond him. Six great gaping windows flanked each side of the ruined nave. 'Peter, think how it must have been,' she persisted, 'when those windows were stained glass saints. Oh, they must have been so proud, those people who built this church. They must have thought it would go on for ever, buying them a place in heaven. And it's come to this.'

Dutton drove past the church and the lane ended at a metal barrier. A weathered notice board said the right of way had been scrapped by the council and it was obvious why. Dutton climbed the barrier and went forward. Sand blew about him, stinging his eyes and finding its way under his shirt collar. The lane fell away to the beach where the remains of the last barrier lay. One day the tide would claim some of it, the sand would bury the rest.

Walkers had made footpaths in each direction from the lane. To the left the sandy path ran on the seaward side of a

190

thorn hedge bent in constant submission to the wind. Then it went precariously close to the cliff and beside a ploughed field. Dutton saw how the cliff had been nibbled away since his last visit. He hoped it would be thought he had fallen and died on this path, to be washed out to sea.

Running back the way he came, scrambling over the barrier, he locked the car and went past the farm and church. This, then, was the moment when he stopped being Peter Dutton. He was clinging to the wreckage of the original escape plan, forging a different version of the next stage of it as there was no hire car to use. It was very unfortunate, he thought, that he could not steal a car when he came to a cottage but he had no idea how to do it and was sure to be caught while trying. From now on he would only do what he knew and understood. A bicycle, maybe? He could ride a bike as far as the main road where he could leave it in a hedge and thumb a lift to Ipswich. Ipswich was still a cardinal idea because its excellent connections by land, air and sea made it a confusing place for someone to disappear.

Dutton trudged on, seeing no one as he went by red brick and thatched cottages but aware that he might be seen. Cover was sparse, a hedge on his right for some of the way, and huge open fields all around. At a slight rise the lane was bordered on the left by a copse. Past that there was a spinney on the right. A pheasant strutted in the lane, a man harrowing was turning a leached field from light to dark. Dutton felt his left shoe begin to rub and blamed sand for getting into it.

He tried to keep up his pace, shielding his face as a car came. Then there was no cover at all. Some more cottages lay ahead but nobody had left a bicycle for him. His blistering heel told him he had come a long way, although the map would argue less than three miles. Shutting out the soreness he clenched his hands and forced himself on. Daylight had almost gone. Even if he were fit and determined to walk it would be impossible when country darkness came. He must beg a lift and trust the driver would not remember him accurately enough to match the descriptions sure to be published later of Peter Dutton, lost on desolate cliffs.

A skein of cottages and bungalows brought him up to the crossroads in Wrentham and he was on the A12, the main road to Ipswich. He felt it would be sensible to get out of the village before attempting to hitch a lift and took up position a little south of it. He never knew how much time he wasted there, trying with receding hope to persuade drivers to stop. With his heel renewing its protest, he began to limp slowly south for no better reason than that was where Ipswich lay. Gesturing at every one of the intermittent vehicles that came along he was equally happy to be taken back up the road to Lowestoft or Great Yarmouth. Anywhere. All that was definite was that he would never return to Southwold or Spinney Green.

Traffic was still obstinately ignoring him when he hobbled up to a telephone box. Its welcoming light came on as he neared it, confirming that day was done. The box was not vandalized and the list of useful numbers intact. After momentary heart-searching Peter Dutton rang for a taxi. He had five hundred pounds in his jacket pocket, but he was not going to make himself a talking point among local taxi drivers by paying for a cab to Ipswich. 'I'm on the A12 at the junction with Gipsy Lane,' he said. 'I want to get to the nearest railway station.'

'That will be Halesworth,' the voice on the telephone told him.

## 27

Carol was jerked awake by the driver shouting that they were in Halesworth. For a second she did not know what it meant. The dream that she was leading a horse through a wood on a hill was a powerful impression for a time. After leaving the bus she asked a boy on roller skates where the station was and he pointed towards the slope that led to the station yard.

No one else was in sight and she drifted on to a platform to seek a timetable and a ticket office. Instead she found a notice saying pay trains were operating on the line, so she would have to buy her ticket on board. Her most attractive option was to get to Ipswich and then change for London where she could get a train to any part of the country she chose. She felt it was imperative to put as much distance between herself and Dutton as she could.

But there was another reason for going to London. She had to sleep somewhere and would look strange without so much as a handbag for luggage. She might well find a bed near one of the big London railway terminals where hotel staff would be used to travellers coping with unexpected overnight stops. She would invent a story about a delayed train, a missed connection, to be ready if anyone bothered to ask. In London they probably wouldn't, in the country she would be noticed.

And then a more interesting idea came to her. She could get a night train somewhere, go to sleep in, say, Paddington and wake up as the Riviera express took her into Cornwall. She didn't think she knew Cornwall, but the journey sounded romantic and had the merit that time spent sleeping was not time wasted. Yes, why not? Dutton wouldn't dream of looking for her in Cornwall and she would have time there to gather her wits and decide what to do next. Out of the holiday season it would be easy to find somewhere cheap to stay, perhaps renting a holiday cottage for a few weeks at the low winter rates. And the west was so much warmer than the south east, the blue suit would be adequate.

The imagined journey to Cornwall and the new life there sustained her as she crossed the footbridge at Halesworth to the platform for Ipswich and London. She had a long wait, the train to Ipswich was not due until 6.42 and it was now only 6.10 by the station clock. The waiting room was locked and there was no respite from the bitter wind. She sat on a bench, hugging herself for warmth.

Carol tried to take her mind off the discomfort by reading her magazine but the wind whipped the pages. Words and pictures were meaningless shapes. She took the silk square from around her throat and tied it over her head, to keep her hair from blowing into her eyes. With her suit collar turned up and her hands slotted into her sleeves as though they were muffs, she sat and waited.

Below the station there were the sounds of traffic and the lights of shops and streets. She tried not to think of the comforts of the twin-bedded room at the Boatman and the good dinner she knew would be served at the hotel before long. She tried, but hunger began to dominate her mind, driving out even the cold. There were no confectionery vending machines on the platform and she thought it unlikely the train would have a buffet bar as it went no further than Ipswich. Consulting the station clock she sprang up and raced over the bridge. Too late to find a shop open but perhaps a take-away café or . . . *anything*. If it came to the worst she could go into a pub and buy a sandwich or a pork pie. Pubs usually had something to eat. But that must be her final attempt because she would make more of an impression going into a pub on her own and she did not want to leave any unnecessary clues to where she had gone.

Another clock made her careful of the time but she spotted a fast-food carton blowing down the gutter towards her and knew she was close to success. Five minutes later she was running back to the station carrying her prize: a hamburger and chips. There had been hot drinks, too, but she could not carry one and run and it was essential to run. A few people had come on to the platform in the time she was away and some occupied the bench she had used. She went further up the platform, sparing them the smell of her food, and dropped on to a seat. Tearing open the package she began to eat greedily. The food was tasteless with a synthetic texture but she did not notice.

The advertised time of the train came and went. People on the other bench muttered about it. Carol finished her food and walked down the platform to find a litter bin for her carton. The train was now more than ten minutes late and there were no staff to say how much longer passengers had to survive the unsheltered cold. Running from the café, and eating, had warmed her and made the wait more bearable. Her mind could reach forward to the next part of her escape. Suppose this delay meant she missed the connection at Ipswich for London? Suppose she got to Paddington too late for the night train to Cornwall?

Standing close to the cluster of people she let their bodies keep the sharpness of the wind from her. No one spoke to her, she might just as well be invisible. They were reminiscing about other fractured journeys and disappointments. She had her back to them, thinking that the less she was studied in detail the better, because one day soon the police might be issuing her description as a missing person and the fewer people who could point the way she had gone the better.

Twenty minutes after the scheduled time the train slowed into the station, to an ironic cheer from the group. Carol was abreast of a smoking compartment and had to move back down the platform a few yards. People were climbing in and out of carriages, the platform was alive with purpose and activity. She found an almost empty carriage and waited while a large woman with a suitcase battled to get out of it. The woman moved away, the door was gaping. And just as Carol was about to step up into the train she saw Peter Dutton.

He was on the platform, no more than three yards away. And he had seen her. He dived forward and grabbed her arm, yanking her away from the carriage. He looked savage. She stifled a cry and then the door was slammed and the train ready to move. Without a word Dutton propelled her down the platform, over the bridge and outside into the station yard. A taxi was there and he flung her into it. The driver looked taken aback and began to speak. Dutton cut him off: 'Southwold.' Only when the car was in motion did Dutton release Carol's arm.

He had discovered her a fraction of a second before she saw him. He had just that long to choose what to do. His disappearing act was doomed if they were to travel down the line in the same carriage. At some point on the journey she would see him. Even if he managed to change carriages on the way, she could spot him at Ipswich. No, the only way out was to behave as though he had been in pursuit of her, to drag her back recalcitrant to Southwold.

That damned driver had nearly ruined it. The man had wanted to talk all the way from Gipsy Lane to Halesworth, refusing to take the hint of curt answers about trains and destinations. When they had arrived the driver said the trains had been running late all day and he'd hang on for a bit to see if any passengers wanted a ride home. Dutton hoped he'd turned that to his own advantage, giving Carol the impression he'd kept the taxi there to take them both back to the Boatman. If she asked where the car was he'd say nothing.

The journey passed in silent misery, the driver flicking glances at Carol in his rear-view mirror. She was slumped, defeated, head down. At the Boatman the driver leaped out to open the door for her, not a courtesy he often bothered with but the curious business at the station and the deadly atmosphere on the way back intrigued him. Dutton was beside them immediately, trapping Carol between the opened door and his own body as though he thought she might make a dash for it. He paid the driver, took Carol's arm in his fierce grasp and pushed her up the steps into the Boatman.

When they got to their room he locked the door and put the key in his jacket pocket. Carol sat on the window seat, looking at the evening-darkened green and the blackness which hid the sea. Neither of them spoke. Dutton switched on a lamp and darted to gather up a piece of paper from her bed. He crumpled it in his pocket. Then he hung his overcoat in the cupboard. She did not look round.

He was pacing up and down, his left eyelid twitching, the room a cage he refused to unlock. Eventually they would have to speak and they would have to face Mrs Moore who had handed him the key at reception on the way in. Her polite enquiry about whether he had enjoyed his walk died on her lips as she took in the extraordinary scene. He didn't care, he could deal with Mrs Moore. Nothing was easier than to step up his story a bit, hint that when he said Carol had been ill he meant she had been in a mental hospital.

He debated the best way to handle Carol herself. His anger at the station was not simulated. It was the destruction of his own plans which caused it, because he could not care less whether she was in Southwold or the South of France. But how should he react now? If she were really ill, as he was going to let Mrs Moore believe, then how would he behave? It was most sensible to look at it that way, then whatever happened next would not seem out of place. And perhaps it would be necessary to let Carol herself believe she had a breakdown before she ran off from Shepherd Road?

He reasoned that if she were genuinely ill then the last thing he would do would be to cause a situation where she got distressed about it and especially in a public place like a hotel. In those circumstances what he would do would be to carry on as though everything were normal. Breaking the silence he announced he was going to take a bath. He locked her in the room as he went out. Because their room was at the front of the hotel their bathroom lay across a passage behind it.

With a sigh of relief she got up from the window seat and moved about the room. She had been waiting for him to explode but the threat had dissipated. Her scarf had slid down around her neck and she unknotted it and stroked the silk. It was easier to fuss about the creases in a silk scarf than agonize about the failure of her escape. Cornwall had no more substance than her unreliable half-memories. She took off her shoes and jacket and lay down on her bed until she felt strong enough to face the disaster without tears of frustration. She wondered how long he had watched her before the train came in, how much he'd enjoyed waiting to pounce, like the cat she had once watched in the Shepherd Road garden with a mouse.

Who was it, she wondered, who had given her away? Dutton could not have stalked her himself or he would have been there sooner. Had someone from the Boatman seen her board the bus and mentioned it to him much later when she did not meet him? And now what? Was she to acquiesce, let him keep her under lock and key when it suited him, be deprived of any further chance to get away? Her stubborn spirit revived. She swung her legs off the bed and sat up, thinking that this very moment might be the time to try again.

Unfortunately she had not watched what Dutton did before he left the bedroom. But she remembered the sound of the cupboard door opening and closing. She looked in and checked his clothes. Everything he said to her was open to suspicion, she had come to accept that; but if it were true that he had gone to bath then he must have taken some clean clothes or his dressing gown with him. The dressing gown was hanging inside the wardrobe, a clean pair of socks, a shirt and underpants were on the shelves. If the shelves had been bare then the answer would have been clear. Instead, there was no answer because she did not know what he had packed. With another sigh she began to close the cupboard door but then shot out a hand to the overcoat and felt inside its pockets. Her fingers clutched the leather tag of a car key.

At the bedroom door she pressed her ear to the wood, straining to hear sounds from across the carpeted corridor. None reached her. Then she telephoned reception and Mrs Moore answered. 'This is Carol Dutton in Room 14. I have got myself locked in and I need to get out to the bathroom. Could you bring your key and free me, please?' She laughed, making light of silly accident.

There was a curious pause and then Mrs Moore said she would come. A minute later there was the scratching at the

198

lock and the bedroom door swung. Carol thanked her, waited until Mrs Moore moved away and then followed her down the passage. She pushed back the door of the bathroom serving an unoccupied bedroom and waited inside until a reasonable time had passed and she could go downstairs without it appearing oddly quick. The stairs led to the reception area and she would have to pass the desk wherever she went next. Luckily the telephone rang as she began down the flight and when she reached the desk Mrs Moore was speaking to a caller and reading her booking list. If she saw Carol, Carol was not aware of it.

Rather than leave by the front door Carol went to the dining room, across a corner of it and through another door that took her into a bar. She was working partly from memory of what she had noticed at tea and partly from guesswork. From a door at the end of the bar she entered a lobby by the door to the car park. Cold hit her like a blow but she did not hesitate, raced through the car park and into an alleyway. She turned right, to avoid South Green where she would be visible from many directions, and wove in and out of streets until, just when she feared her instinct had misguided her, she came into East Green.

Bitter tears welled as she realized the fawn car was no longer there. She had the car key, hard and gritty in her hand, but there was no car. Sobbing, she stood in the yellow pool of a street lamp and stared at the useless key. It lay now on her open palm, there was no point in clutching it like a forlorn hope. She drew it nearer to her face, scrubbed away tears with her free hand and looked intently. She had discovered what she had been too preoccupied to see before, that sand clung to the leather tag. It had wriggled its way into the shabby seams and the pocket where the registration number was displayed.

With resignation she went back to the Boatman. It was becoming too late to do anything else that day. If she telephoned for a taxi to Halesworth she might not get there before the final train to Ipswich, which was supposed to leave at 8.47. Dutton would guess where to look for her. She saw objections to all the alternatives. But the principal one was that she was too weary and too heartbroken to rally again. In the morning, she hoped, she would be more resilient but her priorities now were heat and sleep. Only the Boatman offered these.

Returning the way she had come she checked that the car was not back in the car park and overlooked in her headlong dash to East Green. It was not. She pushed open the back door of the Boatman and went without incident to the landing. The door of the bathroom for Room 14 was ajar and she entered the bedroom with a defensive explanation for her absence ready: that she had been to use another bathroom. She was unchallenged. Dutton was combing his damp hair in front of the mirror and grunted acknowledgement of her arrival.

While he was busy there she opened the wardrobe door and dropped the car key into his overcoat pocket, under cover of taking out her hairbrush. Soon they were in the dining room, he ravenously hungry and she pecking in a half-hearted way. Again there were sympathetic looks from the waitress and again Dutton made a show of animated conversation with Carol. Her disappearance from the locked room was never mentioned. They went to their separate beds without a word. Carol fell asleep straight away, deaf to the ululation of the wind. She dreamt of railway trains and horse riding and driving a very fast car over loping hills. Everything in her dreams was a celebration of freedom.

On Sunday morning she woke early, an unusual quality in the light alerting her to the day. Lying there, facing the wall, she admired the excessively clear light that edged the curtains, then gave her thoughts to the day ahead. After lunch the Duttons must leave the Boatman and trek back to London. She doubted whether Sunday morning would be the most propitious time to run away: buses and trains would be scarce and Dutton vigilant. But she was strong again. She would create her own opportunity out of nothing. She would get a taxi and spend whatever it cost to be driven to Ipswich.

The taste of freedom was lingering, colouring her day as it had coloured her dreaming. With an effort she forced herself to understand that the cost of a taxi as far as Ipswich was prohibitive for someone who had to make less than a hundred pounds support her for an indefinite period. She weighed up the chance of scrounging a lift from a driver going that way. Most of the Boatman's other guests would be leaving after lunch and some would certainly be going in that direction. A lift ought to be possible.

She stretched and rolled over on to her back. And then she saw that she was alone. There was instant relief, abandoned in favour of nervous suspicion about why this should be. It was very early. A clock mounted in the radio on the wall between the beds showed the time was only 7.25. She got up and felt the other bed. It was no warmer than the temperature of the room so Dutton had left it some time. His overcoat had gone from the wardrobe, too, but she was not locked in. Across the passage she ran a bath, returning to the bedroom while it filled. As she did so the brilliant light around the curtain drew her and she held back a handful of velvet to unveil South Green white with snow.

The snow was unmarked, a fine immaculate covering thrown down by the night. There were no footprints leaving the front of the hotel and any that she or anyone else made later would be perfect evidence of their journey. Lying in the bath she rearranged her day, looking for a loophole which meant she could get away and not be snared. Time and again her schemes foundered on the belief that Dutton must have caught her at Halesworth because someone at the Boatman had sent him there. She felt surrounded by spies, unable to trust anyone. She dared not ask for a lift. She either spent too much on a taxi or she relinquished all hope of freedom that day. Put like that, she gave herself no option. The money counted for nothing beside her need to be released.

Dressing, she rehearsed the arguments for making her break that Sunday instead of after she returned to Spinney Green. It came down to the sooner the better. In Southwold she knew the conditions: the gift of the money had bent her prison bars. Dutton was so unpredictable she could not rely on him leaving the cash with her once they were home. The sooner the better.

The clock said 8.00, which she hoped was not too early to

telephone for a cab. She waited and waited for the Boatman reception desk to answer her call, then set the receiver down and went to the window to savour the snow scene. She intended to ring Directory Enquiries and find out the name of a local taxi firm she might call, but perhaps they would not be willing to help. Callers were meant to provide a name and be given a number, strictly speaking operators were not supposed to give any other information. Carol knew she could have found out what she wanted to know easily enough from the reception desk or could have borrowed one of the Boatman's telephone directories but the Boatman itself was a trap. All its staff were labelled in her mind as informers who would give her away to Dutton once he returned.

She wandered about the room, deciding whether to walk to a telephone call box or to the hotel in Market Place to get the information. But then she discovered it was to hand. In the folder by the telephone were the details of the Boatman's facilities and displayed like a decorative border were advertisements for local shops and services. One was for a taxi company. She got her outside line, rang, and suffered a long delay during which she felt rash at expecting a business to answer its phone so early on a Sunday. But then a man's voice was squeaking down the wire at her. She arranged for him to pick her up in fifteen minutes at the end of the alley leading to the Boatman car park. This would prevent anyone at the hotel seeing what she was doing. He wanted her name and she gave him Brown.

Elated, she gathered up her few things: it ought to be practical to take some of them although she and Dutton had shared a suitcase. She could not take it because she would give herself away if she was seen with it. But there were no other bags, so what could she use? The solution was swift. In the room was a metal waste bin with a plastic liner. Nothing had been thrown into it, it was perfectly clean, so she took the bag and laid it on the bed beside her few things. Rolling the clothes up she made them as compact as they would go and fitted them into the bottom of the bag. Her hairbrush and toothbrush were dropped in on top, then she twisted the bag and tied a knot in it. She put her magazine beside the bulbous parcel and looked satisfied.

She asked herself whether to hide them outside the room in case Dutton came back. If they were in the spare bathroom she could fetch them whenever she wanted. But this was not necessary, the time to meet the taxi had almost arrived. She negotiated the landing and stairs without mishap, avoided the eyes of Mrs Moore and carried the parcel down low so that the woman could not see it unless she leaned over the edge of her counter. Then she swung it up in front of her until she was round the corner to the dining room. Mrs Moore and any other spies would believe she was going into breakfast. Again she cut across the room and entered the bar. A woman with a duster made her jump but then she was in the sanctuary of the back lobby.

Confronting the cold was more attractive than meeting anyone entering from the car park. She launched herself into the snow. Footprints and tyre tracks showed there had already been much coming and going. Carol hurried, head bent, across the yard and went left to where the taxi would meet her. Her feet spun and she slowed to a cautious pace over snow which had compacted to ice.

A taxi drew across the end of the alleyway, overshooting so that only its exhaust showed it had not driven on. A slight breeze played with the fumes, sending them along the lane towards Carol. She held the bag and magazine under one arm and teetered the last few yards. Her free hand slid for warmth into her suit pocket. She took a few more steps.

Then a sharp cry broke from her and she was shuffling the parcel and magazine and searching in her other pocket. The truth that struck so cruelly late was that the money had been taken. She could go nowhere.

# 28

The taxi driver, reading his Sunday paper at the steering wheel, never saw Carol Dutton or her panicky flight down the alley and into the Boatman car park. He sat awhile, then got out, stretched and bounded up the steps of the main entrance.

By then Carol was eating breakfast in the dining room, her parcel ripped open and the contents thrown on the wardrobe shelves. Dutton had not returned, the room was as she had left it.

She was quaking as she ordered her breakfast but the decision to come to the dining room had been the right one. Food would make her feel better and eating the meal gave her something to do. Otherwise she would be sitting in the bedroom, waiting. Without money there could be no new schemes.

And without money there could be no newspaper to read, either, until a man alone at a nearby table, catching her reading the back of his, offered it to her when he had finished. She raised her head from it when she heard a car engine start up and saw through the window the taxi swing round in the road and disappear the way it had come. She was grateful that she had thought of giving a false name, it would have been humiliating if the driver had asked in the hotel for a Mrs Dutton. As it was, she had avoided exposing her runaway plan and hoped the episode had not ruined his day as effectively as it had hers.

Upstairs she opened the suitcase and put Dutton's things and hers into it. Then there was nothing to do but hang around, watching the snow melting and teasing her imagination about what Dutton was doing and where he had gone. 'It would be wonderful if *he'd* just run off,' she thought.

A tap on the door brought a maid checking whether the room was free for her to clean. Carol took her suitcase to the residents' lounge, there was no reason to hold up the woman's work. A few other guests were there, watching winter sports on the television and thrilling to the aerial flights of the ski jumpers.

Morning wore on, ski jumpers rose and occasionally fell, and the word 'lunch' cropped up with increased frequency. A bluff elderly man declared that all it required to make perfect this morning of log fires and snowy scenes was a drink, and who was going to join him? A friendly clamour echoed that drinks should be sent for and they were. Carol, invited to order and seeing no purpose in being left out, asked for a gin and tonic and wanted it added to the bill for Room 14.

The waiter said drinks were always charged separately and would she mind paying now? She laughed the matter away, saying her husband had gone out and she had no cash. The bluff man was having none of this. Indicating with the raising of an eyebrow that he thought the waiter was making an error of judgement, he paid for her drink. Her protest and thanks were waved aside by his opinion that it was all his fault, if he hadn't mentioned a drink no one else would have thought of it. The others responded, as on cue, with loud and ironic concurrence.

Eventually everyone drifted off to the dining room, Carol tagging along. She fended off questions about Dutton's absence by saying he 'had to go out' and she expected him at any time. The morning had made people get to know each other and there was conversation from table to table now. All that troubled Carol was that after the meal the rest would be paying their bills and leaving. Until Dutton came she could do neither.

'I am afraid you have got me until my husband returns,' Carol said to Mrs Moore when the last of the guests had driven away. Mrs Moore gave her a guarded smile but said nothing. She left Carol in the lounge where the fire was dying and the log basket empty. The ski jumping had finished and the television was unplugged.

Carol sat near the grate watching red ash dwindle towards

grey, and listened to time passing. Now and then, the silence was snapped by a vehicle crossing the green or by a clatter from the hotel staff. Nobody came to her, she felt utterly disregarded.

Going down the carpeted passage to a door marked Ladies Cloakroom she heard voices in the kitchen discussing her. The first she recognized as the waitress with the sympathetic smiles. She was saying: 'Yes, she's still here. Taken root in the residents' lounge.'

An unfamiliar woman's voice asked: 'What will Mrs Moore do if she won't go? And can't pay the bill?'

A sharp laugh. 'That's what Mrs Moore would like to know. She doesn't like to press her knowing she's ill. I said did she think she'd have to call the police and she said she'd be calling a doctor more likely.'

'D'ye reckon she's really ill, then?'

'Oh, you wouldn't believe how much she's changed. Mind you, she could have done with losing a fair bit of weight. And the amount of food she used to shovel down! Still, dieting is one thing and losing it when you're ill is something else. She's given up all interest in her food, I saw that. Picking at her dinner last night she was, pushing bits around the plate as though two mouthfuls would choke her. Last time I was running in and out of the kitchen for more of this and double helpings of that. And, of course, she never stopped drinking, but now it's a dainty sip of this and just the one glass of that . . .'

'What's meant to have caused it? It's not anorexia, is it?'

'When they came he told Mrs Moore she'd been in hospital and was to be kept quiet. Honestly, we were amazed when we saw her, she looks a changed woman. Then later on he let Mrs Moore know she'd been in a mental hospital. He didn't come right out with it, she says, but she understood what he meant.'

Someone switched on a dishwasher and their voices were extinguished. Carol went into the cloakroom, to be confronted by her own horrified face in the mirror. The women's words were seared into her mind. She was long past believing she must accept everything Peter Dutton told her about herself but it had not occurred to her that he might be telling lies to other people.

And this particular lie was not one which she could easily refute or demonstrate to be untrue. Mrs Moore and her staff had the evidence of their own eyes to confirm something drastic had happened to her and they had swallowed Dutton's explanation. Those sympathetic smiles, the conversations which excluded her, Mrs Moore's doubtful pause before agreeing to let her out of the locked room, all showed that Dutton had been believed. And yet it was he who was behaving in a peculiar way, misleading and concealing and playing with her misery. Whatever was it all for? Exasperated at her failure to understand, she groaned aloud, her hands tearing at her hair as if the pain could compel her brain to deal with the torment once and for all.

Behind her the door moved, shut again. Her next idea was stillborn. It would be pointless to appeal to Mrs Moore, attempt to sell her the silk scarf to raise the fare to London, leave the suitcase as security against the bill to be paid as soon as she could . . . Quite pointless, because Mrs Moore had looked in and seen her behaving like a mad woman.

She splashed cold water on her face, ran a comb through her hair and breathed calmly until she was ready to face the Boatman staff. There was nobody in the passage but as she turned the corner and entered the reception area she came face to face with Peter Dutton. He assumed an expression of concern for her and asked whether she was ready to leave. But most of his talk was with Mrs Moore, and Mrs Moore clearly felt more at ease speaking to him than she did to Carol. The bill had been paid, the suitcase fetched and they had been waiting for Carol. Somehow the history of the day had been rewritten and it was she who was causing all the delay and ought to be apologetic.

Once they left the hotel his show of concern for her was dropped. He reverted to the taciturn Peter Dutton she had endured for most of the past fortnight. It mattered little to her where he had been and why. Rather than hear any of his fictions she declined to ask.

The fawn car moved through the deserted Sunday streets,

207

over the bridge and away towards London. Carol feigned sleepiness and leaned back in her seat. From the corner of her eye she registered wet sand in the welt of Dutton's shoe as it rested on the clutch pedal, abrasions on his left hand. Getting into the car she had noticed the sand which hung damply around the wheel arches and peppered the bodywork. The carpet at Dutton's feet was impregnated with it. On the rear seat the grey coat lay just as it had been left on Saturday. The only difference to the car was the sand which had got into and over it. She remembered the sand on the key ring. She gave herself no marks for guessing the car had been left close to a beach during its time away from the hotel. The hum of the engine and the car's even speed on the empty road coaxed her towards sleep.

With an effort she bent her mind to working out what Dutton had been doing that morning. Clearly, he had been to the beach because it showed on his shoes and, perhaps while he was there, he had scratched his left hand. The injury was recent, a number of raw red lines where blood was drying in dark raised spots. But there was more. She opened an eye and watched the hand as he juggled with the steering wheel while rounding a bend, and she knew what she had only half-noticed earlier. The abrasion was dramatic but in addition to that there was a residue of black stain on the knuckles of that hand and a similar stain on the ball of his right thumb. The hands had been washed, maybe scrubbed, and all that was left for her to see was the ingrained stain that would be hardest to shift.

When she next opened her eyes it was to discover why they were slowing. Dutton pulled into a garage for petrol and, still ignoring her presence, got out to fill the tank and then pay at the cash desk across the forecourt. She sat up and touched the steering wheel. If only he had left the keys in the ignition! Her hand slid down the plastic wheel and then reached for a book on the shelf on the far side of the dashboard. It was a copy of the London A–Z street guide, nothing that would explain any of the mysteries. She flipped it open and found her name written inside the cover. Someone had written it there with small childlike writing.

Then movement made her glance up and Dutton was walking back to the car. Before he came the book was back on the shelf and she was avoiding confrontation by pretending to doze.

The following morning she was wretchedly depressed. Her head ached. The Southwold weekend which had promised so much had only underlined Dutton's mystifying behaviour and not helped her sluggish memory, either. Was it possible, she wondered, that she had been so unhappy that her memory refused to accept who she was and what her circumstances had been? Had Dr Renfrew suggested something of the sort? But she could not be sure whether it was fair to interpret him that way and she would never see him to ask.

The unease she had always felt about being at Shepherd Road was more intense. Coolly, without inflaming her discontent, she listed the things that made her miserable there. Peter Dutton, of course. She did not like or trust him and was sure he did not care for her. Then there was the house. What was there about it to stir her memory apart from the horrifying blood stain on the carpet? Her clothes, some cookery books and some tablets in the bathroom cabinet were the only evidence she had ever lived there. The furnishings and decor must have been Dutton's choice, they were definitely not hers.

'I don't fit,' she thought. And went on to fantasize that it would be wonderful if she turned out not to be Carol Dutton at all. Someone else, someone *appropriate* would come and take her home, and home would be somewhere quite different. She laughed at herself. She was playing the game, the one she'd played in the motorway café. 'Which family shall I choose?'

It was a tempting game. As she had lost her identity why shouldn't she choose a fresh one? She saw the flaw: it wasn't her identity which was lost, merely her memory. Her identity had been returned to her as soon as Peter Dutton claimed her. With a sinking heart she faced the fact that all she knew about herself was what Dutton told her, and she did not trust him.

Among the things she did not trust was his promise to transfer from Dr Andersen to a doctor in Spinney Green. It was a week since Ellie Gray had called on her and she had still not seen a doctor. She wanted to keep herself busy and not sink into despair so she decided to walk down to Dr Hubbard's surgery that morning and ask to sign on. But in a way it was a commitment she did not want to make because she did not mean to be in Spinney Green much longer. She changed her mind about going to Dr Hubbard that day. A little more delay before she saw a doctor could hardly matter. If doctors had been able to do anything for her they would have done it while she was in Princes Hospital.

She switched her thoughts to practical detail, seeking a fresh approach to getting away from Dutton. Money was paramount again, although thirty pounds for a rug was much less attractive now she had known a hundred pounds in her pocket. She came to the conclusion that she must swallow her pride, accept that she was helpless and find an accomplice. She could not contact the elusive Marcia Cohen now that Marcia had left the West End office. Until she phoned again she might as well not exist. Therefore there were only two accomplices on offer: Jean Parker or Holly Chase. The choice was uncomplicated.

Holly was home that Monday while Dan, who also had time off, and Joel, who seldom had work, were putting the finishing touches to the cupboards they had installed in Joel's back room over the weekend. They had no need of Holly and she welcomed Carol Dutton's invitation to join her for coffee. Within moments of entering the Dutton house Holly knew of Carol's state. Her strained look, which suggested the weekend had been anything but a pleasant seaside break, and the air that Carol was stiffening her resolve gave it away. Holly, by profession on the receiving end of confidences, gave Carol time. At last it came out. 'There's no one else so I'm asking you, Holly. I need someone to talk to so I can get things straight and decide what I must do.'

Holly was relieved. It wasn't to be a case of 'tell me what to do' but 'help me decide for myself what to do'. 'What's the problem?' she asked, prepared to give it as long as it needed.

Much later she went home, brimful of Carol's unnerving tale. Dan and Joel were in the kitchen making lunch. 'Where've you been, we thought we'd lost you?' Dan said.

'Next door with Carol.' There was only one thing she wanted to say about it, although it was tough keeping such a repeatable story to herself.

She didn't have a chance to go on because Dan said: 'I can solve your mystery for you. *I* know who Carol Dutton is, Joel just showed me those.' He pointed to Joel's photographs of Carol in her garden.

'And I know now, too. She's the media's Mystery Woman, isn't she? You filmed her in hospital in Leamington.'

'And now she's home and her memory's restored and there's a nice happy ending.'

Holly's cryptic 'not quite' intrigued them but she said no more about Carol Dutton. The tale, though, bobbed in and out of her mind as she went about her day. She doubted she had been much use to Carol, except as an attentive ear. During the afternoon she carried mugs of tea up to Dan and Joel disturbing them putting up the last of the fitments. 'Don't tread on that,' Joel shouted. Holly stopped in time and picked up an implement near her foot.

'What's it for?' It had a rounded star-shaped top on a long steel shank.

'Just a screwdriver.' Joel was now half inside a cupboard. 'They have flat blades but this . . .'

'A more modern type,' said Dan. 'They are used a lot for jobs like this, fixing knock-down furniture.'

'Why? What was wrong with the old type?'

Joel and Dan exchanged superior smiles. Joel said: 'Go away, Holly. Girls don't understand this sort of thing.'

'You mean you don't have the answer,' Holly corrected and went away, avoiding treading on anything else precious. Not long after she called on Carol again. Carol was using a knife to fiddle with the locks on the desk drawers. Holly cocked her head on one side and stared at the desk. She investigated it from several directions. 'What's the back like?'

'No help, I can't get in that way. I'll either have to steal the key or force the drawers which will damage them.'

211

'Or . . .' Holly went crawling into the kneehole, backing out and examining the book shelves which ran down the side of the drawer section. 'Or you could unscrew the thing.'

'Unscrew it? Are you sure?'

Holly swept off the books, revealing countersunk screws. '*Almost* sure.'

'I'll get a smaller knife, I haven't come across any screwdrivers.'

'No, I'll get exactly the type of screwdriver you need.'

Holly said to Joel: 'Would you pass me that screwdriver, if you've finished with it.'

He gaped. Dan said: 'What do you want it for?'

'Oh, just a little job needs doing.' She held out her hand.

'But you didn't even know that *was* a screwdriver half an hour ago!' Joel was incredulous.

'Sure, but I learn quickly.' They had to be content with that.

The desk came apart easily, the toughest bit was undoing the screws. The side panel with the shelves lifted off as one section and then T-brackets under the kneehole were taken off. The drawer section was freed. Although the locks held the drawers in the frame, there was no problem about reaching into the back of them. They were much shallower than their facing panels suggested.

Holly stood the drawer section upright, against a wall. The room was deathly quiet. Holly waited for Carol to move and Carol dared not.

Carol shook her head. 'This is silly, I've wanted so often to put my hand into those drawers and see what the secrets are but now I'm too scared.'

Holly waved a hand at the clock on the mantelshelf. 'You'll be even more scared if this desk isn't screwed back together before he comes home.'

Carol reached into the top drawer. There was the soft sound of paper being shifted and she pulled out a batch of documents and put them on the carpet. Holly said: 'One drawer at a time, so you don't muddle the contents.'

'Yes, everything must go back exactly as it was.' Carol

spread the documents over the carpet. Two were life assurance certificates, one on the life of Peter John Dutton, the other for Carol Mary Dutton. There were National Insurance certificates and other papers relating to their employment. She looked them over and replaced them. She saw nothing which didn't accord exactly with what Dutton had told her about herself.

In the middle drawer were sheaves of paid bills for domestic services and purchases. She handed them to Holly. Holly flicked through, checking there was no other more interesting information hidden among them. A bill escaped and fluttered away. Carol snatched it up. 'It's for the rug. He bought it in Oxford Street on November 29 last year.'

'About the time you went away?'

'Yes.' And also, Carol thought, about the time he needed to cover up the blood stain. She had not mentioned the stain to Holly, afraid of sounding melodramatic. Holly might not have believed it was blood, although Carol, remembering the look of the blood-soaked clothes they had shown her in hospital, was convinced.

In the bottom drawer of the desk was a new and unused bank paying-in book for an account at a bank in Spinney Green, a joint account in the names of PJ and CM Dutton. With it was a torn slip of paper with Carol Dutton written on it in the same handwriting as in the street guide in the car. The paying-in book and signature rested on a bunch of bank statements held together with a paperclip and sent out from a different bank in the West End. For a while these had gone to a flat in South London but from September they had come to Shepherd Road. This account was in Peter Dutton's name only.

Carol studied the most recent sheets which showed the monthly credit transfer which must be the salary from Pegwoods, a standing order which was to pay the mortgage on the house, and a number of other transactions which could have represented anything. The curious thing was that there was money going into the account apart from the Pegwoods money. Carol checked back to the earlier statements and found this was a recent development, dating from December.

Holly, sitting on the window sill, said: 'Has it all been worth it? Have you found anything useful?'

'No, just a further puzzle. There is another source of money apart from the monthly salary and yet the account is always low.'

'Whatever flows in flows right out again? Well, that's money.'

Holly helped Carol lift the drawer section back into place inside the carcass and as she did so there was a scraping sound. They tilted the drawers backwards and something metallic rasped along the wood of the top drawer. Carol picked up a car key.

## 29

Peter Dutton had not gone to Pegwoods that Monday. He left home as usual, snubbed Jean Parker who was taking in her milk, and trotted past the Phase Two houses to the station. He even got the train to King's Cross and squeezed on to the Underground train before he knew he would not go into the office.

At Oxford Circus he stood, buffeted by commuters, in the centre of the platform. When the crush had gone he slumped on to a seat and stayed there while three, four or maybe more trains roared in and out of the blackness. Part of the time he stared down at the floor, seeing only the racing feet – high heels, flat heels, down-at-heels – all dashing by. He felt the lethargy of defeat. Then he sat bolt upright, head tilted back to the tiled wall and eyes fixed on the advertisement opposite, hardly noticing how it disappeared for minutes as each train drew in and replaced it by hard, preoccupied faces surging from the carriages.

Dutton felt sick with anguish, his confident mood of the previous Friday a mocking memory. He was enmeshed in a web of his own making, it was folly to believe he could trick fate: sometime, he was going to be found out. Fate had been toying with him, letting him think he could twist out of the deadlock. It had tempted him with dreams of escape to a new identity and a new life, and then foiled those dreams. His first attempt foundered on the platform at Halesworth, but he had tried again and that had been disaster too.

On Sunday morning, very early, he had left the Boatman and trudged through snow to the car at Covehythe, meaning to drive to Birmingham and dump it in favour of a train as far afield as he could get. Blaming Carol for the coincidence at

Halesworth he had petulantly taken the money from her suit pocket while she slept.

But at Covehythe the car refused to start. Tinkering with it he hurt his hand and became filthy with engine oil. There was no choice but to walk to Wrentham for help and this he had done. By the time he returned to the car to wait for assistance the morning was spent. Sitting in the icy vehicle he had the terrifying sensation that he would be entombed in it as wind ripped at the fragile cliff and hurled sand inland. Grains rolled down the windscreen, gathered in crevices, were inexorably smothering everything.

The mechanic who came was a ponderous untalkative man who looked without comment at the car engine. Dutton saw only the encroachment of sand over the battery, the points and plugs, the engine block. He barely listened to the man's explanation of what had caused the car's refusal to start. He thrust the cash at him and drove away. The first call was the pub at Wrentham for food. Futile to aim for Birmingham – hadn't the mechanic mentioned running repairs and getting to a garage when he got home? How could he have asked whether that meant it wouldn't do to try and escape as far as Birmingham, with its tangle of routes an excellent starting point for a new life?

At Wrentham, Dutton cleaned away the oil from his hands, scrubbing so harshly that skin stung and scratches bled. Then he ate and drank and finally, when he came up against the early Sunday closing hours, drove at dawdling pace to Southwold. He fantasized that Carol would be gone. But he knew that Fate had him there, too: he had left her no money so she could not go. He had given himself no alternative but to fetch her.

Oxford Circus station is always busy, the rush hour worse. Dutton grew conscious the trains were less crammed than they had been, that he had sat there a long time. He studied the Underground map on the wall, took the Bakerloo line for Charing Cross and then walked along Victoria Embankment deaf to the traffic, watching the river forever running away.

He swung round, just short of the dark spike of Cleopatra's Needle, and went back to Hungerford Bridge. Crossing the footbridge he stayed a long, long time leaning over the rail to watch the water below. Boats went by leaving the opaque greenness frothing. Trains on the adjacent bridge rattled along behind his back; people on business hurried singly; gaggles of foreign tourists sauntered; dull-eyed men, each shut into private misery, hung over the rail before shambling off to the South Bank benches or the Embankment Gardens.

The bridge builders had allowed for the slow as well as the speedy when they widened the structure to viewing points. The press of traffic could go on its way unimpeded by dreamers and the unemployed, who had no option but to drag each minor activity to inordinate length to fill the day. Dutton would have been taken for one of the jobless.

He whiled away the morning pretending to read a newspaper over a cup of coffee at the National Theatre. He could hide in there, hide and worry that he was endangered by Marcia Cohen and Irene Yarrow. They wouldn't give up. Marcia because she was a clinging vine and Miss Yarrow because it was her job. Even though Carol was away from Leamington, Miss Yarrow, on behalf of Princes Hospital, would want to know how things turned out for the famous patient. Women! All his life he'd had his actions moulded by them but he had thought he held the initiative when he fetched Carol from hospital, that for once someone was in his control. But it had not lasted. She was stronger than he'd suspected. Her early reliance on him was misleading. She had not needed him. He hated her.

The National Theatre was quiet, warm, consoling, but his cup was removed and he felt obliged to go, too. Outside he walked around the concrete confusion of the arts centre until he came to the Festival Hall and its foyer entertainments. Photographs, pottery, maps – he hovered over each exhibition and then a string quartet began to play so he sat at a table near them, bought a drink and took on the guise of a music lover. Letting the sound go by was enough. He did not have to look as though he was waiting for anyone, or trouble to conceal his idleness. So long as the sound lasted he could sit there unobtrusively and think about anything he chose.

He did not choose but he thought about his wife. Not the

woman at Shepherd Road now but his real wife who went, as he still preferred to say, last November. Dutton tried to picture her normal face instead of the terrifying mask that troubled his sleeping and his waking. Remembering was increasingly difficult. He took from his jacket pocket the wedding photograph.

They were eight years old, those smiles outside the register office, on what had been literally the happiest day of his life. He remembered it in essence but not in detail. Bill Thomas, who had been at school with him and counted then as a lifelong friend, had been one witness, Carol's aunt another. Her parents were in New Zealand and Dutton expected her to want them back for the day or at least to give them the chance to come. 'No, it's got nothing to do with them. I'll write to them afterwards,' she said, and sent them an identical photograph when it was all over.

Bill Thomas, commiserating with her that her family couldn't be there, and astonished to find they didn't know about the wedding, thought she was being a trifle harsh. She never forgave that unguarded remark. Dutton wondered where Bill Thomas was now, what he was doing, whether he had also married. Carol had seen to it that Bill Thomas was excised from their lives, kept away by her abrasive manner.

Carol was so full of her own talk and her own ideas and Dutton was so absorbed in Carol that there was no space for anyone else. Realization of what she had achieved dawned slowly, but even then he could not blame her. She believed she was made of superior stuff and it was natural for her to expect him to aspire to her level and reject the Bill Thomases from the old, poor days in the rented terrace house south of the river. When Dutton resisted dropping old friends she jeered as his mother used to jeer about other things. It was easier to acquiesce, let the silent resentment harden inside.

Family, too – for they both had aunts and uncles and cousins in England – were casually dropped. Invitations were not returned, visits were cancelled at short notice, Christmas cards were ignored. People gave up, especially as a succession of changes of address left them doubtful where Peter and Carol Dutton lived. Each move, from one rented flat to another and then from one mortgaged flat to the next, was an 'improvement' on the last, another step on the way to Carol Dutton attaining the good address and the middle-class lifestyle she claimed was her due. Dutton indulged her, accepting her strenuous argument that she understood these matters and he did not. Unless she caused him a convoluted journey to Pegwoods, he was willing to go along with it. Useless to bemoan the repeated expense of the moves, she was implacable.

'But we *must*, we will never have this opportunity again,' she would say as the estate agents' brown envelopes began to patter through the letterbox once more, each time from a slightly more upmarket address than the one they were living in. 'If we left it to you we'd still be in that squalid little hutch in Battersea.'

'It wasn't squalid.' It was the house where he had grown up. There had been the river view and the power station and the streets he had always known.

'That all depends on one's standards. And one only improves those by taking the opportunities that come along.'

But the opportunities didn't 'come along', she fetched them. 'You don't think what taking these opportunities costs us. Apart from the increased mortgage, which we can't afford, we never have the right furniture for the new place, the carpets never fit, you demand new curtains . . .'

'. . . and there are estate agents' bills and solicitors' fees and removal vans as you keep on saying. We both know all that, but it seems only one of us realizes that what we are talking about is *investment*. You don't think my parents would expect me to sit around worrying about the cost of curtains when I could be moving up in the world like they did, do you?'

That was the only time she mentioned her parents, unless it was to damn the bank for bouncing a cheque written in anticipation of the New Zealand money. And that was the crux of his troubles in those days: the New Zealand money was Carol's private income and the notion of a private income suited her very well. It would have suited her even better if it had been more because she was a young woman determined to live up to her status, as she understood it. Long before the move to Spinney Green she acquired the attitudes which went with life at the better end of the suburb, on the other side of the station from Shepherd Road.

Dutton expected Carol's Shepherd Road phase to last a year, perhaps eighteen months before she was grasping for the next rung of the residential ladder and the brown envelopes appeared. He determined to resist, and made forceful play of the financial strait-jacket they were tied into. The last, bijou, flat had minute rooms so Shepherd Road seemed spacious by comparison and the good wool carpets she had insisted on were left behind, sold for a pittance in a buyers' market.

Yet at the same time the New Zealand money was being reduced as economic vagaries hit her father's business. Dutton was circumspect about relying on receiving much from it. Carol herself was piqued, saying the money ought to be a constant figure (an argument which went unvoiced when her share of profits rose in good times). They had clashed mildly, because for most of the eight years that was how their clashes were. In the early days it had been laid down that Carol determined the way they lived. Now it was too late to up-end the accepted order and begin again, yet his argument was unassailable: they had to tighten belts, cut back, whatever the current jargon was because there was not enough money to do otherwise. She appeared to understand this and the expenditure on their home was curtailed. After the new carpets and three-piece suite the house was left alone; after the rose bushes no more was done about her lavish ideas for the garden.

Other aspects did not change. She continued to urge him to get a better-paid job although her own work had always been temporary and spasmodic. He never knew whether this was because there was no demand for shorthand typists or because she did not care to look for work. He suspected that being a temporary shorthand typist did not chime with being a woman with a private income living in Spinney Green. A bottle of wine with the evening meal fitted the image, and so did frequent restaurant meals and evenings in fashionable wine bars and public houses. They seldom went to the same

220

place more than once or twice, the purpose of the outings was that Carol was prospecting and indulging her yearning for the good things of life. His principal objection was the cost but he did not always bother to say so because it would be thrust aside with the promise that the New Zealand money would bail them out.

She was careless how money trickled away and the more negligent she was the meaner he grew. He saw that happening but could do nothing to influence her. They began to argue about money, whereas they had only ever discussed it. Finally there were rows, neither of them compromising. She frightened him then, taunting that she would get whatever she wanted and leaving him to worry whether that meant she would steal if he did not agree to the expenditure. She had done it once before, making him fret that she had bought an expensive camera when their finances were at a low ebb. After she had teased him to her satisfaction she claimed she had found it by the beach huts in Southwold.

'That's stealing,' he had said, shocked.

She was sardonic. 'No, I found it.' But the tone cast doubt on whether that was true. 'Anyway, it must belong to those boring Harrises. It's too nice for them.'

'We must give it back.'

'We? It's not yours, it's mine now.'

'All right, you must give it back.'

'What will you do if I don't? Hand me over to the police?'

No, of course not, he wouldn't do that. But once the roll of film was used up he gave the camera to Mrs Moore at the Boatman saying he had found it lying around and believed it belonged to some of her guests. The rightful owners were thankful and if they wondered at the delay between their losing it and his returning it, they did not say so. By then he was convinced Carol had not found it by the huts but stolen it from the hotel. He tried to put the matter of the camera out of his mind after that holiday. At the time, he offered to buy her a camera but she said they bored her, and when the photographs they had taken with the Harris's camera were developed she hardly looked at them. The theft was never referred to again, and there were no other occasions when he suspected her.

Dutton always avoided conflict with her. It was easy to tell this with hindsight although the pattern was well established before it occurred to him that it was so. Then, one evening last November, there was an explosive row. To their astonishment he was the aggressor. Why it happened, and why it happened just then, he could not understand. He came home a shade late as the train was delayed and found Carol flitting about the house in a creamy lace dressing-gown. Her fingernails were freshly painted a dangerous red and she had spent part of the day at the hairdresser's. She said she had booked a table for them at a new restaurant some miles away and was about to change into a new dress.

This was not the evening he expected or wanted, but he had always fallen in with this sort of arrangement before. Suddenly he was roaring anger at her extravagance, at her failure to have a meal ready for him when she had been free all day, at the way this sort of thing was always happening, and so on. He could not remember the words nor those she hurled back at him, but what he could not forget was that she rushed at him, fingernails raised in attack, and he flung her aside. The coffee table was tipped over as she fell. Then there was an uncanny quietness.

She lay with her head on the edge of the kerb, an ungainly figure looking up at him in disbelief. She did not move and made no sound but as his hands reached out to her the expression on her face changed to horror.

# 30

Holly broke her silence on impulse next day. She had been to lunch with a pop star who was feeding the *Daily Post* the dirt on his band who were splitting up. It was a tawdry tale, with the more fascinating allegations too libellous for printers' ink, but Holly had concocted two hundred words to accompany the rather good photograph Rain Morgan wanted to run. Now Holly could snatch a break.

She asked the taxi driver for Kington Square, where Rain was enjoying a day off. 'Hi, it's Holly,' she told the entryphone. 'Can I come up?'

'You know I never speak to the press.' The door catch clicked and Holly was admitted to the hall and the climb to the top floor. Rain had opened her flat door, too, and gone back to her exercises. She was a brilliant pink velour shape doing something painful in rhythm with the urgent beat of a record. Holly gave a shriek of laughter, Rain uncoiled and turned down the music. 'Don't laugh,' said Rain. 'And above all don't tell anyone.'

'Trust me. But . . . er . . . you do this all the time?'

'Well, not in the office, for instance.'

'But every day?'

'Not enough days or I wouldn't ache so much.'

She rubbed a protesting thigh muscle. 'They *say* it gets easier. I don't believe them. Coffee?'

'Thanks.' Holly began to dance in her liquid way to the music, as she had danced with Joel. Here she had space and freedom. She broke off as Rain and two cups of coffee arrived. 'There's something exercising my mind and I want to share it with you.'

Rain assumed an attentive pose. Holly told her about Carol

Dutton, ending with the exasperation of finding that the car key discovered in the desk fitted the door lock and not the ignition. 'Maybe it was just as well. There was no sign of a driving licence in her name and I know if she'd got the ignition key she would have wanted to test her conviction that she can drive. All we could do was look inside the car but there was nothing there except a street directory with her name written in it in someone else's hand.'

Rain said: 'If you're feeling protective about Carol don't mention any of *this* in the office either. The newsdesk would have one of their bloodhounds on her doorstep in no time asking irritating questions like "How do you feel?"'

'If I said anything the first question would be why did it take me so long to discover who she was? No, not a word.'

The record came to an end and Rain took it off. 'Dutton's an odd character, I'm not surprised she's frightened of him and wants to get away. Remember that scene in their garden when it seemed he was going to thump her with the spade?'

'I remember the speed with which you got your eye to that knothole in the fence once he began shouting.'

'Good journalistic practice,' Rain said primly. 'You believed everything Carol said?'

'I believe *she* believes it, and we've seen his bad temper for ourselves. If anything, I'd say she was holding back some of it, afraid I might think she was exaggerating.'

Rain ticked off points on her fingers, then said: 'So the general picture is she has no recollection of her past, the few things she thinks she remembers he discounts as nonsense, she's scared of him and would leave if she had the money to buy her escape.'

'Yes. She didn't ask me for money, she didn't ask me for anything but a listening ear. But I am the only person she could turn to and I don't know what to do.'

'Or whether you ought to do anything?'

'I'm sure I ought to try. She's so miserable and trapped. All her sensible practical attempts to help herself have foundered. I am afraid for her.'

'You don't think she's suicidal?'

'No, but how will she be in a few months if the pressure

doesn't let up? I admit I've wondered how I'd feel if she reached that stage. I'm the only person who knows the mess she's in.'

Rain said: 'Getting her away from Dutton doesn't solve everything, does it? She would have to make her living in some way and she can't even type, despite what Dutton says.'

'It's a mystery how she and Dutton ever got together. She doesn't fit in at Shepherd Road – well, OK, neither do I but we can all see why that is. Carol Dutton's problem is hidden behind a lot of lies, Dutton's lies.'

The telephone rang. David Rokeby saying he had been asked to chair a radio chat show and would like Rain to be one of the guests. She chose not to ask what had become of the top television job the nation's favourite pop psychologist had tipped her he had been promised. She had always found it sound psychology never to remind the subject of a gossip column paragraph about anything.

'When?' she asked.

'Recording tomorrow.'

'Who's let you down?'

'Unfair, I'd suggested you in the first place.'

'I'll find out so you might as well say – who was it?'

'Betty Blount. Either she's decided she needs the beauty sleep or else her contract for the breakfast show forbids it. Will you come?'

'On condition you buy me dinner tonight and remind me about amnesia.'

'After your performance in Betty's Boudoir I thought you were the expert.'

'It's serious this time, and you've got several hours to read up the textbooks.' She said to Holly: 'Fate takes a hand. That's David Rokeby, a friend from university days.'

'And a former lover?'

'Would I tell you if he were?'

'Would you have to?'

Holly decided her support for Carol Dutton ought to consist of encouraging her memory to return, a matter in which Dutton was being obstructive. She would ask Carol to talk in greater depth about the things she half-remembered and if there was a way of putting those things to the test then Holly would help her do that. On Wednesday morning she called on Carol before going to work. Carol had a sketch of the garden in her hand.

'Peter agreed last night that I should get on with this. I might as well, it gives me something to do. I've already phoned the garden centre at Spinney Green and asked them to send a man to quote a price for the work,' Carol said. Holly saw the plan was twofold: a skilfully drawn diagram backed by an attractive sketch showing the future view from the Duttons' kitchen window. She couldn't type but Carol Dutton had a talent for drawing. Holly complimented her and they talked about the plan until Holly had to leave. While Carol was taking her mind off her difficulties it was a pity to drag her back to them. Holly put off discussing those shady memories until another day and by then she would know what David Rokeby and the cuttings of the Mystery Woman story had to say about amnesia.

The estimate for the gardening was higher than Carol expected. She resigned herself to Dutton scrapping the project. Disappointed, she went out into the garden to think about cheaper alternatives. The Parkers' back door sounded and Jean was calling to her over the fence. 'You're having the garden done at last, then? I saw the man from the garden centre. I've been telling Peter he ought to see to it, before the summer comes.'

'It's not certain. I've been asking for an estimate of the cost.' And she had been enjoying discussing with the man her design and how to make it a reality. A spark of excitement had come when she recognized how familiar the designing and instructing processes were to her. She *nearly* knew why.

'Tell him you'll have it for your birthday present. That's what I do with Ted and it always works. Well, they never know what to buy, do they?'

Carol was shaken by the realization she did not know when her birthday was. When she asked Dutton about it that evening he told her she was born on June 12. The date suited her very well and she used the ploy Jean suggested. Dutton agreed to pay for the gardening, his only caveat being that she should under no circumstances 'mess about with' his rockery.

Dutton had returned to the office that Tuesday, pretending an upset stomach kept him home the previous day. Mary Partridge, balanced on his desk, remarked that he still didn't look well. Dutton went for one of his lonely lunchtime walks, sitting in a square with a sandwich and then taking the emptier back streets in a circuitous route to Pegwoods. He was nervous of the busy thoroughfares where the woman with Carol Dutton's face might materialize or where Marcia Cohen might latch on to him.

His head was clearer, calmer than for some time. He had not slept soundly on Monday night but tiredness lulled his fraught nerves. He was disgusted with his erratic behaviour over the past couple of weeks. Each time he thought he had decided the shape of his future and how to achieve it, he had gone off at a tangent. He had intended to keep the woman at Shepherd Road, then he had meant to drive her away, then he had planned to run off and leave her. He had been muddled and inconsistent. Floundering from one thing to another had been unconstructive.

That Tuesday, Dutton faced a truth he had never faced before. As long as the woman who now called herself Carol Dutton was alive and her memory could be revived, he was in danger so he would have to kill her. He thought he knew a way.

Leaving Pegwoods early on Wednesday afternoon, saying he had stomach trouble again, he went to see Dr Andersen. Andersen did not have an appointments' system but Dutton was in the waiting room early so he was seen soon after evening surgery started. The doctor asked after Carol, remembering how he had been asked for her medical record by the staff at Princes Hospital in Leamington. No, Dutton said, her memory had not returned although she seemed to have glimpses. Yes, he agreed, she ought to go and see Dr Andersen and be referred to a specialist at one of the London hospitals. His story that he was himself having difficulty sleeping was demonstrably true – the darkened eyes and pallor would have convinced anyone – and he left with a prescription for sleeping pills.

The pot lay in his overcoat pocket that evening while Carol tentatively told him the cost of shaping and planting the garden. He thought it was comical that she was so nervous, so ready for him to stamp on her hopes. He considered them the best possible thing. A well-designed and expertly modelled garden was unlikely to be interfered with if ever he moved away from Shepherd Road. It was an insurance policy. Providing the rockery was not disturbed then all would be well. She was so frightened of him he knew he had her agreement.

As he looked forward to his evening's viewing he wondered how soon the new garden would be completed. Because then he would kill her.

## 31

Carol told him the next evening that the garden centre could start work that week. He was pleased by the speed. It left him little space for doubt or dithering.

He packed her off to bed early with a sleeping pill. She did not resist taking it. He had not expected her to. Patterns of behaviour were so quickly adopted and she would fear that if she crossed him she might forfeit approval for the new garden. Once her bedroom door was closed between them he smiled his cold smile at her foolish state – never quite trusting him, never daring to challenge him.

He knew what it was like, never knowing how a person would react, when you might get away with something and when you might not. First it had been his mother, toying with him so that he could not be sure when she would bully and when she would show no interest in what he did. Later, his wife. He could not keep in step with her moods, was prey to her demands, her rejections. And both women had known what they were doing. Manipulating. Frustrating. Ill-treating. But now he was in no one's power. The power was his, and it was his turn to exercise it on someone weaker.

Dutton went to the bathroom cabinet and emptied down the washbasin most of the contents of a bottle of proprietary cough mixture. Then he carried the liquidizer from the kitchen to the lounge, poured the remainder of the mixture into it and tipped the newly prescribed pills on top. With the television set turned up to confuse the noise, he ground the pills until the mixture was smooth. After a few noisy seconds he was back in the kitchen using a funnel to transfer the liquid to the cough mixture bottle. He washed the funnel and liquidizer and put them away. The bottle he locked in the boot of the car, the empty tablet container he put in his bedroom. Keeping the pot was an afterthought, one of his inspirations. He wiped it clean and left it on the dressing table. Carol would get her fingerprints on it when she moved it to dust. One day that could be important.

He could not sleep that night for a long while. When it came, sleep brought the nightmares and he woke to wander the house. He went back to bed and dozed, again the horrors woke him. Once it was light he got up and went out into the garden. The new plant on the rockery was not taking root. The rain had again washed the earth away to stain the stone. Dutton scooped soil with his fingers and pressed it around the roots but it compacted. Anger heated him. The stallholder had promised the plant would do well on a rockery but he had been cheated. It was dying.

Indoors again he dropped off to sleep on the settee at the very time he ought to have been stirring and making ready for work. The paper boy did not break his sleep, the sound which woke him was Carol opening the door of the room and catching her breath. She did not expect him lying there, he ought to have been on the train to work. He met her surprise, a look which transformed into the face in his dreams. He shrank back on the cushion, petrified until his brain unravelled who she was and where he was and that this was not the hideous thing it seemed.

For her there could be only one explanation: that he had dozed off and overslept. Momentarily startled, she recovered and went to make tea and help him be ready for the next train. And all the while she was marvelling that he had been so frightened of her, as frightened as the afternoon he found her with the spade.

She asked him for the money to pay the gardeners. They wanted half in advance, for materials. He prevaricated. He was so late there wasn't time and yet he did not want to delay the work. She said: 'Leave a signed cheque and I will fill it in.'

He did, dropping it on the kitchen table as he rushed from the house. Then she sat with the cheque in her hand, the hopes once set aside stirring within her. She was there when Holly called. 'I've been given this, it's supposed to be for the gardening.'

'But you're wondering what else you might do with it.'

'Yes.'

'Don't build too many dreams until you know how much is in the account.'

'I'll only take what I was going to pay the gardeners. It was going to be my birthday present, so it's fair in a way.'

Holly said: 'Fill it in and I'll drive you to the bank.' Carol fetched a pen. Holly said: 'There's just one thing – won't the bank think it odd you haven't signed it yourself as this is a joint account?'

They chanced it and drove to the bank at Spinney Green. Holly sat in the car and the minutes slid away until Carol, flushed and close to tears, came running back. 'I feel so humiliated. I was treated like a criminal. The woman clerk asked why I hadn't signed it myself, just as you thought. And I said my husband had gone to work with the cheque book and I had only this cheque and needed cash today.'

'She couldn't argue with that, surely?'

'No one argued, they just looked at me with gimlet eyes, all those clerks with nothing better to do. And she produced another cheque and asked me to make that out instead. So I did, not realizing what was coming. When she had it she didn't pay the money over. She took the cheque away and then the manager came and said my signature didn't match the one they held on record.'

'*What!*'

'He said it wasn't at all like the original and he would not pay out any money. Of course, I said this was ridiculous and he showed me the signature he had. He was right, it's not a bit like mine, but it *is* like the writing inside the street directory.' She groaned, a hand clutching at her hair. 'Holly, what am I going to do? You know why this is so awful, don't you?'

'Because you can't pay for the gardening either now and Peter will find out.'

'He'll find out because the bank manager is going to tell him. The more I begged him not to the more definite he was that he would. And the more I begged the more suspicious I must have looked. I'm sure the man didn't believe I really am Carol Dutton.'

They were silent. Holly took her back to Shepherd Road, unable to suggest anything that might help. She was short of time and dropped Carol off outside her house promising to telephone later. Carol's phone was ringing as she let herself in. 'Hello, Carol!' said Marcia Cohen. 'Sorry about the long silence. I kept meaning to ring but you know how it is. Interruptions all the time.'

Carol did not mean her to escape this time. 'Marcia, when can we meet?'

'You're sounding funny again. Are you sure you're all right?'

'I'm fine. What do you mean by funny?'

'Your voice seems . . . *funny.*' Marcia struggled to explain then gave up. 'It must be the Spinney Green air. I ought to come over and perhaps it will do something for my vocal chords, too.'

Carol said: 'I've got gardeners in for the next few days, so could we meet early next week?'

Marcia's reply was interrupted. 'Sorry, I've got to go. Duty calls and all that. Let's say Monday. I'll phone you that morning as soon as I know where I'll be. I'm only here until the end of this week. Gypsy Marcia on the road as usual!'

She rang off. Carol found her maddening and then thought that she couldn't think that because they were friends. Marcia Cohen was another piece of her jigsaw which did not appear to fit. Worse, Marcia was a will-o'-the-wisp, something that was almost but never quite in reach.

Holly drove to the *Daily Post* with considerable misgivings. She knew, via Rain and David Rokeby and newspaper cuttings about the Mystery Woman, that loss of memory was exactly that and did not encompass a change of personality or taste. She also knew it could not involve a change of handwriting. Handwriting was as individual as a fingerprint, even the most astute forgers could be caught out by the expert eye. The law was rich with examples.

'If people who try to disguise their writing fail, how can

anyone achieve it by accident?' Rain was equally mystified. She ran her finger down the names in her contacts book then asked Rosie, her secretary, to get Professor Doye on the line.

'He's probably in court giving expert evidence in a fraud case, he won't want to be bothered with the sort of silly questions you and I ask,' said Holly.

'He'll be nice – remember how the *Post* got his daughter out of the clutches of that American religious sect?'

'Pay-off time?'

'Right.'

While Rain talked to the professor, who was as happy to hear her as she predicted, Dick Tavett came and leaned over her desk impatient for the outline of stories he would offer at the morning conference. Holly told him what he needed to know, but he replied that it sounded as though Rain was working on something better there and then. 'Professor Doye's always news,' he said with a glint in his eye.

'It's not about him, he's just giving an opinion . . .'

'Fine, about a sleepwalking forger?'

'You're thinking of somnambulism, we're talking about amnesia.'

Tavett trailed a hand where his hair used to be. 'OK, an absent-minded forger. So who is it? A film star? A duke? Someone big?'

'Someone very small,' said Holly. 'And I hate to ruin it, Dick, but this is a private enquiry not a mission for the *Post*.'

Tavett felt for the missing hair again. 'Pity, I like the sound of a sleepwalking duke committing forgery.'

Before she ran into the conference Rain relayed to Holly what Doye had to say. 'As we thought, it was about as foolish as asking whether loss of memory could change your voice or the shape of your nose. Of course, he was too courteous to put it like that but that's the burden of it. What we should be asking isn't why Carol Dutton's signature varied so markedly but why the signature in the book and on the bank records isn't hers. I must go, Dick's savaging what's left of his hair.'

Holly cupped her chin in her hand. Dick Tavett was correct, this was far more interesting than anything they were going to write in the gossip column although not for the reasons he meant. All the items they ran began with puzzles gently teased apart. Each question they started out with yielded an answer and usually experience forewarned them what that answer would be long before they completed the enquiries which proved it so. The optional answers to any questions were very limited.

And yet the harder Holly concentrated on Carol Dutton's problem the denser it became. Up until the moment she came out of the bank it was possible to argue that Carol, obviously deeply unhappy, was exaggerating. If Holly had not already disliked what she had seen of Peter Dutton then she might have been less ready to believe what Carol told her. But the business at the bank destroyed any theory that Carol, however unintentionally, was making things up. Odd and frightening things were happening around her, and Holly wondered how much longer she could stand it.

She thought of her conversation with Rain at the flat and her own comment that the truth about Carol was hidden behind Peter Dutton's lies. And that, she thought, was probably all there was to it. It didn't do to manufacture complex theories, the answer to any puzzle was simple. Often mundane, sometimes startling, occasionally sordid but basically simple. So Holly tried to persuade herself that Peter Dutton had signed his wife's name for expediency when opening the bank account and the deception had only come to light after the account was transferred to Spinney Green. The nagging thought was that Carol insisted the signature the bank held was not like his either and the bank was presumably satisfied about that, too.

With a few minutes to pass before morning conference ended and the hard work of the day began she rang Carol to suggest the useless cheque be thrown away and Dutton given an excuse. Unless the bank manager telephoned Dutton at work she could have a few days grace before a letter arrived and he knew what had happened.

'I've torn it up and I'm going to say I tried to get cash because I thought the gardeners would prefer that,' Carol said. Again she was alarmed at the ease with which she was ready to deceive and lie.

'No doubt they would, that should be plausible.'

'They are going to start work today all the same and I've promised them the money tomorrow instead.'

As Carol put the telephone down she saw the gardeners' van draw up outside the house. Two muscular young men got out, fetched spades from the back of the vehicle and advanced to her front door. Within minutes the new garden for 7 Shepherd Road was under way. By the time Peter Dutton left Pegwoods at lunchtime the patch of weeds at the far end of the plot had been cleared and the route of the path was being marked out with wooden pegs. Dutton expected something of the sort to be going on and would have been upset if it had not. There was a lightness in his step as he sensed things moving to a conclusion. His own part was nearly at an end, this lunchtime should see the next important measure taken. Then it would be a waiting game.

He knew where he was going but not precisely what he would buy. The doubt added piquancy. Weaving through the streets he came to a large health food shop where people were browsing among unfamiliar packages, stealthily reading booklets instead of buying them, or queueing for wholewheat rolls or weighty dark pastries and vegetarian pies. Past the displays of goats' yogurt and packets of raspberry-leaf tea and camomile he came to the corner where the herbal remedies were stored.

Dutton knew the size bottle he wanted, all he had to do now was choose something with an appropriate label. On the third shelf down he found a leaflet extolling the virtues of one company's products. Most of them were things he had never heard of although, if the leaflet was to be believed, they were all staples of medieval medicine. Then a name leaped out at him from the shiny print: feverfew. The company was marketing it as a modern rediscovery for the treatment of migraine, a term he believed was no more than a fancy name for a headache.

Dutton remembered feverfew well enough, that odoriferous plant lurking at the end of his own back garden. He remembered his wife tasting it and the bitterness she complained of. He scanned the shelves and was lucky. The feverfew bottle was the right size. Carol had mentioned several headaches, Dr Renfrew had warned him she might. And now he would have this preventive treatment to hand. He smiled his icy smile. The mixture would be as bitter as the ground-up sleeping pills must be, she would hate taking it but he would stand over her and make sure she did.

She told him that evening about the muddle with the cheque. He sneered at her stupidity, made out a fresh cheque for the garden centre. How foolish she was, letting the gardeners bully her into handing over cash so they could avoid declaring it for tax. Perhaps one of the things she had forgotten was that there was very little honesty about. He went into the garden. The new path was a dark snake over the lawn, from the concrete patio to a far corner.

'It'll look all right,' he said while Carol waited anxiously.

'You'll get a better impression of it once the pond is dug. About here.' She paced out the site in front of the rockery. The path would run between the two. The young men, Phil and Jon, had been scathing about the rockery, criticizing its construction and saying it ought, by rights, to be demolished and rebuilt.

She had been occupied all day and it was not until she joined Dutton for the evening's television viewing that she relived the humiliation at the bank. He had not mentioned a call from the bank manager, presumably a letter was on its way. She decided to wait for the letter and then tackle Dutton about the signature on the bank records. Did it mean he had got someone else to sign her name to open the account, and if so why? He must have realized she could never draw on it so why create the illusion of a joint account?

Whatever his reasons her practical position was that even with a cheque she was unable to get money. Only the branch at Spinney Green, where the account was held, would accept a cheque without a cheque card and she had no card; but the bank at Spinney Green would not accept a cheque she signed. Her eye moved towards the hearth rug. She could still sell that. Thinking about it she went to bed. Before she put off her light Dutton appeared with cocoa and a sleeping pill. Her hand wavered but as always it was easier to do what he wanted than live in fear of his anger.

Dutton watched a programme for another hour and then fetched the cough-mixture bottle from the boot of the car. He tipped the contents of the feverfew bottle down the kitchen sink and refilled it with the ground-up sleeping pills. Before he screwed the cap back on he touched the liquid with a finger and put it to his tongue. It was extremely bitter. After putting the feverfew bottle in the bathroom cabinet and the empty cough mixture bottle in his coat pocket to throw away next day, he went to bed happy. Everything was in hand. No more preparations. When the right time came he would know what to do, and Carol herself would tell him when it was time.

# 32

On Friday things back-pedalled. Only Jon came from the garden centre, apparently to dig out the pond but in practice to collect the money. He came late in the morning, his tousled red head suggesting he had just fallen out of bed. He yawned his way through a cup of tea, pocketed the cheque, made a start on the pond – and then made his excuses, saying Friday was a terrible day, nothing ever got done then, but he'd be back on Monday with Phil and they'd really get to grips with the job then.

Disappointed, Carol cleaned the house. She removed from the dressing table an empty pill container, putting it in the bathroom cabinet. She chose not to throw it away because Dutton was perverse enough to be angry about it. As she put it on the shelf she read the writing on the label, and froze. The prescription had been made up on Wednesday but what had become of the contents? Somehow Dutton had emptied a pot of pills in two days. Maybe less. She did not know how long the pot had been on the dressing table. It didn't appear odd that he should be taking sleeping pills – after all, he was always urging them on her and he had blamed a bad night when he dozed off in the lounge. But the riddle about where so many pills had gone in so short a time made her nervous. She made up her mind to take no more pills or anything else he might thrust on her. She felt once more the panicky urge to run away from him.

She found she was shaking, fought to control herself. It steadied her to remember she was no longer alone. She had Marcia Cohen to look forward to and Holly Chase was her ally. Carol had not seen Holly that morning, or not to speak to. There had been the thump of Holly's front door, a glimpse

238

of her gaily clad figure dashing to her car. Joel was out in the street soon after, walking, camera in hand, towards the other end of the road where new houses were still growing.

Around lunchtime Holly made amends, telephoned to suggest Carol thought hard about those half-memories and then next Wednesday, when Holly had a day off, she would help her put some of them to the test. 'We could go to a riding school I know in the Chilterns and see whether hills and horses really do mean anything to you, if you'd like. But maybe you'll have another idea.'

Jean Parker, coming home from the baker's, invited Carol for a cup of tea. Ted was there, too, taking a break from gromets. Jean handed her the tea and then tipped her head in the direction of Holly's house. 'I see she's only got one in there now. The other one didn't last long.'

Carol said: 'Dan will be back, he's working away for a few days.'

Ted said: 'This one doesn't seem to work at all.'

'He's a photographer,' said Carol.

Ted sniffed. 'Always hanging around.'

Jean gave a meaning look. 'It's not what you expect, is it? In a place like this?'

Carol hopped on to safer ground by mentioning the gardening. 'Oh, they're all the same,' said Jean. 'Get a workman in to do a job and it's all mess and off they go leaving it half done.'

'And it's hand over the money first or they won't start at all,' said Ted.

'I think it will be worth it, though,' Carol said. 'As long as it gets done next week, well before the grass starts growing.'

'Next week,' Jean scoffed.

'You'll be lucky!' Ted shared her view. 'Take your money and vanish, that's what those types do. I'd lay even money you won't see hair nor hide of them on Monday.'

'You see,' Jean said patiently, as though she were telling a child, 'workmen think they can get away with that sort of trick in a decent district because people around here don't like to complain.'

'That's right.' Ted backed her up. 'If they tried it where we lived before they'd be asking to be beaten up.'

Jean glared at him. 'What Ted means is that people wouldn't put up with it.'

'Isn't that what I said?'

Carol left them to untangle whether their last address was truly in such a rough neighbourhood as the unfortunate Ted had let slip. The rest of her day was uneventful, the weekend with its pitfalls lay ahead. Holly's support was giving her strength to hold on, not to jump until she was clear where to go and how to get there. She had Wednesday with Holly to look forward to, and possibly Marcia Cohen before that, and until then the gardening to absorb her interest. Also, Dutton had been easier. So long as she avoided upsetting him she should be able to prevent angry scenes.

Food was running low and on Saturday a trip to the supermarket in the next suburb was due. Carol wanted to go, but Dutton wasn't in favour and as it was cold and raining he used the weather as a good reason for her to stay home. She gave in. The pattern was repeated and he was visiting the supermarket the same day as Holly. But he was already trundling his wire trolley around the shelves while she was parking the car and hurrying through the rain with Joel.

Joel, running ahead to dodge the downpour, waited for her in the doorway of the disused shop next to the supermarket. 'How about this?' he said as Holly, gasping, ran to join him. She shook rivulets of water from her hair. 'Look, Holly, don't you think this would make a terrific studio?'

'Daydreamer!'

'Main road frontage, next to the supermarket – what more could a rising photographer want?'

'The rent money?'

'Yeah.' He shrugged. 'But it's a good daydream.'

They flattened their faces to the glass door, shading their eyes so they could see the extent of the premises. Joel said: 'Of course, I might be prepared to sub-let to help out with the rent.'

Holly caught her breath. 'That envelope.' She pointed. 'On this pile of mail.'

'So what? It's all junk mail, nobody lives here. You know how it is with those free newspapers and circulars – the people delivering have to get rid of the load. They don't care if it makes sense or not, they see a letterbox, they shove something in it . . .'

'I know, I know. But can't you read the name on that envelope?'

He bent his neck. 'How come journalists can read upside down?'

'Trick of the trade. Come on, tell me what it says.'

'It says "Mrs Carol Dutton, 32 High Street . . ." '

'Not the address, just the name. Carol Dutton.'

'The same as the woman next door in Shepherd Road.'

'Doesn't that seem peculiar to you? Why should her letters be going to an empty shop?'

'It's junk mail, it doesn't matter.'

'No, it's over-stamped with the name of the bank that sent it and it was posted in the West End. The Duttons used to bank at a branch there until they moved the account to Spinney Green, she told me.'

'OK, so there are two Mrs Carol Duttons and one used to work in this shop. It's a coincidence, two people with the same name.'

Holly demurred. 'And the same bank? I hate coincidences, I don't *trust* coincidences.'

'Tough,' said Joel. 'There's a lot of it about.' Holly followed him into the supermarket.

Dan came home that afternoon unexpectedly. His wildlife film was progressing well but the weekend's rain proved too much and the producer abandoned work until Monday. He had a lot to tell Holly and Joel about otters. They didn't object, at least it was more cheerful than the murder series. There didn't come a convenient time to tell him anything about Carol Dutton. Joel didn't mention the letter in the shop because he was busy doing a job for *Jet*, and so Holly kept the story to herself. On Monday she was going to make time to talk to Carol fully before going to work, and their plans for Wednesday would be laid as soon as Carol said what she wanted to do. And on Monday Holly would tell her about the letter.

Wet weather persisted all weekend. Only Joel was happy.

The Parkers were annoyed that they could not get out into their garden. Now that Peter Dutton had followed Jean's little suggestions and was seeing to his patch they must look to their laurels, as it were. The Duttons watched a considerable amount of television and read the papers. Daniel Marcus fretted that a continuation of the rain could hamper Monday's filming and Holly read fitfully, her mind frequently wandering away from the book to wonder what might be happening next door.

Through their identical bay windows the occupants of the three houses looked on drizzle and commented on the degree of mud being washed from the unturfed frontages of the Phase Two houses. Then a drain over there became blocked and water pooled. The Parkers were rehearsing in their minds letters of complaint to the council first thing on Monday morning. Dutton enjoyed watching the miniature disaster and the inconvenience it was causing: cars slowed and swung to the wrong side of the road as though it mattered to keep their tyres dry; pedestrians splashed by making wide detours. Holly went out with a stick, jabbed at the offending drain and freed it.

Monday, pleasing everyone, was dry and sunny but the ground was sodden, and when Phil and Jon came their faces were as long as Sunday. It was going to be heavy work digging the pond and they now regretted the misspent Friday. Jon wore the look of a young man who'd had such a lively weekend he had never been to bed – or at least not to sleep. And Phil, who had been less lucky in his entertainment, did not want to hear about it. Jon, though, was regaling Phil and anyone else in earshot with snippets. Lack of sleep had not made his tongue tired.

Towards the end of the morning Phil thought of an alternative to Jon's boastful chatter and asked Carol to lend them her radio. He tuned to the local commercial station and then had to endure Jon singing along with the records being broadcast. Carol got away from the noise as much as she could by taking the newspaper into the lounge to do the crossword. She was expecting a phone call from Marcia Cohen to say where she was working. The tentative arrangement had been for Carol to meet her for lunch that day, but Marcia had left it far too late for that. Perhaps she would ring and suggest Tuesday instead. Carol waited, but the call did not come.

She was interrupted twice. First by Ted Parker shouting over the fence to insist the radio was turned down because his wife had a headache. And secondly when Jon tramped into the house to say they had run into a problem.

'You'd best come and see.' Now that his professional expertise was to be called on, the weekend's fun was forgotten and the face solemn. Carol followed him up the garden to where Phil, leaning on his spade, waited. Phil jabbed the spade into the hole. There was a 'clunk' sound which he did not offer to explain.

Carol said: 'Er . . . what is it?'

'A pipe,' said Jon.

'Sewer, maybe,' said Phil with another clunk.

'Oh.' Carol bowed to their superior knowledge of these matters. 'So . . . er . . . what happens now? You have to dig it out?'

Phil and Jon sucked on their teeth as though her idea hurt. Jon said: 'You don't want to go interfering with a pipe like that, you'd have to take up half the garden to get that out, most likely.'

'Most likely,' said Phil.

Carol peered where they peered. The dark brown pipe with its crazed glazing was several feet down and set to follow the course along the length of her pond. 'What can we do, then?'

'Not a lot you can do,' said Jon in the way of workmen who refuse to solve a problem before building it to terrifying proportions. It would not have astonished Carol if he had said the only reliable recourse was to move house.

Phil shifted the spade and said to Jon: 'Well, of course we could . . .'

'Oh, yeah, we *could*, but that would . . .'

'Sure, but if it's only . . . I mean the lady doesn't want this pipe right through her pond . . .'

Carol said: 'No, she doesn't. So how can we get around it?'

243

'That's it, isn't it?' Phil said. 'I mean, the only thing we can suggest is that you move the pond.'

Carol put a hand to her cheek and thought. Her mind was taking the project back to the drawing board, remembering the other schemes which might be revived. Jon and Phil assumed she was committed to getting them to dig out the offending pipe with all the extra backbreak that would cause. Jon said: 'Must have been an old house on this bit of land sometime, to have a pipe like that.'

'Built to last, them sewers,' said Phil to sow doubt on the practicality of shifting one.

'And, of course, you never know what trouble you're starting if you tamper with old pipes.' Jon added that for good measure.

Phil took pity on Carol. 'I'll tell you what would be your best course, if you don't mind my saying so.' She nodded encouragement. 'Well,' he said, 'if we shift the rockery back to there . . .' he swung out with the spade '. . . and put the pond in front of it . . .'

'Yes,' said Jon, convincing her their double act was rehearsed. 'Swing the whole thing round a bit and take it further up the garden. It would give you a bit more lawn by the house, too.'

Carol smiled. This was her original plan. 'Yes, it would work very well, I'm sure.'

'But your old man built the rockery and doesn't want it touched.' Jon recalled the conversation when he had first come to the garden. 'You can tell him there wasn't actually any choice, can't you.' He gave her a conspiratorial wink.

Phil said to her: 'Reckon you've won this round.'

She held back. Phil said: 'We'd be all right over there, we can see where this pipe is heading and it's not going to affect the rest of the garden. We'll fill in this hole and start further back.'

'Yes,' Carol said suddenly. 'Yes, that would be best.' She paced out the new arrangement, gave exact instructions and left them to it. They refilled the hole, dismantled the rockery setting its plants aside, and then went off to lunch. During her own snack she alternately exulted about the change and

244

worried how Dutton would react. But she reasoned that all would be well once he saw how much better a properly constructed rockery was and how the new siting improved the whole shape of the garden. He would soon forget that first rockery, even though he built it himself.

After lunch she did some cooking and began to read a novel Holly had loaned her. She heard Phil and Jon return through the side gate and the distant sounds of their voices and her own radio. Soon she also heard the ring of her front door bell. Ted Parker, flushed and angry, stood there. 'It's about that radio, Carol. I've been out to them once and now they're at it again. It had better come from you this time. I've got my work to do and I've got Jean lying down with one of her bad heads.'

He was deflated by her total agreement and looked ashamed of making such a fuss. 'I know it isn't half as loud as this morning but it's Jean, you see. Every noise is murder for her.'

Jon switched off the radio at Carol's request and gave a baleful look at the Parkers' back bedroom, unaware that this was the abode of grommets and that the invalid was collapsed in the front bedroom. Had he realized he would have been even more put out. Surely everyone knew you had to have pop music loud, or what was the point? Phil drew his mind back to the digging and Jon took out his ill temper on the sodden earth. Carol retreated to the novel, hoping there would be no more breaks and the pond would be completed and the new rockery built before Dutton came home. She spared a thought, too, for Jean Parker suffering in her darkened room with her headache. Then she began to read.

Moments later she started up as a police car pulled into the kerb outside her house and a young constable went to Holly's front door. Through the wall she heard the rumble of footsteps as Joel came downstairs. There were voices on the doorstep and then a second policeman left the car and the voices were all inside the house. Joel's was raised in anger but the other two were low and dogged. The conversation went on for a long time. Carol wished Holly was there because Holly would have known what to do. She was not happy that

245

Joel would. She wondered how far it would be interfering to phone Holly and tell her what was going on, and decided that if Joel were taken away in the police car it might be reasonable, but not until then.

Another sound broke into the afternoon. She feared the cry came from next door but no, Joel's voice and the other voices were still arguing, cutting across each other with impatience but their tone had not changed. Then she knew the sound came from her garden. Through the kitchen window she saw Phil backing away from the hole, unable to take his eyes from it. Jon was quicker, he was already half-way to the back door. Beneath his red hair his face was shocked into paleness. 'Bloody hell,' he gasped. 'There's a body out there!'

# 33

Carol could not find words. Jon was jabbering about the awful moment when he realized what they were unearthing. Half-sentences trailed, ended in shudders. Carol found herself flopped on a kitchen chair, Jon leaning over her. Had he thought she was going to faint and made her sit? Through the window Phil, in slow motion, was still backing off the dark grave.

Then Jon was no longer with her. His voice was coming from the lounge. She followed, weak-kneed. He had the telephone but his hand was wobbling. 'Bloody hell!' he said again and dropped the receiver. He was staring, utterly confused, at the police car outside. 'How did they . . . ?' He shook his head to clear it.

Carol recovered her voice. 'Next door,' she said. 'The police went next door.' The thrum of voices through the wall confirmed it.

Then the garden was full of policemen and the air full of questions. She could answer few of them. Phil and Jon kept a nervous distance from her. They would sound sympathetic when it came to telling the tale back at the garden centre and around the pubs, but their immediate response was to dissociate themselves from the person who had brought them to such unpleasantness.

The only friendly, familiar face was Joel's. Curiosity had brought him tagging behind the police, who lost interest in him once their enquiries were upstaged by an apparent murder. A strong cup of tea appeared in her hand, she thought Joel had made it.

A voice was saying she would be better off to wait in the lounge and not see what was going on outside. But it was all so remote from reality that it made no difference to her. More police came, some in plain clothes. A middle-aged man wearing a trilby and carrying a bag arrived. Someone looked into the kitchen, saw her and led her into the lounge. She did not know what had happened to Jon and Phil.

A policeman was asking her questions and writing down her answers. Her mind teemed with information, with puzzles and putative answers but they were not connected with the questions which were being put to her. The police wanted to know where her husband was, how long they had lived at the house, who built the rockery, had she any idea there was a body under it? The last question made her grimace. 'Hardly, I shouldn't think I would have let anybody dig it up if I had known.' The police officer did not see the absurdity of the question. He admonished her with a look which said this was no laughing matter.

There was much tramping back and forth through the side gate. Then she was ushered into her kitchen while the police used the telephone. The garden was almost deserted, just three policemen. A vehicle drove off down Shepherd Road, and she guessed the body was being taken away. Covers were being put down in the garden, already there was nothing to see.

She answered more questions, put by a Detective Inspector Morris and a female colleague. The woman police constable sat on the sofa and intermittently asked whether she felt all right as the repetitive business went on. It was all *why*, like listening to a small child. *Why* did you tell the gardeners the rockery must not be moved? *Why* did you change your mind? *Why* was the rockery built there in the first place?

Her answers were all vaguely unsatisfactory. On impulse she told them about the hospital in Leamington, her difficulty in settling into Shepherd Road and the troubled relationship with Peter Dutton. She said she had made attempts to get away, and said why they failed. They let her talk. Clearly it had nothing to do with their enquiry, but there might be some pointers and police were going to be at the house until her husband came home. Their real questions were for him.

Peter Dutton had always wondered how it would happen,

if ever it did. But he had not imagined walking up Shepherd Road and letting himself into the house to find two police officers in his lounge asking him what he could tell them about the body of a woman in his garden. He had pictured himself spotting their distinctive patrol cars as he reached the street corner, so that he would have the chance to flee or, better, to compose his mind as he walked the last few hundred yards.

In real life they took him unawares. He had hung his coat and stepped into the lounge before he saw them. One man stood near the door, the other faced him. Carol was sitting on the settee, avoiding his eyes. There was an atmosphere of menace which told him they were not double-glazing salesmen, they were quite definitely police.

He thought fast. His surprise must be obvious, but that was natural for anyone who arrived home to find these two and this atmosphere. He asked the futile questions anyone would ask: 'Who are you? What do you want?' He was relieved his voice sounded normal.

The younger of the men, a Cockney who looked as though he had settled for the police service after a rough life in the boxing ring, said nasally: 'Detective Inspector Morris, Mr Dutton. And this is Detective Sergeant Patterson.'

Patterson, taller, prematurely grey, had replaced the woman constable an hour ago. He grunted. Dutton assumed an expression which said that this was all very well but what were they doing here?

The Cockney went on: 'I have to tell you that the body of a woman was uncovered this afternoon in your garden. It was buried beneath a makeshift rockery which we understand from your wife you say you built yourself.'

Dutton resented the word 'makeshift' but let it pass. He saw that Morris had chosen his words carefully, allowing him to dodge if he wanted to. But he was not going to play that game because it was pointless: in the end it could be proved, by receipts for the materials, that he had indeed built the rockery. Lying about it could trip him up. The rule was to stick to the truth as far as one might. He could afford to admit to building the rockery because he had already raised the game far higher than Morris knew or would ever know. He could not lose.

Morris asked Carol to leave them and she went to the kitchen, then to her room. She understood she would not be permitted to sit in on the interview with Dutton. It would not do to have one suspect hearing what another had to tell the police, and at the start of an investigation everyone was potentially suspect. A numbing thought struck her. The relief she had felt at unburdening herself to Morris and the woman constable was diminished. Perhaps it would have been wiser not to have told so much. She had said things they could never have guessed, and Dutton would never have told. Her ramblings had made it likely he would be asked about some of them, and she could only fear what his explanations might be.

Downstairs Dutton was showing shock and squeamishness at being told there was a corpse in a back garden and obliquely accused of placing it there. Again he felt he had the advantage of Morris and Patterson: he had lived through this scene in his mind often and they were new to it.

Why had he built the rockery where he did? That was where his wife wanted it, it was part of her scheme for redesigning the garden but she had been ill and only recently been keen to complete it. Why had he forbidden her to let the men move the rockery? How would you feel, inspector, if you'd gone to all the trouble of making the thing for her and then she wanted to tear it down and rebuild it somewhere else? Could he offer any explanation for the body being there. None, absolutely none. Dutton had decided on that 'none' long ago. No romancing about what might have gone on there before the house was occupied, no fancy theories or elaborations.

The Duttons were asked not to go into the garden and both recoiled at the very notion of doing so. Then the police left, saying Dutton could go to work as usual the next day and they would know where to get in touch with him. Otherwise he would hear from them the next evening. 'And the next, and the next,' he thought as he shut the front door on them. He was relieved they had not taken him away for questioning, that his replies had not convinced them of his guilt. He congratulated himself on coping extremely well with the interview – hinting a shade at Carol's delicate nervous state but leaving them in no doubt about her unreliability as a witness. He would have loved to know what she had told them.

They had little conversation, during which neither of them gave much away. They preferred to confine themselves to expressions of horror and amazement. Then they went to their separate rooms to lie awake worrying.

Carol lay still, staring at the blackness of the ceiling. Her thoughts spun. Everything suggested she was living with a killer, however she rearranged the facts she could not escape that. Dutton had known the body was there. Mentioning to the gardeners and the police that he had insisted she should not interfere with the rockery fell far short of conveying how adamant he had been. If they could have seen his determination, or watched his panic on the day she took a spade and he must have thought she was going to dig, or if her words could have illustrated the animal fear in his eyes, then the police could not have accepted his cool rejection of the idea he knew about the body.

And who was this woman who had died and been buried in such a wretched fashion? The police would be sifting the same missing persons' records they had checked when she lay unnamed in a Leamington hospital. Perhaps if they got the right name they would make a link between the woman and Dutton. If not they would consider all the other people who had been connected with the plot of land. No one, in modern times, had lived there but the builder's labourers working on the houses would come under scrutiny. So would people in other parts of Spinney Green who might have had access before the site was cleared for building.

She stopped theorizing and brought the subject back home. The dreadful thing was she so disliked Dutton she did not baulk at believing him guilty of murder. Another story grew in her mind. She must have discovered what he had done and run away but the stress unbalanced her and she suffered a traumatic amnesia from which she had not recovered when she was injured in the road accident. That all fitted: his fear of her, his lack of interest in helping her recover her memory, his determination to isolate her so that if her memory returned she would not give him away.

The room felt stifling, she was thirsty. Making no sound she got up to fetch a drink of water and glided downstairs in the dark. There was enough moon to let her find a glass and run the tap without putting on an electric light. She stayed in the kitchen and drank her water.

Upstairs Dutton was giving in to the terrors he had kept at bay all evening. He had not gone to bed but was sitting on the edge of it, head in hands, restraining himself from moaning aloud. Nightmare had overtaken him. He could get through the days, he was confident of that. Nights were what frightened him. Nights had always been worse. He would survive the days at Pegwoods and the evenings answering police questions and when they took him down to the police station, which they were bound to do sooner or later because there would be no other suspects, then he would come through it stoically. Splendidly. But at night he would be in sleepless despair and that would give him away. Dutton took a deep breath and stood up. This agonizing was useless. Wouldn't it be natural for anyone who was being questioned about a body in his back garden to lose a little sleep over it? Of course it would, a couple of dark patches beneath his eyes would not be confirmation of guilt. Yet supposing the police asked at Pegwoods about his state of health and mind over the previous months, what then? Might a chirruping Mary Partridge, slighted more than once in her advances to him, take her revenge by saying he hadn't been himself and it all dated from when his wife left?

Another deep breath. For heaven's sake keep calm and think straight. His wife left in November, which explained his odd behaviour if any had been noted. She returned in February. All was well, because there was no missing wife to explain away. Unless he had been seen digging the hole in the garden, dragging the body out after it had lain in the lounge long enough for the blood he had not known was there to dry into the carpet and he had faced the fact that she was dead, then there was going to be no proof. Whoever the woman in the garden was she could not be Carol Dutton because Carol Dutton was alive and well and sleeping in the next room.

He nearly smiled. He had been exceptionally clever, far more clever than Morris or Patterson would ever credit. In the end they would be left with another unsolved death on their hands. The dead woman was unknown and so would be the circumstances of her death. All they could be certain of was that the woman was not Carol Dutton.

In bare feet he opened the door and went on to the landing. He did not need to check, he knew she was there but pushing open the back bedroom door he listened for her breathing. Reassured, he slipped downstairs. When he reached the kitchen he switched on the light and the woman sitting at the table screamed. Dutton was scared stiff. He had heard her upstairs, but if she was here then who . . . His hand went to his left eyelid which was nervously alive.

'What are you doing here?' His voice was savage as he disguised fear by attack.

She said nothing. She leaped from her chair, dodged further round the table from him until her back was to the window. She did not intend to say it but the accusation broke from her: 'You did it, didn't you? I know you did it.' Her words alarmed her, she was dismayed at the effect they might have on him.

He laughed, without humour. 'You told the police that, did you?'

Dumb, she shook her head. No, oh no, he mustn't believe that. She felt sick with fear.

He laughed again. 'If you did, they can't have trusted you.'

He approached the table. She was caught in the gap between the table, the end wall and the kitchen sink. He relished seeing her there, like a vulnerable animal waiting for its persecutor to have done with it. He enjoyed the feeling of superiority and power it gave him. Then he had one of his inspirations. He said with sarcasm: 'I wonder how long you can go on pretending you don't remember anything about it? How much longer do you think the police are going to believe that?' And then he went upstairs.

She could not move, as an animal does not dare to move although it has seen danger walk away. She was trembling, violently. Dutton had accused her and she had no way of telling whether he was right. Could she be responsible for that woman's death? The idea was not new, it had come to her earlier when she was telling herself everyone was a potential suspect. With awful premonition she realized that Dutton might blame her and if he did she had no means of refuting it.

# 34

Dutton, afraid of sleep, lay on his bed dozing on and off until the night sky lightened. Then he stayed there, wide awake for a couple of hours, thinking about the day ahead and the trials it would present, the precautions he ought to take.

The police would search the house. At some stage they were bound to and he would have to be welcoming rather than obstructive. He was sure they would find nothing to prove that the woman in the garden was his wife or that he was responsible for her death, but he ran over all the points. The only hazard was the feverfew bottle in the bathroom cabinet. Examining it they might realize its contents were a lethal dose of sleeping pills and not an innocuous treatment for migraine.

Removing the bottle before he went to work was imperative, although it was a pity to pour the mixture away when he was going to need it soon. Nothing that was happening now was deterring him from the course he had set his mind to. He still meant to get the new Carol to take a fatal overdose and die an 'accidental' death, because if she ever remembered her true identity then the corpse in the garden would be named. Until she was dead, he could not be safe.

Wearily he got up and went to the bathroom. It was a nuisance but it would be safest to throw away the mixture, rinse the bottle, drop it in a waste-bin on the way to the station – and then get more sleeping pills and another feverfew bottle in a few weeks time. Then he reconsidered. Getting a second lot of tablets from the doctor would be far more difficult than getting the first ones. The old bottles in the cabinet each contained a small number of tablets, but not enough to make up the massive dose he needed. He thought he might be wise to register with a doctor at Spinney Green after all and try to get some from him. Unfortunately doctors were no longer reliably lavish in dispensing pills and he could find that he'd chosen one who refused to co-operate.

Wasn't there a safe place where he could hide the feverfew bottle until he needed it? Not the desk which the police would open, nor the tin trunk where they would root about among the carpet pieces, and not the car. The cheeky thing would be to bury it in the back garden, a thought which provoked a cold smile. More sensibly he thought of burying it in someone else's garden. The idea was irresistible. He would bury it beneath one of the flowers in the border that separated his house from the Parkers'. There would be weeks of entertainment watching Jean Parker watering and nurturing it until he was ready to whisk it out one dark night and then, when Carol's nerves were nicely frayed and she felt a headache coming on, let it do its deadly work.

He opened the bathroom cabinet, thinking he would bury the bottle before day grew any lighter. But he could not find it. Twice he went through the shelves before he knew what had happened. Carol must have had the beginnings of a headache last night and helped herself to the mixture to ward it off. Dutton struggled to stop himself laughing aloud. Wasn't it extraordinary how capricious Fate would lend a hand?

But he must recover the bottle from her bedside. If she had taken a lot he would clean the bottle and throw it away on his way to the station. If she had taken only a tiny amount then he would bury it in the border for use later. There had been two or three tablespoonfuls in it and the dose for the feverfew was one tablespoon according to the label. He suspected that a tablespoon of his mixture would be fatal, but he would have to go all day wondering whether she would be dead or alive when he came home.

Her door made no noise as he opened it. Light from the bathroom brightened the room sufficiently for him to make out her figure. He went up to the bed. There wasn't enough light for him to see the bottle, so he must feel over the bedside table until his fingers located it.

As his hands stretched out there was a piercing scream and Carol was fighting to get out of bed, away from him. He flung himself out of the room, her shriek reverberating in his skull. With shaking hands he got dressed. By the time the paper boy came he was ready to leave the house, only the knowledge that he must do nothing abnormal cautioned him against going immediately.

He was furious at what had happened. One minute everything was obvious and the next he was thrown into confusion, understanding nothing. Carol was not drugged and dying, she was not even asleep. And he still did not know where the bottle was.

As early as he dared he left the house, desperate to get away from it. At the end of the street he met the postman and took his mail. There was a letter from the bank manager at Spinney Green, reporting that a woman had tried to cash a cheque for several hundred pounds but been refused because her signature was not the same as the one on record. Dutton did not read to the end of it, he tore it up and threw the pieces in a rubbish bin outside the newsagents. If he ignored the matter then the bank would, too.

Carol had locked herself in the bathroom, the only room with a lock, once she heard Dutton go downstairs. She stayed there until she heard the front door shut. She was still trying to marshal her thoughts. All she knew for certain was that she would not spend another night under the same roof as Peter Dutton. Whether he had killed the woman in the garden or not, he had come into her bedroom that morning to kill her. For some time she had lain there hearing him moving about and when the door opened and his dark outline loomed up she had frozen. Then his hands had reached out to strangle her.

Downstairs she made herself a cup of tea, then dressed in the blue suit. Ted Parker was taking in the milk when she opened her front door. 'They say they've found a body in your garden,' he said without preamble.

'Yes, I'm afraid it's true.'

'Who was she?'

She shook her head. It was enough to be quizzed by the

police but to have to answer to the Parkers, too! And there would be more of it. The press would be on her doorstep soon and they would recognize her as the Mystery Woman. Perhaps the police would tell them that's who she was. Either way, they would not leave her alone.

Ted Parker said: 'Are you all right?'

A weak smile. 'As well as can be expected. It has been an awful shock.' A change of tack. 'How's Jean?'

'She hasn't heard about this yet. I thought it best not to say anything while she's poorly. She's sleeping now, I'll tell her all about it when she wakes up.'

Carol got away before he could revert to the body in the garden. She rang Holly's doorbell. Daniel Marcus came, surprised to see her because he was expecting a crew car to take him off on location.

'I'd like to see Holly, if she's got time.'

'She hasn't, but Holly always makes it. Come in.'

Holly appeared from the kitchen, her face both welcoming and concerned. 'Joel told us last night,' she said, sweeping away explanations. 'Come and have some breakfast, you look as though you've had a bad night.'

'I didn't sleep much.' Later, when Dan had gone and Joel was still to come down from his bedroom she told Holly how Dutton had terrified her by coming into her room. 'And there's something else, something I didn't tell you before. He told people at Southwold that I was mentally ill. I'm afraid he will tell the police too.'

'That's ridiculous.'

'But it's the sort of information people accept, isn't it? I know they did at the hotel. Now he's hinted to me that I killed that woman, or at least had a part in it, and that I am pretending amnesia as a cover-up.'

'He can't have told the police or they would be taking more interest in you.'

'They were questioning him until late, I expect they will be back today to see me.' She paused. 'I want to see them, anyway. I can't spend another night in that house with him. I've got to get away so I'm going to ask them if they can arrange that for me. If I tell them what happened in my

258

room this morning they will understand that I really am scared.'

Holly said: 'I'll find you somewhere to stay tonight and then tomorrow we can go and do what we were going to do, just as though nothing else mattered. Your biggest problem is to find your memory.'

Joel appeared then, wearing a sullen expression. 'He's in his garden now,' he snapped. 'Out there looking the picture of innocence.'

Carol jumped, thinking he must mean Dutton. Holly knew better. 'Joel, you stay right in here and keep out of his way. We don't want any trouble with our neighbours.'

Joel snorted. 'Trouble! I'll give him trouble, interfering old . . .'

Holly cut in, explaining to Carol: 'He means Ted Parker. The police were making enquiries because some houses further up the road were broken into and Ted Parker told them Joel was always hanging around and was no doubt the thief.'

'He didn't bother to tell them I was taking photographs,' said Joel. 'They came here yesterday saying I had been noticed down that end of the street. Well, you bet I was noticed. How am I going to go anywhere around here and not be noticed?'

Holly held out a cup of tea to him. 'Didn't I say this was pioneer country?' And then: 'But yesterday wasn't all bad news, was it, Joel? You got some good photographs of the police activity next door and several papers have taken them.'

'All I hope now is they remember to put my name on them and they remember to pay me.' Joel, who was not to be consoled, took his tea and carried it upstairs.

Holly took three ten-pound notes from her purse and put them on the table. 'This is for you, Carol. I know you won't have a penny. Now what I propose is this: stay here this morning and see the police, explain to them you refuse to spend another night at home and when they have finished with you get the train into town and come to my office.'

'The police will want to know where I am going to stay, won't they?'

'Yes, and I expect I can tell you as soon as I have made a phone call.'

She returned to the kitchen a few minutes later saying Carol could tell them she would be at 5 Kington Square. 'I told Rain she owed me a favour for working on the day of my house move, and this was pay-off time.'

The police car drove up then and Carol went to meet its occupants. Morris and Patterson were familiar but the other men strangers. They set about searching the house and garden. Carol watched, there was nothing else for her to do. The search was careful, courteous and thorough. When they came to the lounge she sat on the window sill, out of the way, and was ready with an explanation that the desk was always kept locked. The drawers slid open. She saw nothing in them she had not seen in her own search.

Detective Inspector Morris, recalling her rambling story the previous day about life at Shepherd Road, raised an enquiring eyebrow. 'I thought you said he always kept this locked, Mrs Dutton.'

She felt herself flush. 'It *was* always locked,' she said, and knew how unconvincing she sounded. Dutton had succeeded in making her seem unreliable.

If the inspector had a rejoinder ready it was forgotten. An exclamation from a colleague who had lifted the hearth rug snatched everyone's attention. They gathered round the stain. Carol mentioned how she had herself come across it. Morris remarked drily that it was strange she had not bothered to tell him about it when she had been telling him so much else. Her feeble reply was that she had forgotten.

'Oh, yes,' he said without kindness, 'the famous loss of memory.' She was sure then that Dutton *had* planted the seed of suspicion about her culpability. And she wished unsaid much of what she had given away. Today's questioning was more incisive than yesterday's and she knew that as the days wore on and the scraps of evidence were jigsawed together, the pressure would increase.

The stain was photographed. A test was carried out on it, she overheard that the result was positive. Then the carpet was lifted and carried out to a van. From her window she saw the face of Ted Parker, pressed into his bay and absorbing every detail. She stepped aside before he spotted her. His turn would come, she thought. The police wouldn't ignore him for long.

But before the police went to question Ted Parker or any other neighbours who might have seen anything unusual about the Duttons and their garden, Ted Parker was ringing Carol's door bell. It was mid-afternoon. Morris was recommending a uniformed constable to make tea, and Carol was resigned to another long question and answer session. They all jumped at the urgent sound of Ted leaning on the door bell.

'Quick!' he was shouting as the door was opened. 'Come quick . . .' Two policemen went with him. Morris got up and went to the front door. Carol moved to the window. The constable with the kettle in his hand dithered, no longer sure how many cups were needed.

Morris wanted to get on with the interview, with Patterson taking down Carol's answers. They resumed but everyone had half an ear on what was happening next door: on the agitated voice of Ted Parker, on the arrival of an ambulance, on the stretcher which was carried out to it, and on the alarm which began to sound as soon as it reached the end of Shepherd Road and joined traffic.

A police officer came from next door and reported that Jean Parker had been found unconscious.

'One thing after another around here, you might say,' Morris said in his nasal way.

Patterson grunted. Then: 'Mrs Dutton, how would you explain . . .' And they were off again.

The telephone rang. Marcia Cohen. 'Carol! I've seen that stuff in the *Standard* . . . It's in your street, isn't it? The body in the garden?'

Carol cut across her chatter. 'Where are you?'

Marcia named an office in Chancery Lane. 'I'm sorry about yesterday. I was going to phone you about lunch, wasn't I? Were you very mad at me? The thing is, there's a young solicitor here and he . . .'

Carol pushed in again. 'I'm coming into town this afternoon. We can have tea when you finish work.'

Marcia hesitated. Carol thought Marcia was going to put up an objection, drinks with the solicitor or something like that. Marcia didn't. She said: 'Do you know, you sound really peculiar . . .'

Carol ignored it. She didn't want any digression. 'Shall we meet outside Chancery Lane Underground station. About 5.30?'

'OK. On the Chancery Lane side of Holborn. And you can tell me all about the body then.'

Carol promised.

The police let her go. Towards the end of the afternoon the questions dried up and they let her go. She had given the address in Kington Square, asking that they withheld it from her husband. Patterson wrote the address down.

She waited until they had driven away and then walked down the road after them. It was a novelty to be actually going somewhere. She had never imagined her escape like this, but this is what it was. After all the scheming at Shepherd Road and the agony of Southwold, the reality was an anti-climax. A train arrived as she reached the platform and she was on her way to King's Cross and then the Underground to Chancery Lane and Marcia Cohen. She had set out, excited to be meeting Marcia. Then an aching doubt she barely acknowledged resurfaced in her mind. And she was frightened.

## 35

Carol took up her position. Not the one Marcia Cohen had suggested but across the road from it. There was a Woolworth's and she stood in one of its doorways, pretending to browse but with a view across Holborn. She was determined to get a good look at Marcia Cohen.

It was not easy. Home-going commuters buffeted along the street and down the steps to the Underground. Around each entrance knots of people grew, some buying newspapers, some hanging around waiting for others. Carol kept her attention on the figures that poured out of Chancery Lane, a turning off the main street, and stopped near the station. Within ten minutes she had a handful of women to choose from. Some were ruled out by age, there were several possibles. Some of the possibles were met by friends and moved away.

Carol could not stretch things out too long. She had to trust that Marcia would be more or less on time – she had only a short walk to the meeting point – but she did not know how long Marcia would be willing to wait. Carol pushed it to fifteen minutes and then there was only one of her possibles left.

It was a woman in her middle twenties, short and plump with black hair. She was swaddled in a thick coat and wore high-heeled boots. One foot was tapping with impatience, and she sometimes wandered to the Underground exit and back. She checked everyone who came up the steps into the street. Definitely, she was waiting for someone she expected to come that way.

Carol was trembling in nervous apprehension. When Marcia Cohen came into her consciousness a couple of weeks ago she seemed a lifeline to the past. There were endless questions for her, if only they could meet. The questions were still waiting but before they were put Marcia would answer Carol's secret doubt.

Carol emerged from the doorway and slipped into the crush of pedestrians. Using them as cover she went into the Underground but left them to queue for their tickets. On the other side of the ticket hall she climbed the steps to where the woman who must be Marcia Cohen waited for her. Her heart was loud, her legs leaden.

The short, black-haired woman was directly in front of her as she came to street level. Momentarily Carol thought she had been recognized, but the light in the woman's eyes died and she looked away. Carol did what she had planned. She acted the part of someone at a loss for directions. Then she went up to the woman. 'Excuse me, could you tell me how I get to Fleet Street?'

'Fleet Street? You can take any street on this side of the road to cut through to Fleet Street. It depends which end you want to be.'

'Whichever end the *Daily Post* building is.'

'Then you'll do best to take Chancery Lane. Just up there . . .' And so on, with arm waving.

Carol thanked her and walked towards Chancery Lane. She did not know how her legs held her up. She was badly shaken. The voice and the manner convinced her she had been talking to Marcia Cohen. And Marcia Cohen had not recognized her! Once she rounded the corner she sagged against a doorway for support. Her brain teemed. All the riddles of her life at Shepherd Road were solved: *she was not Carol Dutton*. The doubt she had put out of mind, the impulses to get away had been justified.

She thought she might faint. Her heart was racing, there was a singing in her ears. She forced herself to hold on. She must get to Holly. If she collapsed in the street she would be taken to hospital, and perhaps kept overnight for observation. She walked on down Chancery Lane.

Uncertainty surfaced. She had expected that to be Marcia Cohen, so had she exaggerated the similarity of voice? It was

264

essential to check. She'd go up to the woman and say: 'Are you Marcia Cohen?' Just like that, it was all she needed to know and it was intolerable not to know it. She spun round, ran back towards Holborn.

The woman with the black hair had gone. Carol's face drained. She had no way of knowing whether the woman was Marcia who had given her up and gone home, or someone else who had been met. Feeling limp Carol set off for Fleet Street again. She argued with herself what to tell Holly.

At the newspaper office she had to wait in the reception area for a few minutes. She picked up a copy of the *Standard* which lay on a low table. Joel would be pleased. The front page picture was of a number of policemen and a man with a trilby bending over a hole in her back garden. The accompanying story was brief, the police having given the barest details about the finding of a body in a garden at Shepherd Road and an enquiry beginning.

Holly came bounding out of the lift. 'Hi! I've got the key to Rain's flat, we'll go straight over and she'll be along later.'

'Can you leave now?' She worried Holly was slipping away early for her sake.

'Sure. This place owes me a lot of favours. Besides, this is important.' Holly took her through a back door and into a car park where the bribed attendant had found a space for her.

During the drive Carol persuaded herself not to mention the Marcia Cohen episode. What had happened was inconclusive. She would have been wiser to arrange to meet Marcia at the entrance to her office, not at a popular meeting point. In the morning she could phone Marcia at work and check whether Marcia had been there. She would ask what she had been wearing, whether she had been asked directions to Fleet Street. Never mind what Marcia would think about the questions, they would be put to her. And then Carol would really know.

Carol was thrilled by Rain's flat – its space, its tranquillity, its style. 'This is beautiful.'

'Isn't it?'

'Holly, this is very kind of both of you. You don't know how much I appreciate . . .'

Holly waved her gratitude away. 'Ah, but I do.' She made coffee while Carol wandered around the room treating it like a gallery, looking at and loving the things Rain had gathered around her: the South American embroidery, the African pictures, the swathes of silk from the Far East. The room was much more to Carol's taste than anything she had seen at Shepherd Road. She was tempted to blurt out to Holly that she was not Carol Dutton. Yet denying it would be wild and extravagant, and until she had made sure of Marcia she could not know what was true.

Holly offered her a cup. 'Rain said we were to make ourselves at home so we may as well start with her coffee.'

'Home.' Carol was wistful. If only it were.

Holly read her thoughts. 'It's nice to come here and pretend.'

They talked about what they would do next day. Holly suggested Carol telephone Spinney Green police first thing and ask whether they needed her. If not Holly would meet her in town and they would drive out to the Chilterns and a riding school. Even if it didn't rekindle her memory, Holly said, it would give her a restful day out and she was much in need of that. And there would also, in the private grounds of the school, be the chance for Carol to try her skill at driving Holly's car.

Afterwards, while Holly washed the cups, Carol curled up on Rain's sofa and fell asleep. She dreamed of clear skies and green fields and the scents of summer. It was the best sleep she had enjoyed for weeks.

While she slept Peter Dutton was trudging unwillingly from the station to Shepherd Road. He had passed an unpleasant sort of day because some of the morning papers were carrying photographs of police recovering a body from a garden in Shepherd Road and it was useless to hope his colleagues would not remember he lived there.

'Have you seen this?' Johnson was saying as soon as he went into the office. He was holding up the *Daily Post*. 'What's it all about?'

Lewis had another tabloid. He read out: 'A body, believed to be that of a woman, was recovered yesterday afternoon by police called to a house in Shepherd Road, Spinney Green. It was discovered by landscape gardeners digging a pond.'

'Ugh!' said Johnson with an exaggerated shudder.

Dutton hung up his coat. He'd have to say; they'd find out and it would seem odd if he hadn't told them. 'Yes, I've seen it. It's my garden.'

The other two were stilled as sharply as a freeze frame. They had meant to tease him but never thought it was true. This sort of thing didn't happen to people one knew.

'I say . . .' spluttered Lewis.

'. . . what an awful thing,' finished Johnson.

Dutton felt he ought to expand. He tried to gauge what the average man would do if he found himself with a mysterious corpse in his garden. The average man would theorize a bit, about how the body must have been there before the house was built. But he couldn't do that because he might want to tell the police something different later and it wasn't sensible to say one thing here and another thing there.

The silence stretched. Then Dutton said: 'Well fire away, what do you want to know that it doesn't say in the papers? We've had the police asking questions ever since it was found – I don't suppose a bit more of the third degree will matter.'

Johnson said he was sorry, and took an interest in the papers on his desk. Lewis said he was sorry, too, and it must be rotten. He also found the day's work important. Then Dutton appeared to become engrossed and it was halfway through the morning, when he went to the cloakroom, that the other two spoke again.

Johnson rolled his eyes heavenwards. 'Anybody else would have come in here talking his head off about a thing like that. I've always said Dutton's not normal.'

'Third degree, indeed! He doesn't recognize natural curiosity when he sees it.'

'What do you reckon, though?'

'You mean did he do it? The police can't think so or he wouldn't be sitting here today, would he?'

Johnson said: 'That's true, but they have to have enough evidence before they take someone in, don't they?'

'Anyway, who could the woman be? If he were still saying his wife had left him then we might wonder, but . . .'

They looked hard at each other, the same thought striking them both. Then Lewis said: 'No, we can't go by that.'

'He said it, though. He told us, the day he got drunk. You asked him and he said "Carol's dead."'

Lewis said a word papers like the *Daily Post* don't print. 'We'll have to tell the police.'

'But Dutton's just said *"we've"* been questioned, which means he and Carol were questioned. The police must know whether there's a Mrs Dutton at the house. We'd look pretty silly saying he told us Carol was dead when the police spent yesterday interviewing her.'

Lewis said: 'Supposing there were two Carols? It's a common name, he could have had a girlfriend called Carol.'

The suggestion was not taken seriously. 'Oh, come on, he's not quite the type, is he?'

'I'm not sure there is a type.'

Johnson's mouth was open to reply when Dutton returned. Silence again. At lunchtime Dutton made his usual early move and forced himself to keep to the normal sequence of events. If he were being followed – under surveillance as the police would say – then he did not want to do anything unusual. He bought his sandwich, took it to a square and ate it. Then he trailed around the streets.

His most acute concern was the missing feverfew bottle. The police would never find anything to connect him with the death of the woman in the garden but if they found an innocent bottle containing a lethal dose of a drug they would ask about the intentions of the person who put the mixture there. He erected complicated plans for recovering the bottle, then demolished them as unworkable and unnecessary. Drawing attention to the bottle would be foolhardy. If he could not dispose of it covertly, it was wiser to take a chance that the police would pass over it wherever it came to light.

He turned down a street, a good way from Pegwoods. Oxford Street was behind him but he wasn't sure where he was. On a corner was a pub, a cheerful hubbub emanating from it and coaxing him inside. Breaking his rules, he dispensed with routine and went in. This time he would be disciplined and have only one drink, a repetition of last time was unthinkable, especially on this day of all days.

He waited impatiently to catch the barman's eye and then carried his beer to a space where he could stand near a mantelshelf. There was a mirror above it. As he set his glass down after the first mouthful he saw a reflection which amazed him. Across the room were Johnson and Mary Partridge. She had her back to a wall and was looking up with that irritating coquettish expression. Johnson was leaning over her, darting kisses.

Dutton grew unaccountably angry. He stormed out into the street, setting off in the direction he trusted Pegwoods to be. After a fruitless detour he arrived. Johnson came in shortly after, Lewis was already at his desk. The wordless afternoon proceeded. It was broken by Mary Partridge. She poised on Dutton's desk and went through her familiar manoeuvres while she raised a query on a stock order. Dutton saw the performance for what it was. She was not making up to him at all, she was doing it to arouse Johnson's jealousy.

Dutton slammed his fist down on the desk and roared at her to stop her nonsense. She was stunned into being the gauche youngster she really was. Johnson was saying: 'Steady on, Dutton, she doesn't mean any harm.'

Lewis sat gaping. The girl and Johnson moved, to stand close together. Lewis gaped at this, too. Then Dutton was round his desk, and seizing Mary's arm he threw her out into the passage. She screamed as she thudded into the wall.

Johnson's next words were loud and incoherent. Lewis understood that it was his role to get between the protagonists and prevent anyone hitting anyone. He didn't do it. He sat tight with his mouth open as Johnson swung the first punch, which missed, and Dutton struck back with one which didn't.

More astonished than hurt, Johnson bounced against a grey filing cabinet and then slid down it to the floor. Dutton snatched his coat off its peg and made for the door. The passage was by now full of Pegwoods staff demanding to know what was going on. Mary, her sleeve rolled up, was eager for bruises and already concocting the story that Dutton was jealous of her relationship with Johnson. Dutton pushed through the mêlée and ran.

Johnson picked himself up from the floor mouthing obscenities after Dutton. The manager's secretary stuck her head into the room and they were inadvertently mouthed at her. She withdrew in haste, the scene failed to match up to the happy atmosphere she claimed for Pegwoods.

Johnson rubbed his shoulder where the blow had landed. Lewis closed his goldfish mouth. Johnson regained his chair before he spoke. 'You were right,' he said. And lifted the telephone receiver and asked the switchboard operator to get him Spinney Green police station.

## 36

The shift in tack was obvious to Dutton. The police had been waiting outside the house as he walked home on Tuesday and told him Carol was away, although they did not say where. He had left Pegwoods early because of the fracas but taken care to catch the regular train, passing the intervening time in a café at the station. It was a frail hope but just possible that the police would not find out about the incident.

Once the questioning began he guessed they had, because they were asking about his life there. Well, let them. Whatever they heard about today's outburst it would get them no nearer the truth about the body in the garden. No one at Pegwoods could know the answers.

They took him straight into the kitchen and the interview went on there, a ploy to let the garden and its grave play on his nerves, he decided. Fine. He didn't care. The garden was less horrible to him now than it had been in those early weeks. His strength of will had brought him through those weeks and it would help him now. What he was facing was only to be expected, and it was better to get it over than to be waiting for it in the years ahead. After all, he knew the outcome. The police enquiry would be inconclusive. He had nothing to fear.

Later, when light was dying and the garden no longer clearly visible, Detective Inspector Morris suggested they would be more comfortable in the lounge. Dutton followed. Morris faced him, watching him take in the fact that the stained carpet had been removed for analysis. Dutton's left temple was throbbing.

'Would you like to tell us how the blood got on the carpet, Mr Dutton? Our preliminary tests showed it was definitely blood, now the lab is carrying out the more detailed test which will tell us what sort.' The nasal voice was soft.

Dutton's brain offered fanciful answers but he rejected them. He said: 'You're saying that stain was blood?'

'What do you suggest it was, Mr Dutton?'

'I didn't spill anything, I just bought the rug to cover it up. To me it looked like coffee.'

Morris sat in Dutton's favourite chair, skewed away from the television set. 'I think we ought to go back to the beginning and start all over again, Mr Dutton.' Patterson selected a fresh page of his notebook and the questions resumed.

The telephone interrupted. Dutton took the call. Marcia Cohen. Dutton felt his colour draining and turned his face sharply away from the two policemen. 'Carol isn't here,' he said.

'She was going to meet me this evening but she didn't turn up. Do you know what's happened to her?'

Dutton replaced the receiver, cutting her off. His mind whirled. Marcia Cohen *had* tracked Carol down and Carol had kept it from him. What had Marcia told her? He had no space to think, Morris was waiting to go on.

Towards ten o'clock Patterson tossed in the suggestion that as it was known the woman died only a few months earlier, it was reasonable to assume one or other of the occupants of the house knew she was there. If Dutton himself didn't, could he be equally sure his wife didn't?

Dutton brushed it aside, but it was useful to know the police were already thinking Carol might be guilty and he innocent. He judged it was too soon to push that line himself.

Morris pursued it further. 'Is she in the habit of taking sleeping pills?'

'Quite often, not every night.'

'And do you take them?'

'Occasionally. I got some more last Wednesday.' Damn. So they could have found the feverfew bottle. Well all right, so Carol hated swallowing pills and had ground them up in a spoonful of cough mixture.

'What do you know about this?' Morris brought out the feverfew bottle in a clear polythene bag.

Dutton saw there was very little mixture in the bottle. He stiffened. It could simply mean the police had poured some out to examine it, but on the other hand it might mean Carol had taken it during the day. Morris hadn't told him where she was. Would they keep it from him if she were dead or dying? He battled to concentrate on Morris's questions instead of his own. He gave the prepared answer, saying Carol happened to have an empty feverfew bottle and used that. The lie disgusted him. There would be more because one lie always led to another.

Morris swung the bottle in its plastic prison. 'Does she have migraines, your wife?'

'She suffers from headaches, yes.'

'And she bought this bottle of feverfew to treat them?'

'Yes.'

'And when it was empty she reused the bottle by putting her ground-up sleeping pills in it.'

'I told you, yes.'

Morris steadied the bottle and set it down on the coffee table. 'And when did she do all this, Mr Dutton.' His voice had become dangerously low.

'Oh, some time back.'

'After she returned to live here?'

'No, it was before she went away.'

'Towards the end of last year?'

'October or November, I think.'

'And she hasn't bought any feverfew since?'

'It was very bitter. She didn't like it.' He remembered his wife's face, screwed up in distaste when she chewed the feverfew leaf.

'I see. So this bottle, with the ground-up pills in it, was in the bathroom cabinet untouched since October or November?'

'So far as I know.'

'So far as you know.'

'Yes.'

Morris stroked his boxer's nose. 'You've explained how a lethal measure of a sleeping drug came to be in a bottle with this innocuous label. Perhaps you could tell me how Mrs

Dutton contrived to use this bottle last October or November when the product did not go on the market until February this year?'

Patterson, ball-point pen raised, was looking to Dutton for a sign. Morris's eyes never wavered. The finger caressed the broken nose. Dutton went cold. Fear played along his spine. So she *had* taken the mixture, but Morris didn't believe it was an accidental overdose and by lying about the bottle Dutton had incriminated himself. He put a hand to his flickering eyelid. He fought to control himself. He managed a casual shrug: 'I must be wrong.'

'And Mrs Dutton must have transferred the mixture to this bottle later?' Morris was sarcastic.

'Perhaps the first one broke.' He was relieved his voice was even.

'But there might have been glass in the mixture, she wouldn't risk swallowing that.'

'I don't know what she did, maybe the cap of the first bottle got lost.'

'And maybe she went to the doctor and got some more tablets and made up some more mixture after the first bottle broke.'

'Yes. No. I don't know!' A cold sweat was making his shirt clammy.

'She didn't go to her doctor.'

'All right, she didn't go. I said I don't know what she did.'

'There are a lot of things you don't know Mr Dutton. You don't know how a body got itself buried in your garden, how you chose that spot to build your rockery, how your carpet got stained . . .'

The temple was pulsing, the eyelid twitching. Dutton knew both men were aware of the stress his body was signalling to them. He covered his face with his hands. Lie after lie. Facile, fatal lies. The sort he expected anyone else in a tight corner to tell, but which he believed were beneath him. He was assailed by shame. His brain was screaming but when he next spoke he was controlled. 'Shouldn't you be putting some of these questions to my wife? I mean about the bottle and the pills.'

274

Morris let the seconds slope by. Dutton steeled himself. His question was clever, Morris would have to reveal that Carol was dead or dying. Then Morris spoke. 'Can you suggest any reason why your wife might have wanted to kill Mrs Jean Parker?'

*Jean Parker!* Dutton was incredulous. Too late to wonder whether to invent a motive for Carol, or fake a reaction. The policemen watched. Dutton began to speak, had no voice, tried again. 'Is she . . . she isn't, is she?'

Patterson said: 'Mrs Parker was rushed to hospital after taking some of the contents of this bottle.'

'But how on earth . . . ?'

'Mr Parker asked your wife for some painkillers for Mrs Parker's migraine yesterday and she found this bottle in the bathroom cabinet. The label says it's feverfew for migraine and they thought it might help although it's recommended as a preventive. Mr Parker followed the instructions and gave his wife two doses over a period of time.'

Dutton groaned. Morris said: 'Mrs Dutton tells us the bottle was not in the cabinet when she came home from hospital. She also says she found this empty sleeping-pill container in your room on Friday.' He set it down on the table beside the bottle. 'The prescription was made up on Wednesday and two days later the pills were gone. What would you like to tell us?'

Dutton groaned again. Morris said: 'Is there anything wrong, Mr Dutton?'

Hysterical laughter, then Dutton said: 'There's a body in my back garden, my wife is out poisoning the neighbours and you want to know if there is anything wrong!'

Morris said very softly: 'I wondered whether you thought the wrong woman had been poisoned, Mr Dutton.'

With chilling persistence Morris and Patterson went round the course again. When they left it was with the promise to return in the morning and the instruction that he wasn't to go to work. He tried to unravel what they said that evening, disentangle what they meant. Was Jean Parker dead? No one had answered that, and neither had they said where Carol was.

She could not have taken the sleeping pills, too, but ought he to assume she was in police custody accused of attempting to kill Jean Parker? Or was she in hiding because she was afraid to be with him? Fatigue outweighed fear and he slept. His final thought was that it would be bitter irony if the only woman he ever meant to kill lived happily ever after and his real wife and Jean Parker were both to die by accident.

# 37

Sunlight rippled across the room and Carol opened her eyes to Rain Morgan's flat. She had spent the night on the couch, comfortable and warm and happier than she ever knew she had been. Realization of where she was filtered back. When her eyes focused the pink blob on the carpet at the end of the room uncoiled into Rain performing exercises in a brilliant cat suit.

'Rain?'

'So I am.' Rain sprang up. 'Hope I didn't wake you. I was trying to be quiet but the muscles do creak a bit. Coffee?'

'Please.' Carol stretched luxuriously. Today there would be Holly and horses and tonight she would come back here for a pleasant evening like the previous one when Rain and Oliver West had entertained her with true tales of Fleet Street. Another pleasant evening, unless the police had a different idea.

Showering in the tiny bathroom, traipsing about in a borrowed bathrobe while her hair dried, she took stock. By now Dutton might have pointed suspicion at her, claiming she attacked and killed that woman and caused the stain in the lounge. But how would he go on from there? Would he claim she buried the body and then ran away in a shocked state? Or would he confess he buried it? He had said all along he built the rockery and that would persuade anyone that he knew it was to disguise a shallow grave.

She trembled. Rain said: 'You'll be fine, he won't come here. You've got all day to concentrate on yourself and forget him.' But it wasn't easy and when Rain went off to work leaving Carol to phone Spinney Green police and then Holly,

Carol grew doubtful. At the police station she got a duty sergeant who could not tell her whether she was needed. She interpreted that to mean she wasn't.

Next she rang Marcia Cohen, to put the question that would say as much about her own identity as about Marcia's. She was going to ask whether Marcia had waited for her as arranged, and whether Marcia had given a woman in a blue suit directions to Fleet Street. She found in the telephone directory the number of the company where Marcia was working and dialled, undecided what to say or do if Marcia replied yes to both questions. But there were no answers: Marcia Cohen was off sick. Carol was bitterly frustrated. She had no other way of reaching Marcia.

Carol was about to ring Holly. Instead she walked to the long window which looked over Rain's garden and the glistening rooftops of London. If she went with Holly then Holly would bring her back and that meant eventually back to Shepherd Road. When she was there her spirit was sapped, away she was stronger and independent. She could not impose on Rain and her couch much longer. Besides, there was someone else she wanted to see, somewhere else she wanted to go. If she did not do it today she might never have another chance. She could be involved in police enquiries and maybe even convicted and imprisoned for a crime she could not deny. Years might pass before there was an opportunity to go back to where her memory began.

The phone rang. Holly, asking how she was and whether she was free of policemen for the day. Carol said: 'Yes, but there is something else I want to do.'

'Great,' said Holly. 'We'll do that.' An answering silence down the line. 'Look, Carol, you don't have to be alone.'

'I know, Holly. But I have a feeling that today I might achieve something for myself. You've already made it possible by giving me the money to do it.'

When they rang off Holly sat puzzled, perched in her bay window. Joel said: 'Is something wrong?' He was chirpy, his name had been printed beside the published photographs and a picture editor had phoned to ask him to drop in and talk about doing some work.

'Carol doesn't want to go to the riding school after all, she wants to go off on her own.'

'So?'

'So where? And will she be all right?'

Joel wouldn't share her concern. 'Maybe she's going to collect her mail from that dead letterbox.'

Holly gave a squeal. She had forgotten to tell Carol about the letter. 'No she isn't,' she said, 'but I am.' She was half-way across the room when another thought came and she spun round and picked up the telephone. Rain answered her, in an unwelcoming tone which Holly guessed meant Rosie had been borrowed by Dick Tavett for chores above and beyond the call of duty.

'Hi, it's Holly.'

Rain's tone changed. 'Good morning. You want to know what we made of Carol Dutton last night?

'Yes, how did the interview go?'

'Oh, you know my style. Very subtle, she didn't feel a thing.'

'And she told you exactly what she's been telling me?'

'Yes, and like you I believed her. So did Oliver. She thinks Dutton was going to strangle her to prevent her remembering how the body got into the garden. She says he must want her dead so she could never give away what she knew.'

Holly adopted a jokily superior tone. 'We can all see that.'

Rain said: 'Perhaps, but I'm not utterly convinced. Not in view of all the other strange things. In fact, I've found myself wondering whether he might not want her out of the way because of what she *couldn't* remember.'

Holly dropped the superior tone. Rain had lost her. Rain said: 'I've been thinking about David Rokeby saying amnesia can cut out personal memories but leave skills and general knowledge intact – which seems to be true in her case – and also Professor Doye saying the handwriting on the bank record and in the street guide can't be hers. I wonder if there isn't another element in this mystery, a third person who is the owner of the childish signature?'

'There's a third person all right and she's been lying dead and buried the other side of my garden fence!'

Rain reminded Holly of their earlier conversation when Holly said the truth about Carol was hidden behind Peter Dutton's lies, and when she reported that the gossiping woman in the hotel thought Carol was a changed woman. 'The women at the hotel seem to be the only people Carol has seen lately who used to know her before she was in hospital. And if we were to take their comment literally . . .'

Holly gasped. 'He'd have to be mad to do that. But why would the hospital have handed her over to him so easily?'

'No one would have dreamed he wasn't her husband. I don't know what checks they ran – you'd think they would have tried a few, but life being the stumbling affair it is, they might have messed it up.'

'Something in your voice tells me you are about to put them on the rack.'

'I shall sweetly ask a few pertinent questions about what pertinent questions they put to Peter Dutton. They won't be able to fall back on that line about following the usual procedure because there won't be one. These were unusual circumstances. She couldn't contradict anything he said about her, and neither could anyone else. If he offered some sort of proof that she was Carol Dutton they would have accepted it. If he had the nerve to go through with it, then he was going to succeed.'

Holly said: 'It's a hideous idea.'

'And that's all it is, just an idea. Until I've heard what Princes Hospital has got to say for itself.'

Holly, not to be outdone, said: 'While you do that I'm going to make a few enquiries of my own.'

'I thought you were taking Carol riding?'

'She backed out, she wants to go somewhere on her own. So I am going to collect her mail from a dead letterbox.'

Rain protested she had not been told anything about dead letterboxes.

'A girl has to have some secrets,' said Holly and rang off.

Holly drove to the estate agents and presented herself as a prospective tenant for the empty shop next to the supermarket. She said it might be perfect for a photographic studio. The key was handed over with a warning to be careful locking up because they didn't want squatters in there.

Holly pocketed the letter addressed to Carol and sifted the pile for others but it was the only one. She would keep it until she saw Carol. In the meantime she was disappointed not to be going riding, it had been a good outing to look forward to. Life was kind to people like Dan who had jobs that often took them out of town, and for days at a time. Most of Holly's work was in London, and Spinney Green was, well, just Spinney Green.

She sat in her car, regretting Spinney Green. She thought Joel and Dan would, too, before long. They weren't suburban people. Oh, Dan had never said Spinney Green was a life sentence. He had said it was a house they could afford in a place where property was an excellent investment and they needed somewhere to live. She wondered how long it would have to be – eighteen months, two years? – before one of them could casually mention that it would be good to be right in the thick of London again and weren't those flats at such-and-such-a-place just what would suit them? She didn't doubt she and Dan would be together in eighteen months or two years or very much longer. They weren't like Rain and Oliver and she was thankful for it.

She thought of the Parkers who were also two of a kind and of the Duttons who were not. And she thought of Carol Dutton's face when she drove her into Kington Square, all iced-cake Georgian and plane trees and window boxes dripping ivy. And Carol when she led her into Rain's flat. Expense didn't come into the equation, it was style that mattered.

She chewed over Rain's theory about the Duttons and how everything that had made Carol uneasy at Spinney Green would drop into place if it were right. It was a startling but simple answer and it provided an equally simple answer about who was buried in Peter Dutton's back garden. Yet she could not imagine how, until Carol's missing memory returned, the theory could be proved or disproved.

A traffic warden sauntered by, Holly flashed a cheeky grin and sped away before the ticket was written. Life was made up of lucky escapes – if you were born lucky. She was at traffic lights, humming to herself and looking vacantly at an advertisement for Spa Mountain mineral water when she realized where Carol had gone. In the next second she thought of driving there, and in the following one decided to mind her own business. It would be sufficient to be so sure if the police needed to find Carol. Instead, she went shopping and spent an inordinate amount on a new outfit. Sometimes you *had* to pay for style.

Morris and Patterson did not go to Shepherd Road that morning. They sent a squad car to collect Peter Dutton and take him to the police station. Joel, hearing the car arrive, snatched a photograph of Dutton getting into it flanked by policemen. Then he grinned, turned up the pop music on the radio and went back to his darkroom. He hadn't told anyone yet about the best picture of the lot. He'd actually got a shot, taken from the window of his room some days ago, of Peter Dutton out in the garden and kicking the rockery – foot out, hands flailing and mouth open as though he was cursing it. Well, wait until Dutton was convicted of murder and that one landed on the picture editors' desks! Dewinton and the rest of the crew at *Jet* would be boasting they used to know Joel James.

Shortly after Dutton was taken away more policemen let themselves into 7 Shepherd Road and began another search. At the police station Morris and Patterson conferred.

'They've brought him in, sir,' said Patterson. He was sitting at a desk, Morris leaning against the wall.

'Good. We won't rush, he can wait. Now . . . you've seen the report from the lab on that stain, Pat?' Morris had a cold and his voice was more nasal than ever, conspiring to make him sound surly.

'Human blood on the carpet, sir.'

'Exactly what it looked like, to anyone who realizes that old blood isn't red.'

'Dutton wasn't silly enough to say an animal had injured itself, and neither has he said he or his wife were cut. I should say he's too shrewd to invent an accident now.'

Morris looked down at the papers on the desk. 'Let's see what we've got.'

Patterson obliged. 'The body in the garden is that of a

young woman dressed in what appears to be a thin lacy dressing-gown. There is a fracture to the base of the skull, and the skull is abnormally thin. The pathologist says the injury was caused either with a blunt instrument or a fall on to a hard projection. If someone hit her, then they did it at an odd angle unless she was crouching with her head bent.'

Morris took out a paper handkerchief. Patterson said: 'We favour a fall because the position of the blood stain in relation to the kerb suggests she could have been killed there, either striking her head hard while falling or else by having it smashed on the kerb afterwards. But so far we have no identification, nothing to link her with any reported missing women in the right age bracket.'

Morris blew his nose. 'And so we come to Dutton who would head anybody's list of suspects because of the siting of the rockery he built.'

'He says his wife told him to build it there, and she says she doesn't remember.'

'Tell me what else we know about Dutton.'

Patterson reported that his neighbours and colleagues said he was quiet man who kept himself to himself. Morris's eyes shone. 'Funny how people always say that on these occasions. Ask them under different circumstances and they'd come right out and say he was a miserable sod.'

'Yes, sir.' Patterson ran through the rest of the things they knew about Dutton, ending up with the allegation that he attempted to strangle his wife and apparently put a lethal dose of sleeping pills in a bottle from which she might have taken a headache cure. 'If she had died it would have looked like an overdose, probably accidental unless he contrived a suicide note.'

Morris said: 'A post mortem would have proved she had not taken whole tablets because if they were whole they would not all have dissolved.'

'Dutton probably wouldn't have realized that. Anyway, that's academic because his wife didn't take the stuff, she gave it to someone else.'

'We'll never have enough, without his full and frank co-operation, which isn't on the way, to prove he meant to harm anyone with that bottle. By the way, he lied about his wife giving up taking feverfew because it's bitter. The plant is but not the potion they make from it.'

Patterson pushed a lock of grey hair back from his forehead. 'If he'd had any sense he wouldn't have given us all that rubbish about his *wife* grinding up pills, he'd have said the contents of that bottle were for him.'

Morris's eyes shone again. 'Don't give him any ideas, Pat, he's doing far too well as it is.'

Patterson ticked off the next points on his fingers. 'Mrs Dutton is unlikely to have buried that woman because she's slight and the ground is heavy. She *could* have done it but the odds are against. And that brings us back to Dutton and his rockery.'

The inspector drummed his fingers on the desk, took out the handkerchief again. 'We've either got Dutton killing and burying the woman, or Mrs Dutton doing the killing and Dutton doing the burying – or at any rate building the rockery to conceal the grave. *She* could be innocent of everything, *he* can't be.'

'Sir, there's something I don't understand.'

Morris waited, watching his sergeant pick his way towards the puzzle he was himself confronting. Patterson said: 'Dutton's bright enough to know the rockery gives him away, and the wife can't remember anything, so why isn't he doing the obvious thing and blaming her for the killing?'

'That's what I wonder, Pat. You'd expect him to calculate he could get off a murder charge by saying she did it, but instead of that he's trying to strangle her.'

'And leaving that booby trap feverfew bottle for her to find. You don't think he decided she'd be better off dead than locked away for years?'

'That's a possibility, but not if what she tells us about the life she's been leading since she came home from hospital is true. She says she felt he was imprisoning her.'

Patterson said: 'Nothing from that Leamington hospital about her yet?'

'No, my request for a report from the medical staff got mislaid. Somebody should be chasing it up today. Pat, doesn't it seem peculiar to you that she hasn't been near a doctor since she came home?'

'She says it was never suggested until the social worker came round. She's registered with a doctor at an inconvenient distance and Dutton said she was to leave it to him to sign on with one in Spinney Green. Apparently he hasn't done so.'

'Dr Andersen says she hasn't consulted him since last summer?'

'Yes.' The conversation lapsed. Then: 'You know what the trouble with this case is, sir? Everywhere you look it's Dutton's word against hers. She keeps saying she can't remember and he keeps hinting she's barmy.'

'And whom do you believe? Either of them?'

'Well, sir, he's the violent one – getting into a fight in the office . . .'

'. . . and she's the quiet type who creeps around poisoning the neighbours?'

'What do you make of the allegation he told his colleagues "Carol's dead"?'

'They also said they'd never seen him drunk before. It's hardly going to stand up under cross-examination, is it?'

Patterson grunted. Morris said: 'We'll wait until we hear from Browning at Criminal Records, then we'll have Dutton in and this time we'll get some serious answers.'

Patterson noted a sternness in the boss's eye. The last murder inquiry was still incomplete for lack of information. This one would not fail for that reason, there was perhaps too much information but none of it leading them forward. He said: 'She'll be clean. Barmy, if you like, but clean. Dutton? I don't know, I think we'll hear he's had his fingers in the till. Something sneaky.'

'No violence? We've only heard about violence, you know.'

'Yes, but he likes to think he can use his wits, doesn't he? A bit smarter than the average? I reckon if he's been had for anything it'll be fiddling the books, a bit of fraud.'

'All right,' said Morris with a laugh. 'There's a pint on it.'

A quarter of an hour later Browning rang and Morris

laughed again. 'Bad luck, Pat,' he said to his sergeant. 'Nothing known about Peter Dutton, but guess what?'

'Not the missus!'

'Thieving. Or shoplifting as the practitioners call it to make it sound different from thieving. She got fined at Bow Street magistrates court for pinching a dress from a shop in Covent Garden eighteen months ago.'

Patterson found it hard to take in. 'That just shows how wrong you can be about human nature.'

'This is a very disillusioning line of business. And you owe me a pint. Ready for Mr Dutton, then?'

Peter Dutton's illusions fractured more slowly. The tone of the questions changed but the questions stayed the same: who and how and why? They knew when and watched his distaste as they explained that the degree of decomposition told them that. They knew the age of the woman and how she had died. They watched him as they described her fatal injury.

They floated the idea that he brought a mistress to the house, his wife returned, there was a row and the girlfriend died. They tried every tack to get him to concede an iota so they could force him back and back until he had only the truth to stand on. Inwardly he smiled at their stupidity. He had only ever had the truth. As far as was possible he had stuck to it so there was nothing for him to yield, no safer ground to shift to. He could endure because he had told no direct lies, or none that mattered. The feverfew bottle was a minor disaster, but only a minor one because it had no bearing on his wife's death.

# 38

Carol was talking to Dr Renfrew. The visit was not going as she forecast on her journey to Leamington by train. Dorcas was not on duty and Irene Yarrow was on leave. Renfrew seemed less than delighted to see her, the brown eyes colder than she remembered. She kept asking whether she was keeping him from his patients and he kept saying no, she had picked a good time, it was all right. But it wasn't all right.

He said he was sorry she had not recovered and being at home had not helped. And when he avoided asking her how she had settled down and she began to tell him anyway a little of what had happened, he grew very awkward. Rebuffed and not understanding why, she knew it was best to go. She walked alone down the corridor but then he caught her up to offer as explanation or apology – neither of them knew which – that he had been telephoned by the police shortly before she arrived and he was very sorry if she was in any difficulties with the law but there was nothing he could do to help.

He did not add that he was expecting a local police officer to call in to talk to him more fully. The man had not been explicit on the phone but as he had introduced himself as a detective Renfrew latched on to the idea that Carol Dutton had been involved in something criminal. It would be an interesting court case, he thought, if her defence were to be that she had forgotten the crime. Not an original defence, of course, as some famous criminals had claimed that. But this time there would be strong evidence that she had indeed lost her memory. He had decided not to detain her until the police officer arrived although he saw that was a strange decision to explain.

Carol said: 'Recovering my memory is the only thing that would help me, in any direction at all.'

'I'm sure you will, in time you will.'

She was not heartless enough to ask how much more time and said a final goodbye. The visit was a mistake. Renfrew now appeared inadequate, his words no longer reassuring. A matter of weeks ago she had been heavily dependent on him, and the discovery of his inadequacy would have been disastrous. Now it was merely disappointing. She was heartened by that. He had not diminished, she had outgrown the patient's need for the sympathetic doctor. She had withstood the trials of Shepherd Road, struggling against Dutton and the life he attempted to impose on her. She felt strong and free and full of hope.

After she left Princes Hospital, the *Daily Post* telephoned Renfrew to talk about Carol Dutton and although he shunted the caller off to an administrator he was even more perplexed. Rain Morgan squeezed what information she could from the staff at Princes Hospital and then got Rosie to find the telephone number of Dr Andersen. She was lucky, catching him between patients.

At the end of the call she turned to Oliver, who was sitting at Holly's desk to listen, and said: 'The hospital say they gave Dutton a letter to deliver to Andersen, he swears he has received nothing.'

'Which suggests Dutton deliberately prevented Carol from going to her doctor. What do you do now?'

'Ideally, I'd march Carol straight round to Andersen's surgery, bring them face to face and say to him "Is this Carol Dutton?" '

'That would frighten the wits out of her, she doesn't suspect she's anyone else, does she?'

'If she does it's the one thing she hasn't confided in any of us. You're right, even if I knew where she was this morning and could round her up it would be unforgivable.'

'Conclusive, though. And if the answer were yes then you and Holly would have no excuse not to mind your own business.'

'I don't think for a minute the answer would be yes.' She sat watching Oliver doodle a garden scene.

He said: 'Who is going to mastermind the Carol Dutton Story for the paper once this murder is cleared up? You or Holly?'

'It ought to be Holly, she started all this.'

'You don't want to let Holly get too much credit, she's already after your job.'

'Rubbish.' The sketch had become a rockery with a corpse jutting from beneath it, Peter Dutton skulking, Holly spying over the garden fence, and so on. She pretended to chide. 'That's in very bad taste.'

'Might make a Pegwoods' cover?' He was bringing up the subject of a commission for a Pegwoods' cover with boring persistence. She ignored the remark. He started to say something else on the same theme, but the telephone saved her.

She did not know the caller, it was someone employed at Pegwoods who thought Rain would be interested to hear of the ructions going on there because of their cover for *The Face of Death*. 'I remember you wrote about it a few days ago, when you got people to say what they thought about the cover . . .'

'What's happened now?'

'They weren't very happy about the publicity, so they got on to the design house that did the cover and asked them exactly where that photograph came from. You'll never believe this – it was a genuine photograph of a victim!'

'Are Pegwoods changing the cover?'

'They've got to, there isn't really time but they haven't got any choice. Only advance copies have gone out so far.'

'Did they find out how that awful cover was approved?'

'Well, that's the funny thing. The design house gave the job to one of its new artists who's joined them straight from art school. He's meant to be terribly bright and clever although I should have thought a lot of employers would have been put off on sight because he dresses like a post-punk. Laurie Pegwood met him at his degree show and recommended him to the designers, and now . . .'

Rain and her caller broke down in laughter. When she came off the phone she repeated the story for Oliver's benefit while Rosie was dialling Pegwoods' number. Laurie Pegwood was embarrassed about the matter, not least by his smooth assurances when she had first discussed the cover with him.

'You hadn't really checked anything then, had you?' She was rubbing it in, Oliver relishing the performance.

'It didn't seem serious. I wasn't going to ring up our designers and accuse them of morbid practices.' He squirmed and she let him go on squirming. 'Look,' he said cutting across her, 'what are you going to write about all this? I mean, I don't suppose there's any chance good taste will resurrect itself and . . .'

'There's always a faint possibility but I haven't time to investigate that aspect in depth now.'

'Lunch?'

'One o'clock?'

Oliver looked scandalized. 'You had him at your mercy and you gave in for the price of a lunch!'

'Who says I've given in? There's more at stake than a paragraph in the *Daily Post*.'

When she came back from lunch she was able to tell Oliver that the paper would indeed run the story, but toning down the bits that could lead to the subject of the photograph being identified and the family distressed. 'I explained to Laurie that what was really bothering him was *that*, and the rest was fit to print because publishers are Aunt Sallys and journalism is a knockabout business.'

'How did he take it?'

'With a large vodka and tonic. And then while he was feeling very contrite at having lied to me about checking last week, and grateful to me for offering to tame the story, I got the conversation around to cartoon covers and . . .' She shrugged. 'You can guess the rest.'

Oliver pulled a disappointed face. 'You asked him to let me do a cover and he said no.'

'Certainly not. I asked him and he said yes. What has happened to your confidence in my charm?'

Oliver astonished several people including himself and Rain by hugging her. She disentangled herself. 'But there is a condition. That caricature of him comes off my bathroom wall.'

'And gets ceremoniously burned.'

'No, he asked very nicely if he could have it.'

While Oliver was congratulating himself on Rain's success Carol was walking down the slope of The Parade. There was much to admire: Georgian stucco, a Victorian confection of a town hall, architectural delights. The sun was shining as she went through the main streets enjoying the feel of the town awakening to spring. But how much more exciting to be out in the countryside, the green expanse that had flashed by her train window. The wish was barely formed before a bus pulled in to a stop beside her and she was on her way to Stratford-upon-Avon for its swans and its Shakespeare and its constant sense of occasion.

At Stratford her pleasure was more intense, there was an extra dimension although she dared not name it. If she were wrong, her disappointment would be acute. From Stratford she took a second bus not understanding why this ride must be taken, too, just satisfying an impulse. She left the bus on another whim. A coach drew up ahead of it and women trailed along the drive of a house. Carol followed them. Their voices rang happily among the elms. Cows and horses came up to a wall to watch them go by.

Across a paved yard the women went through a gateway and reached the front of a lion-coloured stone house where centuries of wind had smudged carvings. Soon they were in a great hall, a guide welcoming them in sonorous county tones and reciting the history of the place. Surreptitiously the women fingered what they were asked not to touch, stroking four centuries of patinated oak and friable fabric. Carol hung at the back of the group, tagging on to this outing of a North Warwickshire Women's Institute. No one challenged her right to be there, not by look or word. She was enjoying herself.

And then it happened. The guide led the way into the next room and Carol saw in her mind's eye what lay ahead. The room, the detail of its furnishings and the story the guide would tell about it . . . This was unequivocal memory.

291

From room to room her certainty grew: she had been to the house before, the impulse which had led her there was right as the impulse which had urged her not to give herself into Dutton's hands had been right.

In this great country house there was a familiarity she had never experienced at Shepherd Road or Southwold. The realization was exhilarating, the implications enormous. She had no need of Holly's help, she was finding herself. And she need not telephone Marcia Cohen to check what had happened in Holborn. Marcia Cohen belonged to another life, somebody else's life.

The tour of the house ended, as tours do, in the tea room by the gift shop. The ladies of the WI fell upon scones reckless with cream. Carol felt guilty but when a seat was found for her at a table and her excuse for being there cheerily accepted she became easier. Her companions thought it delightful nerve for her to join in because she couldn't resist it, and as their numbers were light – Audrey's children had chicken pox and Jane was down with a tummy bug – why shouldn't they invite Carol to make up the party?

Tea was served in the orangery, a pretty but noisy arrangement where every laugh bounced off stone-slabbed floors or glass. After a while most of the women went treasure hunting in the gift shop, to buy teatowels bearing pictures of the house or pots of jam which they would take home to compare unfavourably with their own. Carol stayed where she was, alone and thoughtful at her table as the room grew quiet.

One of the waitresses was frowning at her, a thin-featured young woman with pale hair caught back in a rubber band. Carol decided it was time to move. She went out of a different door and let herself into the garden. Beyond urns where early flowers were about to open was a knot garden, a design which had pleased the original gardeners and been kept up without break. Generations of hands had cared for the garden, the hands linking the centuries that had gone and were to come.

Carol paused on coming to a paddock bounding the garden. She was there, stroking the nose of a brown filly, when she heard sounds on the path. The waitress was coming, ahead of her an older woman, a countrywoman in a tweed skirt and stout cardigan.

Only the friction of the filly's nose against her hand proved time was not standing still. The woman came forward until she was very close. Her face wore an expression of wonder and relief. Two pairs of grey eyes stared at each other. 'Alison,' the woman said. 'You *are* Alison.' In the background the waitress nodded. She had known it since the tea room.

Carol's hand dropped and the horse nuzzled her shoulder instead. 'I think you could be right.'

'Wherever have you been? And whatever have you been doing?' The voice was affectionately scolding as she took her into her arms.

It was easy to stop thinking of herself as Carol Dutton, she had always been trying to throw that identity off even if she had not seen it quite like that. There were people around her now who identified her without ambivalence – by her physical appearance, her voice, her mannerisms, all the traits that distinguish one human being from another. She was Alison Marsh, her aunt lived in a cottage a few hundred yards away from the Elizabethan manor house she had visited like any tourist.

She explained what had taken place, hating to dwell on it, more eager to learn her aunt's side of the story. Cautiously her aunt told her. 'You went to London to see off a friend – Sally – from Heathrow for New York. To begin with I assumed you had gone with her because you didn't write. But a letter could have gone astray, you might have been thinking you were owed a letter from me.'

'You didn't know where to reach Sally?'

'No. I knew she had been urging you to go with her and I'd been backing her up. You'd ended an unsatisfactory love affair and I thought the change would do you good. Your car is gathering dust in the garage here, so that appeared to prove you were abroad.'

'I see. But what was I doing in Leamington, where I was injured?'

'I'm coming to that.' Her aunt, treading warily to avoid distress, went on. 'A few days ago a policewoman came to see me and said a handbag with your name and this address on papers in it had been found in Leamington. The police came across it in a house they were searching for stolen goods. The man they were questioning insists he picked it up in the main street in Leamington some months back, although he couldn't say precisely when.'

'So you realized I might not be abroad at all?'

'I'm afraid it looked as though something terrible might have happened. The police said they would treat it as a missing person enquiry, but you can imagine the horrible things that were running through my mind.'

'But my photograph was in the papers, and I was on television – how did you miss seeing me?'

'When was this? It all sounds rather dramatic.'

She told her aunt when it was and after a bit of calculation and reminiscence about a jumble sale cancelled because of reasons beyond the organizers' control, her aunt was able to check the date of the sale. 'The jumble sale – and your starring role on television – were the week when the villages around here had the power cuts. Well, there's your answer. No heat, no light, no hot food, no jumble sale and definitely no television.'

'But I was in the newspapers, too.'

'I didn't see you. I was probably too busy groping about in the half-dark looking for candles to be reading a newspaper. Besides, have you ever recognized anybody from a newspaper picture? I remember that picture of me in the evening paper the year I was chairman of the village Women's Institute, it was so awful even my best friends . . .'

They filled in some more of the gaps over the next hours, looked at photographs and recited family history and Alison's own. Her aunt took her up to her room, a quaintly-shaped cottage room decorated with flair. Clothes hung in a cupboard, and there were books. She admired the room with its low window that looked past honeyed Cotswold buildings and along a wooded valley.

Her aunt laughed. 'Goodness, you don't remember you designed this room? That this is what you do for a living?'

'I remember nothing about that – not about work or social life or anything I ever did or anyone I ever knew.'

So her aunt started at the beginning and told her how she studied interior design and then did freelance work in London although she was often drawn back to the countryside. 'You worked for all sorts of clients on all sorts of projects. You seemed to be doing very well, but then you went down with a broken heart, gave up your flat in London and came here. You'd got around to talking about trying London once more – and then Sally began pressing you to go to the States with her . . .'

They went down the twisting dark oak staircase, her aunt telling tortuous tales and throwing out scraps of information to tempt her memory and Alison trying to fit it all in. She felt this must always have been a good place to come back to, after her parents died, after her love affairs went wrong. It was a happy background to her life, a proof of worth and identity which everyone ought to be blessed with and so few were. A homing instinct had brought her back to it at last.

She accepted the sherry her aunt offered and they settled in front of a log fire while a room or two away her aunt's help – the pale-haired girl who had been a waitress in the tea room – was preparing supper. For minutes at a time she was able to push Shepherd Road right out of her mind, but inevitably she came back to guessing what was happening there.

She made a phone call. 'Holly, it's me, Carol. Only I'm not Carol, I'm Alison.'

Holly did not sound as amazed as she ought to have done. Alison sketched in the outline of her day and Holly told her how Rain had spoken to the hospital and Dr Andersen because the situation had made her suspicious. She had phoned Holly that afternoon and they had discussed what they ought to do next.

Holly went on: 'I've got a letter from your bank for you – I mean for Carol . . . This is too muddling!'

'You'd better give it to the police, it wouldn't make sense for me to have it.'

Holly recovered from her confusion. The Carol Dutton story had been interesting, the Alison Marsh one irresistible. Holly arranged to interview her for an article to appear when the time was right. They both knew the timing depended on Dutton being tried for a criminal offence, perhaps the murder of the woman in the garden or perhaps abduction of Alison.

After their conversation Alison delayed making her next phone call, to Spinney Green police. She had torn herself free of the misery of Shepherd Road, but talking to Holly had brought it to the forefront of her mind. She was outraged at what Peter Dutton had done to her and the cynical way he had done it. His reason seemed obvious: the woman in the garden must be his wife and he had killed her. But she wondered how difficult it would be to convince the police in a telephone call, and she worried that Dutton might even now find a way of incriminating her.

## 39

The interview ended abruptly. Sergeant Patterson was unclear whether this was the boss's way of keeping his suspect on the hop or whether it had more to do with a promise to his wife to go to a parents' evening at the school. Dorothy Morris was not a woman the boss cared to cross.

If Peter Dutton was bewildered by the angry instruction to go home and be there when he was wanted, he concealed it. His temple throbbed but the only other sign of emotion all day had been when he confessed Carol's guilt.

Walking home past Spinney Green station and up the rise to Shepherd Road, Dutton agonized whether he had done the right thing. But the rockery had been built on the exact spot to protect the grave – how could he ask Morris to accept that as coincidence? Blaming Carol and limiting his own involvement to disposing of the body seemed the neatest way out. He did not know what happened to people who buried bodies unofficially. Did that mean prison, too?

The problem was still with him as he rounded the corner of Shepherd Road and saw the police patrol car outside his house. Dutton staggered, losing his balance. He was afraid he had been tricked: Morris had pretended to send him home for the night but was actually waiting to pounce, catching him off guard and forcing an admission from him when there were no witnesses.

Dutton darted down the side of one of the completed Phase Two houses and stumbled across unfenced, unmade back gardens. His breath was coming fast and painful. He got to the far end of Shepherd Road and reached the building site which was currently the limit of the cul-de-sac. Ducking behind embryo houses and heaps of bricks and other materials he reached open land, the continuation of the strip which ran at the back of his own garden. He was sure that if he could cross the land unobserved and get to a street on the far side he could dodge the police. Unfortunately, he could not see any access to the gardens on the far side.

He was crouching there, assessing his chances of climbing a fence without being spotted, when a lorry arrived and dumped sand. The noise was an assault on his ears – pop music on the cab radio, the roar of the tipping machinery, the thunder of the load of falling sand. Dutton, hidden by a patch of weeds which would soon be someone's Shepherd Road garden, squinted at distant fencing. He worried that he would be seen, might have been seen already. He knew what people were like in these parts – so suspicious that a man loitering at the back of their properties would have the police station telephone ringing in no time.

The lorry changed key as it finished dumping and prepared to leave. With the quickest of reflexes Dutton was on his feet and hurling himself into the back of the truck. If he could not go one way, he would go another.

He lay flat, face downwards as the vehicle gathered speed along Shepherd Road, not daring to check whether the police car was still parked. Pale houses with dark bay windows raced beside him. He felt sick. At the corner the lorry slewed, then plunged into traffic. Dutton was rolled around without mercy. A few hundred yards on he raised himself to a crawling position, praying for a chance to jump out if traffic lights or any other impediment persuaded the driver to slow.

On his knees he saw the police car. It was travelling a couple of vehicles behind the lorry. Dutton flattened himself, unsure whether he had been seen. A second later he knew. The police car created a gap in the traffic, swung to the offside, switched on its wail and gave chase. Dutton's face contorted in a soundless cry. His nails gouged livid scallops in his palms.

Maybe the lorry driver had his cab radio turned up too loud to notice, maybe he had a guilty conscience. Either way, he saw no reason to stop and sped down the road, past the railway station, past the baker's and the newsagent's, on into the classier part of Spinney Green. The driver aimed, finally, for the open gates of a building supplier's yard and bounced high over the pavement to reach base.

The police car came to a jerking stop across the yard entrance and two uniformed men got out. Dutton, his suit streaked with vomit, shrank back into a corner of the truck wishing for invisibility. The policemen dragged him out.

At Spinney Green police station Patterson said to him: 'Trying to run away were we, Mr Dutton?' Dutton hated him for his patronizing tone. He did not reply. His clothes were filthy and stank. He thought there was almost as much dirt on him as if he had been buried. He wished he were dead.

Morris came, not altogether sorry to be headed off on his way to the parents' meeting. 'Well, well,' he said and unconsciously echoed his sergeant, 'trying to run off, were you? I wonder why that was?' He knew. One of his men at 7 Shepherd Road chanced to be craning into the bay to look for a colleague coming to relieve him and saw Dutton's panic at the sight of the parked patrol car.

The questions had a new edge to them. Dutton had done today what they hoped he would have done tomorrow. Panicked. Cracked. Morris knew all along he would have to sometime, that throbbing temple and the twitching eyelid had told him. They were incontrovertible proof of a guilty mind, no matter how blandly Dutton stood up to interrogation.

'Empty your pockets,' Morris snapped. He blew his nose while Dutton obeyed. Car keys, handkerchief, money, comb, cheque book, credit card. 'And the rest or we'll do it for you.' Dutton brought out the two things he wanted to leave in his jacket pocket.

Patterson reached forward to the table across which they faced their quarry. He picked up the wedding photograph, passed it to Morris. Then he selected the slip of paper with two words on it: Carol Dutton.

No one spoke. Morris and Patterson were registering that the photograph looked like a typical bride and bridegroom pose. It might well fit the silver-plated frame recovered from Dutton's desk at Pegwoods along with letters sent to his wife by her parents. The queer thing was that, after a passing resemblance, they could see the woman was not Mrs Dutton. If Dutton's marriage to Carol was a later marriage, then why would he be carrying around the photograph of his first wedding?

Before they groped towards any answers the telephone rang. Morris was told the fingerprints people had finished at Shepherd Road and there was only one print in the house which matched Carol Dutton's as recorded at Criminal Records Office. *'What!'*

Patterson leapt. Morris listened to the rest, then signalled Patterson outside. 'What's up, sir?'

'Carol Dutton's fingerprints. They've found only one in the house that belongs to her.'

'But that's impossible.'

'Exactly. The one they found was on a light fitting . . .'

'Sir, that must mean . . .'

. . . that the woman we've been interviewing isn't Carol Dutton. I don't think I need say we don't have to look for the real Carol Dutton.'

'No, sir.' He thought for a moment. 'Do you think the Carol Dutton we've met has any idea about this?'

'The hospital confirms what she says about her condition, so she can't. Her misfortune is that she believes she's Dutton's wife. I look forward to the relief on her face when we tell her she's not. We don't often have good news for people.'

Patterson replied that he was looking forward to hearing Morris tell Peter Dutton when they went back into the room.

Presented with the *fait accompli* Dutton knew there was only one way open to him. He fell back on the truth, most of the truth and nothing that wasn't the truth. He thought that was safest, it was when people elaborated that they got into deep water.

'It was an accident,' he began. Morris's eyes were unconvinced above the boxer's nose. Patterson nearly yawned. 'Honestly,' Dutton said, trying for their sympathetic attention. 'We had a row and she fell and . . . and then she was dead and I didn't know what to do.' Sweat was shining on his forehead.

'Most people would call an ambulance,' Morris suggested.

'But I panicked. Don't you see? I lost control, I couldn't believe what had happened and I didn't think anyone else would believe me.' He saw he had been right, they didn't.

Dutton clutched at the eyelid with the dancing nerve. He gabbled that he had buried his wife's body and then, when he had seen her on television, it was like . . .

'A miracle?' offered Patterson sarcastically.

'Well, yes, I suppose that's more or less what I thought.' He could see they were not men who believed in miracles.

Morris said: 'How long do you think it would have been before you were killing the second Carol Dutton? When her memory came back? Or when you grew tired of the game? You had already done that, hadn't you? You tried to strangle her in her bed two nights ago.'

Dutton whimpered. He buried his palpitating face in his arm, his denials were muffled.

Morris had more to say. 'We'd have noticed, you know. A second dead woman at 7 Shepherd Road would have been very awkward for you to explain away. Your first idea was smarter, wasn't it? Pouring a lethal dose of sleeping pills down her throat?'

Patterson said: 'Then it would have been just another accident, wouldn't it?'

Dutton clung limpet-like to his story that his wife had died by accident. He explained about forged cheques and forged letters and deceiving Princes Hospital and everything else he had done, but he would not budge from the story that his wife died by accident. Morris and Patterson bullied and snarled, cajoled and charmed. Within the rules by which they worked they used everything. But Dutton was unshakeable. He regained his composure and that air of superiority which they had disliked from the first meeting.

'You don't have to convince me, you have to convince a jury,' Morris said and charged him with the murder of Carol Mary Dutton.

When he'd been taken to the cells there was a telephone call for Morris, a call from the woman who would never again introduce herself as Carol Dutton. Patterson interrupted a yawn to comment on the good news that the mystery of her identity was solved. He hoped he had disguised the yawn. Morris could work all night, he'd had enough. Patterson said: 'And tomorrow we hear from the legal boys if there's any way of getting Dutton for the death of Jean Parker, and what we can do to him for the way he acquired Carol the Second.'

'Meanwhile you can buy me that pint you owe me.' Morris had a mischievous glint in his eye.

'What pint?'

'The pint I won when Carol Dutton's fingerprints turned up at Criminal Records.'

Patterson gave him a look which betrayed all the indignation of a six-year-old about to shout: 'That's not fair!'

It wasn't, but it wasn't exactly a lie, either.